Mysteries

Enid Blyton

The Ring O'Bells Mystery
The Rubadub Mystery

·PARRAGON·

This edition published in 1996 for
Parragon Book Service Limited
Units 13–17 Avonbridge Industrial Estate
Atlantic Road
Avonmouth, Bristol BS11 9QD
by Diamond Books
77–85 Fulham Palace Road
Hammersmith, London W6 8JB

First edition published 1992 for Parragon
Book Service Limited

Printed and bound by Caledonian International
Book Manufacturing Ltd, Glasgow

Contents

The Ring O'Bells Mystery

First published in a single volume in hardback in 1951 by
William Collins Sons & Co Ltd.
First published in paperback in 1967 in Armada

Chapter One

They Couldn't Go Back To School

'I thought those three children were going off to school today,' said Mr Lynton. 'Why aren't they down punctually to breakfast?'

'Oh, Richard – isn't it *tiresome* – Snubby and Diana aren't well,' said Mrs Lynton. 'They've both got temperatures – and I can't send Roger back in case Snubby and Diana are going to have something infectious. The school would not take him back if so.'

'Good gracious!' said Mr Lynton, exasperated. 'After four long weeks of Easter holidays, when there has been nothing but noise and racing about, and that dog Loony under my feet all the time – now we get another two or three weeks of it, I suppose!'

'Oh, well, Richard, we can't help it if they fall ill,' said his wife. 'Snubby really *must* be feeling bad – he can't even eat a sausage for his breakfast, and you know how fond he is of them.'

'It won't hurt him to starve for a week,' said Mr Lynton hard-heartedly. 'I'm not wasting any pity on Snubby. I've never known anyone eat as he does. They can't make a penny profit on Snubby at school, I'll be bound!'

He gathered up his papers and went off to catch his train, looking rather gloomy. He had been looking forward to a little peace in the house, with the three children enjoying themselves away at school. Now it looked as if they wouldn't be gone for another week or so, possibly longer.

Mrs Lynton went up to see Snubby. He groaned when

she came in. 'I do feel bad, Aunt Susan. And do you think you could possibly take Loony out again? He keeps wanting me to play and I can't bear it. He's such a very *scrapey* dog this morning – scrapes the clothes off me, and scrapes the rugs off the floor, and–'

'I know, I know,' said his aunt soothingly, pulling the clothes straight. 'There's not much about Loony that I don't know already. Now try to get a little sleep till the doctor comes. I'm going in to see Diana.'

Diana was feeling bad too. Mrs Lynton felt her hot hands. 'I think you've both got a touch of 'flu,' she said. 'What a pity, just at the end of the holidays!'

Roger still seemed all right, though he was in bed too, as he had just a slight temperature. He had been able to manage a little breakfast.

The doctor came at half-past ten, and tripped over Sardine, the cat, on the stairs. 'I'm so sorry,' said Mrs Lynton. 'I should have warned you! Sardine, if you do that again, I'll send Loony after you.'

'Dear me – who's Loony?' asked the doctor, and knew immediately, as Loony came racing down the stairs after Sardine, nearly sending him to the bottom.

He was a nice, cheery doctor, and the children liked him, though Snubby and Diana could only raise rather feeble smiles when he made his jokes.

'Ha! I suppose this is all faked just to get out of going back to school!' he said, taking Diana's hand to feel her pulse. 'I know these tricks! I've half a mind to order you up and about!'

'I couldn't possibly get up,' said Diana weakly. 'I got up in the night to get a drink and I could hardly stand.'

'Well, don't worry,' said the doctor cheerily. 'You've only got a touch of this wretched 'flu that's going round. You'll soon be all right.'

'Well, thank goodness it's only 'flu and not scarlet fever

10

or anything like that,' said Mrs Lynton, when the doctor went downstairs with her again.

'It's a pretty nasty 'flu, though,' said the doctor, looking for his gloves. 'Now – where did I put my gloves?'

'Loony! *You've* got them!' said Mrs Lynton sharply to the black spaniel. 'Drop them! Bad dog!'

The doctor got back his gloves at last. 'Well, as I was saying,' he said, 'it's a pretty nasty 'flu. Keep them in bed till I say they can get up – and then, I'm afraid, they ought not to go back to school for another ten days or so. They'll feel pretty washed out afterwards. Perhaps you could get them away somewhere.'

'I'll see what I can do,' said Mrs Lynton. 'Well, thank you, Doctor, I'll be seeing you tomorrow then.'

Roger was soon as bad as the others, and the amount of grumbling and groaning that went on was terrific. Perhaps the most miserable person in the house was Loony the spaniel. He wasn't ill, of course – but he simply couldn't understand why the three children were kept in bed and didn't appear to want his company at all!

'He's awful,' complained Diana. 'If I let him in, he goes mad, and I simply can't stand it, I've got such a headache – and if I don't let him in, he scrapes at the door and whines till I do. Can't Snubby have him in his room? He's Snubby's dog.'

'He doesn't want him either,' said Mrs Lynton. 'I'll send him out for a long walk with the baker's boy this afternoon. He's very fond of him, and would love to take him for a walk.'

'I don't mind Sardine so much,' said Diana. 'She doesn't stamp about like Loony. But I don't like it when she sits on my tummy and kneads me carefully with her claws as if I were a bit of dough. Oh, Mummy – I do feel bad!'

11

'Poor old girl,' said her mother. 'You'll soon feel all right again. Don't worry!'

Mrs Lynton had put Roger in a room by himself when Snubby had fallen ill, hoping that perhaps he wouldn't catch it. But now that it was certain he was in for the 'flu as well, she moved him back into his own room with his cousin Snubby. They both felt so miserable that she was sure they wouldn't get up to any tricks together just yet!

The illness ran its course, and in a few days all three were feeling decidedly better. 'If only my *legs* weren't so wobbly!' said Snubby. 'They feel as if they were made of jelly. Will they ever get all right again, Aunt Susan?'

'Of course. Don't be silly,' said his aunt. 'Anyway, *I* know you're much better because you asked for a sausage for breakfast this morning. Tomorrow you'll probably ask for three.'

'Woof,' said Loony, who always knew the word 'sausage' when he heard it. He put a big black paw on Snubby's bed, and looked mournfully at his master. He hadn't understood Snubby at all for the last few days. Snubby hadn't been pleased to see him – he hadn't yelled and laughed as usual – he hadn't even been pleased when Loony brought him a half-chewed and very smelly bone.

Snubby patted Loony's smooth, silky head, and fondled the black, drooping ears. 'I'm feeling better now, Loony,' he said. 'We'll soon be out for walkies again.'

'Woof!' said Loony excitedly, and leapt with one bound on to Snubby's middle. But that was more than Snubby could stand, and soon Loony was being taken sternly out of the room by Mrs Lynton.

'I think the children had better go away for a change of air,' Mrs Lynton said to her husband that night. 'They are all much better, but I feel rather tired myself now. I could get Miss Pepper, my old governess, to look after them for a bit, I know. She's very fond of them all.'

12

'Good idea,' said Mr Lynton warmly. 'I know what Snubby was like after he'd had a chill once – do you remember? He appeared to be twice as full of beans, and three times as full of cheek. I don't feel I could stand that after four or five weeks of him here.'

'Yes – that was the time when he managed to get up on the roof, wasn't it – and emptied a can of water down the dining-room chimney,' said Mrs Lynton. 'I remember how startled I was. Well – I think I'll ring up Miss Pepper and see what she thinks about it. She's very good at handling the three. She doesn't stand any nonsense.'

Miss Pepper said yes – she would take the three children off Mrs Lynton's hands with pleasure. It was a long time since she had seen them – not since they had all stayed at Rockingdown with her, and plunged into peculiar adventures!

'You'll see that they don't get up to mischief at all, won't you?' said Mrs Lynton anxiously. 'You know what they are – so headstrong and lively and daring. They want firm handling.'

'You needn't worry,' said Miss Pepper. 'Now where did you think of sending them? By the sea?'

'Well, no,' said Mrs Lynton. 'The doctor says somewhere inland, but not too low – and somewhere fairly warm. He doesn't want them paddling or bathing or doing anything like that just yet. Can you suggest anywhere?'

There was a pause. Then Miss Pepper spoke doubtfully. 'Well – I do know a place. It's got a lovely name but it's not as pretty a village as it sounds. Have you heard of Ring O'Bells Village?'

'Yes – isn't it that very old place, near the town of Lillinghame?' said Mrs Lynton.

'That's right,' said Miss Pepper. 'I've a cousin who keeps a little boarding house there – I'm sure she would be pleased to have the children.'

13

They talked about the idea for a little while. Ring O' Bells sounded just right to Mrs Lynton. There were riding stables nearby, where the three children could hire horses and hack round the countryside. There were walks up the hills and through the woods. Miss Pepper was sure the air would do them good.

'Right,' said Mrs Lynton, thankful to have settled everything so easily. 'Will you telephone your cousin, Miss Pepper, and arrange everything? The children can travel this week, the doctor says – so I could pack them in the car, and drive over to you – and then drive down to Ring O' Bells. It really is a lovely name, and sounds so *peace*ful somehow.'

'Yes,' said Miss Pepper, wondering if it would be quite so peaceful when Loony and the three children got down there. Thank goodness there wouldn't be that strange circus friend of theirs there too – the boy Barney and his monkey, Miranda!

Chapter Two

Ring O' Bells Village

'Ring O' Bells Village!' said Diana delightedly, when she heard the news. 'Oh, mother – it sounds lovely. I should like to go there. It sounds as if it's out of a nursery rhyme.'

'Are there bells or something?' demanded Snubby, who was now up and looking more himself, though he was very pale under his thatch of red hair. Even his mass of freckles seemed to have faded. 'I'd like to ring church bells – you know, pull those ropes and make them play a tune.'

'It's not as easy as all that,' said his aunt. 'Well, I'm glad you are all pleased. You'll be able to ride, anyway, and you all like that. I believe Ring O' Bells is an interesting old village, too, with all kinds of stories and legends about it.'

'Good!' said Roger. 'I like places like that. You never know when you might find out about something mysterious.'

'I don't want you to go smelling out any mysteries or anything,' said his mother. 'I just want you to get well enough to go back to school as quickly as possible, so as not to miss any more of the lovely summer term than you need.'

School didn't appeal to the children very much just then. 'I believe I'd faint if I had to go and sit in a maths class now, Aunt Susan,' said Snubby, trying to sound pathetic. He had enjoyed being fussed over by his aunt.

He had no parents, and his Aunt Susan was the nearest he had known to a mother.

'It's much more likely that your maths master would faint,' said his aunt unsympathetically. 'He's probably thanking his stars that he hasn't had to cope with you yet this term, Snubby.'

'I'm afraid I shan't get much of a report this term, Aunt Susan,' said Snubby, still looking pathetic. 'I mean – if I get a bad one for a change, you'll quite understand, won't you?'

'It won't be a change,' said his aunt. 'Have you forgotten last term's report already? Shall I quote some of it for you?'

'No,' said Snubby hurriedly, suddenly remembering a few very nasty bits. He changed the subject. 'When do we go? I say, it'll be fun riding again, Aunt Susan – though I don't know if I'll be able to get on a horse now. My legs still feel peculiar.'

'Well, let the others ride then, and you wait till your legs let you mount,' said his aunt hard-heartedly. Snubby sighed. The time of being petted and fussed and coddled was over. He could see that. Well, it had been very nice while it lasted!

They all set off one day after breakfast. The three children looked pale, but they were in high spirits. It was fun to be going away to a strange place. Diana thought pityingly of her friends, swotting away at school. It was almost worth while having that awful 'flu, to be going away unexpectedly like this.

Mrs Lynton drove the car with Diana beside her. At the back were Roger, Snubby and, of course, Loony. Loony's great idea in a car was to stick his head as far out of the window as possible.

'Go faster, Aunt Susan,' urged Snubby. 'I want to see

what Loony does when his ears stand out straight behind him in the wind.'

'Don't talk to the driver,' said Diana. 'And don't let Loony hang out of the window too much. He'll get a chill.'

'He won't,' said Snubby. 'He never gets chills. He didn't even take the 'flu from us!'

They picked up Miss Pepper on the way, and then Diana went to sit at the back of the car with the two boys. They were all pleased to see the tall, trim woman, with her eyes twinkling as usual behind her glasses. She had a very nice smile that quite altered her rather prim face with the straight grey hair brushed away from it.

'The three children are not *quite* as lively as usual,' said Mrs Lynton, 'but you won't mind *that* of course. Loony, I fear, is much the same as ever – perhaps a little madder, if anything.'

Loony was delighted to see Miss Pepper. He put his paws up on the back of her seat and snuffled lovingly down her neck. Then he pawed at her hat and she clutched it in haste.

'Is Loony still fond of taking brushes away and hiding them?' she asked.

'Yes!' chorused the children. '*And* towels now too, Miss Pepper.'

Miss Pepper groaned and made a mental note to keep her towel in a drawer, and not hanging by her washbasin. She liked Loony but he really was a trial. She wondered how her cousin would put up with him. Oh dear – she hadn't thought of that!

It was a long drive to Ring O' Bells Village. They had a picnic on the way, and then, in the afternoon, Diana, Roger and Snubby lolled together in the back of the car and fell asleep. They were already tired with their journey. Loony stuck his head further and further out of the window, then his shoulders, and enjoyed himself thoroughly.

'We're getting near the village now,' said Miss Pepper, looking at the map on her lap. 'See those hills? Well, Ring O' Bells is behind them, on the south side, so it's very warm, though fairly high.'

They rounded the foot of the hills, and came in sight of the sprawling old village. The houses were made of white stone, and looked very solidly built indeed. The children woke up as they came into the village, a little way up the slope of the great hill.

'We're almost there,' said Miss Pepper, turning to them. 'Look – that's Hubbard Cottage. When I was here as a little girl I really thought Mother Hubbard lived there. And over there is a very old show-place called Ring O' Bells Hall – it was once a mansion, built in the sixteenth century. It's now on show to the public, with a lot of the old original furniture in it. It's got a secret passage too.'

'*Has* it!' said Diana in delight. 'Are the public allowed to see that, too, Miss Pepper?'

'Yes, on payment of an extra sixpence,' said Miss Pepper. 'They make a lot of money here in the summertime, because people come from all over the place to see Ring O' Bells Village and hear its old legends. There are one or two old cottages in Ring O' Bells Wood that really might have been where Red Riding Hood lived!'

'Ring O' Bells Village – Ring O' Bells Wood,' said Diana. 'Mother Hubbard – Red Riding Hood – a secret passage! I say – this sounds exciting!'

'I dare say it's all quite ordinary to the people who live here,' said her mother. 'Look – there are the riding stables. I'm sure you'll be there more than anywhere else, helping with the horses and getting yourselves even dirtier than usual!'

18

The riding stables looked nice. They too seemed old, and a bit tumbledown at the back, but the horses in the paddock were spruce and well groomed. The children felt their spirits rising high.

At last the car drew up in a lane off the main road, outside an old solid-looking stone house. It was quite big, and rather rambling, as it spread away at the back into an odd wing or two and some outbuildings. Hens ran over the garden, and ducks quacked from somewhere not far off. A dog ran barking to welcome them, its tail wagging furiously.

'A golden spaniel,' said Snubby, delighted. 'Hey, Loony – meet your cousin. Do you know his name, Miss Pepper?'

'Yes – it's Loopy,' said Miss Pepper, with a chuckle, and everyone roared with laughter. Loony and Loopy – what a pair of names – and what a pair of dogs too!

Loopy seemed practically as mad as Loony in the way he pranced about and barked and fawned over everyone. They might all have been long lost friends of his! Miss Pepper's cousin hurried out to greet them, smiling. She was like Miss Pepper, but shorter and fatter, and her smile was not quite so wide and cheerful. Still, the children thought she looked quite jolly – and anyway she had a very nice dog, who would be good company for Loony.

Soon they were all indoors, sitting down to a fine meal of home-made bread, scones and cakes, with home-made jam, and home-made honey in dishes. Mrs Lynton saw with approval that the three children seemed to have suddenly recovered their enormous appetites. Diana's cheeks began to glow a little and she chattered as fast as the boys.

Loony and Loopy sat impatiently beside first one child and then another, hoping for titbits. Occasionally they

19

sniffed each other approvingly, though Loopy growled if Loony got a titbit he thought *he* ought to have.

'And now–' said Mrs Lynton when they had all finished, 'now, you three – you're to go straight to bed. You have had a long and tiring drive, and I can see that Snubby's legs are turning to jelly again.'

All three protested – but not very violently. Secretly they all longed to get between the sheets and lie down in comfort. Snubby felt surprised at himself for wanting such a peculiar thing, and wondered seriously whether he wasn't suddenly turning into an old man.

It wasn't long before they were all in bed, and Diana's eyes closed almost at once. She shared a bedroom with her mother that night, but Mrs Lynton was going off early the next morning, to drive herself home. Then Diana would have her room to herself. The boys shared one. Loony shared it too, of course. He would never be parted from Snubby at night.

'Have you got an old rug or something to put on Snubby's bed?' Miss Pepper asked her cousin. 'Just so that the dog won't spoil your nice blankets, you know. I'm afraid he *will* sleep on the boy's bed. I do hope you won't mind.'

'I would have minded last year,' said her cousin, producing an old rug from a chest. 'But since I've had to put up with Loopy I've learnt a lot of things. I won't let him sleep on my bed – but he insists on sleeping on my couch. Here you are, Becky – take it to Snubby. What a name!'

'It's because of his snub-nose,' said Miss Pepper, escaping with the rug. Snubby was already asleep. So was Diana. Roger opened his eyes just a little to say good night and then he too was asleep. His mother peeped in as Miss Pepper arranged the old rug on Snubby's bed for Loony to lie on.

'I do hope you'll all have a peaceful, restful time,' she

said. 'I shouldn't think anything much ever happens here, does it?'

'No, nothing,' said Miss Pepper. 'It's a funny old dreamy, half-forgotten place. We shan't have any excitement at all!'

She shouldn't have said that. It was just *ask*ing for things to happen, of course!

Chapter Three

Mother Hubbard's Cottage

For once, not one of the children awoke early. Mrs Lynton was away before even Snubby had opened his eyes! They didn't even hear her car purring down the lane, and they didn't hear the hens clucking, Loopy barking, or the rooks cawing as they sailed overhead.

Snubby only woke because Loony insisted. Loony was tired of hearing everyone awake and astir, and of being shut up in a bedroom with two sleeping boys. He scraped at the door but nobody came. He heard Loopy barking and suddenly gave a loud answering bark.

Snubby awoke with a jump, but Roger went on sleeping peacefully, his head under the bedclothes. Snubby sat up and looked at the time. Twenty-five-past *nine!* Good gracious! Whoever heard of such a thing? He leapt out of bed, quite forgetting to test his legs as he usually did, since they had become so curiously jelly-like. However, they behaved very well, and didn't let him down or even wobble. He went to the window, Loony licking him madly, his tail wagging nineteen to the dozen.

It was a brilliant morning in early May. Snubby's bedroom looked out on the back garden of the house, and there was plenty to see there! Dozens of hens scrabbled about. Three great geese cackled in a corner. Ducks swam on a round pond in the field just outside the garden, upending themselves in their usual ridiculous way.

A cat sat sunning itself on a wall, keeping a wary eye open for Loopy, who was always under the impression that he could leap any wall. He couldn't, but the cat was always afraid that he might. It stuck one leg up in the air and began to give itself a thorough morning wash.

'Now this is just the kind of place I *like*,' said Snubby, rubbing his hands. 'Plenty going on. Is that a goat I see beyond the duck pond – and two little kids? And surely that's a grey donkey? I'll have a ride on him today.'

'Woof,' said Loony, trying his hardest to see out of the window too. Snubby lifted him up. He caught sight of Loopy down below, sniffing hard at a smell of some sort, and almost leapt out of the window in his excitement. His sudden barking awoke Roger.

'Come on, Roger, get up!' said Snubby eagerly. 'It's awfully late. This is a wizard place. All kinds of animals and things. Loopy's down there, longing for Loony to join him.'

'Well, let him then,' said Roger, fending off Loony as he tried to cover him with licks. 'Can't you teach your dog to stop washing everyone he loves? I'm dripping already. Shut up, Loony, keep your tongue in your mouth!'

Snubby opened the bedroom door, and Loony shot downstairs, taking the stairs in almost one bound. He slid across the polished hall on his four feet, neatly avoided a little table there, and gave Miss Pepper a real shock as she came in from the garden. Before she could say a word, Loony was hob-nobbing excitedly with Loopy, who at once began to show off.

'Couple of mad creatures,' said Miss Pepper to herself. 'I suppose that means that the children are now awake.'

Judging by the thuds upstairs, they were. Miss Pepper called to her cousin, 'Hannah! The children are awake at last. I'll get the milk out of the fridge for them. They do so love it icy-cold.'

'Oooh,' said Snubby, who in two minutes' time appeared dressed at the dining-room door, and was gazing with joy at the table. 'Ham and tomatoes! And what's this? Hot sausage rolls! For *breakfast!* I say – are we going to be fed up, like the doctor said? I heard him tell Aunt Susan to feed us up well.'

'Yes – you're going to be fed up,' said Miss Pepper, smiling. 'I hope I shan't be – by the end of these few days here!'

'Ha ha – joke!' said Snubby politely. He sat down. 'I don't need to wait for the others, do I? Do I begin with porridge?'

'You do,' said Miss Pepper, serving him out of a dish on the food-warmer. 'And take plenty of cream – plenty! Doctor's orders. You've gone skinny and I don't like you skinny.'

'Gosh! Can I really take as much cream as I like?' said Snubby, reaching for the big jug with its pattern of flowers all down it. 'All my life people have been telling me to go carefully with the cream!'

Hannah Pepper came in after a while to see that everything was all right. She seemed pleased to see the three children tucking in. 'They won't be long putting a bit of flesh on again,' she said to her cousin, who was now knitting by the window. 'But don't let the dog have any cream. He's fat enough as it is.'

'He's only licking a drip off my fingers,' said Snubby. 'Hallo, here's Loopy. Have a lick, Loopy?'

But cream was no luxury to Loopy, and he disdained it. He sniffed at Loony's mouth to smell what other food he had received. Loopy was very ready to welcome Loony, but he didn't mean him to have anything more than his fair share!

'Can we go and have a snoop round the place, Miss Pepper?' asked Diana, when they could not possibly eat any more. 'You don't need to come,' she added hastily, feeling that it would be nicer to snoop round by themselves. 'And is there a book about Ring O' Bells we could read? A guide book or something?'

'No. But I dare say the woman at the old mansion we passed yesterday – Ring O' Bells Hall, it's called – can tell you all you want to know,' said Miss Pepper. 'Can't she, Hannah?'

'Yes, she can,' said her cousin, who was now clearing away the breakfast things. 'It's a pity she's not a native here – she's a stranger really, who read up all about the old place, and put in for the job as caretaker and guide to Ring O' Bells Hall when it was decided to open it as a show-place. Still, she certainly knows all the history of the place, and explains it very well – better, maybe, than one of the villagers could have done it.'

'We'll go and have a good look all round,' said Roger, feeling the sun warm on his face, as it streamed through the window. 'I'm going to enjoy this unexpected holiday. Can Loopy come with us, Miss Hannah?'

'Oh, *yes*,' said Miss Hannah thankfully. 'Do take him. He's under my feet all the time, and he *will* keep running off with the mats. Now just look out of the window – if he hasn't got somebody's towel too this morning!'

Snubby had a feeling that it was Loony not Loopy who was responsible for the sudden appearance of the towel. He got up in a hurry to fetch it, only to meet Loony running through the hall with another towel dragging behind him!

'Loony! This is not your home!' scolded Snubby, in a low voice. 'It's somebody else's place. If you start dragging towels about, you'll be sent away. Do you hear? Then we shall play with Loopy, not with *you!*'

Loony's tail went down, and he put on his most mournful expression. Snubby put the two towels back in their places, and went downstairs. This time he met Loopy carrying a mat in his mouth, evidently taken from the dining room, where there were many rugs laid down to cover the old wooden floor.

Snubby didn't interfere with Loopy. Let him take his own rugs! It was no business of Snubby's. Anyway, the more mischief Loopy got up to, the less Loony's mischief would be noticed!

The three children set off together. They went down the sunny lane, already sweet with the scent of the first drifts of may blossom. Cowslips danced in the nearby fields, and primroses lined the ditches by the road. The brilliant blue of the germander speedwell shone beneath the hedges. What a lovely place Ring O' Bells was!

They came to the white stone cottage that Miss Pepper had called Hubbard Cottage. The name was on the gate. The children stood there staring. They supposed Mother Hubbard might have lived *some*where when she was alive – and why not here?

The door opened and an old woman in a red shawl and printed skirt appeared, shaking a duster. She looked so exactly like Mother Hubbard that the children gazed in delight. She smiled at them.

'You visitors here?' she said in a pleasant brogue. 'You've brought the good weather with you!'

Loopy scrabbled at the gate, trying to get in. This sounded like the kind of old woman who was generous with titbits. Loony put his paws on the middle bar and looked through.

'Ah – there's Loopy,' said the old woman. 'I'll find him a bone – and one for the other dog too.'

'She really *might* be Mother Hubbard,' said Diana in excitement. 'I wonder if *she's* got a dog. We'll ask her.'

They opened the gate and went up the tiny stone path, edged with polyanthus and wallflowers, and stood at the little door, waiting. They peered inside the cottage. It was dim, and they could hardly make out anything.

'Come away in,' cried a voice, and they went cautiously in, their eyes finding it difficult to get accustomed to the dim light after the brilliant May sunshine outside.

The front door opened straight into a little room. Mother Hubbard, as they all called her, was in a room beyond. Diana clutched Roger's arm. 'Look – the cupboard!' she whispered. 'She's got a cupboard!'

Mother Hubbard was at an open cupboard, that went back into the thick stone wall of the cottage. But it wasn't bare! It was filled with pans and dishes and jugs of all kinds – it was, in fact, her larder, set in the cool stone wall. She brought out two bones for the dogs.

'Did you ever have a dog?' asked Diana suddenly as the old lady came back into the sitting room, or parlour.

'Dear me, no,' said Mother Hubbard, looking surprised at the sudden question. 'Not of my own, if that's what you mean. I've lived with my old grandad nearly all my life, and he don't like dogs, never did. I like them, mind you – I've always got a bone for one that comes along. Old Grandad don't mind, so long as they don't go worriting him out in the garden there.'

It was astonishing to hear this 'Old Mother Hubbard' actually had a grandfather out in the garden. 'Could we see him?' asked Roger. 'I expect he's very interesting, isn't he? He could go a long way back in history, couldn't he?'

'Well, he says he's over a hundred years old,' said Mother Hubbard. 'He's asleep now, look – you come and talk to him some other time. He knows a rare lot about Ring O' Bells – more than that woman at Ring O' Bells has ever read or heard of, I can tell you *that!*'

This was interesting, and rather exciting. 'We'll certainly come back!' said Roger. 'And thanks most awfully for the bones!'

Chapter Four

Ring O' Bells Hall

As the children went past the strange little 'Mother Hubbard' Cottage, they peeped over the high garden wall of stone, just to see if they could spy 'Old Grandad' there.

They saw a tiny old man fast asleep in a chair, propped up with cushions. A long clay pipe dangled in one gnarled, wrinkled hand. He had a little fringe of fluffy white hair round his head, which otherwise was quite pink and bald. His nose was a mere button, but his eyebrows made up for that. They jutted out fiercely and shaggily, snow-white and thick, almost hiding his closed eyes.

'He looks fierce, except for his nose,' said Diana in a low voice. 'Look at his mouth, with its stuck-out lower lip, and his chin with the funny bit of white beard on it. Do you suppose he really *is* a hundred years old?'

'He looks *two* hundred,' said Snubby. 'Get down, Loony, you ass. I warn you, Grandad won't stand any nonsense from a silly young thing like *you*. Get hold of Loopy, Di – he looks as if he's going to leap over the wall.'

'We'll certainly come back and talk to him,' said Roger. 'A hundred years old! The things he could remember! He's a bit of living history.'

They went on their way, and soon came to Ring O' Bells Hall. It was a big, grand building, but rather grim looking, built of such solid grey-white stone that it looked as if not even a bomb would disturb it.

It had two towers, one square, and one round, which seemed peculiar to the children. A stone-flagged path led up to the great door, which was studded with iron nails. It was open.

The children went in with the dogs. A cold voice greeted them. 'Dogs not allowed inside, please. Tie them up outside.'

'But they'll bark their heads off!' protested Snubby.

'Then don't come in yourselves,' said the voice. At first they could not see who was speaking, because the great hall of the building was dark, lit only by a slit of a window at one end, and the dim light that came through the front door.

Then they saw that there was a table set at one side of the hall, and a woman sat there, knitting. She was dressed very neatly in plain black, and her grey hair was strained away from her white face, and put into a bun at the back. She was rather shapeless, and her hands looked very big and bony as she clicked her knitting needles in and out.

The children didn't like her face very much. The mouth was set in what was meant to be a smile, but the small black eyes above it were hard and unsmiling as they looked over at the three children and the dogs. How old was she? She might have been any age, Diana thought.

'We thought we might see round the Hall,' she said, at last. 'Are we allowed to?'

'Yes, but not with the dogs,' said the woman. 'Not allowed, as I told you. This place has some very valuable old furniture and ornaments in it, and no animals are allowed inside. They might cause great damage.'

'Well, that's fair enough, I suppose,' said Roger, and he took Loony and Loopy outside. They didn't mind going in the least, because neither of them liked the great cold Hall, nor the small cold woman. Roger tied them to a post, put their bones down beside them, and left them, hoping that they wouldn't begin barking.

They paid their fees to the woman. She put down her

29

knitting, rolled up her wool, and wrote down the sums of money in her big account book, which lay open before her.

Then she got up. The children followed her round the mansion. It felt a dead, forgotten place, and everywhere struck cold, that lovely warm May morning. Diana shivered. She didn't like any of it much.

The woman recited long strings of facts about the old place, but she didn't make them sound very interesting.

'In 1645 Hugh Dourley lived in this Hall, and it was he who first caused it to be called Ring O' Bells,' she droned on.

'Why?' asked Snubby, his interest caught at last.

'He had a peal of bells put in the south tower,' said the woman, beginning to gabble. 'He rang them when he had anything to rejoice about. But one night they rang themselves, so it's said – and it wasn't because there was anything to rejoice about, either. His eldest son had been killed, and he didn't know. But the bells rang at the very moment of his death.'

This sounded rather weird. The children were now at the bottom of the square south tower. A small spiral stairway went up, and they wondered if they might climb it.

'Yes, climb up if you want to,' said the woman. 'You'll see the bells hanging there, high up. They say they're still the same ones that Hugh Dourley put in, but it stands to reason they can't be.'

The children climbed up the stairway. It was steep and narrow and twisted sharply, so that it was difficult to climb without slipping.

At the top of the stairway was a small platform. The children looked up, and saw, high above their heads, a cluster of bells, hanging silently on what looked like thick ropes.

Snubby stared at the bells, and his hands itched to ring them. Snubby always liked anything that made a loud noise.

'Can we ring them?' he asked, feeling, of course, perfectly certain of the answer.

The guide-woman looked shocked. 'Of course not,' she said. 'Whatever would people think?'

'I don't know,' said Snubby. 'We could ring the bells and find out.'

'There aren't any ropes to *ring* the bells,' said Diana. Sure enough, there were no long ropes hanging down to the little platform they stood on. The bells hung high up on their own short ropes, and there was no way of ringing them at all.

'They'll never ring again,' said the guide. 'People say they'll ring only when enemies come to Ring O' Bells, but that's nonsense. How can bells ring if there's nothing to peal them with?'

'And what enemies could come here, to this little out-of-the-way place?' said Diana. 'Roger, isn't this a strange tower, with its tiny spiral staircase, and its long-forgotten bells, unable to ring ever again.'

'You sound very dismal,' said Roger. 'Like me to throw a stone and make one of the bells ring?'

'Now, now,' said the woman sharply. 'Don't talk like that or I shall have to ask you to go.'

'I'm only joking,' said Roger, grinning. 'What else is there to see?'

The history of the old place was full of boring recitals of this person and that person, who happened to have lived in the house. The children followed the guide about, yawning, but one piece of information made them prick up their ears.

'The Lady Paulet had a secret chamber made in the fireplace here,' droned the guide, as she took them into

31

a small room with an enormous fireplace. All the rooms had big, old-fashioned fireplaces. The children had actually been able to stand upright in some of them, their heads and shoulders up the wide chimney. There was no soot, because it was years now since Ring O' Bells had been lived in.

'A secret chamber!' said Roger. 'Where?' He gazed at the big fireplace, and could not imagine where any secret room could be.

'Look up the chimney,' said the guide. 'You will see what looks like two steps there, cut in the wall of the chimney. If you go up those steps, and then put out your hand, you will feel a cavity behind the fireplace there. It is big enough for a man to step inside and hide.'

'Can we go and see?' asked Snubby, eagerly, visualising a proper little secret room, with perhaps a small table and a bench, as dark as pitch.

'If you like,' said the woman, and she produced a torch, which she held out to them. Roger went first. He shone the torch up the wide chimney, and saw the two rough steps hewn there in the side. He climbed up and began to feel about for the cavity the woman had mentioned. He soon found it. It was a fairly big hole, taller than he was, and he found that he could easily step into it.

But that was all he could do! There was no room for anything except just his own body! It wasn't so much a secret room, as a secret place to hide in, just big enough to take a man – and woe betide him if there should happen to be a fire on the hearth!

'He'd be suffocated, or would be cooked,' thought Roger, getting down thankfully, and handing the torch to Diana. He gave her a shove up. She didn't like the cavity at all when she felt it and shone her torch there. She wouldn't go into it.

'Ugh! It's horrid!' she said. 'It feels so dirty too. Fancy

hiding there! Why, it would only just about take a grown-up.'

Snubby went next, and he, of course, insisted on squeezing himself right into the cavity, and feeling all round it, just in *case* there was something else to find. But there wasn't. It was just what it was meant to be – a temporary hiding-place for some man in danger. Snubby found that he could sit down in it too. The others got impatient and called to him. 'Snubby! Come along! You'll get filthy.'

Roger was very dirty through getting into the cavity. He hadn't realised it might be so filthy. As for Snubby, when he finally jumped down on to the big stone hearth, and appeared before the others, they could hardly believe their eyes. He looked like a sweep!

'I say – Miss Pepper's going to have something to say to you,' said Diana. 'Keep away from me, for goodness' sake. You look awful – and you smell awful too. Just like you to get dirtier than anyone else, Snubby. Keep *away* from me, I said!'

Snubby blew down at himself, feeling rather dismayed to see his coating of dirt. He glanced at the guide and caught a look of pleasure on her face. 'Horrid old thing!' he thought. 'She only encouraged us to get into that cavity because she thought we'd get black, and be told off when we got home.'

He went near to her and banged himself violently as if to get rid of the dust and soot. Some flew over her, and she started back in disgust.

'You'd better go home and clean up,' she said.

'Oh, no!' said Snubby at once. 'OH, no! We haven't seen the thing we want to see most – the secret passage. Where is that? We want to see it, please.'

Chapter Five

The Secret Passage

'No – you go off home and clean yourselves,' said the woman crossly. 'I've had enough of you. You'll mess up all the clean rooms if you go about like that now.'

'Well, it was your fault,' said Snubby, banging himself violently again, and making the soot fly. 'You must have known that place was filthy. Come on – we paid you an extra sixpence each to show us the passage. Where is it?'

'You come back clean tomorrow and I'll show it to you,' said the woman. But Snubby could be very obstinate when he wanted to.

'I'll walk all over the Ring O' Bells Hall banging off my soot, if you don't show us,' he announced, and gave himself such a blow on the chest that everyone sneezed because of the soot.

The woman scowled and said no more. She went back to the hall and took a bunch of keys from a hook. She selected one and led the way to a panelled room, which she unlocked.

'The secret passage was made in the year 1748,' she said. 'Or so the chronicles say. This room was panelled then, and an entrance to the passage was made behind the panelling. It runs behind it for a little way, and then curves downwards into the foundations of the house.'

'Does it go to the cellars?' asked Roger.

'No. It avoids those, and ends blindly,' said the guide.

'What was the use of it then, if it didn't lead anywhere?' asked Snubby. 'What a pity!'

'It was probably used as a hiding-place,' said the guide.

'More people could crowd into it than into the small cavity behind the fireplace. Now – can any of you find the secret passage?'

They looked round the panelled room. It was dark, because the windows were heavily leaded and not very large. The ivy that grew outside obscured the light even more.

Snubby began tapping over the panelling. He gave a triumphant cry at last. 'It sounds awfully hollow here! Tap it, you others. Then tap this bit. Can you hear the difference?'

They could. One panel sounded hollow, the other sounded solid. The woman watched them, looking bored.

But Snubby could not find out how to enter the secret passage. He pushed this and pulled that, but nothing happened at all. He turned to the woman at last.

'Tell us where it is exactly. It's very cleverly hidden.'

'Watch,' said the woman, and she went to an enormous tapestry picture over the mantelpiece. The children went with her. 'But the panelling sounds solid all round here,' protested Snubby. 'We tapped it.'

The woman said nothing. She reached up to the dim face in the old picture. The face wore a helmet, or what looked like a helmet, pushed back over its forehead. The woman pressed a stud in the helmet and then stood back.

The great picture slid silently to one side – about four inches only – but enough to show a small panel of wood that looked just a little different from the others.

The woman put her hand firmly on the small panel and pressed it to one side. It slid along under her hand, leaving a tiny space, just big enough for a hand to go into it.

'Feel inside the space,' she said. They all groped there, feeling curiously excited as they did so. There was something mysterious about this – a secret planned long ago

35

by a clever brain, a secret well hidden, and perhaps of great use more than two centuries before.

Each of them felt a knob in the space behind. 'Now you – press it,' said the guide, tapping Roger on the arm. He pressed the knob hard and it yielded suddenly beneath his hand. At the same moment something rattled softly behind the panelling not far off.

'That knob releases a lever which in turn enables us to press back a bigger panel,' said the woman, going to the panelling from behind which the rattle had come. She pressed her hand against a big panel, and it gradually slid into the wall, sliding neatly behind the panel next to it. A hole yawned there at last, big enough for a man to squeeze into. The woman shone her torch into the hole.

'There you are,' she said. 'Not much to see, really. Just a passage behind the panelling. It runs along beside it for a few feet and then goes downwards to the blind end I spoke of.'

'I want to go inside,' said Snubby, of course, and he put one leg into the hole.

The woman pulled him back roughly. 'No!' she said. 'No one is allowed to go inside. Now surely you don't want to get dirtier than you are! Get back at once.'

Snubby struggled away, and tried his hardest to get into the dark hole. He badly wanted to follow that secret passage. Why did it go to a blind end? Was it only a hiding-place, then, not a passage? He didn't believe it.

The woman got angry. 'I shall report you,' she said, still holding Snubby by his coat. 'Do you want me to lose my job? Now, you just do as you're told. And listen to those dogs of yours barking! Something's up. You'd better go and see what's the matter.'

Snubby heard Loony and Loopy barking and he reluctantly got back into the room. But he made up his mind about one thing – he was going to explore that secret passage before his holiday was ended!

All three rushed out into the front garden of Ring O' Bells Hall to see what was exciting the dogs. It was only another dog! He had come trotting by, and had smelt the two bones belonging to Loony and Loopy. He had also seen that the other two dogs were tied up.

He had apparently nipped up to them and taken one of the bones before either Loony or Loopy had seen him. Then he had sat himself down well out of reach and proceeded to crunch up the bone.

This, of course, made the two spaniels go nearly off their heads with rage and desperation, and if their leads had not been very strong, there is no doubt that the four-footed thief would have been chased out of the country!

As it was, all they could do was to bark madly, almost strangling themselves with their leads. Snubby ran at the thief-dog, and he tore off, leaving the bone behind him.

'Take your dogs away,' called the woman from the door of Ring O' Bells Hall. 'And don't come here again with them. Anyway, you've seen all there is to see.'

The children went off, the dogs still on the lead, straining after the scent left behind by the other dog. Snubby got cross. 'Stop it, Loony – you're almost pulling my arm out. You've got your bone back, so what's all the excitement about?'

Diana suddenly looked white. Roger noticed it and took her arm. 'Come on, old girl,' he said, 'we'll get back. This is the first day since the 'flu that we've taken much exercise or had much excitement. You looked fagged out. Lean on me and we'll go home.'

They were all very glad to get back to the house. Miss Pepper was there, looking out for them. Lunch was being laid, but alas, none of them felt quite like it after their rather peculiar morning.

'You all look very tired,' said Miss Pepper reproachfully. 'Whatever have you been up to?'

'Only talking to old Mother Hubbard and getting the dogs a bone, and seeing over Ring O' Bells Hall,' said Snubby, sinking down into a chair. 'And examining secret hidey-holes in fireplaces and secret passages behind panels and–'

'Oh, Snubby! You surely haven't been doing all that?' said Miss Pepper. 'And what in the world has made you so dirty? *Look* how dirty you've made that cushion. You look as if you've been up a chimney or something.'

'Good guess!' said Snubby. 'Oh, Miss Pepper – *must* I go and change and have a bath and all that? I do suddenly feel so tired.'

He wasn't pretending. Miss Pepper patted him kindly, and then was horrified to find a cloud of sooty dust rising into the air out of his shoulder. Dear, dear – trust Snubby to arrive home in some sort of dirty state. But she hadn't the heart to make him change even his coat.

They ate rather a poor lunch, mostly because they had had a late and very good breakfast. Then they dragged themselves off to have a rest in their beds. Snubby managed to undress himself and throw his sooty things down to Miss Pepper. Then, rolled round in his dressing gown, he fell fast asleep.

'That 'flu really did take it out of them, poor things,' said Miss Pepper to her cousin Hannah, as they sat sewing together peacefully that afternoon. There wasn't a sound to be heard from the children. Loony was on Snubby's bed, of course, and Loopy was out in the garden, making futile leaps at the cat on the wall.

'You've done enough walking for today,' said Miss Pepper firmly, when the children came down to tea, showing signs of a healthy appetite. 'Just potter about the

38

garden after tea. You can feed the chickens for Miss Hannah and collect the eggs.'

However, Loony and Loopy made up for the lack of energy on the part of the children, by indulging to the full their craze for purloining mats, towels and brushes, and when the children arrived back in the garden after feeding the hens, and looking for eggs, they found half the mats and towels in the house strewn over the grass. Somebody's hairbrush sat in the middle of a clump of polyanthus!

Loony got a spanking with the hairbrush and retired under the sofa, sulking. Loopy, who had never seen anyone spanked with a hairbrush before, rushed away in horror and didn't appear till suppertime.

'By the way,' said Miss Pepper, at supper, 'do you ever hear from that strange friend of yours – Barney. He was a circus boy, wasn't he – and had a monkey called Miranda.'

'Yes,' said Roger. 'We don't *very* often hear from him. He's been all over the place since we last saw him. We ought to hear soon, though. Good old Barney.'

'Who's this?' asked Miss Hannah, with interest. 'Barney? I've not heard of him before.'

'Oh, he's a circus boy we made friends with,' said Roger. 'He's a nice chap. Mother likes him, so you can guess he's all right. He's got no mother, but he's hoping to find his father one day. He's got one somewhere – an actor, he thinks. But you should see Miranda, his monkey.'

'No thank you,' said Miss Hannah, with a shudder. 'I can't bear the nasty little things. I hope you won't hear from your friend just yet, anyway, if he's got a monkey.'

But they did hear from Barney – the very next day too.

Chapter Six

News from Barney

The three children didn't wake quite so late the next day. In fact, though rather on the late side, they were down for breakfast with Miss Pepper and Miss Hannah.

And by Roger's plate was a letter in Barney's characteristic handwriting – large, sprawling, slanting all over the envelope! Good, good, good!

Roger snatched it up. 'I say – a letter from old Barney! Funny we should have been talking about him last night. I wonder if there's any chance of seeing him.'

He tore open the envelope and read the letter aloud, with Diana and Snubby hanging on every word.

'DEAR ROGER,

Just to say I'm out of a job again after a very good one indeed. What do you think I've been doing? Looking after a troupe of monkeys in a circus! Right up my street, of course. Miranda's had a grand time – putting on no end of airs, and bossing all the monkeys in the troupe.

Well, I made a good bit of money, and I thought it would be nice to see you all again. The only thing is – won't you have gone back to school by now? If you have, it's no use, of course, and I'll have to try and see you all in the summer. But if you're not back yet, let me know, and I'll hitch-hike along to you, no matter how many miles it is. Can't neglect my old friends like this too long, else they'll be forgetting me!

So long – and here's hoping to see you.

BARNEY.

Miranda sends warm love.'

All three looked at one another in glee. 'Good old Barney! Dear old Barney! We'll have to get him along here to Ring O'Bells Village, and see him again for a bit. What a bit of luck we aren't back at school yet!' Roger rubbed his hands joyfully.

'Barney can't come here with his monkey,' said Miss Hannah firmly. 'I'm having no monkeys in my house. If the boy likes to ask someone to look after his monkey for him, I'd be pleased to have him here, for your sake – but no monkey. That's flat.'

'Oh!' said all three. They knew perfectly well that nothing in the world would persuade Barney to leave Miranda with anyone else. It was quite unthinkable.

'He could perhaps lodge somewhere in the village,' said Miss Pepper, seeing the children's disappointed faces.

'Yes. Though as it's May and so fine and warm he'd probably just as soon sleep out of doors,' said Diana, remembering that Barney didn't need a roof over his head, as ordinary people did. 'He'll find a barn or hay-stack or something.'

'Very well,' said Miss Hannah. 'But I will not have the monkey here. Becky, you'll see that it doesn't come here, won't you?'

Miss Pepper nodded at her cousin. 'Yes, Hannah. Don't worry – the monkey shan't come here – though it's not a bad little thing at all. I didn't mind it after a bit.'

Miss Hannah gave a mild snort. 'Well, I should never, never take to a monkey,' she said. 'And at my time of life I'm not going to try.'

The children went out into the garden after they had made their beds and tidied up. Diana took her fountain pen, and Roger had note-paper and envelopes. Snubby,

41

as usual, merely looked on and made unhelpful remarks about what to say to Barney.

'Dear Barney,' wrote Diana:

'Thanks awfully for your letter. You'll be surprised at our address, but we've had 'flu, and we've all been sent away here for a change, Snubby and Loony too. Loony didn't have the 'flu though, of course. There's a dog here, called Loopy, who's very good company for Loony, because he's just as idiotic.'

'Tell Barney how he takes all the mats out,' put in Snubby.

Diana took no notice. 'I wonder if I've spelt "idiotic" right,' she said. 'Yes, I think I have. I'll go on now.'

She went on with the letter, with Roger and Snubby looking over her shoulder, breathing down her neck.

'We all felt pretty awful after the 'flu, and . . .' she went on writing. Snubby interrupted.

'Tell him my legs felt just like jelly,' he said.

'*Do* you think that would interest him?' said Diana scornfully. 'Who cares about your jelly-legs? And do stop panting down my neck. You feel like Loony.'

Loony heard his name and bounced up at her, so that her pen made a deep mark across the letter. 'Blow you, Loony – it was such a nice neat letter and now look what you've done. Anyway, Barney will guess it was you. Get down!'

'Go on, Di – you've just written: "We all felt pretty awful after the 'flu," ' said Roger. 'Are you going to tell him how to get here? He won't have any notion of where this place is.'

'If he's going to hitch-hike, what's the good of telling him?' asked Diana. 'I'll just say, "Show this address to anyone you're hitch-hiking with, and they'll tell you if you're going in the right direction or not." '

42

'Tell him about the secret passage,' said Snubby. 'He'll like that.'

'You seem to think I'm writing a *book* or something.' said Diana, exasperated. 'And *will* you stop breathing down my neck. I'm going to end the letter now. It's long enough already.'

She finished it. 'We're here with Miss Pepper, you remember her, don't you? We're staying with her cousin, Miss Hannah, who doesn't like monkeys, so you won't be able to stay with us, worse luck. But we can arrange something when we see you. Lots of love to darling Miranda

Your friends,

Diana, Roger and Snubby.

P.S. – Loony sends his best woof.'

They all signed their names, and Diana heaved a sigh of relief. 'There – that's done. I do hate writing letters, but it's nice to be able to tell Barney to come. *What* a bit of luck we're not back at school!'

They posted the letter, and speculated for some time as to when Barney would get to them. 'He'll get our letter tomorrow,' said Roger. 'And maybe he'll start straight away. If he hitch-hikes as cleverly as he usually does, he might be here any time after tomorrow.'

This was very cheering. Everyone felt much better somehow, now that they could look forward to seeing Barney and Miranda.

They pictured Barney's wide-set startlingly blue eyes in his brown face, and Miranda's dear little monkey face. Yes – it really would be fine to see them both again.

On the way back from the post, they passed Mother Hubbard's Cottage. The old lady was out in the garden, picking polyanthus. She smiled at them.

'Good morning, Mother Hubbard,' said Snubby, quite forgetting it wasn't her real name. Roger and Diana gave him a punch, one each side. He was taken aback. 'Oh – er – I mean – well, good morning, Mam!'

The old lady laughed. 'Call me Mother Hubbard if you like,' she said. 'It's no matter to me what I'm called. And I've certainly got a cupboard, though it isn't bare.'

'Is your Grandad asleep today?' asked Roger, remembering the old, old man with his fierce, shaggy eyebrows and fluff of white hair round his head.

'I'll see,' said Mother Hubbard, and disappeared. She soon came back. 'No, he's not asleep,' she said. 'You go out and talk to him. He's got a wonderful memory, though he repeats himself sometimes. He remembers what happened years ago, better than what happens these days. Why, he forgets what he had for dinner as soon as he's eaten it, poor old man!'

They had to leave Loony and Loopy tied up outside, of course. Old Grandad didn't like dogs. Mother Hubbard took them out of her back door into the little garden beyond. Old Grandad was there, sitting up in his cushioned chair, smoking a long clay pipe.

'Good morning,' said the three children, marvelling again at his immense eyebrows. They could hardly see his eyes because of them. They wondered how *he* could see. Diana secretly thought that he looked a little like an old English sheepdog, with its shaggy hair over its eyes!

'Good morning to you all,' said Old Grandad, and pointed with his clay pipe to the ground. 'Sit you down, and tell me your names and who you be. I've not set eyes on you before.'

They told him their names. He chuckled when he heard Snubby's. 'Ah, they call you that acause of your turn-up nose, don't they? And do you see *my* nose? Button of a thing it is – and so they used to call me Button. And Button I be now, to my pals – Button Dourley, I am, and Button Dourley I'll die. I misremember my rightful name.

44

Mebbe it was John, mebbe it was Joe. But my nose named me, just like your nose named *you*!' And the old fellow pointed his pipe at Snubby and went off into a peculiar cackle of laughter, rather like a hen makes when she has laid an egg.

What he said interested the children very much. They sat up, all ears, when he told them his name. It wasn't the 'Button' so much, it was the surname – Dourley. Where had they heard it before? It rang a bell in the mind of each of them.

Diana remembered first. 'Hugh Dourley!' she said, out loud. 'Of course – Hugh Dourley.'

The old man heard her, and his shaggy eyebrows drew down even farther over his eyes. He pointed his pipe at Diana.

'That's my name you said just now, young lady! It was Hugh – that's right. It wasn't John or Joe – it was Hugh. How come I forgot it? But how do you know that, young lady?'

Diana was remembering how she had heard the woman at Ring O' Bells Hall telling the history of the old mansion. What was it she had said? Oh, yes! 'In 1645 Hugh Dourley lived in this Hall, and it was he who first caused it to be called Ring O'Bells,' she had droned.

Diana answered Old Grandad. 'We heard there was a Hugh Dourley who put in the bells at Ring O' Bells Hall,' she said. 'It's such an unusual name – Dourley – I remembered that long-ago Hugh Dourley, when you said *your* surname was Dourley. That's all.'

The old man had sunk back into his chair. His eyes were closed all but a slit.

He opened them suddenly and leaned over to children as if he had a secret to tell. 'Hugh Dourley was my Great-great-great-great-grandad,' he half-whispered. 'I don't know how many Greats. Yes, I'm one of the Dourleys of

Ring O'Bells. I know all about that old place – I know things nobody else knows. Maybe I'll tell you a few – just a few. Shall I?'

The three children were thrilled beyond   s. They looked at Old Grandad, and at last Diana spoke.

'Would you really tell us about Ring O'Bells Hall? It's such an old, mysterious place – full of secrets. We saw that secret chamber in the old fireplace, and–'

'Oh that,' said Grandad scornfully. 'That's a poor thing. I doubt if anyone ever hid up there.'

'And we saw how the tapestry moved, so that the lever could be worked to free that big panel,' said Snubby. 'But the woman there wouldn't let us get into the secret passage behind.'

'Ah, many's the time I've been in that,' said Old Grandad, with a chuckle.

'What's the use of it?' asked Roger. 'Was it just a hiding-place, not really a passage? Does it go to a blind end, as the woman said?'

'A blind end!' said the old man, astonished. 'No, that it doesn't. Blind end indeed! What would be the good of that? No, no, young sir – that was a way of escape from the house centuries ago. Times were good and bad in those days, just like they are now – and the folks at Ring O' Bells never knew when enemies might come – or gangs of roaming thieves – or folks after revenge. Those were cruel days, so I've heard my old Grandad say.'

'*Your* old Grandad!' said Diana, in amazement. 'Good gracious – that must go right back into history. How old were you when your Grandad told you these tales?'

'That's getting on for a hundred years ago now,' said

ctoria was on the throne, and a bonny
she was too. It's said she visited Ring O'
nce, but I misremember that.'

'Do go on,' said Diana. 'How old was your Grandad
when he told you these tales?'

'Oh, he were a youngster,' said the old man with a
curious high chuckle. 'He were only sixty mebbe, or there-
abouts. But he'd heard plenty from *his* old Granny, and
the tales he told you wouldn't believe!'

The children stared at him, watching his eyes go slit-
like under their shaggy eyebrows as he wandered far away
back into a past that seemed as near to him as the present
day of May sunshine and warmth. How curious to be so
old – how strange to read the pages of history in your
own mind, instead of in a book!

Diana patted the gnarled old hand softly. 'Are we
making you tired?' she said. 'Can you tell us any more?
What did your Grandad's old Granny tell *him*?'

The old man began to pour out a jumble of strange
tales. 'In the days when there were wolves round about
here,' he began, and immediately they seemed to be back
in Red Riding Hood's time!

'In the days when there were wolves, there came a hard
winter. Ground were so hard that my old Grandad said
sparks could be knocked out of it if so be you hammered
it! But that's a tale, o' course. Well, one night the wolves
came in a howling flock to Ring O'Bells, looking for
cattle, looking for chickens, aye, and looking for humans
too.'

'How horrible!' said Diana, with a shudder. 'Surely this
must be long long ago?'

'I told you, it were in my Grandad's Granny's time,'
said the old man, impatient at being interrupted. 'Folks
were asleep, and the wolves got nearer. They got to

48

Mother Barlow's cottage in Ring O' Bells Wood, and they smelled the old woman. And there they stood, howling–'

Old Grandad leaned forward suddenly in his chair, making the children jump. 'And what do you suppose happened?' he said, his cracked old voice rising high. 'Why, them bells in Ring O'Bells Hall rang out loud and clear! They did so – loud they rang, and woke everyone up.'

He sank back, and said no more. 'And I suppose the people heard the wolves howling, when they awoke, and went to drive them off, and rescued poor Mother Barlow?' asked Diana, after a minute or two. She felt that she *must* hear the end of the story.

'Ay, that's it,' said Old Grandad, seeming to wake up again. 'But here's the peculiar bit, Missy – no one rang those bells – they rang theirselves!'

Diana gave a little shiver. 'That's what the woman at the Hall said,' she remembered. 'She said the bells rang themselves when Hugh Dourley's son was killed one night – and ever since then they rang themselves when enemies came. And as the wolves were enemies of the little village, I suppose it was right for the bells to ring themselves again! How very weird!'

'Have they rung at other times?' asked Snubby, who was very thrilled by all this.

'Oh, yes – there was the time when the outlaws came creeping up at night,' said Old Grandad. 'And the day when soldiers came to take old Dourley off to prison – that were in my own Grandad's time. Many's the time he's told me that tale. Out rang the bells, all of a sudden, and old James Dourley escaped down the secret passage.'

'The secret passage – the very one we saw yesterday!' said Roger. 'It can't possibly have a blind end then.'

'The soldiers went after him,' went on the old man.

'Down the passage they went, climbing in one after another – but he got away.'

'Where does the passage go to?' asked Roger, getting quite worked up with all these old stories.

'You ask Mother Barlow,' said the old man, and he gave his curious high chuckle again. 'She knows all right.'

The children looked at one another, puzzled.

'But – you said Mother Barlow lived in the time when there were wolves,' said Diana. 'She's not alive now.'

'But she'm there all right,' said Old Grandad. 'In her old cottage. *She* knows, I tell you. Ah, she knows. Old Grandad doesn't give away too many secrets.'

This was most exasperating. The old man must be wandering in his mind, Diana thought. Perhaps he was tired out with all his talking, and was muddling up past and present.

'Don't *you* know where the secret passage goes to?' asked Diana, trying again. 'Does it go to the cellars of Ring O' Bells Hall? Or does it go to–'

'It goes to Mother Barlow,' said the old man obstinately. 'That's where it went when I was a boy. Me and Jim, my brother, we went down there once – and we found some old books.'

'Old books!' said Snubby excited. 'I say – have you still got them?'

'Where did you find them – in the passage – or at Mother Barlow's?' asked Roger, feeling that the old man was getting muddled.

'Down in the passage,' whispered the old man, as if this were a secret. 'There was a little old cupboard there – hidden away – and me and Jim, we opened it. There were books and papers there – and a little old carved box – and I misremember what else.'

'Did you take them?' asked Snubby, after a pause. 'They weren't really yours, so I suppose you didn't.'

The old man took another long look back into the past. He began to mumble excitedly.

'Wasn't Jim and me of the Dourley family? Wasn't we Dourleys ourselves, even though we lived in a little cottage, and not at Ring O'Bells Hall? Who knew about them old things? They weren't no value. We thought mebbe some old Dourley had hidden them there long since – and we was Dourleys too, so why shouldn't we have them?'

The children could think of many reasons why the old man and his brother should not have had them, but they said nothing. What they really wanted to know was – were these old treasures still in existence!

Diana spoke to the mumbling old fellow, who now seemed to have got quite lost in the past. She spoke very gently, as if he were a child.

'Old Grandad – don't worry yourself about all this. You took the things, and brought them back. Have you still got them?'

'Aye, we took them back,' said Old Grandad, and a gleam came into his watery eyes. 'Jimmy had the box and I had the books.'

'What were the books about?' asked Roger.

The old fellow snorted. 'How was I to know? I couldn't read. I never did have no learning, but I wasn't any the worse for that.'

This was disappointing. Diana tried again.

'What happened to the books, Grandad? Have you still got them?'

'You ask my granddaughter,' said Old Grandad. 'She've got all my things now. But what's the use of them old books – she've burnt them long ago, no doubt!'

'Grandad, *do* tell us exactly where the secret passage goes,' begged Snubby.

The old man scowled at him so ferociously that Snubby drew back in alarm.

'Me and Jim got thrashed for going there,' he said. 'We boasted about it, see – and Mr Paul Dourley, who had the Hall then, he took us and he thrashed us till we yelled for mercy. He said if we told what we knew about it, he'd have us sent away from Ring O' Bells village, sent right away to a foreign country where we'd work as slaves. So Jim and me, we held our tongues. I'm not talking no more about it. You might get summat done to me, you might. Who be you, anyways?'

His voice rose, and he half got out of his chair.

'Why – you know who we are,' said Diana, scared. 'We're just three children. Your granddaughter told you our names and everything. We wouldn't do anything to hurt or harm you.'

But the old man was now so wrapped up in the past that he could no longer place the children in the present. He peered at them, as he sank back in his chair again.

'Who be you? Strangers come to pester me, and get my secrets! Prying and poking and worriting me!'

His voice rose high, and his granddaughter, Mother Hubbard, heard it. She came hurrying over.

'Now, now, Grandad – don't you go exciting yourself! Don't look so scared, children. He's been telling you some of his old tales, hasn't he? He always gets excited then.'

'He thought we were trying to pester him and pry secrets out of him,' said Diana, almost in tears. 'But we were just very interested, that's all.'

'Of course you were,' said Mother Hubbard. 'Now don't you worry. Grandad didn't always do right in his time – he's got a guilty conscience sometimes, poor old man – and when it begins to work, he gets afraid. He'll soon forget!'

She tucked the old man back into his cushions, and led the three children into the house. They looked round, wondering if they would see any old books. They didn't quite like to ask just then, after having upset the old grandfather.

'I must go back to the old man,' Mother Hubbard said, taking them to the little front door. 'You come along again whenever you like. You'll be welcome!'

Chapter Eight

A Morning in the Village

The children wandered off down the road, feeling rather bemused with all they had heard. They came to Ring O' Bells Hall, the two dogs racing round them in delight. They had gone nearly mad at being untied at last, though Mother Hubbard once more supplied them with bones to gnaw and keep them quiet.

They stood still and looked at the old stone mansion.

'I shouldn't have liked to live there,' said Diana.

'Those small windows, the dim light inside, the stone floors and walls, so very cold – ugh! It must have been a very uncomfortable place to live in.'

'And never knowing if the bells were going to ring out by themselves!' said Snubby. 'I should have been scared stiff. How *did* the bells ring by themselves? Who rang them? I mean – bells can't *really* ring themselves.'

'Don't let's talk about it,' said Diana, with a shiver. 'I expect it's all made-up tales, really. Things like that don't happen.'

The woman who acted as guide came out to sweep down the front path, and saw the children standing there.

Loony ran up to her at once and frisked round her in his usual friendly fashion. She swept out at him crossly with her brush.

Loony never could resist a brush. He leapt at it, trying to bite it, quite thinking that the woman was playing some sort of game with him.

Loopy then thought he would join in too, and the

54

woman got really angry, and half frightened. She hit out with the brush, and the dogs went quite mad with joy.

'Loony! Loopy! Come here!' called Roger at last. The dogs came obediently, and the woman glared at the children.

'Don't you bring them here again,' she said threateningly. 'I'll report you if you do.'

'Who to?' asked Roger. 'Do tell us! Is there a Mr Dourley you can report us to? We'd like to meet him, if so. We want to ask him questions about that secret passage!'

The woman stopped her sweeping and looked at Roger.

'That secret passage? What questions are there to ask? You've seen it, haven't you?'

'Yes – but you said it led to a blind end, and we've heard that it doesn't,' said Roger.

'Well, you heard wrong, then,' said the woman. 'It does. I've seen it myself! It's been walled up now, so it's no longer really a passage. It just comes to a blind end.'

'Oh,' said Roger. That seemed all there was to say. He hadn't thought of that solution. Secret passages were often walled up when they were no longer in use. It *was* quite likely that this one would be too, especially as Ring O'Bells Hall was now a show-place and no longer lived in.

'Do you know where the passage led to?' asked Snubby.

'To nowhere,' said the woman promptly. 'The roof had fallen in, and it was impassable – no one could get through it.'

'But where did it *once* lead to?' persisted Snubby.

'I don't think anyone knows that,' said the woman, beginning to sweep again, keeping a wary eye on Loony and Loopy, who were watching her brush longingly. 'It's not been used for centuries, I should think. Anyway, no one would want to explore the ruined old passage – the roof was likely to fall in at any moment, all the way along.'

'It's a long passage then?' asked Roger. But the woman didn't answer. She merely gave an impatient snort, shook the dust out of her brush, and disappeared into the dark hall behind her.

'She's a bad-tempered creature, isn't she,' said Diana. 'Well – I suppose she's right. The passage got dangerous, was of no use, and was walled up when the Hall was taken over as a show-place. I dare say the old house wasn't lived in for years, and everything was in an awful state. Some society or other must have bought it and opened it to show to tourists or trippers.'

'It's a pretty strange place, I must say, all furnished with old, forgotten things that seem to stand and dream in the rooms,' said Snubby.

The other two stared at him, surprised. 'You've gone all poetical or something,' said Roger.

'No, I haven't,' said Snubby, blushing at the idea of being called poetical. 'That old place seems to have got hold of me somehow. It's mysterious, with its hidden chambers and secret passages and bells that ring themselves. I'd just hate to spend a night there.'

'Well, nobody's asked you to,' said Roger. 'So don't worry!'

'Look – Loony's gone into the Hall!' said Diana suddenly.

'Loony, Loony, Loony!'

Loony came tearing out with a brush in his mouth, looking very pleased with himself indeed.

'You idiot!' said Snubby, and took it from him. It was a small, hard brush, used for stair-carpets and mats.

Snubby took it cautiously back to the front door and peeped inside. There seemed to be no sign of the guide-woman so he tiptoed inside to replace the brush somewhere.

An angry voice made him jump. 'Now then! I can see you, coming in to snoop round without paying! If I have any more bother with you children and your dogs, I'll go straight to the police station and ask them to warn you about your behaviour!'

Snubby saw the woman at the back of the hall looking rather like an angry black witch against the light that trickled in through the slit-window there. He fled, and the others roared with laughter at him, as he came out at top speed, almost falling over the two delighted dogs.

'Heard the bells, or something?' inquired Roger. 'My word – your legs must have got over their jelly-feeling, or they wouldn't have taken you so fast just then. Talk about being jet-propelled!'

'Oh, stop it!' said Snubby crossly. 'Let's go and get some ice creams or something – if they've got any in this old village! They've probably never even heard of them.'

They went on down to the village. Diana began to talk about Old Grandad. 'It's like turning the pages of history to hear him talk,' she said. 'Wasn't it extraordinary, though, the way he mixed everything up – the past and the present – and thought we were people out of the past come to find out his old, old secrets and punish him. Poor old man.'

'Fancy him going down that secret passage and finding those old books and that carved box,' said Snubby. 'I suppose the box has gone long ago – he said his brother took that, didn't he? But it's quite likely that the *books* are still about somewhere.'

'He would probably have been scared in case anyone found out that he'd taken them,' said Roger, 'and he'd have hidden them away for years. Then he probably forgot

57

about them, and his granddaughter found them when she kept house for the old man.'

'And quite likely put them on the rubbish heap,' said Diana. 'Fancy the old fellow not being able to read! How tantalising to have exciting old books like that and not be able to read them!'

'I don't expect we'd be able to, either,' said Roger, making his way to a small village store that appeared to sell everything. 'I expect the words are in that peculiar old writing where all the letter s's are f's.'

'Or maybe in Latin,' said Diana. 'Well, Snubby could translate that all right, couldn't you, Snubby? You're good at Latin, aren't you?'

Snubby gave her a punch. Everyone knew that the remarks about Latin on Snubby's report were most sarcastic. Latin was not Snubby's best subject.

They sat down and had ice creams. They were very good ones too, made of real cream. After that they had glasses of orangeade, and felt much better.

'I'm almost forgetting we've had 'flu now,' said Snubby, sucking up his orangeade through a long straw. 'I feel much more myself.'

'What a pity,' said Roger. 'A little of you goes a long way, Snubby. Too far.'

'Don't be funny,' said Snubby. 'I don't feel well enough yet to punch your head when you make one of your fatheaded remarks – but I soon shall!'

'Woof,' said Loony, putting a paw on Snubby's knee. Snubby looked down. 'What do you want? You don't like orangeade.'

'Maybe he's thirsty,' said the shopwoman, and she put down a dish of water for the dogs. They lapped noisily.

'Oh, thanks!' said Snubby. 'That's nice of you!'

The shop bell rang and somebody came in. Diana nudged Roger.

'Somebody out of a fairy tale,' she whispered. It was a little old woman in an old red cloak. A ragged hood hung down her back.

'Red Riding Hood grown old,' whispered back Roger. Diana nodded in delight. Yes – Red Riding Hood grown old – and maybe still living in the same cottage as in her childhood. It wasn't possible of course – but it pleased Diana to fancy it!

'A pound of butter, please – and an ounce of black pepper – and a bag of flour – and a jar of your own honey,' said the cloaked customer, in a small clear voice. She turned to look at the children as she stood waiting.

She had curious eyes – almost green, Diana thought. Her mouth was the mouth of an old woman, fallen in and toothless, but her eyes were still very bright. Her hair was snow-white and still curly, and she smiled and nodded at the children.

'Good morning,' she said, in her small, rather child-like voice. 'Are you visiting here?'

'Yes,' said Diana politely. 'We're staying with Miss Hannah Pepper. We've had 'flu so that's why we're not back at school yet. Do you know Miss Pepper?'

'Oh yes,' said the old woman. 'I worked for her mother years ago. You tell her you've seen me – she'll remember me all right.'

'I will,' said Diana. 'What is your name?'

'Barlow,' said the old lady. 'Naomi Barlow, and I live out in Ring O' Bells Wood.'

'Barlow!' said all three children at once. They had immediately remembered what Old Grandad had said. 'Ask Mother Barlow!' Could this old woman be the same Mother Barlow he was thinking of?

Before they could make up their minds to ask her, the old lady was away out of the shop with her bag of goods. Diana turned to the shopwoman.

'Er – we've heard today of a Mother Barlow,' she said. 'I suppose – I suppose *that* wasn't Mother Barlow, was it?'

The shopwoman laughed. 'Dear me, no – Mother Barlow lived long ago – before my time! She lived where old Naomi lives now – in Ring O' Bells Cottage away out in the wood.'

Chapter Nine

Talk at Tea-Time

The children paid their bill and walked slowly back to
Hannah Pepper's cottage. 'Ring O' Bells Cottage away
out in the wood!' repeated Diana two or three times.
'This is all getting more like a nursery rhyme place than
ever – or a fairy tale!'

'Did you notice the curious greenish eyes that Naomi
Barlow had?' asked Roger rather sheepishly. 'Witches
have green eyes – or they were supposed to.'

'Don't be silly,' said Snubby. '*She* wasn't anything like
a witch – she was a nice old thing, I thought.'

'I didn't say she was a witch, or even *like* one,' said
Roger. 'I just pointed out that she had unusual eyes. I'm
not idiot enough to believe in witches nowadays.'

'*I* thought she looked exactly what Red Riding Hood
would look like when she grew old,' said Diana. 'With
that old red cloak and ragged hood. You could imagine
Red Riding Hood keeping the cloak for years and years
and years.'

'She'd probably grow out of it,' said Snubby, getting
rather tired of this conversation about green eyes and
witches and cloaks. 'Let's get home quickly. I'm *just*
beginning to feel my legs going a bit wobbly again.'

'You and your legs,' said Diana. 'There doesn't look
anything wrong with them to me.'

Miss Pepper insisted on their having a rest again that
afternoon, though Snubby, whose legs seemed to have
made a miraculous recovery, wanted to go and hire a
horse for riding over the countryside.

'Well, you can't,' said Miss Pepper. 'You're to have a rest.'

'Couldn't I just have a quarter of an hour's rest and then take Loony for a walk?' asked Snubby. 'He's awfully fat. He *needs* a long walk this afternoon.'

'I agree with you,' said Miss Pepper. 'He's much too fat – and he does need a long walk. I'll take him myself this afternoon, with Loopy – though my name will probably be Dotty, when I come back – I shall certainly be driven crazy with two mad dogs capering round me.'

'Ha ha – joke,' said Snubby automatically. He didn't think much of Miss Pepper's jokes. 'No, Miss Pepper – I'd rather have Loony on my bed with me, thank you. You can take Loopy.'

'Thank you very much,' said Miss Pepper. 'Now *will* you go upstairs at once and do as you're told? I warn you that if you start being awkward, I shall go back to an old punishment of mine, and you won't like it.'

'What's that?' asked Snubby, with great interest. 'I'm sure I shouldn't mind your punishments very much, Miss Pepper.'

'Right,' said Miss Pepper. 'We'll try this one then – no jam or cake at tea – only bread and butter.'

This didn't sound so good. Snubby hastily went up the stairs, with Loony at his heels. He felt sure he would be far too hungry at tea-time to relish a silly punishment like that.

He was more tired than he knew, and slept solidly till tea-time, with Loony stretched over his legs, sleeping too. Loopy could not imagine where Loony disappeared to in the afternoons and, after hunting vainly for him in all kinds of unlikely places, including the coal-hole, he went off happily with Miss Pepper for a walk.

Snubby was very glad that Miss Pepper said nothing about his having no jam or cake at tea, when he sat down at tea-time feeling extraordinarily hungry after his long sleep.

'Hot scones!' he said, touching the warm dish. 'Goody! Home-made butter and home-made honey! Couldn't be better. And what's that over there? New currant-bread? Oh, I say – whatever shall I begin on first?'

'Don't sound so greedy, Snubby,' said Diana, helping herself to a scone. 'And don't gobble. You've got plenty of time before you reach the cake stage.'

'Shut up,' said Snubby. '*You* can teach me about gobbling any time!'

Miss Hannah looked across at Miss Pepper, and gave her a small smile. 'They're rapidly recovering from the 'flu,' she said.

'They are,' said Miss Pepper. 'Snubby, will you tell Loony to remove himself from my feet. I think he's under the impression that he's sitting on yours, and he's really very heavy.'

Loony removed himself, and Loopy immediately took his place. Miss Pepper put up with it. She didn't like to ask Hannah to tell Loopy to remove *himself*. The dogs always seemed to play this kind of 'musical chairs' at meal times.

'I wonder if old Barney will come quickly,' said Snubby. 'I wonder if he's got our letter yet.'

'Of course he hasn't,' said Diana. 'We only posted it this morning.'

'Did we really?' said Snubby, astonished. 'You know, this holiday's beginning to act like all holidays – time seems to get all muddled up – and then, whoosh – the whole holiday's gone before you've even got it by the tail.'

'Don't talk such nonsense, Snubby,' said Miss Pepper – but Diana and Roger knew exactly what Snubby meant.

'Miss Hannah,' said Diana, remembering the green-eyed old woman in the village shop, 'do you know an old lady called Naomi Barlow?'

'Dear me, yes,' said Miss Hannah. 'She worked for my dear old mother years ago – and a very good worker she was too. I remember her from when I was a small girl. She must be quite old now.'

'She lives in Ring O' Bells Cottage,' said Roger.

'Yes,' said Miss Pepper suddenly. 'That's the little cottage in the woods – the one I always thought must belong to Red Riding Hood.'

'Old Naomi Barlow has a red cloak and hood,' said Diana. 'She probably had them when she was much younger and you might have seen her. Miss Pepper. I expect that's what made you think of Red Riding Hood Cottage.'

'Do you know anything about old Mother Barlow who used to live in the same cottage years and years ago?' asked Roger.

'No,' said Miss Hannah. 'I've just heard the name somewhere, that's all. How did you hear about her?'

'We talked to Old Grandad this morning,' said Diana. 'You know – Mother Hubbard's grandfather.'

'Mother Hubbard?' said Miss Hannah, surprised. 'Whoever is she?'

'Well, that mayn't be her right name,' said Roger, 'but she lives at Hubbard Cottage and she *looks* exactly like Mother Hubbard. She's got a very old grandfather – he says he's over a hundred years old – but he looks more like two hundred to me.'

'Don't be absurd, Roger,' said Miss Pepper. 'I know who you mean, of course. I don't know his real name – everyone calls him Old Grandad.'

'His real name is Hugh Dourley and he's related in some way to the old Dourleys who used to live in Ring O' Bells Hall,' said Diana. '*He* told us about Mother

64

Barlow. He said she knew all about the secret passage under Ring O' Bells Hall.'

Miss Pepper looked bewildered – but her cousin followed what Diana meant. 'What a lot you seem to have found out in a day or two!' she said. 'I do remember a bit more about old Mother Barlow now. She must have lived about eighty or ninety years ago – when Old Grandad was a bit of a boy.'

'He *could* have known her then,' said Diana. 'Oh, what a pity she's not alive now – she could have told us all the secrets of Ring O' Bells Hall. Perhaps she even knew who it is that rings the bells to warn the village of danger!'

'Oh, that's an old, old story, almost a legend,' said Miss Hannah. 'The bells haven't rung during *my* lifetime! And you may be sure that if ever they did ring, they were rung by human hands. It was people like old Mother Barlow who put about these peculiar old stories. She was supposed to be a witch.'

'Was she *really*?' asked Diana. 'Oh, Miss Hannah! Then no wonder Naomi Barlow's got green eyes – she takes after Mother Barlow, the witch!'

'Don't take all this too seriously,' said Miss Pepper. 'These are only old tales and legends, with possibly no truth in them at all. Mother Barlow was probably a kindly old woman, who knew a good bit about herbs and the roots of plants, and could make medicines and ointments to cure all kinds of ills. That would be quite enough to make her a witch in the eyes of the ignorant village people!'

'I do like this place,' said Diana. 'I really do like places that are old and full of long-ago tales. Bits of real history are wrapped up in them, and it's so exciting to unwrap them and discover what they are.'

'As for Old Grandad, he's like a real live history book,'

said Roger. 'Why, he even told us a tale about wolves coming to Ring O' Bells Village!'

'That may be quite true,' said Miss Hannah. 'There is a place outside the village called Wolfwick – only a glen now with a cottage or two – where the wolves were supposed to gather in winter time.'

'I wish we could wake up one morning and find ourselves back in the past,' sighed Diana. 'Just to see what it was like. We might see Mother Barlow going by the window on her way to work.'

'And we'd see a sprightly youth with his brother, capering by to go to work in the fields,' said Roger with a grin.

'Who would they be?' asked Diana.

'Old Grandad and his brother Jim,' said Roger. 'I know it's impossible to think of Old Grandad ever being young, but he must have been.'

'And we might hear the bells ringing in Ring O' Bells Hall one night,' said Snubby. 'And if we could see into the old place, it would be full of the old Dourleys who lived there – children like us, but dressed differently.'

'And their dogs,' said Roger. 'Spaniels like Loony and Loopy, I expect. They were used a lot for country sport.'

Loony and Loopy had got up immediately on hearing their names. They came from under the table, wagging their tails eagerly, putting heavy paws up on Snubby and Roger.

'Are you tired of this silly conversation?' said Snubby, pulling Loony's long ears.

'We seem to have sat here a long time,' said Miss Pepper, pushing her chair back. 'Have you all finished?'

'Well, there's nothing left to eat,' said Snubby. And he was right. Every plate was empty, the whole of the currant-loaf was gone, and the big new fruitcake had disappeared too.

'I should think you'll be able to last till breakfast-time

now,' said Miss Pepper hard-heartedly, and was quite surprised at the chorus of, 'No, Miss Pepper, *no*!'

Chapter Ten

Barney Starts on a Journey

Next day the children went off to the riding stables and asked for horses to hack round the countryside. The owner was a youngish woman with a face so like a horse that it quite astonished the children.

She wore her hair tied down at the back of her neck like a horse's tail, and had a laugh like the whinny of a horse. But she was very nice indeed, and soon sized up the children's ability.

'You can have Tom Tit Tot,' she said to Snubby, who wasn't as big as the other two. 'And let me warn you, he stands no nonsense, so don't play the fool with him.'

He was a good little pony, sturdy, with white socks and a star on his forehead. Snubby liked him.

Diana had a quiet horse called Lady, and Roger had a fine-looking one called Heyho. The children had put on jodhpurs, yellow jerseys and riding coats – but they were far too hot, and left their coats hanging up on nails in the stables.

They walked their horses through the gate and into the road. 'Take the road up the hill and down through Ring O' Bells Wood,' said the riding mistress, when she saw them off. 'It's a beautiful ride, and good going for the horses.'

It was a most magnificent day. Birds sang joyously, lambs, fat and frisky, leapt about the hillside, the hawthorn was out everywhere like snow-drifts on the hedges. The trees were in new leaf, tender and green, and daisies sprinkled the grass all around.

'Oh Maytime, fold thy fleeting wing,
And let it be forever spring!'

sang Diana, as she cantered over a daisy-strewn path,
away up the hill.

They had a good gallop that morning. The horses were
fresh and happy, and the children were good horsemen.
They went almost to the top of the hill, which was long,
but not very steep and enjoyed the magnificent view
below.

'There's Ring O' Bells Village,' said Diana, pointing
with her whip. 'And look – aren't those the towers of
Ring O' Bells Hall – one square and one round, peeping
above the trees?'

'Yes – and there's the church,' said Snubby. 'Its spire
is sticking right up, not far from the Hall. Can we see
Miss Hannah's house from here?'

They couldn't. The wood stretched between them and
the house and hid it. It was a big wood, full of beech and
oak, some of the trees very tall and spreading.

'Look – there's a thin thread of blue smoke rising up
from that corner of the wood over there,' said Snubby
pointing. 'There must be a house in the wood.'

'Well, we know there is,' said Roger. 'Ring O' Bells
Cottage is there – where Naomi Barlow lives.'

'Oh, of course!' said Snubby. 'It's really not very far
from Ring O' Bells Hall, is it, tucked away in that corner
of the wood?'

'It's much farther than it looks,' said Diana. 'Can't you
picture old Mother Barlow down there in the cottage,
perhaps a hundred years ago, bending over her black iron
pot, boiling up all kinds of herbs and roots and things?
Perhaps the people of Ring O' Bells Hall bought their
physics from her – their ointments and medicines and
lotions.'

'A green-eyed witch,' said Roger. 'All the books say that witches or anyone distantly related to the Little Folk have green eyes. I'm sure Naomi's old grandmother, or whoever she was, was a witch, and that's why Naomi has green eyes.'

The horses stamped impatiently, and Loony and Loopy appeared from the rabbit holes they had been excitedly examining.

'Come on,' said Snubby. 'We sound a bit cracked when we talk like this. We none of us really believe it!'

But in their secret hearts they wondered if there *was* some truth in the old, old stories, and if bits of that truth were not still hidden here and there in this beautiful, ancient countryside. Diana, especially, wanted to believe it – it was romantic and exciting and mysterious.

They rode back through Ring O' Bells Wood. The path was broad, and the horses knew it well. Occasionally the children had to dodge twigs and low branches by bending this way and that. The wood was rather silent, and although sunshine came in here and there through the branches of the trees, their way seemed dim and shadowy.

'I wonder if we pass Ring O' Bells Cottage,' said Diana. 'It must be somewhere near here.'

'I can see smoke from a chimney, anyway,' said Snubby. 'It must be quite near. We shall pass it!'

But they didn't. A little path ran off the main path, and wound away between the trees. That must be the way to the cottage. Diana glanced at her watch.

'We oughtn't to stop and have a look at the cottage today,' she said regretfully. 'It's getting so late and we promised to have the horses back by half-past twelve. Anyway, it's a very narrow path for horses. We'd better bring the dogs up here for a walk one day, and have a good look at the old place.'

'Right,' said Roger, turning his horse down the broad

path. 'Come on. There's a good clearing there – we'll gallop!'

It was a good ride, and all three enjoyed it very much. The horses enjoyed it too, and the two dogs trotted home happily, their long pink tongues curling out of their mouths.

What a lunch the children ate! Miss Hannah looked on, quite dismayed, as they demolished a huge stew and an even huger treacle pudding.

'Becky, we can't let them go riding every morning if this is how it makes them eat!' she said comically.

'You can always do plenty more potatoes,' said Diana.

'I did you four each as it was,' said Miss Hannah. 'Well, well – you'll certainly feel better after today!'

They were tired that night, though. They only had a very short rest that afternoon, and by the time eight o'clock came not one of them could keep his eyes open. Even the dogs, tired out by their long walk, lay motionless on the hearth-rug, Loopy's head resting on Loony's black body. They were very fond of one another.

As they undressed, the two boys wondered about Barney. Had he got their letter yet? Would he, by any chance, arrive the next day? What fun if he did!

'Di!' called Snubby through the door. 'We're talking about Barney. He might come tomorrow, if he's got our letter.'

'Well, that's the very earliest he could arrive!' said Diana, getting into bed. 'We'll look out for him. Good old Barney. I wonder what Loopy will say to Miranda. He's never seen her. I should think old Loony will go mad with joy.'

Barney *was* on his way! He had got Diana's letter that very morning, and had read it with delight. He had no idea where Ring O' Bells Village was, of course. He had

71

been sleeping in a caravan lent to him by one of the men he knew, and all he had to do was to tidy it up, and return the key to the owner. Then he was ready to leave.

Barney travelled light. All his possessions were in a big red handkerchief, tied up in a knot, and either slung over his shoulder on the end of a stick, or carried knotted about his arm.

Miranda, of course, travelled on one or other of his shoulders! She sat there, a little bright-eyed creature, with an old, wizened-looking face, and a host of youthful ways. She was as mad and playful as a kitten.

'Now, Miranda, we're off on our travels again,' Barney said to her, as they set off together. 'You've had a mighty fine time lately – bossing all the other monkeys and pretending you're Princess Miranda, too high and mighty to do any performing in the ring!'

Miranda chattered back at him gaily. Barney listened seriously as if he understood every word. He certainly answered her as if he had!

'Well, I'm glad to hear you enjoyed yourself so much. Now who do you think we're going to see? Guess!'

Miranda bounced up and down on his shoulder, chattering again.

'Quite right, Miranda! We *are* going to see Diana, Roger and Snubby,' said Barney. 'And don't forget Loony!'

Most excited this time, Miranda gave another bounce or two. She recognised Loony's name, and a picture of the little black spaniel flashed into her monkey mind. She chattered excitedly, and nibbled Barney's ear.

'Now then, now then,' said Barney. 'Careful with that ear. You've already taken the edge off it.'

People turned and smiled as they saw the big, loose-limbed boy walking down the road, with the little monkey on his shoulder. Barney was very striking to look at, with his brilliant blue eyes set in his brown face. His hair was thick, the colour of ripe corn, and he looked the picture of health.

He took Diana's letter from his pocket, and looked at the address. He thought he had better try and make for the big town of Lillinghame, rather than for the village of Ring O' Bells. It wasn't likely that any lorry or van would be going to that little village, but one might go to Lillinghame, or near it.

He stood by the roadside, with Miranda on his shoulder, thumbing passing lorries. At last one stopped and the man beckoned him up to the seat beside him.

'That a monkey?' he said. 'Is she tame?'

'Oh yes,' said Barney. 'Salute this kind gentleman, Miranda.'

Miranda saluted smartly, bringing her tiny paw up to her forehead and down again. The man laughed.

'Well, I've given many people a lift, but never a monkey. This will be something to tell my little boy at home tonight. Where do you want to go to, mate?'

'Do you know Lillinghame?' asked Barney.

'Never heard of it,' said the driver disappointingly. 'Where is it?'

'It's in the county of Somerset,' said Barney, looking at Diana's letter. The man whistled.

'That's a long way, chum. You won't get there before tomorrow, unless you're lucky. I'm going about fifty miles on your way, then I turn off. You'll have to pick up another lorry then, going in your direction.'

'Right. Thanks,' said Barney, and off they went on the first stage of his long journey to Ring O' Bells.

Chapter Eleven

Hitch-Hiking all the Way

Barney and Miranda enjoyed the ride. They both liked the fresh air in their faces, and Miranda enjoyed the fussing and petting she got whenever the lorry stopped, and the driver had a minute to spare. He was very proud when she actually went to sit on his shoulder whilst he drove.

'She's got her paw down my neck, under my collar,' he said to Barney. 'I say – I suppose you wouldn't sell her, would you?'

'No, I wouldn't,' said Barney at once. 'For one thing I'm too fond of her – and for another she'd pine away and die if she left me.'

He hopped down after they had gone about fifty miles, and the driver rattled on, waving goodbye to him and Miranda, quite sorry to part from them both. Barney went to a roadside café to get something to eat, and to ask where was the best place to wait for lorries to thumb.

'Wait here, mate,' said the café owner, polishing his cups till they shone. 'This is a good pull-up for lorries – there'll be a lot along presently. Where do you want to go?'

'To Lillinghame in Somerset,' said Barney.

'You're a long way from there,' said the man. 'Let's see now – you want to take the Biddlington road – and get a lorry to drop you off at Biddlington. Then, if you're lucky you'll get a ride right into Somerset, and be able to pick up another lorry to Lillinghame.'

Lorries drove in soon after that, and the men got down

74

for snacks and a cup of coffee. The café owner introduced Barney and Miranda, and inquired whether anyone could take them on their way.

'I'm going that way,' volunteered a middle-aged driver, 'but I don't know as I can do with monkeys sitting beside me. I never did take to them.'

'Can I sit at the back then, out of your way?' asked Barney, anxious not to lose the lift. So it was agreed that he should sit at the back among the crates that the lorry was carrying.

It was very uncomfortable indeed. The floor of the van was hard, and the crates were even harder, the van shook as it rattled over the roads at a good speed, and poor Barney began to feel very bruised indeed. He was thankful when the van slowed down and the driver yelled to him.

'Better get down here, lad. I'll be taking you out of your way if you go any farther with me.'

Barney shouted his thanks and jumped down quickly with Miranda. The van rattled away, leaving him standing on a broad deserted road.

His luck was not so good after that. Not many lorries came by, and only a few private cars, which took no notice of him. Nobody wanted a monkey in a car!

Barney trudged on, mile after mile, thumbing each lorry or van that passed. He came to a small town and had something to eat, for he was getting very hungry. He bought Miranda a banana and some raisins. She loved raisins and spent a most enjoyable time picking the pips out of each before eating them.

The only thing was that she took it into her head to poke the pips down Barney's neck! 'Stop it!' said Barney in disgust. 'Miranda, I'm surprised at you – nasty, sticky, messy pips like that! I'll take your raisins away if you do that any more.'

Miranda stopped putting the pips down his neck, and spat them into the road instead. Barney laughed and went to stand at a good corner for thumbing traffic.

Nobody stopped for him until an enormous removal van came slowly by. Barney thumbed it hopefully. The two men sitting in front took no notice, but then one of them suddenly caught sight of Miranda on Barney's shoulder.

He nudged his companion, and the big van stopped.

'That a monkey you've got, mate?' yelled the driver.

'Yes!' yelled back Barney, and went to the front of the van.

'You go at the back of the van then, and tell Alf,' said the driver, with a broad grin. 'He's daft on monkeys. He'll let you go into the van and sit with him, if you'll let him play with your monkey.'

This was a bit of luck. Barney ran to the back of the van. A small man, with moustache rather like a walrus's was already looking out to see why the removal van had stopped so suddenly. When he saw Barney with Miranda he grinned in delight.

'They told you to come along and look for me, didn't they?' he said, nodding his head towards the front of the van. 'They know I'm cracked about monkeys. Come along in, lad, and make yourself comfortable. Where do you want to go to?'

Barney told him. The little man took down a map and had a look at it. He put a dirty fingernail on a certain spot and handed it to Barney. He held out his arms to Miranda, and the little creature leapt straight into them. Barney was surprised.

'They all know me,' said the small man, winking at Barney. 'I go to the Zoo whenever I'm back in London, and you should see the monkeys when they spot me coming along. They all crowd to one side of the cage, the

76

nearest they can get to me, and put their tiny hands through the bars for their titbits. Talk about dogs! Give me a monkey every time! As for cats, you can have the lot. Now a monkey is—'

He went on chattering without a pause, and soon Miranda began chattering too. Barney looked up in amusement. The two of them looked distinctly alike! The man had a little wizened face, with monkey eyes, and his moustache looked like thick whiskers. He was enjoying himself thoroughly.

Barney had a much more comfortable journey this time. The van was full of furniture, and he and the little man reclined at their ease in big soft arm-chairs whose springs gave to every bump on the road. Barney felt as if he could go to sleep at any moment!

He had looked at the map, which he didn't understand at all. He knew all he needed to know – that he had to get off at the third big town, and then see whether he could get a lift from there to Lillinghame. He could walk after that.

The little monkey-faced man was almost in tears at having to part with Miranda when the van drew up at the town where Barney had to get out. Miranda clung to him as if she too hated to part with him, but when she saw Barney stepping down from the van, she was on his shoulder with one enormous bound. She waved to the disconsolate little man.

'Well, you certainly gave him a treat, and got us a welcome lift,' said Barney to Miranda, as he waited at the corner for another lorry to come by. It was getting rather dark by this time. Barney began to wonder if he would get to Ring O' Bells Village in time to see the children.

It was quite dark when a small, closed van came by. As it passed a lamp-post Barney saw the name on it.

'PIGGOTT, ELECTRICIAN.' He stepped out and thumbed it.

It accelerated at once, swerved past him and went on. Barney was used to this sort of thing and stepped back to the pavement. Then he saw that the van had stopped some way down the road. He wondered why. Perhaps it had stopped for him, after all?

He went to see. He soon saw that the van had a puncture in one of the front wheels. The driver was already out of his seat and looking at it.

'Bad luck, mate,' said Barney, going up. 'Want any help? That was a pretty sudden puncture.'

'This wheel's been a bit of a nuisance lately,' said the man. He was short and plump, but that was all that Barney could make out in the dark. 'Do you know anything about changing a wheel? I don't want to get my hands filthy, and all the garages will be shut by now. I'll make it worth your while if you can change this wheel for me.'

'Yes – I know how to change wheels,' said Barney. 'And if you'd give me a lift to Lillinghame, if you're going there, sir, that'd be payment enough. I just want a lift, that's all.'

The man hesitated. He struck a match and looked at Barney as if he wondered whether he might be taking on a rogue or a ruffian for a lift. When he saw that Barney was only a boy, he looked relieved. 'Right,' he said. 'You change my wheel and I'll take you to Lillinghame. I go right through it.'

Barney was pleased. He set to work, whilst Miranda sat on the roof of the van and watched. She disappeared after a while, and the man looked round for her.

'Where's that monkey of yours?' he asked. 'I don't want her in my van.'

'Miranda!' called Barney. There was a scuffle from

inside the van, and then Miranda's face appeared at a small open window in front of the van, just by the driver's seat.

'She went inside!' exclaimed the man. 'Get her out quick!'

'She won't do any harm to anything, sir,' said Barney. Miranda had now disappeared again inside the van. She was very inquisitive and liked to explore and examine any strange place as thoroughly as possible.

Suddenly there was an agonised shriek from her inside the van. Barney snatched up a torch the man had lent him, and thrust it inside the opening in the front of the van. He was just in time to see something white moving quickly at the bottom of the van. Miranda was crouched at the back, squealing in fright.

Barney watched to see if the moving white thing appeared again, but he could see nothing but boxes and sacks. Then he felt himself roughly pulled away and the torch snatched from his hand.

The driver shouted at him. 'Come away from there, you and your monkey. Don't mess about with my goods.

'All right, all right,' said Barney, surprised at all the excitement. 'Here, Miranda, what's frightened you?'

The monkey had now climbed out, and had scrambled on to Barney's shoulder, trembling. Something had obviously given her a fright.

'Shall I finish changing the wheel, sir?' asked Barney. 'Sorry my monkey got inside. She's always so inquisitive.'

The man hesitated, then spoke roughly. 'All right – finish the wheel, but buck up about it. I don't want to be all night on the road!'

Chapter Twelve

Journey's End

Barney finished changing the wheel in silence, with Miranda clinging tightly to his shoulder, still very scared. The boy was remembering the white moving thing he had seen in the van. What was it? It was something that had frightened Miranda very much, that was plain. Was it something alive, or what?

'Thanks,' said the man, when Barney had finished. 'Here's some money. I won't give you a lift after all. I've changed my mind.'

'Oh no, you haven't,' said Barney, and he slipped quickly into the seat beside the driver. 'A bargain is a bargain. I don't want money. I want a lift. Now don't try to turn me off my seat, or my monkey will fly at you. She can bite hard.'

The man said something under his breath, stood still for a moment and then climbed up into his own seat. He let in the clutch, and away they went into the night, the van's strong lights raking the road in front of them.

Neither Barney nor the man said a word. Miranda made no sound, but clung to Barney tightly. She didn't like this man beside him.

'Here's Lillinghame,' said the man at last, and stopped. He said no more at all, but watched Barney get down. Barney looked up in the darkness into the white blur of the man's face.

'Thanks,' he said. 'Tell me one thing before I go. What have you got in your van that frightened my monkey so much?'

'Pah!' said the man, fiercely and angrily, and drove off so suddenly that Barney almost fell to the ground. He laughed and patted Miranda.

'Whatever's in that van is a mystery,' he said. 'And if you could talk really *properly*, Miranda, you could tell me what it was. Nasty little fellow, wasn't he?'

Barney walked on until he came to a signpost. He heaved a sigh of relief, because on it, lighted now by the moon which had sailed out from behind a cloud, was the name he wanted – RING O' BELLS!

'Good,' said Barney. 'I haven't done so badly to come all the way here in one day. The thing is – it's too late to find where Roger and the others are now – so we'll just walk into Ring O' Bells, Miranda, and see if we can find somewhere to sleep.'

As he walked down the road, the moon sailed into great black clouds that were coming up from the west. Soon rain fell, and Barney pulled up his coat collar. He debated whether to shelter under a hedge or not, but decided to go on. The rain might not last long.

He trudged on, with Miranda now tucked under his coat. She hated the rain. He came to another signpost at a fork in the road. 'RING O'BELLS two miles.'

That didn't seem far to Barney. The rain was now only a drizzle, so on he went, whistling very softly. Tomorrow he would see his friends. He hadn't seen them for weeks and weeks. It would be good to meet them all again.

He walked down the road and along lanes, past small cottages and one or two farmhouses. Then after passing into Ring O' Bells Village, which was now silent and dark with not a light to be seen, Barney stood still and debated with himself.

Where now? The rain had begun to pour again, and he didn't somehow fancy a night under a hedge. He might find a haystack and burrow into that. So on he went, bending his head to the pelting rain.

He came to a great building, its black shadow making the night even darker. He wondered what it was. If it was a church, perhaps he could creep into the porch and sleep there out of the rain. He walked cautiously up the flagged path, and then stopped.

He could hear voices – low voices. Where were they? Barney slipped into the shadow of a bush. He waited. Then he heard a door closing very quietly, and some one came up the flagged path in soft-soled shoes. Then someone went to the gate – and then, to Barney's amazement, he heard a car starting up outside!

He hadn't noticed any car outside. It must have been driven well into the shadow of the hedge, or he would surely have seen it. He ran on tiptoe to the gate. Someone stood there, lighting a cigarette, unaware that there was anyone watching nearby. As the match flared up, Barney recognised him!

'It's the man who gave me a lift to Lillinghame – the man whose wheel I changed for him!' he thought. 'Short and plump – and with very black eyebrows and jutting chin. I caught sight of his face when we passed a lamp-post during the drive. I wish I'd taken more notice of him now. What's he up to?'

Barney watched the little van disappear up the road, its red light getting fainter and fainter. He wondered if he ought to have taken the number, but the rear light was far too dim to allow him to read anything on the back of the car.

He turned back to the building behind him and wondered what it was. It couldn't be a church, he thought. Was it a private house?

The rain stopped. The moon came out again, and Barney stepped quickly into shadow. Then he caught sight of a big notice set up near the front door. He went on tiptoe towards it.

He read it carefully. Well! After all, the building was only an old show-place – a museum or something, Barney thought. He wondered if he could shelter inside somewhere. He was wet, and would like to take off his coat.

There must be someone inside, surely, because he had heard voices – and yet, only one man had gone to the car. So perhaps he had better not try to get in. He might be arrested as a thief, if he were found.

Barney had no sooner thought this than he heard the sound of cautious footsteps inside the front door, near the noticeboard. He slipped round to the side of the house. He heard the door open, and then it was shut very quietly. Someone came down the flagged path, keeping to the shadowed side.

The someone gave a little cough, and Barney stiffened in surprise. That was a woman's cough! Whatever could a *woman* be doing wandering about in the darkness like this? The figure soon disappeared into the shadows of the lane, and then there was silence.

Barney went to the front door and tried it. Locked, of course. He went all round the place, but found every window locked or shuttered.

The moon shone down through one window as he peered inside. 'Gracious! It's all furnished – it's not empty, or full of cases and things like museums usually are,' said Barney, in surprise. 'I wish I could get into *this* room – I could sleep very comfortably on that old sofa!'

Ivy grew very thickly indeed on one wall. Barney looked up at the thick green screen and noticed a window on the first floor. It *looked* as if it might be open.

He tried his weight on the ivy stems. They were as thick as small trunks, and held his weight easily. So up he went like a cat, testing each ivy stem as he climbed.

Miranda climbed beside him, flinging herself up and down the ivy in a way that Barney very much envied.

He got to the window and found that he was right. It was a small casement window, and because the fastening was broken, it could not be shut. It had swung open and Barney saw that he could easily get inside, once he had got astride the windowsill.

He pulled himself up. Miranda shot up to his shoulder at once. She had seen the half-open window and had guessed Barney was going to enter there. It wasn't long before they were both in the old room behind the open window.

The moon went in and Barney stood still in the darkness. He waited till the moon came out again and then saw that he was in an old-fashioned bedroom. An enormous four-poster bed stood in the middle of the room, almost shut in by side-hangings that were slightly pulled back with tarnished gilt girdles.

Barney tiptoed to the door and opened it. He found himself on a gallery that ran round a great room below, overlooking it. All was silence. Not even a mouse pattered across the floor.

Barney found the stairs and went down. They were shallow stairs that swept down in a curve, right into the big room below. Smaller rooms opened off it. Barney peeped cautiously into each, but there was nobody there, and not a sound to be heard. It did seem quite safe to sleep upstairs in that great four-poster!

A screech made him jump, and Miranda gibbered in fright. But it was only a barn owl outside, screeching to frighten the fieldmice into sudden movement, so that it could see them and pounce.

Barney decided to go upstairs again. He was damp and very tired. He didn't think it would matter if he slept on that great bed. He would take off his shoes and his wet coat. Perhaps there would be something up there that he could wrap himself in.

He went up the wide stairs, and came to the gallery again. He found the bedroom through whose window he had climbed. He looked around in the moonlight for something to wrap round himself.

There was an old table in one corner, covered by a tablecloth of some kind. Barney couldn't see what colour it was or what it was made of. He fingered it, and it felt thick and warm. He pulled it off, took off his coat, and wrapped himself round in the tablecloth. It certainly was nice and cosy!

Miranda tucked herself into its folds, glad to think they were going to bed. She was tired out with her long and exciting day.

Barney slid his shoes off his feet. He felt his socks. Blow, they had holes in them already – just as he wanted to visit his friends too. Well, perhaps he had better wear shoes and no socks, then the holes wouldn't be noticed!

He got on to the bed. It was high, rather hard, and not really very comfortable, but it was bliss to poor, tired Barney. Dragging the tablecloth closely round him, he put his head on the pillow and immediately fell asleep.

Not very far away, at Miss Hannah's house, Diana was lying awake, wondering if Barney would come the next day. Little did she know that at that very moment he was fast asleep in the middle of the old four-poster bed in the best bedroom of Ring O' Bells Hall!

Yes – Ring O' Bells Hall. That was where Barney had ended up for the night. Wake up early, Barney, or you'll be discovered – and then what trouble you'll be getting into!

Chapter Thirteen

Up in the Bell-Tower

Fortunately for Barney he did awake quite early the next morning. The sun shone directly into the window, and a bright beam rested on his face. It woke him, and he sat up blinking in the yellow sunlight, wondering wherever in the world he was.

He soon remembered. Yes – he was in some old building – some kind of show-place. He had better get out quickly! He woke up Miranda, who was fast asleep in the rug, her tiny face hidden in her paws. She opened her eyes, and made a little chattering noise.

She ran up Barney's chest, as he sat up on the bed, and sat cuddled into his shoulder, pulling at one of his ears, and putting her monkey face against his cheek. He fondled her lovingly.

'You're the best little companion in the world!' he said, and tickled her. 'Aren't you, Miranda? Say – do you know who you're going to see today?'

Miranda chattered back eagerly, and Barney nodded solemnly. 'Quite right – we're visiting our friends. Now we'd better think about going. Better not shin down the ivy this time, in case someone sees us. Let's go and see if there's a back door we can open. We could slip out cautiously then.'

Barney replaced the tablecloth on the table. It looked very crumpled but he couldn't do anything about that. He put on his shoes, but stuffed his holey, rolled-up socks into his pocket. He felt his coat. It was quite dry, so he pulled that on too. There was a mirror on the wall, and he looked into it.

'Just look at that scarecrow in there, Miranda!' he said to the listening monkey. 'You might not guess it, but it's me! I wonder if there's anywhere I can wash here – or didn't these old places run to a bathroom? I guess not.'

He took a comb from his pocket and combed back his bright hair. Then he straightened the covers of the big four-poster bed, and went into the gallery that ran outside the room, overlooking the enormous room below.

He walked quietly, but there was no one about. Miranda leapt about from table to chair, from chair to chest, chattering and excited. Any strange place always pleased her.

Barney was not very interested in the old building. It meant very little to him, for he didn't know much of history. He thought some of the big wooden chairs looked extremely uncomfortable, and marvelled at the suits of armour that stood here and there round the wall. He stood and looked at one.

'Pretty small, isn't it, Miranda?' he said to the monkey. 'I could just about get into it, but only just. I reckon the old-time men couldn't have been as big as we are – tiddley little things they must have been. And fancy walking about in that, clanking all the time!'

He came to the back door, which was a massive affair, though not as enormous as the front door. He looked round for Miranda. 'Come on,' he said. 'We'll slip out here.'

There was no chattering in reply, and Miranda didn't come flying on to his shoulder. Barney looked round the room he was in. It was a huge kitchen, furnished just as it might have been two or three hundred years back. Where on earth was Miranda?

Miranda was off on a little exploration of her own. She

hadn't realised that Barney was looking for a way out. She thought he was exploring too. She had completely disappeared.

'Miranda!' called Barney softly. 'Blow you, Miranda! Where have you got to?'

He heard a little noise somewhere and went quickly in its direction. He came to the foot of the big square tower, though at first he had no idea what it was.

All he could see was the little spiral staircase going up. Up to where? Perhaps another bedroom, Barney thought. He stood and listened. Surely that tiresome little monkey hadn't gone up the stairway? A noise from above made him certain that she had.

And then another noise made him jump. Somebody was unlocking a door! 'It's the big front door!' thought Barney, scared. 'Somebody's coming in. I shall be caught.'

He glanced round. There seemed no sensible place to hide – and anyway he must get hold of Miranda and keep her quiet, or she would certainly give the game away.

He began to climb the little spiral staircase quickly, his rubber shoes making no sound on the stone. Up and up he went, and at last came to the little platform at the top. He gazed up and saw the silent bells hanging far above his head.

And up there, looking down at him cheekily, was Miranda! She was playing hide and seek with him! He had taught her that – but now she had chosen a most unfortunate time to play it!

'Miranda!' he said, in a whisper. 'Come on down! Quick!'

Miranda immediately disappeared. Barney craned his neck. Where could she be? And how had she got up so high. It was too far for her to leap.

He was in the tower. Barney could hardly see anything

88

except the bells high up, gleaming and silent. He felt up the wall with his hand and at last came to something he had guessed must be there.

There was a row of footholds in the stone wall of the tower on the south side. The stone was hollowed out at set places, so that a foot or hand could be inserted for climbing up. Barney slipped his hand into one hold and found that it was hollowed in such a way that his fingers could grip quite well.

He gave a little groan. Now he would have to climb all the way up in this half-darkness to get Miranda! Once she was playing hide and seek she wouldn't come to him unless he found her and cornered her. He stood on tiptoe and felt for the handholds above his head. He slipped his hands in, and then put his toes into the ones below.

He felt for the next holds and put his hands there, clutching hard with his strong fingers. It was not a very pleasant way of climbing up the steep walls of a stone tower – but Barney was used to acrobatic feats of all kinds, and he didn't really find it difficult.

As for Miranda, she must have discovered the footholds at once and climbed up easily, with glee. Barney went steadily up, slipping first his hand into the stone hollows, and then his feet. At last he was up to the bells. Now – where was Miranda?

He couldn't see her anywhere, nor hear her either. He looked cautiously round in the dim light. The bells, looking remarkably big and bright now that he was so near them, hung near his head, held by their ropes. He strained his eyes to see beyond them.

He caught sight of a pair of gleaming green eyes looking down at him. Miranda! 'You little scamp!' muttered Barney, exasperated. 'How did you get beyond the bells?'

He felt about for another handhold and found it. Then his hand found the end of a thick rope. He felt it cautiously. It didn't seem to be loose. It seemed to be fastened tightly. Was it to help a climber to go up above the bells?

Barney pulled at the rope, and it felt very firm and safe. He swarmed up it, through what looked like a hole in the roof of the tower – and found himself in a most curious place!

It was a small square room above the bells. It would have been completely dark if it hadn't been for a slit-like window set in the south side, that let in a bright ray of sunlight. Now Barney understood why the bells had gleamed so brightly when he was standing below them. This beam of sun had penetrated into the room, and a little piece of it had pierced through the hole of the floor, and fallen on the upper surface of the bells.

'So that's why they shone so curiously!' thought Barney, looking round the little stone room. There was a low bench there, very small, and a heap of what looked like rags. There was an old wooden candlestick with the remains of wax still in the bottom.

'This must have been a hidey-hole long ago,' thought Barney, kicking the rags which looked as if they had once been a rug or blanket of some kind. Miranda at once ran over to them and cuddled herself up, peeping out comically.

'I'm not too pleased with you, Miranda,' said Barney severely. 'Making me climb up all that way to get you. And now we've got to climb down again – but this time you'll be on my shoulder, and keep there – see?'

He looked out through the slit-like window. The whole countryside lay before him, smiling in the bright May sunshine. Not a cloud was in the blue sky. It made Barney long to be out there.

He suddenly felt very hungry indeed. 'Come on,

Miranda,' he said. 'We'll go and find Snubby and the others, and get some breakfast.'

Miranda knew the words breakfast, dinner, tea and supper very well indeed. She leapt on to Barney's shoulder and held on to his collar.

He let himself down through the hole in the floor, found the guide-rope, and then felt for the first footholds in the stone wall of the tower. It was easy to climb down, and soon he was standing far below the gleaming bells, on the little platform at the top of the spiral staircase.

He listened. He could hear what sounded like someone beating a mat. Perhaps the caretaker of the building was at her morning work. He might be able to slip out past her.

He went down the stone stairway very silently and carefully. He peered out at the bottom. No one was to be seen. He made his way to the front door. He caught sight of a woman in one of the rooms, dusting the old furniture. She had her back to him, so Barney took his chance and fled to the open front door. He was out in the sunshine in a trice, rejoicing to feel the warmth on his head and shoulders.

He saw the name of the old building on the gate, Ring O' Bells Hall. 'So that's where I slept for the night,' he thought. 'Ring O' Bells Hall, in Ring O' Bells Village. Very nice too!'

He debated how to find his three friends – but his difficulty didn't last long. Up the road came Roger, Diana, Snubby and the two dogs!

Barney yelled loudly. 'Ahoy there! Here we are!'

Chapter Fourteen

A Happy Meeting

Shouts, squeals, laughter, barks, chattering, back-slapping – what an excitement and scurry there was, as all the friends rushed together once more!

'Barney! Dear old Barney! We did hope you'd come today!'

'Miranda! You're just as sweet as ever! Oh, she's leapt on to my shoulder!'

'It's grand to see you all – Diana, you've grown. Snubby hasn't. Hallo, Roger – it's good to see you.'

'Woof, woof, woof!'

'Barney, you're a bit taller – and as brown as ever! Oh, do listen to Miranda chattering! I know exactly what she's saying!'

'When did you come? How did you get here?'

'Where did you spend the night? Oh, I say – the dogs have both gone mad.'

'Woof, woof, WOOF!'

It certainly seemed as if both the dogs had gone completely off their heads. Loony recognised Barney and Miranda at once, of course, but Loopy didn't know them, as he had never seen them before. But when he saw what a tremendous welcome the excited Loony gave them, Loopy felt he must certainly join in.

He almost outdid Loony in his excitement. He leapt up and barked and licked and wagged and rolled over, and altogether behaved like two Loonies rolled into one. Loony himself got rather annoyed with him at last. These were *his* friends, not Loopy's. What did Loopy mean by behaving like this?

Loony gave the surprised Loopy a sharp nip as if to say, 'Keep off! This is *my* welcome, not yours!'

Miranda leapt from one shoulder to another, delighted and so excited that she hardly knew what she was doing. She suddenly dropped down on Loony's back, and rode him as she always used to do. Loopy seeing this, got the surprise of his life. He backed away at once.

Miranda sprang from Loony's back on to Loopy's, and the golden spaniel ran for his life, with the cheeky little monkey jigging up and down on his back. He whined in panic.

'Woof, woof, woof! Roll over, woof!' barked Loony, running after him. So Loopy rolled over on his back, which, of course, was a sure way of dislodging Miranda. Before either dog could pounce on her she was up on Barney's shoulder again, chattering for all she was worth.

The children's excitement died down at last. They linked arms with Barney and strolled back to Miss Pepper's, quite forgetting that Miss Hannah had said she would not welcome any monkey to her house. Barney mentioned that he hadn't yet had any breakfast, and was hungry.

'Could we stop and buy some food somewhere?' he asked. 'And I'd like to buy some socks. Mine have got holes in them. I don't want to appear with holey socks.'

'You *have* got particular!' said Diana. 'You never used to mind things like that.'

'No,' said Barney, and didn't like to say that he was so proud of his friends that he wanted to be like them, and look decent if he could.

'Better come to Miss Hannah's and we'll ask her for something for you,' said Roger. 'Look at those dogs and Miranda! What a time she'll have with them!'

93

Miranda was sitting on a wall, holding a long twig, and was poking this at the dogs every time they tried to leap up at her. Loopy by now had decided that she was a very peculiar kind of cat, and he meant to have some fun with her.

Miss Pepper was in the front garden, picking flowers. She was delighted to see Barney. 'Just the same startlingly blue eyes and brown face!' she thought to herself, as she went to meet him. 'What a striking boy he is!'

'Miss Pepper,' said Roger when the greetings were over, 'Barney hasn't had breakfast. Can we get him some?'

'Of course!' cried Miss Pepper, and took them all inside. Miranda came too. Miss Hannah came out of the kitchen, when she heard all the excited voices – and stopped dead when she saw Miranda on Barney's shoulder. She gave a piercing scream and ran back to the kitchen, slamming the door behind her. Barney felt astonished. The others, of course, guessed at once what the matter was.

'Oh – of course – she hates monkeys!' said Roger. 'Blow – we all forgot. Miss Hannah – it's all right. I'll take Barney back to the garden, and the monkey too.'

So poor Barney was ushered back to the garden and given a deck-chair to sit in, whilst the rest went back to pacify Miss Hannah and get a meal of some kind for Barney.

Loony and Loopy remained with Barney. Loony had already given him about five hundred licks, but he still had plenty to spare, and Barney had to wipe his face with his handkerchief every minute or so.

Then Loopy began to show off to Miranda. He rushed indoors, got a mat from the hall and dragged it out at top speed, falling over whenever his hind legs got caught on it. He placed it in front of Miranda, who promptly dropped down on it and sat there.

Loony watched jealously. He also disappeared into the house, and when he came back he held a large bath-towel between his teeth. He deposited it on the rug. Miranda at once took it and draped herself round in it with a very naughty air indeed.

'Woof,' said Loony to Loopy and disappeared again. He brought back somebody's hairbrush, and Miranda brushed her fur vigorously with it. Barney roared with laughter. Off went Loopy for another mat.

When Roger and the others appeared with food for Barney, the grass looked most peculiar, strewn with mats and rugs and towels, a hairbrush and a broom, which Loony with much trouble had managed to drag out by the head.

'Good gracious,' said Miss Pepper. 'Just look what those dogs have done! Are they showing off to that little Miranda?'

Diana collected everything and took mats, brushes and towels back into the house, laughing. Those two dogs! Nothing was safe from them when they took it into their heads to be silly.

The three children exchanged all their news with Barney. Barney told them of the jobs he had had since he had last seen them. They sounded remarkable to the children, even though they were used to their circus friend's doings.

'I told you I managed a troupe of monkeys – with Miranda's help,' said Barney, munching away at bread and ham. 'My word, she *did* boss those monkeys! Before that I had charge of an elephant. He was grand, that elephant.'

'What was his name?' asked Diana.

'Mr Little,' said Barney with a grin. 'He was enormous,

but very gentle and deft. You wouldn't believe it, but if you put cups and saucers down in rows in front of him, he'd walk among them without even touching a cup!'

'What else did you do?' asked Snubby.

'I took a job with a man who owned two roundabouts,' said Barney. 'That was a messy job, though. I had to oil them and see to the works. I didn't do that long. The man was mean and bad-tempered. I went to a good little job after that.'

'What was it?' said Roger.

'It was in a little theatre,' said Barney. 'Not much more than a shed, really. Different travelling companies hired it for their shows. It was my job to manage the lights and the scenery.'

'I know why you took that job,' said Diana suddenly. 'It was in case your father might come there and act!'

Barney nodded. He was always on the look-out for anyone who might be his father. He felt sure he would know him, though how, he didn't know. He didn't feel so bad about not having a father or mother now, though, because he had three good friends, and had even shared a little of their home-life at times. A home and people meant a great deal to Barney, who had none. Still, he had Miranda – she was all the world to him!

The children told him their news too – how they had had the 'flu, and had been sent away for a change and they told him about the mysterious Ring O' Bells Hall, and the secret passage and legend of the bells.

'My word! Those must be the very bells I climbed past when I went to hunt for Miranda in the tower!' said Barney, and told them about the little room above the bells. Then he remembered the strange episode of the night before, when he had seen once again the man who had given him a lift, and had heard him talking to some-one in Ring O' Bells Hall.

'What was he up to, do you think, at that time of night?' asked Barney, eating the very last bit of cheese, and feeling pleasantly full. He drank his glass of milk, and got out his hanky to wipe his mouth. Before he had made friends with the children he had always wiped his mouth with the back of his hand!

'Goodness knows what anyone would be up to in this old village!' said Roger, puzzled. 'And Ring O' Bells Hall is always shut up and locked at night. Nobody is there!'

'Well, someone was definitely there late last night,' said Barney. 'And, as I say, I know who one person was, because it so happens he was the man who gave me the lift! I said I wanted to go to Lillinghame, never dreaming anyone would be going to Ring O' Bells itself. But apparently he was. He must have gone in his car, and I followed painfully on foot, not knowing he was away in front of me!'

'It's strange,' said Diana. 'And you say you heard a woman cough too – well, I should think that must have been the bad-tempered woman who guides people round the old place, and gives lectures on it. The one who showed us the secret passage but wouldn't let us go down it.'

'Perhaps she's got something down there she doesn't want anyone to see,' said Barney idly. 'After all, she's the caretaker, she can forbid people to snoop down there – what's to prevent her from hiding away anything she likes!'

'Do you mean that, Barney?' asked Diana, after a pause. It suddenly seemed to fit in with their idea of the woman, and with her behaviour.

'No – not really,' said Barney, giving Miranda a piece of an orange. 'I just said it. Why? You seem to have gone all serious about it.'

'You know – I think we ought to examine that secret

passage,' said Roger. 'Just to make sure there *isn't* something peculiar going on down there!'

Chapter Fifteen

A Wonderful Day

Miss Pepper came out and interrupted this most interesting conversation. 'Barney, have you had enough?' she asked. 'Sure? Well, listen. My cousin Miss Hannah really *is* scared of monkeys, she's so scared she's quite likely to faint if Miranda comes near her. It's a pity, but there it is. So I thought as it's such fine weather you could all go off for the day together, and take your meals with you.'

'Wizard!' said Snubby and Roger at once, and Diana's face shone. Barney got up politely and smiled.

'Nothing I should like better,' he said. 'And I quite understand about your cousin, Miss Pepper. I won't come further than the front gate in future.'

'It's very nice of you not to mind, Barney,' said Miss Pepper. 'Hannah is very sorry about it – and she's packing up a most exciting lunch and tea for you to take with you, just to make up to you for her unfortunate dislike of monkeys.'

'Goody!' said Diana, pleased. 'Where shall we go? I know! Let's go through Ring O' Bells Wood, and walk through the bridle path all the way to the top of the hill where we rode to yesterday. It would be heavenly.'

'Woof,' said Loony approvingly. He had heard the word 'walk', which always seemed to him to be one of the most sensible words in the language of humans. 'Bone' was another and 'Dinner' was the third. A conversation made up of these three words, with perhaps 'Biscuit' and 'Chocolate' and 'Rats' and 'Rabbits' thrown in occasionally would have interested Loony very much.

'Let't go and see old Red Riding Hood in Ring O' Bells Cottage on our way,' suggested Snubby. Barney looked surprised.

'Who's she? I've never heard of an *old* Red Riding Hood before,' he said. 'All the ones I've seen in panto-mimes have been young.'

'Well, wait till you see ours,' grinned Snubby. 'And wait till you see her green eyes! We think she's the grand-daughter of a witch.'

'Don't be idiotic, Snubby,' said Roger. 'Di, hadn't you better go and see if Miss Hannah wants a bit of help with the sandwich-packing? There's a lot to cut up and pack, I should think!'

Diana went. Miss Hannah was pleased to see her, and let her arrange slices of tongue on the bread cut for sandwiches. There seemed quite a mound of cut slices! 'Have I cut enough?' asked Miss Hannah anxiously. 'My cousin said you all ate twice as much out of doors as in, and that scared me a bit. I don't want you to go hungry.'

'We shan't,' said Diana, eyeing the loaded table. Sand-wiches, sausage rolls, hard-boiled eggs, bread and butter to go with them, tomatoes, lettuce, slices of thick, solid fruit cake, biscuits in a packet, bars of chocolate – good gracious, what a picnic it would be!

She gave Miss Hannah a sudden hug. 'You're awfully nice,' she said. 'As nice as Miss Pepper. Thank you very much.'

Miss Hannah went red with pleasure, and put an extra lot of butter on the bit of bread she was buttering. She liked these children, noisy though they were, and quite mad at times. But they had nice ways and good manners and were always ready to help. You just couldn't help liking them, even that monkey of a Snubby. That reminded Miss Hannah of Miranda and she gave a shudder.

'Do see that the monkey doesn't come anywhere near me, won't you, Diana?' she said beseechingly. 'Why, the very thought makes my legs turn to water!'

Diana glanced with interest at Miss Hannah's legs, but they seemed just the same as usual – not even wobbly as Snubby's had been. She finished putting the tongue in the very last sandwich.

There was so much food and drink that Miss Hannah had to find three satchels to put it in, for the boys to carry. Snubby didn't see why Diana shouldn't take her share of the carrying and said so.

'I'm *going* to take my share of the load, Snubby,' said Diana. 'But you might at least let Miss Hannah go on thinking you're a perfect little gentleman – though how anyone can think that, I really – '

She had to stop and laugh, because Snubby picked up a cushion to smother her. Anyway, who could quarrel or bicker on such a day, when they had got Barney and Miranda back with them, and a whole day's picnicking in front of them!

'I hope you won't be lonely, Miss Pepper,' called Snubby kindly as they set off down the front path.

'Oh, it'll be quite a *nice* loneliness!' called back Miss Hannah. 'Don't you worry about us. We shall get on quite well without you.'

Miranda was on Barney's shoulder as usual. The two dogs, their tails wagging furiously, capered round and round, getting in everyone's way. They knew by the satchels on the boys' backs that this was to be a long, long walk!

It certainly was a wonderful day. The four children and the animals went up through Ring O' Bells Wood, and when they came to the little path that led off to Ring O' Bells Cottage, they debated whether or not to go and have a look at it, or to call on their way back.

'On our way back,' decided Roger. 'Old Red Riding Hood might give us a glass of milk or something then. We shall probably be thirsty on our way home.'

'All right,' said Diana. 'Come on – up the broad path we go. Loony, that's not a rabbit-hole – that's where a tree had been uprooted.'

They walked through the wood, which was dim and cool on this hot May day. Bluebells were coming out everywhere, and lay like pools of shimmering amethyst among the trees. The children sniffed the sweet smell, with just as much enjoyment as the two dogs sniffed rabbit-smells.

'Look at those wind-flowers – there are hundreds of them!' said Diana. Barney stood with her and watched the pretty, star-like flowers dancing in the wind. Barney didn't know many flower-names, and he liked to learn them. Diana knew such a lot! She enjoyed teaching Barney. He was a very willing pupil, with an excellent memory.

They had their lunch on the very top of the hill, overlooking the valley. Far away in the distance they could see the gleam of the Bristol Channel, thrusting up from the sea. It was dazzling silver in the sun, though it would turn blue later in the day.

'This is a most magnificent lunch,' said Barney, biting into a hard-boiled egg. 'Where's the salt? Anyone remember it?'

'I did,' said Diana, and gave him the screw of paper with the salt inside. 'Look out – don't let the wind blow it all away.'

The four children worked their way through most of the food. They left very little for tea. 'We really ought to stop eating,' said Diana, examining what was left. 'We're sure to be hungry for tea, and we've eaten nearly everything.'

'Perhaps old Red Riding Hood will offer us tea,' suggested Snubby.

'Why should she?' said Diana. 'I should think she'd be scared of four like us. We've got frightful appetites. Everyone says so.'

'Snubby only said that because he'd like to finish everything now,' said Roger, and gave Snubby a poke in his fat middle.

'*Don't*!' said Snubby, in alarm. 'I've eaten too much to be jabbed in the middle.'

This was the kind of silly, friendly talk that Barney enjoyed, and got nowhere else in his life. Most of the circus children he knew were rough and cheeky, and the adults he had lived with had no use for simple friendly talk like this. Barney listened to every word and enjoyed it. How nice to be a family and know each other so well! He thought he was very lucky to be friendly with this one.

The dogs had their share of the food, and Miranda ate a banana daintily, peeling it herself. She threw the skin on the grass. 'Now then, Miranda, manners!' said Barney sternly. 'Pick that up at once. We don't leave litter about.'

Miranda picked up the banana skin and hopped on to Roger's shoulder. She suddenly stuffed it down his neck, and leapt away chattering with glee at his yell of dismay. He put it into the bag of bits and pieces that was to go into one of the satchels and be taken home to be burnt.

It was a long lazy day, and by the time three o'clock came they were red-brown with the hot sun, all except Barney, who was already so brown that he couldn't possibly get any browner!

'It's time we went back,' said Roger lazily. 'Where are those dogs? It's a good thing rabbit-holes aren't any bigger, or both of them would be wandering lost for ever in a maze of warrens!'

'They never learn they can't get down,' said Diana. 'If

I were a rabbit I'd sit a little way down the hole, where I could see Loony's black face poking down at me, and laugh my head off at him.'

'That's just what rabbits probably do,' said Snubby. 'I've often wondered what it is that makes Loony go so dippy about digging out rabbit-holes – he's probably feeling furious with a grinning rabbit sitting a little way down.'

The dogs came back at last, their noses sandy, and their tongues hanging almost to the ground! They flopped down beside the children.

'Up you get,' said Roger, getting up himself. 'We're starting back on the way home. We're making a call on the way, Loony, on Red Riding Hood. Look out for the wolf!'

They walked leisurely down the long slope of the hill, and reached the wood. The bluebells were a deeper blue now, and the wind-flowers no longer danced because there was no breeze. It was very hot indeed.

'I could do with a drink of water,' said Roger. 'If I had a tongue long enough it would be hanging out on my chest!'

'Here's the little path that leads to Red Riding Hood's Cottage,' said Diana at last, and they turned down it and walked till they came in sight of the little house.

'Honestly, it's a fairy-tale house!' said Diana, as they came near. She was right. It was. It looked as crooked and tumble-down as a cottage in a tale, its chimneys were surprisingly tall, its windows small and diamond-paned. Bluebells grew right up to the little wall that surrounded it.

'There's an old well in the garden,' said Diana, pointing. 'I say – isn't it an adorable place. I do hope old Red Riding Hood is in!'

Chapter Sixteen

Ring O' Bells Cottage

They opened the little white gate and walked up a tiny flagged path to the front door. It was painted blue, as were the shutters outside the windows. Diana knocked.

'Come in!' said a voice, and Diana opened the door. Inside was a small room, perfectly square, with a big fireplace at one end. The uneven floor was of stone. Old Riding Hood was standing over the fire, stirring something in a pot.

But she wasn't wearing her old red cloak and hood, so she didn't look like Red Riding Hood any more. The cloak hung on a nail nearby.

Naomi Barlow looked out of her green-grey eyes at the children. They were disappointed to see that her eyes didn't seem nearly so green as they had imagined. Still, she looked a bit of a fairy-tale person still, with her white apron, red shawl, and snow-white hair.

'Well! If it isn't Miss Hannah's visitors!' she said. 'Sit you down, and I'll get you some home-made biscuits. I'm sorry I've no milk to offer you, for you must be rarely thirsty this hot day. Would you like some ice-cold water out of my well?'

This sounded good. 'Yes, please,' said Roger at once. 'Can I go and get some? Is there a bucket on a chain, and a handle that winds?'

'Yes,' said Naomi. Then she suddenly caught sight of Miranda on Barney's shoulder. 'Why, the little mite!' she said, and left her pot and came over to Barney. 'I once had a monkey of my own. It was left for dead by a circus that once came to Ring O' Bells. I took it and nursed it and it lived with me many a year.'

She fussed over Miranda, which made Loony and Loopy jealous. She seemed quite at home with children, dogs and monkey. They all liked her.

Roger went out with Barney to get the water. They took a large white jug that Naomi had given them.

'What an enormous well for such a small place,' said Roger, in surprise. 'I bet it's deep.'

It was. It was so very deep that neither of the boys could see the water. Roger took a stone and dropped it down. It was quite a time before he heard the splash. He peered down.

'It's a nice well,' he said. 'It's got ferns and things growing all the way down the sides. I bet the water's cold!'

He and Barney wound the bucket down till it reached the water. Then they wound it up again, the chain making quite a noise. They took the bucket off and emptied the water into the big jug. 'Feel it,' said Barney. 'Absolutely icy-cold!'

They all enjoyed drinking the crystal-clear cold water, and eating Naomi's home-made biscuits. They tasted of cinnamon, and were very spicy indeed. She put some into a bag for them.

The children asked to see round the cottage. 'There's not much to see,' said old Naomi. 'Just three tiny rooms! This is my parlour-kitchen, where I cook and sit. And this is my bedroom.'

The bedroom was even smaller than the kitchen. The children looked at the flat stone floor, and thought how cold it must be in the winter. The kitchen was the same, set with big, solid, white flags, a little uneven here and there.

'And this is my store-room,' said Naomi, opening a

door off the kitchen, and showing them a cupboard of a room. She had made it into a store-room, and there were jars of pickles, jam, honey spices, and all kinds of things. It too had a cold stone floor, and even on that hot May day, it seemed chilly to the children.

'That was my bedroom when I was a girl,' said Naomi. 'I slept there for years. Then when my old Dad died and Ma followed him, I made it into a store-room. Barlows have lived here for years upon years – four hundred years, so I've heard tell. But there won't be a Barlow here after me, more's the pity.'

It was a quaint, peculiar, uncomfortable old cottage, too dark with its too-small, leaded windows, and probably far too cold, with its solid stone floor, in the winter. But, as Diana said afterwards, 'it had a lovely *feeling* about it, it was full of old thoughts and old doings, and past and gone days.'

'Mother Barlow must have lived there too,' said Snubby, as they went home. 'I'd like to have known her. I do wonder why Old Grandad kept saying, 'Ask Mother Barlow, ask Mother Barlow,' the other day, when we wanted to know where the secret passage went. Why should *she* know so much about it?'

'Because she probably used it, and caught him!' said Roger. 'I say – what about Barney's lodgings tonight? I was thinking he'd be coming home with us, but of course he can't. We'd better ask in the village if there's anywhere for him to sleep!'

So they asked, first at the village stores, and then at the various addresses that the woman there gave them.

But although many would have been willing to take Barney, nobody wanted Miranda. In vain Barney and the others sang her praises, said she was quite harmless, and very sweet and good-mannered – nobody would have Miranda!

'She'd bring fleas,' said one.

'She'd bite my baby,' said another.

'I don't hold with monkeys,' said a third.

And so it went on – no, no, no, till the children got quite desperate.

Barney, of course, didn't mind. He was used to sleeping anywhere, in a caravan, in a tent, under a hedge or a haystack.

'Don't you bother about me,' he kept saying, but the children did. Diana pointed out that great clouds had rolled up again and threatened the same downpour of rain as the night before.

'You simply *must* be under cover,' she said

'All right,' said Barney. 'What's the matter with me sleeping in the Ring O' Bells Hall again? Nobody sleeps there, and I shan't do any harm.'

'Well, you could,' said Roger. 'I can't see what it would really matter. What's the time? I believe it would still be open. Let's go and see. If it is, we'll pay and go in, and find a better place for you to sleep than the four-poster bed you spoke about. We can leave you there!

The woman looked sourly at them when they arrived in the hall, having tied up the two dogs securely. 'It's just upon closing time,' she said.

'There's five minutes to go,' said Roger firmly, and he placed the money on the table, 'We want to show our friend around.'

The woman caught sight of the monkey. 'Not with that monkey!' she said. But the children had already marched on down the hall.

'Show me the room where that secret passage is,' said Barney suddenly. 'I'd like to see that.'

'Right,' said Roger. 'But we can't look at the passage because you have to pay extra for that, and I don't want

108

to go back to that bad-tempered woman! Now let's see – which room was it?'

They went into two or three and then found the little room into which the secret passage opened. Roger showed Barney the big tapestry picture which could be moved to one side in order to open the tiny panel that had to be used to move the lever that freed the big panel.

'Sounds like the House-that-Jack-built to me!' said Barney, with a grin. 'Move the picture to open the panel to move the lever to free the panel, to–'

'It does sound a bit complicated,' said Roger, 'I tell you what – we'll come one day and explore that passage all by ourselves. Though how we're going to do it without that woman suspecting, I don't know.'

'Have to come one night then,' said Barney. Diana shivered.

'I only hope the bells don't ring then!' she said.

'They wouldn't. We're not enemies!' said Snubby. 'I say – that would be a bit of an adventure, wouldn't it – to explore a secret passage one night!'

'I think I'll sleep in the little room here for the night,' said Barney, looking round. 'There's a big couch with cushions – though they look pretty hard – and I could take that cloth off the table over there to put round me. You wouldn't believe how warm the table-cloth was last night! I shall be very comfortable here.'

A voice came sharply from the hall. 'I'm just closing the place. Will you please come, or you'll be locked in!'

'She doesn't guess that one of us *wants* to be locked in!' whispered Snubby in glee. 'So long, Barney. Sleep well. See you in the morning.'

'Take old Red Riding Hood's biscuits for your supper,' said Diana, pushing the paper bag into Barney's hand. 'And here's the rest of the chocolate. Come up to Miss

Hannah's in the morning and wait outside the gate. We'll bring you breakfast.'

'Thanks,' said Barney, gratefully. The others went quickly out of the room and looked round the hall. The woman could be heard locking up somewhere at the back. Now was their time to go, before she realised that only three were departing instead of four!

'Good night!' called Roger, in a stentorian voice and Snubby and Diana joined in. There might have been a dozen of them, not three!

The woman made no answer. The children went out quickly, grinning at one another. It was easy! They untied the impatient dogs and went off up the road to Miss Hannah's rambling old house.

'Barney will be all right in that little room,' said Roger, glancing up at the overcast sky. 'Here comes the first big drops. Hurry!'

They hurried, glad to think that Barney and Miranda wouldn't have to sleep under a hedge. They ran in at the gate, and were welcomed by Miss Pepper.

'*Just* in time!' she said. 'I was afraid you'd be caught by the storm. Did you have a good day?'

'Wonderful!' said Diana. 'Where's Miss Hannah? We want to tell her that the food was absolutely super!'

'Wizard,' said the boys, together. 'We ate it all!'

'What have you done with Barney and Miranda?' asked Miss Pepper, as they went indoors. 'I hope you found him lodgings of some kind.'

Roger grinned. 'Yes – we did. He'll be quite comfortable, Miss Pepper. He's got a *very* nice little room of his own, with nobody to disturb him at all!'

Chapter Seventeen

In The Middle Of The Night

Barney certainly had a nice little room of his own! He felt quite glad to be there, too, when he heard the thunder crashing and the rain pelting down. The caretaker-woman had gone, slamming the front door behind her. He was quite alone, except for Miranda.

Barney waited for the slamming of the front door, and then he stood up. He didn't want to go to bed yet! He wondered if there were any books about that he might read.

He had crouched by a chest waiting for the caretaker to go, ready to open the lid and slip inside, if she came near. But she didn't. She apparently thought that all the children had gone, and that the place was quite empty.

'And now I'm master of Ring O' Bell Hall,' said Barney, out loud, as he wandered through the great mansion. He went into the kitchen and marvelled at the enormous cooking stoves there. What meals they must have cooked in the old days here! He went idly to the tap over the great wide sink and turned it on, not expecting any water to come out.

But a stream of cold water splashed at once into the sink. Barney found an old tankard on a shelf and filled it. He drank deeply, for the night was hot and he was really very thirsty. He rinsed out the tankard and put it back. He supposed that water was laid on for the caretaker to use. Well, that was lucky for *him*!

He found some books in a panelled room that looked like a library. In fact, he found about two thousand books.

They lined the shelves from floor to ceiling, most of them leather-bound. Their colours were old and faded now, and looked as if nobody had ever read them.

Barney took one or two down. They were printed in old-time lettering and he found them too difficult to understand. He put them back carefully, noting that they were very dusty. The caretaker-woman needed to take her duster round a bit more, he though!

It was dull all by himself, and he was glad when he felt sleepy. He ate all the biscuits and the chocolate that Diana had given him, and then got another drink of water. He gave Miranda a drink too, and a few raisins to eat.

'And don't you put the pips down my neck this time, and don't you spit them out, either!' he said. 'Put them into your paw and give them to me.'

So for once in a way Miranda was very polite, and spat each pip into her tiny brown paw, and handed them solemnly to Barney, who just as solemnly put them into an ashtray on one of the tables.

When it was almost dark, he took the tablecloth off the table a carried it to the big couch. He arranged the cushions for his head and then lay down. He pulled the big cloth over him. It was heavy and warm – too warm after a while, and Barney had to push it partly off him.

Miranda cuddled into his jacket, putting her little paws inside his shirt. He liked to feel them there. He blew softly on the top of her head.

'Good night, Miranda. Sleep well, and we won't wake up before morning!'

But he was wrong – they did!

Miranda woke first, and lay cuddled against Barney, her ears twitching. What had awakened her? She lay listening, and then settled down again. But before she had fallen asleep once more, her ears twitched again. This time she scrambled out of Barney's coat and sat on the head of the couch. She chattered a little in a very small voice indeed.

She awoke Barney, and he sat up, feeling for Miranda. Where had she gone? He heard her low chattering nearby and put out a hand to touch her. She nestled into his arms at once.

'What woke you, Miranda?' Barney whispered. 'Something disturbed you. What was it. It's the middle of the night. Did you hear a mouse or a rat?'

On the night air came the sound of the church clock striking some distance away. Doing – dong – dong.

'Three o'clock,' said Barney. 'There's still a lot of the night left, Miranda. Go to sleep.'

And then he too heard a noise. At first he thought he must be mistaken.Then it came again. Where was it? Surely it wasn't in the room? It was a curious noise, and it came and went in spasms. What did it sound like?

Barney decided that the noise certainly wasn't in the room. He felt in his pocket for the torch that Roger had lent him. He switched it on. The beam flashed round the room. It was quite empty. There was nobody and nothing there.

The noise could not be heard outside the little room where he had been sleeping. He soon made certain of that. He then went carefully round the room, stopping and listening at various points.

He came to one place where the noise sounded loudest. He flashed his torch on the spot. It was the panel which Roger had pointed out to him as the one that opened into the secret passage. He pressed his ear to it.

Now he could hear the noise much better, when it came. It was a curious, spasmodic noise, fairly regular, but too far away to make out whether it was made by a machine, or by a human being or animal, or by water – in fact Barney couldn't make it out at all. It came

113

spasmodically, but it was always the same when it did come – a series of quick sounds more or less regularly spaced. Barney guessed they came up from the secret passage, and were altered considerably before they reached him because of the distance and the hollowness of the secret passage.

He didn't know how to open the secret passage, so he couldn't find out anything. He went back to lie down on the couch, with Miranda beside him.

'Might as well go to sleep,' he told the little monkey. 'We're not likely to find out anything by just listening to those sounds for hours. But – I think we certainly ought to examine that secret passage, Miranda. What do you suppose is down there?'

Miranda hadn't the faintest idea. She cuddled down again and went to sleep. So did Barney. Whether the noises went on again or not, he didn't know and he didn't care.

Barney awoke in good time in the morning and got up cautiously, in case the caretaker had come early. But the whole building was silent. There was not even the mysterious sound he had heard in the middle of the night.

He wondered if he could have dreamt it. No, he couldn't, he remembered it too well. He stole into the kitchen to put his face under the tap and to get a drink.

Miranda pretended to hold her paws out to the tap, but she didn't get wet. She wasn't fond of water!

'You're a fraud,' said Barney, drying himself on his big red handkerchief. 'No, I'm not going to dry your paws when they're not even wet. You wash your hands properly then I will.'

He went back to the little room where he had slept and made it tidy, draping the tablecloth over the table again. He wondered if the caretaker would notice how crumpled it was, and be puzzled. He didn't think she noticed much though, judging by the layers of dust she had left here and there.

He went into the hall to watch for her coming. He didn't like to go out of the back door, leaving it unlocked, in case she was suspicious.

He hid behind the big chest and waited. She should be coming soon. In a little while he heard her footsteps coming down the path outside, then she slid the big key into the door and opened it.

As soon as she had disappeared into one of the rooms Barney slipped out with Miranda. Nobody saw him. He made his way to Miss Hannah's house and stood by the front gate, waiting.

Snubby rushed out to him. 'Barney! I've been watching for you. We're in the middle of breakfast and I'll bring a tray out for you here. You can sit in the garden, Miss Hannah says, if you'll promise not to let Miranda off your shoulder.'

When the others come out after breakfast Barney told them of his peculiar experience in the middle of the night. 'I can't imagine what it was,' he said. 'It was a silly sort of noise. I can't place it, and yet I feel I know it and have heard it many times. But, of course the hollowness of the passage must make it sound very different from what it really is.'

The others listened, amazed and thrilled. 'Did it *really* come from behind the panelling, Barney?' asked Roger. 'What's down there then? That woman says the passage is walled up, so whatever is there can't be very far down!'

'It sounded a good way down,' said Barney. 'Are you all game to explore it?'

They were – though Diana sounded a bit quavery. Snubby felt very brave sitting out there in the bright sunshine, discussing weird noises that happened in the night – but he couldn't help wondering if he would feel quite so brave in the dead of night!

'That woman would never let us go down in the day-time, that's certain,' said Roger. 'So it means we must explore after she's gone home. But we can't very well slip out before supper, or Miss Pepper would want to know what we're up to with you. We'd better come after we're supposed to be in bed.'

They debated it solemnly, and decided it would be best to go then. Miss Pepper and Miss Hannah went to bed very early, about nine o'clock. The children could easily dress and slip out. Nobody would know.

'Right,' said Barney, finishing his breakfast. 'That's settled then. Tonight about half-past nine. We'll do the "This is the-House-that-Jack-Built" business – move the picture that slides the panel that works the lever that frees the panel that opens the passage that lets us go down, that brings us to – '

'What?' cried the other three eagerly. But Barney shook his head. 'That's as far as I can get,' he said. 'We'll know the rest of our little story tonight, I hope. Now if you've got to do some jobs for Miss Hannah, I'll take the two dogs for a walk. They're pawing at me as if they want to get my jacket off! All right, all right, Loony and Loopy. I'll take you for a walkie-walk and get some of your fat off!'

He went off with the two dogs, whistling his lovely clear whistle. The others went back to help with the various jobs.

'Tonight – at half-past nine!' thought Diana, with a little shiver. 'It's exciting – but I do feel a little bit scared!'

Chapter Eighteen

Down the Secret Passage

At half-past nine that night Miss Pepper and Miss Hannah were both in bed, and Miss Hannah was fast asleep. The children were ready to go and were debating whether to take Loony or not.

'Will he bark the place down if we don't take him?' whispered Diana.

'Yes,' whispered back Snubby. 'We'd better let him come. I'll carry him downstairs so that his great paws don't make a noise.'

So Loony was carried downstairs, puzzled but very good and quiet. Loony slept on a couch in Miss Hannah's room, which was fortunately in another wing of the house, so he heard nothing.

They all heaved a sigh of relief when they were safely out on the road, walking softly in the moonlight. They soon arrived at Ring O' Bells Hall, and Barney let them in at the front door. He closed it quietly.

'Have you heard those noises again?' asked Snubby. Barney shook his head.

'No. Not tonight. Not a sound. Come on, let's go to the little room and get going.'

They went to the room where Barney had slept the night before, and where the entrance of the secret passage was. All of them had torches, and they shone them on the big tapestry picture on the wall.

'See that face with a helmet pushed back on the fore-head?' said Roger in a low voice. 'Well, watch – I press it just *here* – and see what happens!'

The picture slid quietly to one side, exposing the small panel. Roger pressed on it and the panel slid aside in its turn. He put in his hand and felt for the knob. He pressed that too, and at the same moment a small rattling noise came from behind another panel some distance away on the wall.

Barney looked startled. 'That's the lever freeing the other panel, so that we can push it to one side,' whispered Diana. They went to the second panel which was large. Roger pushed against it hard, and to Barney's surprise it slid to one side, passing neatly under the panel next to it, disclosing the yawning hole that was the entrance to the secret passage.

Loony gave a tiny yelp. He couldn't understand all these curious happenings by the light of torches. 'Shut up,' said Snubby, tapping the dog's head. 'Don't say a word, Loony.'

Roger thrust his torch inside the panelling and tried to see the passage. But all he could make out was a dark and narrow way behind the panelling.

'Shall we get in and follow the passage now?' whispered Roger. 'It's all quiet – nothing to be heard at all!'

'Right – you go first, Roger, then Diana can go, then Snubby and I'll follow with Loony,' said Barney. 'It's so narrow we'll have to go in single file.'

Roger got in, lifting his leg over the panelling. He stood in the passage, which smelt dusty and musty. He moved along a little way and one by one all the others got into it too. Loony was lifted in by Snubby.

He was surprised and very subdued. He thought this was a most peculiar evening!

'Where's Miranda?' whispered Snubby.

'She wouldn't come into the hole,' whispered back Barney. 'She was scared. She'll be all right in that room. She'll wait for us.'

118

The passage was indeed dark and narrow. It went behind the panelling of the room for about twelve feet and then turned abruptly to the left. It then went downwards by means of very shallow steps, down and down and down.

Roger was in front, keeping his torch level so that its light flashed on what was before him. Once he stopped, and the whole line bumped into one another.

'What's up, Roger?' asked Diana anxiously.

'Look,' said Roger, and flashed his torch on two tiny wooden doors set in a hole in the wall at one side of the passage. 'A cupboard! Perhaps the very cupboard where Old Grandad found those books and the carved box!'

He opened the doors, expecting the cupboard to be empty. But it wasn't. What it held was rather surprising. Nothing old, but something very new and modern. There were torch batteries, candles, a little tin of paraffin oil, and a dozen boxes of matches.

'What strange things to store here,' said Diana, looking at them. 'I suppose they've been left here ever since the passage was walled up – maybe they were useful for exploring it before the roof fell in and they closed it.'

'That was a long time ago,' said Roger. He shut the cupboard doors thoughtfully and went on once more, picking his way slowly. The passage was much wider once it left the panelling. Roger reckoned that it was really a tunnel now, going underground. Possibly it had left the house behind and was no longer underneath it. The caretaker-woman had told them that it avoided the cellars, which, presumably, spread themselves under the house.

He suddenly stopped again, with a short exclamation. The others did their usual bumping. Loony whined.

'You might give us warning when you're going to stop so suddenly,' grumbled Snubby under his breath. 'What's up now?'

119

Roger was flashing his torch on what looked like a brick wall in front of him. It stretched from ground to roof. 'Here's the wall that woman told us of,' he said. 'The passage *is* bricked up then! Look at that! We can't go any farther!'

This was bitterly disappointing. None of the children had really believed in their hearts that the woman had spoken the truth. But she had. There was the wall! If there was any more of the secret passage it must be on the other side of the wall, and she had said that the roof had fallen in there.

'What a swizz!' said Snubby.

'What about the noises Barney heard? We haven't come across anything that could make them,' whispered Roger. This was passed back to Barney.

'Funny,' said Barney. 'Where could they have come from then?'

'Let's go back,' said Diana. 'I don't like the smell down here.'

So back they went, turning themselves round and having Barney for leader this time. They passed the unusual little cupboard but didn't open it again. Then they were up behind the panelling, and in a moment or two were climbing out of the passage and into the room beyond.

Roger pressed the panel back into place. A rattling noise came as it slid back. That was the lever moving back against the panel to prevent anyone opening it unless they pressed the hidden knob behind the picture. Roger then slid back the little panel, and wondered how to move back the picture into place. He couldn't find out, so it had to be left out of place.

'Perhaps that woman will think she left it out of place herself, if she notices it tomorrow,' said Diana. 'I say – what a disappointment. I don't quite know what I

120

expected to find, but I expected *some*thing. But we didn't even hear one of Barney's noises!'

'Sh!' said Barney, suddenly. 'I believe I did hear it again – just then. Hush, everyone!'

They all stiffened, and listened hard. Yes, there *was* a noise – a few quick, regular sounds, far away and hollow-sounding. It *did* seem as if it came up the secret passage, muffled and distant.

'There you are,' said Barney. 'I began to think I'd dreamt it – but I hadn't.'

And then they suddenly heard another noise – quite a different noise, that made them go tense and clutch one another.

It was only a small sound – a tiny jangle of a noise – as if – as if one of the bells up in the tower had moved, and its clapper had bumped against it!

'That was a bell-noise,' breathed Diana. 'And it came from the tower. Oh, don't say the bells are going to ring themselves!'

And then it happened. The bells rang out, jingled and jangled, clashed and rang away up in the tower! Diana clutched Roger so tightly that her nails went into the flesh of his arm. Loony howled dismally.

The bells suddenly stopped. The echo of the clanging died away, and Diana sank down on the couch, trembling. Snubby was petrified and couldn't move. Barney and Roger spoke together softly.

'Who rang them? There's nobody here but ourselves.'

'And anyway there are no ropes to pull. Why did they suddenly ring?'

'In the old days it was said that they rang because enemies were coming. Surely the bells don't count us as enemies! They couldn't have rung against *us*!'

'Bells can't ring themselves,' said Roger, trying to convince himself that they couldn't. But they *had* rung themselves! The children had heard them.

A little scared, whimpering noise made them all jump.

'Oh – *poor* little Miranda!' said Diana, picking the tiny monkey up. 'Did the bells scare you too? Never mind. It's all right now.'

'Do you think we dare to go and look in the square tower, just to see if anyone has rigged up ropes to peal the bells?' asked Roger, after a time. They were now all sitting close together on the couch, trying to recover from their fright.

'I'm not going,' said Snubby promptly. 'They might begin to ring again and I'd have a double fit!'

'I'm going to see,' said Barney and walked off. Roger followed him rather reluctantly.

They soon came back. 'No ropes at all,' said Barney. 'The bells are all quite still. There's nothing to be seen. Well – I don't know who the enemies are – but *I* can't see or hear any. The bells made a mistake *this* time!'

'*Listen*,' said Diana urgently. 'I can hear something. I can really – out in the hall there.'

They listened tensely. They heard a key being thrust into the front door, and somebody opened it. There were voices – footsteps! The door closed softly.

'The bells were right!' whispered Snubby. 'These must be the enemies!'

Chapter Nineteen

All Very Peculiar

'We must hide!' said Barney. 'They may come in here.'
Fortunately the footsteps went into the kitchen, and the
children could hear water running. They looked round
the little room desperately. They didn't dare to leave it
in case they were seen.

A great chest stood in one corner, and a smaller one
in another. Barney lifted up the lid of the large one. 'Get
in,' he whispered to the others. 'There's room for three
of you. I'll get into the other with Miranda.'

They got in hurriedly, making as little noise as possible.
Snubby dragged poor Loony in, tapping him fiercely on
the head every time he showed an inclination to growl.
Barney slipped inside the other chest. But Miranda ref-
used to come! She shot away from him in the darkness.
She hated being shut up anywhere.

Barney gave a little groan. He hoped Miranda would
keep out of the way of the 'enemy' whoever they were.
What in the world were people doing here at this time of
night?

They had only just hidden themselves in time. Footsteps
– two pairs – came into the room where they were hidden.

'Where is he?' said a man's voice.

'I'll take you to him.' It was a woman's voice that
answered – the caretaker! Barney lifted up the lid of his
chest a fraction and listened.

He heard the now familiar rattle behind the panelling
as the lever fell back to release the larger panel. Ah –
they were going down the secret passage then. Why?

There was nothing there. It was blocked up not very far down. Barney was puzzled. The woman had apparently not noticed that the big picture was out of place, which was a relief.

He saw her by the light of the man's torch. He couldn't see the man very well, but noticed that he had a bag, a small attaché case of some kind. His voice was deep and rough. He didn't sound at all pleased.

Loony growled suddenly – a deep, blood-curdling noise from the depths of the large chest. The woman and the man stood still, as if transfixed.

'What in the name of goodness was that?' said the man at last. 'What a fearful noise!'

From above his head came a small gibbering sound. That was Miranda, of course, telling Loony to be quiet! It made the man and woman jump violently. The man swung his torch upwards, but Miranda had gone. She gibbered from the opposite side of the room now.

Loony growled again, and was immediately stifled by Snubby.

'There's that frightful noise again,' – said the man. 'It's enough to give anyone the creeps. What's the matter with this place?'

'Nothing,' said the woman, in a trembling voice. 'I've never heard these noises before. But it can't be anything – just – just owls or something.'

'Owls don't make blood-curdling noises like that,' said the man, switching his torch into the yawning hole in the panelling. 'Well, come on – do we really have to get in here?'

The woman gave a sudden scream, and Barney almost dropped the lid of the chest in surprise. Now what was happening?

Miranda had sat herself on a shelf near the woman's

head, and had pulled at her hair. No wonder she screamed.

She made the man jump, and he became angry. 'Stop it!' he growled. 'We're getting nerves or something. What's the matter now?'

'S-s-s-something pulled my hair,' the woman quavered.

'And so will I if you don't stop all this play-acting,' said the man. He gave the woman a shove and she went into the secret passage more quickly than she had intended to. He followed. Barney could hear their steps going along behind the panelling, and then down the shallow steps underground. He opened the lid wide and jumped out, padding across the floor to the opening in the panelling. He put his head in and listened.

But except for a scraping kind of noise which he couldn't make out, he heard no more. All was silence. Where had the two gone?

He ran lightly to the other chest and opened it.

'Come on,' he said. 'Now's our chance to go. They've gone down the secret passage, goodness knows where or why. We'd better clear out. I don't like this much.'

The others gladly scrambled out. They shut the lid down and ran quietly in their rubber-soled shoes to the door. They sidled into the dark hall and made for the front door, which they knew was directly opposite. Barney thought it would be safe to switch on his torch for half a second.

They came to the front door and Barney opened it quietly. He would have to leave it open because he couldn't risk making a noise when he closed it. He suddenly put out a warning hand to the others.

'Be careful. There may be a car waiting somewhere,' he said. 'We don't want to be seen.'

He looked sharply out to the road, and made out a dim red light – the rear light of a car!

125

'We'll go round the house to the back,' he whispered. 'We can squeeze through a hedge and into the lane farther up. Come on. Don't make a sound!'

They all breathed more freely when at last they were some way up the lane, having squeezed through the hedge halfway down the garden of Ring O' Bells Hall. Loony was completely bewildered. What kind of game was this, played so late at night? He was tired of being tapped on the head by Snubby when he wanted to growl.

'Don't say anything till we get back to Miss Pepper's,' said Roger, in a low voice. So, feeling that there might be ears listening in every hedge, the four of them hurried quietly back.

They went to a little shed in Miss Hannah's garden and crowded in there together. 'What an evening,' said Roger, blowing out a deep breath of relief at being somewhere ordinary and safe. 'Those bells ringing out all by themselves like that – and then the woman and the man coming, exactly as if they were the enemies foretold by the bells.'

'I wonder if anyone else heard them – the villagers, for instance,' said Diana.

'Some of them may have,' said Roger. 'But the village is a little way away, isn't it – and as the bells are not swung loosely on ropes, but only jammed up there tightly together, they wouldn't sound nearly as loud as they would do if they were pulled and rung properly. They jangled, more than rang.'

'They did the best they could,' said Diana soberly. 'I was awfully scared. I suppose the "enemy" didn't hear them because they were coming in the car, and must still have been some way away. I wonder if they would have come into the Hall if they *had* heard them.'

'Of course not,' said Roger. 'Clever bells – to warn us

but not them! I say – this is all very *peculiar*, isn't it? What's down that secret passage?'

'You mean *who* is,' said Diana. 'That man said "Where is *he*?" not "Where is *it*?" There's someone down there, doing something.'

'I don't know where, then,' said Roger. '*We* went right down to the brick wall, and there wasn't anyone. And, as far as I could see, there was absolutely no other passage or cave or anything. Just a tunnel.'

There was a silence. Everyone was thinking. 'Shall we go down the passage again some time and have another snoop?' asked Roger at last.

'No,' said everybody, very firmly. The idea of getting down there again at dead of night, with those bells nearby likely to ring all by themselves at any minute, didn't appeal to anyone.

'I tell you what we *could* do,' said Snubby suddenly. 'We could try and and find out where the *other* end of the secret passage is, and then explore it backwards, so to speak – to the other side of the brick wall.'

Everyone thought this was a very bright idea. Roger gave Snubby a little pat on the back. 'Now that *is* an idea,' he said. 'We might find something out then.'

'Yes – but wait a minute. We don't know where to look for the other end of the passage,' said Diana, after a moment's thought.

'We must go and ask Grandad again,' said Roger, promptly. 'Maybe he'll tell us this time.'

Diana suddenly yawned, and that set the others off. The church clock struck twelve, very solemnly indeed.

'We ought to go to bed,' said Diana. 'We'll never wake up in the morning. Where's old Barney going to sleep? He can't go back to Ring O' Bells Hall, that's certain.'

'I shouldn't think he wants to, either,' said Snubby. 'I know I wouldn't.'

'Well, I don't,' said Barney. 'Those bells rather shook me. I just can't understand it. Poor little Miranda is so frightened that she's not moved since I tucked her into my shirt. She must have had a fit when she heard them jangling out!'

'I had a pretty good fit myself,' said Snubby. 'Well, what about Barney. Couldn't he sleep here for the night? In this shed?'

'Yes – just for tonight,' said Roger, considering. 'I don't know if Miss Hannah would mind, but as we can't ask her now, we'll just say Barney *can* sleep here. After all, Miranda isn't likely to pop in through her window or anything.'

Barney was very tired. He arranged some sacks to lie on, and Diana found an old garden rug to cover him. 'We'll go in now,' she said. 'You'll be all right, Barney, won't you?'

'Fine,' said Barney, curling himself up. 'You go and get into bed – you'll be getting 'flu again, or something! See you tomorrow.'

'Yes – and we'll find the other end of the passage *some*how,' said Snubby. 'And down we'll go.'

'Though I expect we shall find the roof *has* fallen in, as that woman said,' remarked Roger, remembering.

'Anyway, we'll have a shot at finding it and exploring,' said Barney sleepily. 'Good night, all of you.'

Loony gave Barney one last lick on the nose and sniffed at the sleeping Miranda under his shirt. Then he trotted off quietly after the others. What an evening! He would have something to tell Loopy next day, no doubt about that!

Chapter Twenty

Grandad's Old Box

Neither Miss Pepper nor Miss Hannah had heard the bells ringing the night before. Diana didn't ask them straight out, but the children felt that they *had* to discover if they had been heard.

'I thought I heard bells ringing in the night,' Diana said casually at breakfast-time. 'Funny!'

'You must have been dreaming,' said Miss Pepper. 'Mustn't she, Hannah?'

'Yes – she probably heard the church clock striking,' said Miss Hannah. 'It has a lovely tone. Do you want a fourth sausage, Snubby?'

Snubby did. 'My appetite's coming back,' he informed Miss Hannah.

'*Coming* back!' she repeated horrified. 'You don't mean to say it's even worse than this?'

'He's just greedy – it's nothing to do with appetite,' said Diana. Snubby aimed a kick at her under the table, but Diana had already drawn her legs well out of the way, and there was a sudden agonised yelp from poor Loony. This meant Snubby getting hurriedly down from the table and crawling underneath to comfort him and apologise.

'*You'd* better have the last sausage, Roger, as Snubby had disappeared,' said Miss Pepper, whereupon Snubby came back again in a hurry.

'What are your plans today?' asked Miss Hannah. 'Riding? Walking? Lazing?'

'We thought we'd go and have a talk with Old Grandad

again,' said Diana. 'And then perhaps go for a walk. Do you want any errands done, Miss Hannah?'

'No, I don't think so,' said Miss Hannah. 'You'll do all your usual jobs first, I know – beds and so on.'

'Oh, of *course*,' said Diana. 'And you do know you've only got to ask us to do absolutely anything for you and we'll do it.'

'Like a shot,' said Snubby, finishing the last sausage. 'I do like the way you cook sausages, Miss Hannah – nice and *bursty*.'

'What extraordinary things you say, Snubby,' said Miss Hannah. 'Have you finished? Because if you have you might remove Loony from my feet. He's so heavy.'

Loony was removed, and Loopy followed. Diana got up to go and fetch Barney's tray of breakfast things. She had already been out to see him, and had taken him a very fine breakfast. Miranda was sitting licking marmalade off a piece of toast. She offered it to Diana.

'No thanks, darling Miranda,' said Diana. 'You can have it all. I don't want even one lick. Barney, we'll come out as soon as we can. We've got a few things to do.'

'Right,' said Barney. 'I'm going to mend that bit of fence that's broken. I must do *some*thing in return for my breakfast!'

'Oh – Miss Hannah *will* be pleased,' said Diana. That was so like Barney. He always felt he simply must repay any kindness as soon as ever he could.

About eleven o'clock the four children, Loony, Loopy and Miranda were all going up the lane to Hubbard Cottage. They stopped at a little shop to buy a tin of tobacco for the old man they were going to see. The woman knew quite well what he smoked, which was lucky.

They walked up to the front door of the cottage and knocked.

'Come away in!' called Mother Hubbard's voice, and

in they went. Mother Hubbard was there, scrubbing her floor. She was pleased to see the children. She got up, wiping her hands, and smiled at them.

'Could we see Old Grandad?' asked Diana politely. 'We've brought him a little tin of tobacco.'

'Well, if that isn't kind of you!' said the old lady, and she took the tin. 'I wish you *could* see him – but he's got one of his poorly turns and he's in bed.'

'Oh,' said the children, and looked so disappointed that Mother Hubbard felt sorry.

'There's nothing *I* can tell you or do for you instead, is there?' she asked.

'Well,' said Diana, and paused. She looked at the others and they nodded. 'You see, it's like this – Old Grandad told us about some old books he once had, and we wondered if he still had them and would lend them to us.'

'Old books?' said Mother Hubbard, frowning as she tried to remember. 'Let me see – those must have been thrown away years since.'

'Oh – *what* a pity!' said Diana, disappointed.

'When I came to look after Old Grandad, he had a wonderful lot of rubbish,' said Mother Hubbard. 'And I had a good turn-out and threw a lot away. But I did put some into an old box of his. You can rummage through that if you like, and see if you can find any old books there. He wouldn't mind!'

'Oh, *could* we!' said Diana delighted. 'We'd love to. We're so interested in Ring O' Bells Village, you know.'

'Yes – it's a strange old place,' said Mother Hubbard. 'Do you know what Old Grandad said to me this morning? He said he heard the bells at the old Hall ringing last night. The things he do think! Why those bells haven't rung for years – they've got no ropes to pull them with.'

'Didn't you hear the bells too?' asked Roger.

131

'I sleep sound,' said Mother Hubbard. 'And if I heard bells ringing at Ring O' Bells Hall, I'd think I was off my head. Will you believe it, when Fanny Tapp came by this morning, and I told her what Old Grandad said, she made out she'd heard them too, and was proper scared in the night. The tales some folks make up!'

The children listened to all this and said nothing. So others had heard the bells too!

'You come along into my washhouse,' said Mother Hubbard. 'I've got Grandad's box there. And would you like some of my gingers? I made them yesterday.'

The 'gingers' turned out to be nice, hard, ginger biscuits, almost as good as Naomi Barlow's cinnamon biscuits. The children followed Mother Hubbard into the little washhouse, munching the biscuits.

There were shelves round the washhouse and Mother Hubbard pointed to an old brass-bound box. 'That's Grandad's,' she said. 'Can you lift it down?'

'Yes, thank you,' said Barney, and lifted it down. It wasn't very heavy, so there couldn't be much in it.

A loud call came from the little front garden and Mother Hubbard hurried off. 'That's the baker,' she said. 'You undo the box and see what you can find. If there's books there, you can borrow them.'

The children opened the box. It had a simple catch to fasten it. They bent over the open box, excited. What would they find?

They found very little. There were a few roughly carved wooden figures, which probably Old Grandad had done himself and was proud of. There was a funny old ship, its sails in rags, its mast broken. There was an old wooden pipe, and what looked like a home-made whistle.

'Not much here,' said Roger. 'Wait – here's a book!'

He took it out. It was bound in leather that was warped and discoloured with damp. Many of the pages had stuck together. The children pored over it, trying to pull the pages apart.

'Be careful – you'll tear them,' said Roger. 'Blow! This book is in that difficult old lettering. We can't possibly make out much – and look how messed up the pages are – we can hardly read anything anyhow.'

They all pored over the book, trying to make out a word here and there. They couldn't even find out the title. It was in flourishing letters, so decorative that the children couldn't read them.

'No good,' said Roger, disappointed. 'Still – if Mother Hubbard will let us, we'll borrow it, just in *case* we can make out something. Though how we could ever find out if the secret passage is mentioned here I simply don't know!'

'Found anything interesting?' asked Mother Hubbard, appearing again. 'Nothing but rubbish there, I expect. Oh, you've got an old book. Borrow it, if you like.'

'Thank you,' said Diana. 'We'd like to. I hope Old Grandad will be better soon.'

'I'll tell him you've been, and give him the tobacco,' said Mother Hubbard. 'Goodbye – and keep the book as long as you like.'

They all went out. Barney took Miranda out from his jacket. He had hidden her there in case Mother Hubbard or Old Grandad didn't like monkeys. She had been as good as gold. The two dogs, each with a bone from the old lady, welcomed the children as if they had been away for a week. Roger laughed and untied them.

'Old Grandad doesn't like dogs,' he told them, 'so don't bark your heads off like that, or he'll come after you with a stick!'

They went to the village for an ice cream. Snubby was carrying the book, dipping into it as he went. He suddenly stood still and said 'HA!' in a most excited voice.

133

'What are you ha-ing about?' asked Diana. 'Found a recipe for cooking sausages or something?'

'Look at this,' said Snubby, and the others crowded round to see. Snubby had got the book open at the very last page. He pointed to the inside of the back cover.

'There's a kind of pocket there,' he said. 'And there's something in it – a map – a map, I should think. Let's sit down somewhere and find out.'

They went into a field and sat down. The dogs ran off to the rabbit-holes, delighted. Miranda went with them – not to look for rabbits, but to jeer at the two digging dogs!

Snubby drew out a paper from the old pocket inside the back cover of the book. 'It's parchment,' he said. 'Gosh, I hope it doesn't fall to pieces in my hand!'

'Give it to me,' said Diana. 'I'm more careful than you are.'

With deft, gentle fingers she unfolded the parchment, and spread it on her lap.

It had been folded in four, and the folds were already cracking.

'It's a map!' said Diana, thrilled. 'Look – a map of Ring O' Bells Hall! Oh, if only it would show the secret passage!'

They all pored over it in excitement. The map was not so discoloured and faded as the pages of the book, and the children could easily make out the name at the bottom. 'Dourley. Ring O' Bells Hall.'

'It's genuine!' said Roger. 'Now we really *may* find out something!'

Chapter Twenty-One

A Little Hunting Around

They did find out something. They found out quite a lot. It might be difficult to decipher the old printing on the pages of the book – but it was much easier to read a plan or map.

It seemed to be a plan of Ring O' Bells Hall, showing all the ground floor. The two towers were indicated, one as a square, one as a circle at each end of the Hall. Bells were drawn in the square showing that that was the Bell Tower.

'Where's the little panelled room where the secret passage begins?' said Roger.

'Here,' said Diana, and pointed to it. 'That must be it – it's off the hall, and near the kitchen and it's small.'

'Is the secret passage shown?' asked Snubby, bending his head over the map.

'No,' said Diana, in disappointment.

'There's a letter P in the room,' said Roger, pointing. 'Why? P for passage, of course. It *is* a P, isn't it?'

They all agreed that it was. But the P only told them what they already knew – that there was a passage leading off the little panelled room!

'Well – it's a thrilling old map, and beautifully drawn – but it doesn't tell us what we want to know,' said Roger, in disappointment. 'I suppose there isn't anything else in the old pocket inside the back cover, Di?'

Diana looked, inserting her fingers gently. She gave a little exclamation. 'Yes – I believe there is!'

Very slowly and carefully she drew out another piece

of parchment, much smaller than the other. It was folded in half. With fingers that suddenly shook, she opened it. Everyone bent over it at once.

At first they couldn't make it out. It seemed to be merely the plan of some bit of countryside. Then Snubby's rather dirty finger poked down at the paper.

'P!' he said. 'P again. P for passage. Look, it begins here, by this house, or whatever it is.'

'I should think it's meant to be Ring O' Bells Hall,' said Diana. 'It's roughly the shape – you know how it sticks out at the back, so to speak. Well, all right – we'll say that P is for Passage – the secret passage. How does that help us?'

'Can't you *see*?' said Snubby impatiently and he jabbed at the map again. 'There's a faded red line leading from that P – look, there it goes – right from Ring O' Bells Hall, over the stream, through the wood – and ends at this other P here!'

'Gosh – you're right, Snubby!' said Roger. 'It *is* the *passage* – must be! But it doesn't go over the stream, of course – it goes under – and under the wood – and it seems to end at some little building, if that's what this square indicates.'

'What building would that be?' said Diana, thinking. 'Could it be – Ring O' Bells Cottage?'

'It could be – and is!' cried Roger. 'Of course, of course. Don't you remember what Old Grandad kept saying, when we asked him where the secret passage went to. "Ask Mother Barlow, ask Mother Barlow!" It went to her cottage, of course, that's why we had to ask her – though she's been dead for ages. He'd forgotten that.'

'And Naomi Barlow lives there now,' said Diana. 'I wonder if *she* knows anything about it. But I say – where in the world does the secret passage end in her cottage? Don't you remember the solid stone floor in each of the

136

rooms? There didn't seem anywhere for a passage to open.'

'There wasn't,' said Snubby. 'I'd stake anything that no passage is under the floors of Ring O' Bells Cottage.'

'Yet this old map certainly shows the passage ending there,' said Roger, puzzled. 'Perhaps it ends somewhere nearby – in the wood, under a trapdoor, or something like that.'

'Yes – that might be so,' said Barney. 'Anyway, we know the way the passage takes now – it runs from the panelled room we know, avoids the house, goes straight under the garden, runs to this stream, goes under it – must be pretty deep there, I should think, or the water would seep through – then under the wood, and up to the cottage, ending somewhere about there.'

'Gosh – it's wonderful!' said Snubby, too thrilled for words. 'What do we do next?'

'I'll tell you what we do next,' said Diana, a marvellous idea suddenly filling her mind. 'We go to Ring O' Bells Cottage, and ask Naomi Barlow if she'd be kind enough to let Barney sleep in her little store-room, with Miranda – because we can't find a place for him in the village!'

'And he can snoop round, and ask her questions and see if he can find the passage!' said Snubby. 'What a brainwave!'

'She loved Miranda – she would say yes, I'm sure,' said Diana. 'Let's go and ask her immediately after lunch.'

Feeling very thrilled indeed, they all went home to enjoy a good lunch. Barney had his out in the garden with Miranda, who spent a most enjoyable half-hour peeling the skin off a tomato and eating it.

After lunch they set off for Ring O' Bells Cottage. They were almost there when they saw Naomi Barlow hurrying along, looking like old Red Riding Hood again, because she had on the red cloak! She greeted them kindly.

'I hope you weren't going to see me, children. I am going down to clean out the church, and shan't be back till six.'

'We *were* going to see you,' said Diana, disappointed. 'We were going to tell you that we simply can't find *any*where in the village for poor Barney and his monkey to sleep in at night – and Miss Hannah won't have him because she's afraid of monkeys. So we wondered, we just wondered if – '

'I'd let him sleep in my little old cottage!' finished Naomi, and she smiled. 'Of course he can – he can have the room where *I* used to sleep for years when I was a child. You remember the store-room I showed you? He can sleep there – and I shall have a pet monkey to fuss over again.'

'Thank you, Mam, very much indeed,' said Barney gratefully.

'You go up to the cottage now, and set the store-room to rights,' said Naomi. 'Tidy it up, and put down the old mattress you'll see in one corner. That'll save me doing it when I come back tired.'

'You *are* kind,' said Diana. 'We'll love to do that – and is there any job you'd like us to do for *you* – clean the windows, or anything?'

'Oh, no – the only other things you can do is to help yourselves to my cinnamon biscuits!' said old Naomi with a laugh. 'They're in that big tin on the mantelpiece. Now I must hurry. You go along to my cottage – you'll find the door isn't locked.'

She hurried off, looking more like an old Red Riding Hood than ever. The children looked at each other in delight. Could anything be better! A bed and shelter for

Barney and Miranda in the very place where the other end of the secret passage began!

'We're in luck's way,' said Diana, as they turned down the little path to Naomi's cottage.

'Yes – we can have a good look at the floors in each room to make sure there's no passage below,' said Roger. 'I wish we could do something in return for the old woman's kindness.'

'I shall pick some bluebells and put them about the cottage,' said Diana, and she went to pick a big bunch. The boys went on with the dogs, Miranda on Snubby's shoulder for a change.

They came to the cottage. The door was not locked, and they opened it and went in. 'Let's have a good look round first,' said Roger. They were examining the kitchen floor when Diana came in with her bluebells.

'Found anything?' she asked, putting the flowers into a jug, and looking round for some water. She found some in a pail. There were no taps, of course, because Naomi had to draw her water from the well outside.

'Look at this floor,' said Roger. He was on his knees, examining it closely. 'I could bet anything that these stone flags haven't been disturbed for hundreds of years! You can't shift a single one. They're set so close together too. If there *is* a passage underneath, it can't be got at by us, that's certain.'

The floors were the same in every room, solid and firm, though uneven. The stones were hollowed where much treading had been done. 'Shows how old they are,' said Roger, marvelling.

They went into the store-room and tidied it for Barney. 'It smells nice,' he said, sniffing at the pickle jars and jam. I shall like sleeping here. I shall dream of dinner with pickles, and tea with jam!'

They found the old mattress, and put it on the floor.

There really wasn't much room for anything else then. It was just a cupboard of a room, but Barney was not at all particular.

'Well, that's done,' said Diana. 'Now what about having a good look round the garden and in the wood nearby, just to see if we *can* find anything else – an old stone trapdoor, or something – hidden under grass, perhaps.'

They went out into the sunshine. First they searched the little garden, but there was obviously nothing there. Then they went out of the gate, separated, and examined every inch of the ground all round the garden. But there was nothing to be found there either.

'It's maddening,' said Diana. 'The entrance *must* be somewhere. Barney, you must get into conversation with Naomi Barlow tonight, and see if *she* knows anything. It's so long since the passage was used, apparently, that people seem to have forgotten all about it. But she may have learnt something from Mother Barlow.'

'Right. I'll do my best,' said Barney. 'Now what about one of those cinnamon biscuits?'

'Oh, yes,' said Snubby and lifted down the tin. They each took one and put the tin back, though Loony and Loopy clamoured for one too.

'Certainly not,' said Snubby firmly. 'You were not included in the invitation to help yourselves to biscuits. Anyway, you've had a wonderful afternoon, scrabbling round the wood.'

'Let's go back to tea now,' said Diana. 'I'm hungry.'

So back they went to one of Miss Hannah's good teas. How they hoped that Barney would be able to find out something from old Naomi Barlow!

Chapter Twenty-Two

Barney Has An Idea

The four met the next morning in the garden at Miss Hannah's. Snubby had Barney's breakfast tray all ready, and he carried it out, with Roger and Diana running in front to greet Barney and Miranda.

'Did you find out anything?' asked Diana eagerly. 'Did Naomi tell you where the passage began?'

'No, she wouldn't,' said Barney. 'At first she said she knew nothing about it all – the passage was known only to a very few at any time, and those were the Dourlays themselves. Then she said it wasn't in existence now as far as she knew.'

'Blow!' said Roger. 'Not at all helpful. Didn't she *really* know anything?'

'Well, it was strange,' said Barney slowly, 'when I tried to press her a bit about it, because I couldn't help feeling that she knew more than she said, she got all upset, and said something rather peculiar.'

'What?' asked everyone at once.

'She said, "I'd forgotten the drowning for years, and now you've made me think of it. I shall have my nightmares again. I tell you that passage has never been used since the drowning. It's gone, it's gone!" '

The children listened to this in astonished silence. What could it all mean?

'What drowning?' wondered Diana. 'And why hasn't the passage been used since the *drowning*? Whatever has it got to do with somebody being drowned? You can't drown in a passage.'

'There's just one explanation,' said Barney and he lowered his voice. 'It may be wrong, but it's the only one I can think of. Where do you drown? In water. And where is there any water near Naomi's Cottage? Only in the well.'

There was a pause. 'I still don't see any explanation,' said Roger. 'What do you mean?'

'I mean this,' said Barney, 'and it may sound farfetched, but I think it's worth going into. Suppose that secret passage has its outlet in old Naomi's *well*? And somebody, who was being chased, used that passage and instead of being able to get out of the well, fell down and was drowned? If it had happened when Naomi was very young, and she heard of it, she would never forget it. It would give her nightmares. Maybe even the story of it, if told to her as a child, would be enough to make her dream.'

'I think you're right,' said Roger. 'It all fits together. But good gracious – how could a secret passage open into a well?'

'I don't know,' said Barney. 'That's for us to find out. If there *is* an opening down that well – and we all know how very deep it is – there must be some way of getting up or down it – some footholds of some kind – iron staples driven into the wall, perhaps. We could soon find out.'

'This is very, very exciting,' said Snubby, rubbing his hands together. 'We'll have to be careful not to miss our footing, though – or there'd be a nasty splash!'

'Don't say things like that,' said Diana with a shiver.

An impatient voice suddenly called from the house. 'Children! Whatever are you doing? Are you *never* coming to breakfast?'

'Good gracious – we forgot all about it,' said Roger in surprise. 'Fancy *you* forgetting too, Snubby. Unbelievable!'

'We'll be out as soon as we can, Barney,' said Diana, and the three of them tore in with the dogs at their heels.

They all had to go riding that morning, because they had arranged it the day before. Barney went too, wearing old jodhpurs belonging to Miss Hannah's nephew, who was now grown up and gone away. He was a perfect horseman, having been trained to the saddle from his babyhood. The children admired him as he rode. Good old Barney, he was a marvel!

As they rode, he told them about his night at Ring O' Bells Cottage. 'I slept in that tiny room,' he said, 'and I dreamt of food all night long, the smells were so delicious. Snubby, you ought to try taking a few pickle jars and spice jars to your bedroom. You'd have wonderful dreams. You'd probably be eating all night long in them.'

Everyone laughed. Snubby considered the idea seriously and thought it a very good one. He debated whether to subtract a few bottles and jars from Miss Hannah's larder and give the idea a trail.

Nobody noticed the scenery very much that morning because they were so excited at the idea of examining the well.

They talked and talked about it, and at lunch that day Diana could hardly eat anything, she felt so full of anticipation. However, neither Roger nor Snubby were in the least affected, so the lunch was not wasted.

That afternoon they all went up to Ring O' Bells Cottage with Barney. 'Old Naomi is going off to finish cleaning the church,' he said. 'It would be a good chance for us to have a look at the well.'

The cottage was empty when they arrived. Naomi had gone. The children made sure of this and then went straight to the well. They looked down.

It certainly *was* a very deep well. Roger dropped a

stone down again and the listened for the splash, which seemed to be a very long time coming.

'There it is,' said Barney at last. 'Now, let's look for a way down.'

The little ferns grew so thickly in the well walls that it was difficult to see even the bricks. Barney felt about, leaning over the well side. Diana held on to him, scared of his falling down.

'I've got something!' said Barney at last. 'There's a kind of iron loop here. Wait – I'll pull out these ferns.'

He pulled them out and then the others could see what he meant. A loop of iron was fixed to the wall. It seemed very firmly fastened in. Barney gave it a tug.

'Well – if this is a foothold to use when going down, there should be others in a row down the wall. I'm going over to see.'

'Oh, Barney – don't,' said Diana.

'I'll get a rope from the store-room and tie it round Barney's waist,' said Roger, who also didn't like the idea of Barney going down the well. 'We'll tie the rope to the well post, and hold on to it ourselves, letting Barney down bit by bit, as he finds something to hold on to.'

They got the rope and Barney let them tie him. Secretly he considered this rather silly, for he was a first-rate acrobat and climber – but he could see that Diana was very scared.

He went over the side, treading on the iron loop he had found. He put his foot down cautiously and felt about among the ferns. He found another loop!

'Got it!' he called back cheerfully to the others. 'This must be the right way down. No wonder nobody knew of it, it's so well-hidden by the ferns.'

Ferns did not grow very far down, however. Barney found it easier to feel the iron loops after a time. One or two of them fell away as he trod on them and gave him a little shock. The others heard them splashing into the water, and held very tightly to Barney's rope. Diana's heart beat fast. Oh, dear – this was very dangerous! Surely they ought not to do it? But they must find out, they must!

Barney went down a very long way. 'Can you see the water yet?' yelled Roger, his voice sounding most peculiar down the well.

'Yes – just,' called back Barney. 'I say – I can't feel any more loops for my feet. Blow – don't say the rest of them have rotted and fallen away!'

He felt about again, shivering, for it was icy-cold in the dank, dark well. No – there were no footholds at all below where he was. He called up to Roger.

'Roger! I've not got a torch with me. Tie yours carefully on a bit of string and let it down. I want to see if the entrance to the passage is anywhere here, as there aren't any more footholds.'

The torch came down, twisting round and round on its string. It only just reached Barney! He took it and switched it on. Ah – now he could see!

He sent up such a yell that the others nearly let go of the rope. Miranda, who hadn't gone down the well with Barney, looked down into the darkness anxiously.

'What is it?' shouted Roger, his voice echoing all the way down.

'There's a hole here, right in the side of the well!' called Barney. 'I bet it's the entrance to the secret passage! I say – what a marvellous idea to have a way of escape leading to a well. Nobody would ever dream of that! I'm going in!'

'No, no!' almost shrieked Snubby. 'Wait. We want to come too!'

'Not Diana,' came back Barney's voice.

'I don't want to come!' cried Diana. 'Anyway, someone

must guide the rope and hold it as you each go down. I'll do that.'

Barney stepped into the black hole, flashing his torch. He could see nothing but a tunnel underground. Gosh – this was exciting! They really had found the other end of the secret passage now. Would it lead back to Ring O' Bells Hall, as it showed on the map?

Roger came down next, feeling for the loops with his feet, and holding on to others with his hands. Then Snubby, who left a frenzied Loony behind. Diana had a job to stop Loony and Loopy from leaping into the well.

Soon all three boys were standing in the narrow hole. It was merely a round gap in the brickwork of the well. Did the water ever reach as high as that? Probably not. The spring from which the well water came must be very deep under the earth indeed.

'You can see what old Naomi means by someone drowning now, can't you?' said Barney. 'Probably someone came hurrying along this tunnel in the dark and didn't realise he'd come to the end. He must have run straight out of the hole and dropped down into the well.'

'Horrible!' said Roger, shivering with excitement, cold and horror. 'Come on. Let's explore the tunnel. But hadn't we better keep quiet, in case there's somebody else about? There may be someone down the tunnel at the other end!'

'Yes. Keep quiet then,' whispered Barney. 'Come along. I'll use my torch, and you can follow.'

So down the weird tunnel they went, following each other in the darkness. What a strange adventure!

Chapter Twenty-Three

Underground

For some way the tunnel ran straight and level. The roof was low in places and the boys bumped their heads till they got used to looking out for a sudden dip in the roof. They trailed on, with only the light of Barney's torch. The tunnel smelt dank and musty, and Roger hoped the air was good enough. If it was bad they might faint and fall down!

'Just as well we left Di behind to raise the alarm if we don't get back,' he thought.

The tunnel took a sharp bend, and ran downwards instead of level. The boys went on steadily. They all wished they had warm coats on, for they felt very chilly indeed. Suddenly Barney stopped and pointed with his torch to something.

A tree-root had penetrated through the roof of the tunnel and hung down in front of them! It looked very strange.

'We're under the trees now,' said Barney in a whisper. 'We shall soon leave the wood behind and come to the stream. I bet the tunnel takes a big dip under that, to get away from the damp river-bed!'

It did. It suddenly went down very steeply indeed, and became wet and muddy. The roof dripped water. Barney shone his torch on it. 'Look,' he said. 'Someone reinforced the roof just there with great stones. They've made a kind of stone arch. A good thing too, or the roof would have crumbled very quickly.'

They went on again, and then came to a full stop.

'Blow! said Barney, shining his torch in front of him. 'The roof *has* fallen in here – look!'

So it had. A great mass of rubble lay in front of them, and there was a broken hole in the roof.

'It might not be very serious,' said Roger. 'Let's just scrabble a bit and see if we can get through.'

It was difficult to 'scrabble' with only their hands, but they soon found that Roger was right – the fall was only trivial. They could make a way through at one side, by piling the earth and stones in the middle of the fall.

They went on again. Then Barney spoke in a low whisper, almost in Roger's ear. 'We must be getting somewhere near Ring O' Bells now – better be very cautious.'

The tunnel now began to slant upwards a little, and curved to the right. Then another roof-fall stopped them. This time it was a bigger one. The three looked at it in silence.

Then, from behind the roof-fall came a noise – a spasmodic noise of quick, regular sounds, painful to hear – the noise that Barney had heard, distorted and muffled by distance and by the fact that it had come up the secret passage to the little panelled room. No wonder Barney hadn't recognised the noise.

It was very simple to recognise now that it was near – just the other side of the roof-fall. It was a man coughing painfully – cough, cough, cough, – pause – cough, cough, cough – pause – cough, cough.

Then there was a dreadful groan, and the man on the other side of the roof-fall muttered something in a broken voice.

'He's terribly ill, I should think,' whispered Barney. 'He ought to have a doctor. What's he doing down here, do you suppose?'

'Kidnapped, probably,' said Roger, also in a whisper. 'As for a doctor – that's probably who we saw when we

148

hid in the chest the other night – do you remember the man with a small bag? He was probably a doctor called in by the woman.'

'But wouldn't a doctor be amazed to be taken to a patient hidden down here?' asked Snubby.

'He's probably a doctor who attends the gang or whatever it is that kidnaps people and hides them here,' said Barney.

'Look,' said Roger, straightening himself up. He had been bending down, peeping here and there. 'Look – there's a little space in this mass of rubble – you can see right through it.'

Barney bent down and put his eye to the space. He could make out part of the clothed body of a man, tossing and turning. He could not see his face.

'Shall I speak to him and ask him who he is?' whispered Barney. The others nodded. They felt sure the man was a captive, a prisoner, probably kidnapped and held for some reason or other.

Barney spoke through the hole. 'Hallo, there! Who are you?'

The man beyond stopped moving at once. He now appeared to be sitting up.

'Who spoke?' he whispered, in a croaking, frightened voice. 'Who is it?'

'Never mind,' said Barney. 'Tell us who you are. What are you doing here?'

'I've been kidnapped,' groaned the man. 'I'm a detective, and I've been spying on a gang who are known to be kidnappers. They've got *me* now – and now they want to get out of me all I know – then they'll bump me off. So I'm not telling.'

He fell back and began to cough again, a dreadful tearing cough. The boys knew he must be very ill. They didn't doubt his word at all.

149

'Shall we try and get through to you, sir, and – get you out this way?' asked Barney, realising as he said it that it would be quite impossible to get such an ill man along the tunnel and up the sides of the well.

'No. No, I can't even stand,' said the man, beginning to cough again. 'Listen – they'll kill me if they think I've been talking to anyone, so be careful. Listen to what I say.'

'We're listening,' said Barney.

'Three of the gang are coming here tonight to try and get out of me, for the last time, all that I know about them and others,' said the man hoarsely. 'They'll be here at eleven. Can you hide till they come, and then warn the police? Tell them its Detective Inspector Rawlings who's sending the message.'

'Right – and then if the three are down here in the secret passage, they'll be nicely rounded up,' said Barney, seeing it all. 'A very good plan, sir.'

'Does the caretaker-woman feed you?' asked Roger, through the hole. 'Is she in it too?'

'Everyone's in it!' said the man. 'I knew they were using this place for their headquarters, but I'd no idea there was any secret passage here. There's many a poor fellow's been put down here!'

He coughed so badly that he couldn't stop. Barney and Roger and Snubby felt distressed. 'If only we could get to him to help him – but this wretched roof-fall is too big to shift without tools,' said Barney. He called through the hole in a pause between the coughs.

'We're going now, sir, but we'll do exactly as you say. Goodbye!'

They made their way carefully back, clambering over the side of the other roof-fall when they came to it. They were at last beside the well, and heard Diana calling in a despairing voice.

'Barney! Roger! Snubby! Oh, do come back! Roger, what's happened?'

'Poor old Diana!' said Roger, suddenly realising what a long time they had been, and how scared Diana must be. He yelled up.

'Hallo, Di! We're back all safe and sound, with news for you!'

'Thank goodness!' came Diana's voice, sounding very tearful.

Barney felt for the rope end hanging down the well and tied it round his waist in case he fell. 'I'm coming up. Diana!' he called.

He was soon up, going hand over hand up the well wall, climbing like a cat. Miranda leapt chattering on to his shoulder as soon as he appeared, fondling and caressing him lovingly. Loony and Loopy threw themselves on him barking.

'I feel like doing that myself, Barney,' said Diana, with tears of relief in her eyes. 'You *have* been gone a long time.'

'We'll get Roger and Snubby up and then tell you our news,' said Barney, and he turned to look down the well. Snubby was already coming up. Roger soon followed. All three shivered with the cold, and were glad to feel the hot May sun on their shoulders.

They told the astonished Diana all that had happened. She could hardly believe her ears.

'*Well*! To think that kidnappers use the old Ring O' Bells Hall like that! I suppose that's why that woman put in for the job and got it – it would be easy for any gang to get in and out, and use the secret passage for hiding things and people in, if they had someone actually here all the time, watching over their prisoners, ready to let the gang in and out of the place!' Diana paused for breath.

'Yes – no one would ever guess that an old show-place

like that in a country village would be such a cunning headquarters,' said Roger. 'One of the gang must, of course, have heard about that secret passage and seen its possibilities. And to think that no one could go down there because the woman was always on guard!'

'There's one thing I don't understand,' said Barney. 'We went down that passage, but we came to a brick wall, bricking it up. There was no one there then, yet I heard that man coughing the night before. Where was he?'

They all thought hard. 'All I can say is that some of the bricks in the wall must be easily removable,' said Roger, at last. 'After all, we didn't examine the wall very closely. It must be possible to take out enough bricks to get through. I'm sure we shall find that's right. It's all very clever and very well planned.'

'It's a bad look-out for that detective tonight,' said Snubby. 'He won't tell what he knows, that's certain – so they'll either bump him off, or leave him there to die. He's ill enough to pop off at any time, I should think.'

'So should I be, down in that cold, dank, damp, chilly place, shut up day and night with no air to breathe,' said Barney. He sat on the wall that ran round the old well, and thought for a minute or two.

'I'm seeing a lot of things now,' he said. 'You know when I got a lift in that van which took me to Lillinghame, but which I saw later on, outside Ring O' Bells Hall, late at night? Well, there was something in that van which terrified Miranda when she got into it. All *I* could see was a sort of white thing that seemed to run about on the floor of the van – but it was probably the detective's hand out of its covers! I expect he was lying there under sacks and things, probably doped with something.'

'Yes – it looks as if the prisoner was brought here that night,' said Snubby. 'Poor wretch! What a long time to spend down there.'

'We must make our plans now,' said Barney. 'And – we must make them very, very carefully.'

Chapter Twenty-Four

That Night

They did make their plans carefully. They talked everything over bit by bit, and discussed exactly what would
be best to do.

'No good saying a word to Miss Pepper,' said Roger.
'She would be scared, go to the police, and they'd do
exactly what the detective doesn't want – go in immediately to rescue him, and then that woman would warn the
gang, they wouldn't come tonight, and not one of them
would be captured.'

'For that same reason I think it would be best to stick
to what the man said, and not warn the police till the
gang are actually down the passage,' said Barney. 'The
police might act too soon.'

'All the same, I think the poor ill man ought to be
taken up immediately,' said tender-hearted Diana. 'He
might die.'

'I don't think another few hours would hurt him – and
he'd be pretty wild if he thought we hadn't done what he
told us to,' said Roger. 'No – I think we must do exactly
what he said – wait till the gang is there, and then rush
for the police station.'

'Where are we going to watch for the gang to come?'
asked Snubby. 'In Ring O' Bells Hall?'

'Yes,' said Barney. 'We might be spotted, anywhere
outside. You never know. There are plenty of good
hiding-places inside. Those chests, for instance.'

'I don't like those,' said Snubby. 'I feel sort of cooped
up there.'

'Right. We'll find somewhere else then,' said Barney.

'But listen – we don't take Loony. If he growls he'll certainly give us away again.'

Loony heard his name and ran up at once, wagging his tail violently. Snubby patted the silky black head. 'All right,' he said reluctantly. 'We won't take him. But he'll howl like anything.'

'Well, he'll have to,' said Barney. 'This is too serious a matter to spoil for the sake of taking Loony.'

'What about Miranda?' asked Diana. 'She gibbered like anything the other night.'

'She'll be all right tonight,' said Barney. 'I'll put her collar on, and a lead, so that she has to stay on my shoulder. I will see she doesn't utter a sound.'

'All right. We hide, and we wait, and we watch to make sure the gang are safely down the secret passage,' said Roger. 'Then we rush and get the police in – is that right? Suppose they don't believe us?'

'They will if we say the detective's name,' said Barney. 'Detective Inspector Rawlings – they'll know about him and will have been informed that he has disappeared. Anyway, I'll jolly well *make* them believe us.'

'Those bells knew what they were doing all right, when they rang themselves the other night,' said Snubby suddenly. 'Talk about enemies! I'm not awfully looking forward to waiting in Ring O' Bells Hall tonight, I don't mind telling you. I'm scared of those bells.'

'Well, don't come then,' said Barney. 'Stay with Diana. I'm not letting her come.'

Diana was relieved. She had thought she really *ought* to come, but she didn't want to in the least, If Barney said she wasn't to, well, that was that. She would stay at home with Loony – and Snubby too, perhaps.

No – Snubby was going, whether he was scared of the bells or not. 'You can't keep *me* out of it,' he said, putting on a most courageous voice. 'I may not want to come very much, but I'm jolly well coming, all the same!'

'Good for you,' said Barney. 'Where's the police station? We'd better know all these details – the shortest way to get to it from Ring O' Bells Hall, and all that. Pity we can't telephone them – but they'd probably think it was a spoof call. Anyway I don't remember seeing telephone wires anywhere near the Hall.'

'What time shall we be there?' said Roger. 'The detective said the gang would arrive at eleven. We'd better be there at ten, and watch out for them. We shall have plenty of time to arrange our hiding-places.'

'Yes – ten o'clock,' agreed Barney. 'Gosh – this is all frightfully exciting, isn't it? I never thought anything like this would happen when I popped down here to see you for a few days.'

'Excitement must be very good for 'flu,' said Diana. 'I feel perfectly all right now. I bet Snubby still thinks of his poor wobbly legs though!'

'I do not!' said Snubby indignantly. 'Except that I keep feeling awful pangs of hunger all day long, I'm just exactly the same as usual.'

'I thought you *usually* felt pangs of hunger,' began Diana, and then was interrupted by Roger, who had just looked at his watch.

'Wheee-ew! I say! It's half-past five! Would you believe it? We've missed tea at Miss Hannah's now. It will be all cleared away when we get there. What shall we do?'

'No wonder Snubby began talking about pangs of hunger,' said Barney. 'I'm feeling some myself.'

'Let's go down to that village shop and see if they'll give us something,' said Diana. 'We could at least get ice creams. I do hope Miss Hannah won't be too wild with us.'

They found the shop open and were able to buy buns,

ice creams, chocolate and orangeade, so they didn't do too badly. The dogs had an ice cream each too, for being so good and patient all the afternoon. Miranda had half of one, because Barney said they sometimes gave her a tummy-ache and he didn't want her whining that evening!

They went back to Miss Hannah's. Barney went too. He planned to wait in the shed till the time came for him to join the others and go to Ring O' Bells Hall. He would have supper with them first.

'It's such a wonderful evening perhaps we could have a sort of picnic supper out in the garden,' suggested Diana. 'I believe it's all cold tonight.'

It was – so they were allowed to take their plates into the garden and sit on the grass, with Loony and Loopy and Miranda greedily watching every mouthful. Miranda was too clever at snatching, and Barney had to speak to her very severly. She hid her face in his neck and made little mournful noises. Diana wanted to fuss over and pet her, but Barney wouldn't let her.

'No Diana. She's getting spoilt with all the fuss everyone makes of her. A scolding will do her good. Do you know, at Naomi's last night she actually went to a bottle of cherries, took the lid off – unscrewed it, mind you – and began to take out cherries with her paw. And Naomi let her! No wonder she's getting spoilt.'

'She's such a darling, though. I do so love her,' said Diana. Loony was immediately jealous and came and put his head on her knee, looking up at her mournfully out of melting brown eyes.

'Go on with you!' said Diana, tapping his nose with her spoon. 'It's cupboard love! You want a bit of my blancmange.'

Loony looked at her, got up and trotted indoors. He came out with Miss Hannah's lovely green bathtowel, treading on it as he ran, and tripping himself up. He put it down at Diana's feet, as if to say, 'You're not very kind to me – but look what I do for you!'

'You're very naughty,' said Diana. 'Now I've got to get up and put it back again. No, Loopy, no – you are *not* to feel you've to play a silly trick too. If you dare to go in and bring out the hall mats I'll SMACK you!'

They almost forgot what was going to happen that evening as they had their picnic supper and played about with the dogs and Miranda.

Miss Hannah and Miss Pepper watched them through the window. They were having their own supper in peace. 'How nice to be young and carefree like that!' said Miss Hannah. 'No worries, no serious cares – just able to pop into bed and shut their eyes and sleep till morning without a single worrying thought.'

She would have been amazed if she had known the worries and cares the children had that night. They were certainly not going to be able to go to sleep with no worries till the morning. Snubby, in fact, felt that his life was full of fears and worries as the evening drew on!

'Snubby, you're looking tired,' said Miss Pepper, seeing a worried frown on his face. 'You'd better pop off to bed straight away.'

'Right,' said Snubby, thinking that he might as well get two hours or so of sleep before he had to face the darkness and silence of Ring O' Bells Hall. He went up in such a docile manner that Miss Pepper was most surprised, and a little alarmed. Surely Snubby was not sickening for something else?

Nobody was late that night. Barney said good night and went out of the gate, presumably to go to Naomi's. He slipped back through the hedge at the bottom of the garden, and made his way to the shed with Miranda. He settled himself quietly on some sacks to await the striking of the church clock. They were all to set off at ten.

Snubby fell asleep, but neither Diana not Roger did. They both felt extremely wide awake. Diana half wished she was going, then changed her mind as she thought of seeing the 'gang', whoever they might be.

'It's almost ten,' whispered Roger to himself. 'I'll wake Snubby. I do hope Loony will be all right without us.'

Snubby sprang up. He whispered goodbye to a most surprised Loony, thrust him into Diana's room and then, while she was making a fuss of him, fled downstairs with the others. They were out in the moonlit garden just as Barney walked out of the shed, and the clock struck ten.

'Good work,' said Barney in a low voice. 'Got your torches? Come on then. Don't put them on though – we can easily see in the moonlight.'

They walked down to Ring O' Bells Hall, and waited while Barney shinned up the ivy and got into the room with the four-poster bed he once slept in. He ran down into the hall and opened the front door to them. They all crept in and shut the door again.

'Let's go into that room over there, and wait,' said Barney. 'I've just remembered, there's a big cupboard there. We could leave the door of the room open, and watch through the crack for the gang to come in – and then pop into the cupboard till they're gone down the secret passage. Then we'll hare up to the police station.'

They went to the room and pushed the door open. Then they got the most terrible shock! There, seated round a candle on a table in the room, were three men and a woman!

The gang must have come early! Run, Barney, run, Roger and Snubby. Run for your very lives!

Chapter Twenty-Five

Headlong into Trouble

Barney and Roger were right in the room before they realised that there was anyone there. Snubby had suddenly paused, seeing a light, and had tried to pull back the others, but they were right in the room by then, and were seen.

The men leapt to their feet at once, staring in astonishment and anger. Roger was petrified, but Barney saw at a glance the danger they were in. He turned to run at once.

'Stop!' shouted one of the men. 'STOP, I say. Who are you? COME HERE!'

In real fear the boys fled out of the room. What a blow! All their wonderful plans were shattered! They would be lucky if they escaped themselves now.

'Separate – hide – quickly!' panted Barney. He darted off towards the kitchen. Snubby fled into a nearby room. Roger made for the little panelled room where the entrance of the secret passage was. The chest! He would hide there.

He felt about in the darkness when he got into the room. Ah – here was the chest! He lifted up the lid and got in. The lid fell with such a noise that he trembled. Surely the men would have heard it.

Snubby didn't at first recognise the room he was in – then as he looked round, panic-stricken, in the moonlight that flooded through a window, he saw that he was in the room that contained the secret chamber up the chimney.

He tore to the fireplace at once, just as he heard the

men outside the room. He pushed himself into the wide chimney, and felt frantically for the steps at the side. Thank goodness, it was the right chimney! He climbed up, and squeezed himself into the dirty, musty, secret cavity.

Only just in time! The three men burst into the room, holding brilliant torches that drowned the silver moonlight. 'He came in here!' cried one. 'I saw him.'

'Then he's here still,' said another man grimly. 'There's only one door – the one he came in by. We'll find him all right!'

Snubby trembled so much that he really wondered if his legs would hold him upright. They didn't! They gave way beneath him and he slid into a sitting position! The men heard the noise he made, sliding down to sit. 'Listen – he's quite near!' said one, and opened the door of a cupboard. It was empty, of course.

'*I* thought the noise came from somewhere over here,' said another man, walking to the fireplace. He poked his head up the enormous chimney and flashed his torch there. Snubby almost groaned. He expected to feel his foot pulled roughly, and to be hauled out.

But the secret chamber was meant to hide people properly, and it did. Not a sign could be seen of the hidden boy in the light of the torch. Only if the man had known of the chamber could he have seen Snubby, by climbing up one of the steps himself. But he didn't know it.

The woman did – but she had gone after Roger! The men hunted all over the room, opened chests and cupboards, looked behind curtains – and finally gave up the search. 'He couldn't have come in here,' they said.

'Lizzie!' called one of them. 'Where are you? Have you found those kids?'

'I've found one of them!' she called back. 'He's in this chest!'

She had heard the banging of the lid and had rushed into the little panelled room. She could see at once that the only hiding-place was in one of the chests. She lifted the lid of the small one. It was empty.

Poor Roger was crouching down in the other, hardly daring to breathe. He heard the lid of his chest lifted, and a torch was flashed in quickly. Then the lid was slammed down immediately – and he heard a key turn in the lock!

Roger clenched his fists. Now he was out of things – locked up well and truly. It was an idiotic thing to do, to let that lid bang down! He could have kicked himself.

The men came into the room and the woman tapped the chest with her torch. 'Here's one anyway,' she said. 'Safe and sound for the moment. What about the other?'

Roger heaved a sigh of relief. So they thought there were only two of them – they couldn't have seen Snubby! Where in the world had he gone? If only he could nip out and go to the police, things would still be all right. But would Snubby be brave enough to do that?

The three men and the woman began a search for Barney. 'Who *are* these kids?' demanded one of the men. 'And what are they doing here at night?'

'They're probably a couple of young hooligans who got in somehow and thought it would be a lark to steal a few things,' said the woman.

'Well – it's just too bad for them, but I'm afraid we shall have to take them off with us tonight and dump them somewhere where they won't be able to split on us for a long, long time,' said one of the men grimly.

'We've *got* to find the other fellow,' said another man. 'Listen – what's that?'

It was Miranda! She was hiding with Barney, not far from the foot of the square tower. He had got behind a great heavy curtain, and was crouching there, his heart

162

beating far too loudly for his liking. Miranda felt that he was scared, and she was scared too.

She didn't like being on a lead when she was frightened. She leapt a little way up the curtain, felt the pull of the lead and fell back again. Barney didn't dare even to whisper to her. She began to gibber a little.

He decided to undo the lead. She might feel happier then. So he slipped the catch and freed her. She was off and away at once. She leapt to the top of a cupboard and ground her teeth in a peculiar way she had when she was both frightened and angry. This was the noise that the men had suddenly heard.

One man flashed his torch in Miranda's direction, and was amazed to see a little monkey there. 'A monkey!' he said. 'The owner must be in this room then. Quick, search everywhere!'

Barney felt concerned. Sooner or later they would come to his curtain. He had no illusions about these men. They were tough and cruel. It would go hardly with any of the boys if they were captured.

He decided to worm his way behind the curtain to where the foot of the tower was. If he could sprint up the steps to the platform, he might find a corner to hide in – some niche the men wouldn't see. It was a forlorn hope but the best he could think of.

The men were on the opposite side of the room, examining every cupboard. Miranda chattered at them angrily, keeping well out of their reach.

Barney came to the end of the curtain. He made a dash for the tower. He rushed safely through the open doorway and sprinted up the stone staircase, round and round and round. Miranda heard him and with a bound she was after him, scuttling up on all fours.

Barney groaned when he saw her. No matter where he

hid up on that little shadowy platform, Miranda would chatter and give him away!

Then a brilliant thought shot into his head – that little room above the bells! He could get up there, and be perfectly safe. He had only to threaten to push down anyone who came up after him! Nobody could ever get him out of there.

He began to climb up the straight wall of the tower, finding the hand and footholds in the stone quite easily, for he had used them once before. Miranda sat chattering angrily on his shoulder. She couldn't understand any of these peculiar happenings at all.

The men raced up the spiral staircase too, with the woman behind. 'You'll get him – there's only a platform at the top – hardly anywhere to hide!' she panted.

But when the first man reached the platform and flashed his torch round, there was no one to see! He shone his torch into one or two shadowy corners – nobody there!

He heard a noise above his head and flashed his torch there in surprise. He was just in time to see Barney's legs disappearing, as the boy clambered through the hole in the roof, from which the bells hung.

'Look there!' he said startled. 'The fellow has actually shinned up this steep wall and climbed through the roof. Can he escape from there?'

'No – unless he squeezes out of the window and flings himself to the ground – where he would certainly be killed,' said the woman. 'We don't need to worry about *him* now! We can shut and lock the big door at the front of the tower, and he'll be as much a prisoner as the other fellow in the chest. Nicely out of our way!'

One man looked doubtfully up at the hole in the ceiling. 'There must be footholds up the wall,' he said. 'I've a good mind to try and shin up myself, and knock the fellow on the head to make sure he doesn't worry us for some time.'

Barney heard all this, of course. He kept well away from the hole, in case one of the men had a revolver. He didn't trust these fellows – he had upset their carefully laid plans, and goodness knew what they would do to him if they had the chance.

He called boldly down. 'I can hear you – and I tell you this – if any of you climb up here, I'll knock him down to the stone platform! I've got the advantage of any of you up here!'

There was a silence. 'He's right,' said one of the men in a low voice. 'He could reach out and strike anyone down, once they got up to the top. Well, we'll do as you say, Lizzie – lock the tower door at the foot, and leave him here to stew!'

'Well, that's the two of them then – and the monkey,' said another man. 'Now let's get about our business. We'd better go down and see our friend. Lizzie says he's pretty bad tonight, so maybe he'll be willing to listen to us.'

Barney heard them go down the spiral staircase. He heard the heavy door at the bottom slam, and he heard the grating sound of the big key being turned in the lock. He sat up in the little room above the bells, gritting his teeth together. All their plans were spoilt! They were prisoners instead of setting someone else free!

'Shall we go down or not, Miranda?' he said. 'Better go down, perhaps, and see if they *really* have locked the door.'

He put his head down to look out of the hole. The bells gleaming in the light of his torch, hung just below him, still and silent. Barney flashed his torch down beside them, trying to see the platform below.

Miranda suddenly gibbered in fright, and clutched at his arm. With all her small monkey strength she tried to pull him back. Barney was surprised. Whatever was the matter?

Chapter Twenty-Six

The Warning of the Bells

'Why are you suddenly so frightened, Miranda?' asked Barney in surprise. 'I'm not going to fall down.'

But still the little monkey gibbered and pulled at him. Barney sat back and looked at her. 'Now what's all this about?' he said. 'Why be in such a state because I put my torch out of the hole?'

He put his torch out again, and by accident it touched one of the bells, which gave out a very small sound – ding!

Miranda went quite mad. She leapt to the window sill as if she were going to go out. Then she leapt back to Barney, squealing pitifully and pulled at him. What *could* be the matter?

'Are you afraid of the bells, Miranda?' asked Barney at last. 'Did they scare you when they rang all by themselves that time? Look – I'll touch them – they won't harm me!'

He stretched out his hand and tapped one of the bells, which said, 'DING' a little more loudly. Miranda scampered into a corner, put her arms across her face, and rocked herself to and fro, moaning as if she were human.

Barney was really nonplussed. He had never seen Miranda like this before. He flashed his torch on the scared, miserable little monkey and pondered. Why? Why? Why?

And then he suddenly knew! Of course! Why ever hadn't he thought of it before?

'Miranda, come here,' he said softly. 'I know why you

are so frightened – you're frightened of the bells, aren't you? Miranda – *you* rang them before, didn't you – when we all thought they had rung themselves? You were up here, exploring – you didn't know what the bells were, or what noise they made – and in your usual inquisitive way you leapt on to them – and set them swinging. And they rang! They jingled and jangled and wouldn't stop!' Miranda still went on moaning to herself. Barney was sad for the little monkey. He went on talking in his quiet, soothing voice.

'You leapt from one to the other in panic, didn't you, Miranda – and you made them ring madly and wildly till you were almost frightened out of your skin. Now you can't bear me even to touch them! Poor little monkey. Come here, Miranda.'

Miranda came, making funny little noises. She cuddled into Barney's arms, comforted by his soft voice, though she couldn't follow what he said.

'There's nothing to be frightened of, Miranda,' said Barney. 'They're only bells. Well, well, well, – so they didn't ring themselves the other night – *you* rang them, though you didn't guess what a noise they would make.'

He sat there with Miranda in his arms, thinking back to the night the bells had rung and frightened them all so much. Then his thoughts slid back to this unfortunate night. They had had high hopes – and now here they were, captured and locked up! He was pretty certain that Roger, anyhow, was captured, and he couldn't imagine Snubby remaining uncaught for long.

Barney thought of the ill man down at the bottom of the secret passage. He thought of the three men and the woman – the 'gang' as the detective had called them. Now they would be able to get out of their unfortunate prisoner all the information they wanted – they would probably leave him there to die – and get away in safety themselves.

How long had they been using this place as their head-quarters? How many plots had they hatched here, how many people had they imprisoned down in the secret passage beyond the brick wall?

Barney wished he knew what was the best thing to do. How could he warn anyone that something was amiss at Ring O' Bells Hall? Was it possible to squeeze out of the window and climb down the ivy, if it grew strongly there?

Then, as he sat there, just above the bells, an idea came to him. Why didn't he think of it before? It was the only thing to do!

He would ring the bells himself! Not as Miranda had rung them, jingle-jangling them in fright – but ring them fiercely and loudly and urgently without stopping! He would rouse the whole of the village! He would bring the police hurrying to the Hall. He would terrify everyone so much that SOMETHING would have to be done!

The another thought struck him. The bells would warn the men too. They might come rushing up, and get away, if they had a car. Barney thought hard. They would now be down in the secret passage, far below the foundations of the house – beyond the brick wall, which must have a way through it somehow. They couldn't possibly hear the bells there!

'The bells will warn the whole village – but not the men.' Barney decided exultantly. 'It's an idea – a wonderful idea. Miranda, darling, I'm going to give you the fright of your life, I'm afraid – but it can't be helped. I'm going to ring the bells!'

Barney lay down flat on the floor of the little tower room. He leaned out of the hole, and stretched his arms down to the short ropes on which the bells were tightly hung. He caught hold of them.

He rang the bells. How he rang them! Surely never,

169

never before had those bells rung so wildly, so madly, so insistently.

'Jingle, Jangle-jangle, jing, jing, JING, jangle, JANG, JANG, jingle, jing, JING, JANG, JING, JANG, JING, JANG. . . .'

The noise up in the little tower was terrific. Miranda gave a loud howl and bounded to the window. She was out of it in a trice. Barney didn't notice. His head was down through the hole, and he was pulling the short ropes for all he was worth, panting hard.

Roger, down in the chest, heard them, and was terrified. The bells! Ringing by themselves again! They must know that enemies were here, right in the very house. He crouched down in the locked chest, trembling, wondering if the men could hear them too.

Snubby heard them, half-standing, half-sitting in the secret cavity of the old fireplace. He was in a most uncomfortable position. When he heard the tremendous loud noise of the bells, breaking the silence so suddenly and urgently, he almost fell out of the secret chamber. He sank down till he was sitting flat again. He shook so much that even his teeth rattled in his head.

'The bells!' he thought to himself. 'The bells again! How do they know? How do they guess that enemies are here?'

Neither he nor Roger imagined that it was Barney who was ringing them. They didn't even know that Barney was up in the tower.

Snubby was far too frightened to move out of his hiding-place. For all he knew the men might be waiting somewhere to pounce on him. He was quite, quite determined not to stir from the secret chamber. How well he knew now what fugitives had felt when they crammed themselves into this little secret hidey-hole. Now that he heard the bells ringing, he was all the more certain that nothing,

nothing, nothing would make him leave the chimney-place!

The men and the woman down below in the secret passage heard almost nothing of the bells. The place where they were now, beyond the brick wall, was sound-proof to the jangle of the bells so high up in the tower. All they heard was a slightly tinny noise from somewhere which didn't make them suspect any danger at all.

But the sound of the bells went far and wide over the countryside. The jangling leapt out of the old tower and penetrated into cottage windows, and into dog kennels, and into the barns. This was no hurried, flurried spell of ringing such as the bells had given before—it was a summons, a warning, a signal of danger!

Dogs barked. Cows lowed. Cats fled to corners. Men threw the bedclothes off and leapt out of bed. Women screamed. Miss Hannah and Miss Pepper awoke in a hurry.

Diana comforted the amazed Loony, while Loopy put himself in a cupboard.

Diana was frightened. Those bells again! What was happening down at the Hall? Were the boys all right?

The two policemen at the police station, dozing in their chairs, sprang up, astonished, at the sound of the bells. One reached at once for his helmet.

'Something's up!' he said. 'Where's Joe? Tell him to phone through to Lillinghame, just in case we need their help. 'Something's up! Just listen to those bells!'

Down towards Ring O' Bells Hall went a crowd of scared, wondering villagers. Some of the men had pitch-forks, some had sticks. Why did they bring them? They didn't know! Something was up, at the Hall—and till they knew what it was they were taking no chances.

The police joined them on bicycles. 'What's to do?' the villagers shouted to them. 'Who's ringing the bells?'

But the police knew no more than anyone else!

They came to the Hall. It was in complete darkness. Not a light was to be seen in any room. But still the bells clashed out urgently.

'Someone must be in the tower, surely!' cried a man.

'The bells ring themselves,' said an old man somberly. 'Always did!'

'Here's a car!' cried a woman, shining a torch on to a big car shoved right up against the hedge, not far from Ring O' Bells Hall.

'Ha!' said one of the policemen. 'Here – where's Joe! Joe, you take charge of this car. Take out the key, to start with. Now then, where's Bill? Oh, there you are – we're going to get into Ring O' Bells Hall, if we have to break the door down!'

The police hammered at the great front door of the Hall. Barney couldn't hear the noise, up in the tower room, but Roger, hidden in the chest, heard it, and Snubby, trembling violently up the chimney, heard it too. He felt sick. Now what was up?

He heard a stentorian voice outside the front door.

'OPEN IN THE NAME OF THE LAW!'

But the front door, of course, did not open. It trembled under the hammering the policeman was giving it, but it remained firm. The policeman tried again.

'OPEN IN THE NAME OF THE LAW!'

'It's the police,' thought Snubby, and was flooded with relief. 'The police! They heard the bells and they've come! I'll open the door to them. Oh, WHAT a relief!'

172

Chapter Twenty-Seven

Plenty of Excitement

Snubby forgot his fears. He scrambled down from the secret chamber, almost falling headlong into the great fireplace. He rushed across the room, out of the door and into the hall. Very little moonlight entered there, and it looked very dark. But Snubby was feeling extraordinarily brave now.

He ran to the front door, tripping over a mat or two. He turned the great handle and swung the door back.

The police had powerful torches, and they flashed them on to Snubby at once, not quite knowing what to expect. They gaped when they saw a sooty-faced boy of about twelve, grinning joyfully at them!

'Here – what's all this?' said the first policeman. 'What are you doing here? And who's ringing those bells?'

'I don't know,' said Snubby. 'Gosh, I'm glad you came. Those bells are ringing to say that enemies are here. Look out, won't you!'

The villagers began to crowd in too. The policeman swung round. 'Where's Joe? Joe, keep these people back. May be danger here for all we know.'

The bells went on ringing madly. Barney was doing the thing properly! He had rests every now and again, but he made up his mind to go on ringing them till something happened.

The two policemen went to the foot of the square tower. They meant to find out who was ringing the bells. Snubby followed some way behind. He was quite certain they were ringing themselves, and he didn't particularly want to go near bells that behaved in such a strange manner.

The police unlocked the door at the foot of the tower. They went up the spiral staircase cautiously, torches in hand. They came out on to the platform. Barney saw the light of their torches immediately, and withdrew his hands from the bell-ropes. He looked down warily. Who was this – enemy or friend?

To his great relief, he saw the dark-blue uniform of the police. He almost fell down the hole with joy. The bells gradually stopped jangling, and the first policeman called up in a stern and commanding voice.

'You up there! What do you think you're doing, ringing bells in the dead of night? Who are you?'

'Wait a moment and I'll come down and tell you,' called Barney. He slipped through the hole, held the guide-rope, found the first footholds and climbed down the tower wall like a cat. The police watched him in astonishment. He leapt down beside them.

'Another boy!' said the first policeman. 'Now you just tell me what all this is about, young fellow!'

'It's serious,' said Barney. 'Very serious. Did you ever hear of someone called Detective Inspector Rawlings?'

This unexpected question made both the policemen gape in surprise. 'What do you know about *him*?' rapped out the first one.

'I'll tell you,' said Barney, and tried to tell his extraordinary story as shortly as possible. It took the policemen some time to grasp what he was trying to tell them.

'Secret passages – Rawlings behind a brick wall down there – ill, perhaps dying – the gang here tonight – who *are* they, anyway? And where are they? Tell us, boy, quick!'

'I'm trying to tell you,' said Barney impatiently. 'But what you don't realise is that it's all very urgent. The men are down there *now* with Rawlings. You can catch them and rescue him, if you're quick! That's what he planned for you to do, with our help. But things went wrong, so I rang the bells to get somebody here.'

At last it dawned on the policemen that things really were urgent. They went down the spiral staircase, almost falling over Snubby, who was half-way up listening to what Barney was saying, with very great interest. So it was old Barney who had done all that bell-ringing! Gosh!

'Hallo, Snubby – where's Roger?' called Barney, catching sight of Snubby.

'No idea,' said Snubby.

'Who's Roger? Another of you?' asked the policeman, marvelling at coming across so many boys in the middle of the night.

'He's my cousin,' said Snubby. 'When we were chased, we all separated and hid. I don't know where Roger hid.'

'I'll take you to the entrance of the secret passage,' said Barney, and he guided the two policemen to the little panelled room. 'The passage begins here,' said Barney. 'I'll just – '

But he was interrupted by a terrible noise in the chest nearby. Roger had heard Barney's voice and was clamouring to be let out! He knocked with his heels on the floor of the chest, hammered with his fists and yelled at the top of his voice. 'Let me out! I'm here. Let me out!'

'Bless us all!' said the policeman, startled. 'What's that now? Who's in there? Is this a pantomime, or what?'

'It's Roger,' said Barney thankfully, and he unlocked the chest. Roger sprang up like a jack-in-the-box. 'What's happened?' he cried. 'I heard the bells.'

'Tell you later, Roger,' said Barney. 'Look, did you hear the gang go down into the passage?'

'Yes,' said Roger, 'the three men and the woman.'

'Have they come back yet?'

'No,' said Roger. 'I thought they might when I heard the bells. But they shut the secret panel, and I reckon the noise of the bells didn't reach them enough to scare them. The tower is a good way away from here. I heard them, of course.'

'Where's the secret panel?' said the first policeman. Barney showed him how to slide it back. He was most astonished.

'Such goings on!' he muttered, and was about to stick his head into the hole, when Barney pulled him back.

'Wait – they're coming back. I can hear them. Better be careful, they're tough.'

Sure enough, the sound of voices and footsteps could now be heard. Silently Barney slid the panel into place again, and they all stood waiting. Could they catch the whole gang – or would the first one give warning so that the others would run back?

A most unfortunate thing happened. The second policeman felt a sneeze coming. It was a large sneeze, he knew that. He groped for his handkerchief, feeling as if he were going to burst – which is practically what he did do, when the sneeze came. It was quite colossal, and almost blew Snubby to one side. He jumped violently.

The first policeman gave an angry mutter, then everything was silent again. There was now no noise from behind the passage. The 'gang' had evidently heard the explosion and had stopped to consider the matter.

The men apparently eventually decided that the woman had better go and investigate. Soft footsteps came up to the closed secret panel. In a moment or two it slid quietly back a crack, and the woman shone a torch through the crack.

When she saw the silent group in the room she shut the panel with a scream, and called back to the men. 'It's the police! They're here!'

She stumbled back in panic. The first policeman slid back the panel with a bang and shouted down the passage. 'You come on here, and give yourselves up. You're cornered. It'll be the worse for you if you don't come now.'

A loud and sarcastic laugh came up the passage. 'Sez you! Come and get us! Anybody coming down this passage will be neatly picked off!'

That made the policeman hesitate quite a bit. He considered things for a moment and then called down again.

'Bring Detective Inspector Rawlings up here at once.'

'Sez you!' said the mocking voice again. 'He'll be a nice little hostage now, won't he? He's ill, you know, and he needs a doctor badly. We'll give you your inspector if you let us go. Otherwise – well I doubt if he'll last till the morning!'

As if to underline what they said, a terrible rasping cough came up the passage way, muffled by distance, but still dreadful to hear.

'He *is* very ill, sir,' whispered Barney.

'Well – what are we to do?' said the policeman, exasperated. 'No one can go down there without being in grave danger, that's certain. If only we knew of another way to out-flank them.'

'I know another way, sir,' whispered Barney. 'This secret passage runs a long way – up to an old woman's cottage – it comes out half-way down her well.'

The policeman began to think he must be dreaming. 'Where's Joe?' he said, turning round. 'Joe, stay here and see no one escapes this way. You've got your truncheon, haven't you? You know what to do. I'm going with this boy.'

Leaving the useful Joe behind, the two policemen followed Barney, Snubby and Roger to the front door, where an excited crowd of people were still waiting.

'You can go home,' said the first policeman gruffly.

'You'll be told the news tomorrow. Can't tell you anything. Here you, Jim – go and telephone to Lillinghame and tell them we do want them, and the quicker the better.'

'We'd better wait till they come, I think, sir,' said Barney. 'This gang is pretty desperate, according to Detective Inspector Rawlings. I've got a plan, if you'd like to hear it.'

'Come back into the Hall then, and we'll listen,' said the policeman. He and his companion, and the three boys went into a nearby room. The policeman sat down and turned to Barney. 'Go ahead,' he said.

'Well, sir,' said Barney. 'We know another way into the secret passage, which leads to where the inspector is lying. There are two roof-falls which we shall have to deal with. He is just behind the bigger of the two. Now, what I propose is this – '

He paused, thinking. 'Go on, then,' said the policeman, and Snubby and Roger bent forward, wondering what plan Barney had thought of.

'These men won't know we're coming from the opposite direction,' said Barney. 'They won't be expecting that. They'll just be keeping guard on the other end of the passage – so, if we surprise them from the opposite end, we'll capture the lot!'

Chapter Twenty-Eight

A Very Nice Evening's Work!

'Pah!' said the policeman. 'They'll hear us coming.'

'I'd thought of that,' said Barney. 'Could you arrange with Joe or somebody to create a disturbance up this end, so that all the gang would think they were going to be rushed, and would have their attention on this secret passage here – '

'And not be watching the other end!' cried Roger. 'So that we could break in there and take them from the rear. Good work, Barney!'

'Ah I see,' said the policeman. 'Yes – quite a good idea. But how shall we make sure that there's a disturbance this end at the same time as we want to break through?'

'Easy,' said Barney. 'Set a definite time, sir – and we'll count on the disturbance being set in motion here at that time, we'll know the gang will be guarding the secret passage here, and we'll be able to break through behind them nicely!'

'Yes – it sounds all right,' said the policeman. 'What time shall we say?'

'Let me see – it'll take a little time to get to Ring O' Bells Cottage,' said Barney, calculating. 'And then down the well, and along the tunnel – remove the roof falls, or it will be difficult for all of us to get through. I should think if you said in two hours' time, sir, that would be about right.'

'Good – say three o'clock then,' said the policeman, consulting his watch. 'All these goings on in the middle of the night! Where's Joe? He'd better be told about this, and told to set his watch by ours.'

'I'll tell him,' said Roger, and went off to the useful and very solid-looking Joe. He promised to create a terrific diversion at exactly three o'clock.

'Shouting and hammering and such-like?' he said. 'Yes, I can do that all right. I'll have some of the Lillinghame fellows with me, too, by then.'

The Lillinghame men arrived in another two minutes. There were four of them.

'Where's Joe?' said the Ring O' Bells policeman. 'I want two of you Lillinghame fellows to stay with him. He'll tell you what's up. And I want you other two to come with me. I'll tell you the tale as we go. We mustn't hang about here any longer.'

They set off with the three boys. Barney had suggested taking a couple of spades, and these were borrowed from one of the villagers.

As they were going along the road, a little dark shape dropped down from a tree on to Barney's shoulder. 'Miranda,' he said thankfully. 'So you've come back. I was so worried about you. I knew you were terribly scared.'

'Who's Miranda now?' asked the first policeman, feeling that he couldn't cope with much more. He shone his torch on her and gave a jump. 'A monkey? What next? Is she coming with us too?'

'She is,' said Barney cheerfully. 'I'm not losing her again tonight! She nearly went off her head when she heard those bells!'

They walked quietly through the wood to Naomi's cottage. There was no light in her windows. She was in bed and fast asleep.

'To the well, sir,' said Barney in a low voice. He lowered himself over the side and went quickly down, holding on to the iron loops that stuck out from the brickwork.

180

The first policeman stared in horror, flashing his torch down.

'Here – what's all this? Surely we haven't got to go down here? Why, it's a very deep well!'

'It's quite safe,' said Roger, and he went down too, followed by Snubby, who was now almost speechless with excitement. What *would* the boys at school say to all this?

The police followed very reluctantly. The two spades were let down on string. At last everyone was safely through the hole in the side of the well, and started on their way through the secret tunnel.

Nobody liked it much, though the three boys didn't find it quite as strange as the policemen because they had been that way before.

The spades came in useful at the first roof fall, which was soon tackled so that everyone could go through easily. As they came near the second one, Barney stood still and warned the policeman behind him.

'We're almost there. What's the time, sir? It's not three o'clock yet, is it?'

'Five minutes more,' said the policeman.

'Well, we'd better get as close to the second roof fall as we can – the inspector is lying just behind that – and wait for three o'clock. We may hear something of the commotion above. We may not, of course, but we shall at least hear some exclamation from the men, and possibly hear them leaving the place where the inspector is and going through the brick wall.'

'How do they get through that?' inquired the policeman, feeling rather dazed.

'I don't know, sir – I guess they can take out enough loose bricks to get through all right,' said Barney. 'Now, we'd better move on, sir. It must be almost three.'

They moved silently up to the second roof fall. The crack through which Barney had seen the sick man had disappeared. The rubble had shifted a little and covered it.

The dreadful cough came rasping through the roof fall to the ears of the waiting company. 'He sounds very ill,' whispered the policeman uncomfortably. 'Poor chap. We must get him off to hospital at once.'

There were muffled voices to be heard behind the roof fall. Then, in the far-off distance, came echoes of some kind of noise. The men on the other side of the roof fall started up at once.

'What's that!' said one of them, in a loud voice. 'They're coming! Quick, up the passage! Got your gun, Charlie? We'll soon show them we mean business!'

There was silence after that, except for the distant noises that kept echoing through to the watchers by the roof fall. They came from the valiant Joe and his helpers, no doubt, making their 'commotion!'

'Quick, sir – where are the spades? Let's got through now,' said Barney urgently. Soon the spades were at work on the rubble, and in no time at all a way was cleared through. Beyond was a small, widened-out chamber in the tunnel, with a rough bed, a bench, candles, and a jug of water. On the couch lay a man, breathing heavily.

'Inspector Rawlings!' said the first policeman. 'We're here!'

The ill man turned bloodshot eyes to the company crowding into the little chamber. He smiled feebly. 'Good,' he said, 'good. Get them, Brown. They're tough, so look out. Keep those boys back, though.'

He began to cough again. Silently the policemen crossed to the brick wall that enclosed the other side of the little hidden room. There was an opening there big enough for a man to get through.

Barney had a look at it. Yes – it was as he had expected. Certain bricks were loose and could be easily removed.

He was about to follow the last policeman with Roger and Snubby when he was pushed back.

'No kids in this,' said the policeman's voice, rough but kindly.

'I'm not a kid,' said Barney indignantly.

'You're to keep out of this,' said the policeman. 'You'll only cramp our style. Do as you're told, youngster.'

Barney knew when orders had to be obeyed. He sat down beside the man on the couch, who had now closed his eyes and seemed to be in an uneasy sleep. He breathed so loudly and with such difficulty that it was painful to hear him.

'We're out of the most exciting part of all,' said Snubby gloomily.

'You wouldn't like it a bit if you were in it,' said Roger. 'I wonder what's happening. Hark!'

There was suddenly a loud disturbance up the passage, shouting, yelling, and the woman was squealing. It went on for some time, and then a policeman came grinning down to the secret room. He stuck his red face through the hole in the brickwork.

'All finished!' he said. 'They were waiting for Joe and the others to attack from above – and we crept up behind and were on them before they could even turn round. They never heard us at all. I'm not surprised, with the din old Joe was making.'

'Are they all caught?' asked Barney in delight.

'Yes – and we've got the woman too – Lizzie the Go-Between,' said the policeman. 'We've been after her for a long time – and here she was at Ring O' Bells under our very noses. Come on up. We're sending a doctor down here now, and the poor old inspector will have to be taken up above and put into hospital. He's in a bad way.'

'I'm all right,' said a weak voice, and the ill man opened

183

his eyes. 'I feel a lot better now I know the gang is arrested. I know a lot about them, and a lot about their friends. I – '

He began to cough. 'Now don't you say a word, Inspector,' said the policeman kindly. 'Don will soon be here.'

He beckoned to the boys, and they climbed through the hole in the brickwork. The policeman then climbed into the little hidden room, to stay with the inspector till help came.

Up the passage went the boys, and behind the secret panelling. A helmeted head was poking inside the open hole in the panelling. 'Oh, it's you boys,' said the head. 'Come on, now.'

The boys climbed out. There seemed to be quite a crowd of people in the little panelled room – any amount of policemen, the woman, the three men belonging to the gang, and a man they saw was a doctor. He disappeared into the secret passage at once, carrying a small black bag.

The three men and the woman were handcuffed. They all looked angry and sullen and the woman looked scared. She was astonished when she saw the boys. She recognised them at once.

'You!' she said, hissing at them. 'So it was *you*, prying and snooping and – '

'Shut up,' said one of the gang sharply. The woman subsided, but she glared all the time at the boys as if she would like to bite them.

'A very nice evening's work,' said one of the men from Lillinghame, who seemed to be an inspector, and very much in charge of the proceedings now. 'A nice little haul – and a prospect of further hauls, when we get some information from Inspector Rawlings!'

'You go home now, you kids,' said the policeman who had directed proceedings in the tunnel. 'We'll see you tomorrow. You've done well. Now go home and sleep – if you can!'

Chapter Twenty-Nine

All Good Things End!

It was all very well to say: 'Go home and sleep.' For one thing there really wasn't very much of the night left, and for another thing, who in the world could go to bed and sleep peacefully after such an adventurous night?

Feeling very much awake and on top of the world the three boys left the Hall and went up the road once more. Miranda was on Barney's shoulder, rather subdued by all the queer happenings of the night.

'She'll never like bells again,' said Barney, fondling her. 'Will you, Miranda? She must have made for the window in the tower, and vanished out of it.'

'Diana will be wondering what's been happening,' said Roger. 'I'm surprised she and Miss Pepper and Miss Hannah didn't come down to see what the matter was.'

There were lights in the front room, when the boys arrived. Diana was looking out for them anxiously, with a worried and angry Loony by her side. The spaniel hurled himself on Snubby like a cannonball as soon as he came into the hall, and Loopy followed suit. For a few minutes nobody could make themselves heard through the excited barking.

'Boys! What *has* been happening? How *could* you go off like that without telling us?' cried Miss Pepper. 'Diana told me such a peculiar tale that I could hardly believe it. What *is* all this about secret passages and bells and a sick man and – '

'We can tell you everything now, Miss Pepper,' said Roger, grinning. He looked pale and tired but very cheerful. Barney looked the same as usual. Snubby looked incredibly dirty, through having stayed so long in the secret chimney cavity. Miranda was not to be seen. She was curled up inside Barney's shirt, and not even a paw was showing. Miranda was too tired for words!

Bit by bit the strange story came out. Miss Hannah's eyes nearly dropped out of her head. 'Such goings on!' she said. 'I never heard such things in my life.'

Barney explained about the bells, and how he had rung them to awaken the village and perhaps startle the police, and how marvellously his plan had worked.

'The bells woke *us* up,' said Miss Pepper. 'I was really scared. I couldn't help remembering the old legend. I couldn't imagine there was anyone in the tower at that time of night, ringing the bells – and fancy its being *you*, Barney!'

'Gosh, I did ring them hard,' said Barney. 'They absolutely deafened me. I had to ring them by their short little ropes, you see, so I was almost touching them. I'm certain sure it was Miranda who rang them the first time – by accident, I expect. She probably jumped down on to them without knowing they would jangle, then got terrified and did a lot more jumping.'

'Poor Miranda,' said Snubby, and put his hand inside Barney's shirt to feel the warm little bundle. Miranda didn't stir.

Miss Hannah had got some cake and milk and they all ate as they talked. 'Funny how hungry an adventure makes you,' said Snubby. 'I haven't felt hungry like this for ages.'

'Fibber,' said Diana. 'You're always saying that. Goodness, Snubby, I did have an awful time here all alone, wondering and wondering what was happening to you. I simply couldn't bear it – and Loony was a frightful nuisance. I had to hold his nose into the cushion when he began howling in case Miss Pepper heard him.'

'Woof,' said Loony mournfully, looking reproachfully at Snubby.

'It's dawn,' said Diana, looking out of the window. 'The sun will soon be up. I shouldn't think it's worth while going to bed, is it, Miss Pepper?'

'Certainly it is,' said Miss Pepper, who was feeling rather dazed with all she had be told. These children! It was really *dangerous* to look after them. You simply never knew what they would do next.

She got up. 'Come along,' she said. 'Get into bed just as you are, dirt and all! Just slip into your pyjamas and crawl in. Sleep till twelve o'clock if you like.'

'Good gracious – we'll be awake *long* before then!' said Snubby, and got up, yawning loudly.

They were not awake long before then. They all slept till past eleven o'clock, and they would not have awakened then if Loopy hadn't given such a fusillade of barks that they all sat up with a jump. Snubby rose to the window and looked to see why Loopy was barking so madly.

'It's the police!' he said excitedly. 'Three of them – all looking very important. Come on – get dressed and come down.'

'You'd better wash your face, Snubby,' said Roger. 'Hey, Barney, stir yourself a bit more!'

Barney had actually been allowed to sleep on a couch in Roger's room, with Miranda tucked into his arms. Miss Hannah couldn't bear to send him out into the shed, and most heroically said that Miranda could sleep on the couch too.

Soon they were all downstairs, and the police welcomed them with broad smiles.

'What have you come for?' asked Snubby eagerly.

'Oh, just to see if we could persuade you three boys to join the police force,' said the inspector smiling. 'I feel you'd be a real help.'

Snubby really believed this. He gazed exultantly at the inspector. 'Gosh – not go back to school, do you mean?'

'Fathead,' said Roger, and gave him a poke in the ribs. 'Don't you know a joke when you hear one?'

'Oh,' said Snubby, and looked so bitterly disappointed that the three policemen guffawed with laughter.

'We came to clear up a few points,' said the inspector. 'How did you come to guess there was any funny business going on at the Hall?'

Barney told them how a man had given him a lift, dropped him at Lillinghame – and then, to his surprise, he had seen him again at the Hall that night.

'I know it was him – he had the same van, with "PIGGOTT, ELECTRICIAN" on the side,' said Barney. The policemen looked at one another and nodded.

'Just what we wanted to know,' said the inspector, and wrote it down. 'We've had our eye on Piggott for some time. He's always making peculiar little trips to the Bristol Channel and round about here. Now we know why. When his pals come up to the Channel with one or two men on board who want to get into the country and keep hidden till they've got papers, Piggott is at hand. And when a little kidnapping is done, Piggott is again at hand with his van. It probably has a false bottom. We'll examine it carefully.'

'To think that such things go on!' said poor Miss Hannah, who really was upset at all these sudden happenings.

'Another thing we want to clear up,' said the inspector, 'is about the bells ringing the first time. Who rang them then?'

'Miranda, my monkey, I think,' said Barney.

'Were you in the Hall with her?' asked the inspector. 'I understand it was at night.'

'Yes, sir,' said Barney, looking very uncomfortable. 'I'd nowhere to sleep, so I shinned up the ivy and slept in a four-poster bed there. I suppose I did wrong, sir.'

'You did,' said the inspector. 'But I understand you're a circus lad, without a home – you sleep anywhere you can.'

'That's right, sir,' said Barney. 'I hope you won't hold it against me, sir. I didn't do any harm.'

'It won't even be reported,' said the inspector. 'You're a good lad and a brave one. Have you anywhere to sleep now?'

'Yes,' said Miss Hannah surprisingly. 'He's going to stay here with me until the other children leave in about a week's time. I'll look after him.'

Barney looked at her in grateful surprise. Diana gave Miss Hannah a sudden hug, and Snubby yelled 'Hurrah!' Roger rubbed his hands joyfully. Now they would all be together properly. Good old Miss Hannah!

'Well – if he's under your care, he'll be all right,' said the inspector, with a twinkle. 'There won't be any more borrowing of four-poster beds – or, er – tablecloths! We noticed how creased and crumpled they were when we found the four-poster bed had been slept in – and that couch downstairs.'

'Barney's all right,' said Snubby loyally. 'You can always trust old Barney, sir.'

'I think I agree with you,' said the inspector, giving Barney a little nod. He asked a few more questions and then shut his notebook. 'That's all,' he said. 'And I wish you a very happy week – without even the *smell* of an adventure to spoil it!'

'Oh, sir,' protested Snubby. 'Adventures don't spoil things. I say – could we go to the Hall today, and get

190

down that secret passage again – we didn't really examine the hole in the brick wall properly, or the secret room beyond. Did you see that little cupboard, sir, with the candles and things?'

'Oh, yes,' said the inspector. 'We probably saw as much as you did, though not quite so soon. Those candles were kept there, I imagine, to light the secret room when it was occupied. You can certainly go down to the Hall if you wish, and explore anything you like – on one condition.'

'What's that?' asked Roger.

'That you will ring the bells at once if you find any prisoner, crook or suspicious person hiding in any secret cavity, chamber, passage or room,' said the inspector solemnly.

'Good gracious,' said Miss Hannah, half-alarmed. The children laughed.

'We promise!' they said, and took the three policemen to the front gate. The children watched them go ponderously down the road, while they stood there talking. Loony and Loopy got tired of it and ran off.

Presently Miss Hannah called to them. 'Are you coming in to brunch?' The children turned in surprise.

'Brunch?' said Diana doubtfully. 'What's that?'

'Just a mixture of breakfast and lunch,' called back Miss Hannah cheerfully. 'It's nearly twelve o'clock, you know – too late for breakfast, too early for lunch – so you'll have to make do with brunch.'

Brunch proved to be a really wonderful meal, beginning with bacon and eggs, going on to tongue and salad and finishing up with tinned pineapple and cream. Snubby approved highly.

'Why don't we always have brunch?' he said. 'I say, Barney – Miranda's helped herself to a handful of pineapple chunks. Greedy thing – I was going to have a second helping!'

Miranda sat nibbling her juicy pineapple chunks, her bright monkey eyes keeping watch on Snubby, as if she were afraid he might snatch them from her. Loony put his head on Snubby's knee. Loopy immediately put his head on Snubby's other knee.

Snubby sighed happily. 'Gosh – another whole week of brunches and rides and games with Loony and Loopy and Miranda, and Barney living with us here – it's too good to be true.'

'Woof,' agreed Loony, licking Snubby's bare knee. Loopy at once licked the other one.

'Well,' said Barney, reaching for his glass of lemonade, 'good luck, everyone – and here's to our Next Adventure!'

The Rubadub Mystery

First published in a single volume in hardback in 1951 by
William Collins Sons & Co Ltd.
First published in paperback in 1970 in Armada

Chapter One

Plans For a Holiday

'Snubby!' called a cross voice. 'SNUBBY! Didn't I tell you to tie Loony up?'

Snubby came flying downstairs to his aunt. 'Oh, Aunt Susan, I did! Has he got loose again? Oh, I say – did he make all that mess in the hall?'

The black spaniel sat in the middle of a few sheets of torn-up newspaper, his tongue hanging out. He looked exactly as if he was grinning.

'That's your uncle's morning newspaper,' said his aunt. 'He hasn't even read it yet. Snubby, you know that we're very rushed trying to get everything done before we leave today. I really *can*not have Loony rushing about loose.'

'I'll shut Loony into my room, Mother,' said Diana, coming up. 'And I'll lock the door and put the key in my pocket. Then Loony will be safe.'

'Well, nothing else in your room will be safe!' said Mrs Lynton. 'Do what you like with him – but keep him out of my way this morning! We shall never get off this afternoon, your father and I.'

The Lyntons were going to America for a few weeks. The three children and Loony the dog were going off to the sea with Miss Pepper, Mrs Lynton's old governess. She often had charge of them when the Lyntons had to go away.

Snubby had only arrived the day before, having spent the first week of the holidays with some other cousins. He had no parents and spent his time staying with various relations – but of them all he much preferred the Lyntons. He was very fond of his Aunt Susan, and admired and respected his Uncle Richard. His uncle, however, neither admired nor respected Snubby.

'I consider that boy to be the world's worst nuisance,' was his continual description of poor Snubby.

Loony was led upstairs by a firm Diana. Sardine the cat was waiting for him at a turn of the stairs and leapt at him. He sprang back, almost pulling Diana down the stairs, and she squealed.

'This house is a mad-house,' said her father, at the top of the stairs. 'Where's Miss Pepper? Can't she take you all into some quiet corner till we've gone? America will seem a place of utter peace and quiet after this. Really, when you children come back from school, it's . . .'

'Oh, Daddy – you always say that,' said Diana, hauling Loony up by his lead. 'You know you'll miss us when you go. Daddy, I wish you'd take us with you to America.'

'Not on your life!' said her father, horrified. 'You'd probably all fall overboard, to start with – and Snubby would spend his time down in the engine-room with Roger . . .'

'Oh, I say, sir – should I be allowed to?' called Snubby. 'That would be smashing.'

'Where do you get those awful words from?' said his uncle. 'Can't you talk Queen's English?'

'I bet the Queen says "smashing" sometimes,' argued Snubby. 'I bet she . . .'

'Move aside and let me pass,' said his uncle impatiently. 'What with Diana and the dog on the stairs, and now you – and is that Sardine I see waiting for me to fall over her as usual – this is a real mad-house.'

'Richard dear – do come down and help me with the labelling,' called Mrs Lynton. 'We'll go into the study and shut the door and the windows, and see if we can't keep out all the riff-raff!'

'Gosh – fancy Aunt Susan calling us riff-raff,' said Snubby indignantly. 'Hey, Aunt Susan . . .'

A door slammed down below. Snubby gave it up. He helped to push the reluctant Loony along the landing to Diana's bedroom.

Miss Pepper was there, pulling clothes out of the drawers and cupboards. The children were to go to the seaside the next day, and Miss Pepper was trying to do a little sorting and packing in between helping Mrs Lynton.

'Hallo, Miss Pepper,' said Snubby, as if he hadn't seen her for a month. He gave her a sudden squeeze round the waist. She gasped.

'*Don't*, Snubby! Why so affectionate all of a sudden? What is it you want out of me now?'

'Nothing,' said Snubby, looking hurt. 'I just felt sort of thrilled – holidays, you know – no more work for ages – going off to the sea tomorrow. What's the place we're going to, Miss Pepper? Nobody's told me anything yet.'

Roger came marching in, his arms full of swimsuits. 'Here you are, Miss Pepper,' he said, putting them down on the bed. 'I've found three swimsuits each. Is that enough?'

'Good gracious yes,' said Miss Pepper. 'Oh, don't let Loony get hold of them. Snubby, take him away.'

'He's supposed to be locked up here in Diana's bedroom,' said Snubby.

'Well, he can't be,' said Miss Pepper decidedly. 'I'm doing a lot of sorting out in here and I don't intend to be locked in with Loony or any other mad dog either.'

'He's not mad,' said Snubby. 'Are you, Loony?'

Loony promptly lay down on his back and pedalled his feet in the air, looking sideways for Snubby's admiring remarks.

'Bicycle away,' said Miss Pepper to Loony. 'Stay there on your back and pedal for the rest of the morning. That will suit me nicely.'

'Nobody's told me *yet* where we're going tomorrow,' said Snubby plaintively.

'Well, you only came yesterday,' said Roger. 'And considering that you spent practically the whole evening describing the cricket match you played in last Saturday, and told us about every run you didn't get, and how many sweaters the umpire wore, and what you'd do if *you* were chosen for the Test team, and . . .'

'That's not funny,' said Snubby. 'Miss Pepper do tell me about tomorrow.'

'Well, we start off early, and we catch the train to Woodlingham, and we change there, and we catch another train, a slow one, to Rockypool, and then we get a taxi to Rubadub,' said Miss Pepper. 'There – now you know, so stop asking me.'

'Rubadub! I don't believe it! There's not a place called Rubadub!' exclaimed Snubby disbelievingly.

'There is,' said Diana. 'It's marked on the map. I think it's a super name. I love thinking I'm going to stay at Rubadub. Miss Pepper used to stay there when she was small – didn't you, Miss Pepper?'

'Yes,' said Miss Pepper, emptying another drawer. 'Diana, sort these out and put them over there. Yes, I often stayed there. It was the funniest little seaside village you ever could imagine then. Only a few shops, no pier, no promenade, a few cottages – and the old inn. You'll never guess what it was called!'

'Rubadub Inn?' said Roger.

'No. It was called Three Men in a Tub!' said Miss Pepper 'You know the old rhyme – "Rubadub-dub, Three men in a Tub." Goodness knows why the inn should have been named that, but it was – and still is. Actually Rubadub village was called that because of a strange whirlpool place set between some oddly-shaped rocks. One is like a scrubbing-board, and down below it the water boils and swirls and bubbles . . .'

'As if it were in a wash-tub, I suppose!' said Diana. 'Rubadub, See how we scrub . . .'

'That's right,' said Miss Pepper. 'The whirlpool is called Rubadub Pool, and so the village got its name, I suppose.'

'It sounds jolly good,' said Snubby approvingly. 'I like the sound of all this, I must say. An inn called Three Men in a Tub, and a whirlpool called Rubadub Pool – I say, do we stay at the inn, Miss Pepper?'

'We do,' said Miss Pepper. 'I stayed there as a child and it was very comfortable. My niece stayed there last year and she sent such good accounts of it that when your mother suggested somewhere for you all these holidays, I thought of Rubadub.'

'It'll be nice to stay in a dear little old-fashioned seaside village,' said Diana. 'No pier, no promenade, no . . .'

'Oh yes, there's a pier now *and* a promenade, and plenty of things going on,' said Miss Pepper briskly. 'And there's an enormous Secret Harbour built there, too, round beyond Rubadub Pool – where new submarines are tried out. Oh, Rubadub is no longer a tiny, sleepy village!'

'I say! A Secret Harbour!' said Snubby, thrilled. 'I should like to go over that.'

'I said "Secret",' said Miss Pepper. '"Top Secret" too, Snubby. So well guarded that no one, not even an inquisitive lad like you, could possible get near it. So get that out of your head.'

There came a call from downstairs. 'Miss Pepper! Can you come? There are a few things I want you to do.'

'Coming, Mrs Lynton!' called Miss Pepper, and hurried out of the room. Loony immediately jumped up to go with her and leapt after her, quite forgetting he was tied to the bed-rail by his lead. He almost choked himself.

'It all sounds super,' said Snubby, comforting poor Loony. 'I'm sorry Aunt Susan's not coming, though. But I don't mind if Uncle Richard doesn't. Sooner or later I always seem to get a whacking from him.'

'You got two, last hols,' said Diana. 'One for letting

Loony chew up his best slippers, and one for cheeking him.'

'Don't remind me,' said Snubby. 'I have to think twice now before I say anything to Uncle Richard in case he might think I am cheeking him. It's an awful nuisance.'

'It's a jolly good thing,' said Roger. 'You want keeping down, young Snubby. And while you're about it, you can think twice before you cheek me, too. Oh, blow you, Loony – how did you get those swimsuits off the bed?'

A loud sound rang through the house, and the three children and Loony gave cries of joy. 'The gong! I thought it was never going!'

'Race you downstairs! Come on, Loony!'

And down went an avalanche at top speed. Mr Lynton groaned. 'How *pleased* I shall be to see the coast of quiet, peaceful America. This house is Bedlam – never a moment's peace anywhere!'

Chapter Two

Getting Ready

Mr and Mrs Lynton were to set off in their car after the meal. Everything was ready. The cases were packed and labelled. Big *Queen Elizabeth* labels were tied on, or pasted on. The tickets were safely in Mr Lynton's wallet.

He was smiling as he said good-bye. He shook hands with Miss Pepper. 'Don't stand any nonsense,' he said to her. 'And keep Snubby in his place. We'll write from New York. You've got our hotel address, haven't you?'

'Yes, thank you,' said Miss Pepper. 'Have a good time, and don't worry about the children. They'll be quite safe with me down at Rubadub. I'll see they don't get into mischief.'

'No mysteries, please, and no adventures,' said Mrs Lynton, kissing her old governess. 'Keep an eye on that, won't you – you know what extraordinary things can happen when these three are together.'

'Goodbye, Mother! Don't forget to write!'

'Goodbye, Aunt Susan! I hope you don't get a storm that wrecks you!'

'Goodbye – and we'll be very good, so you needn't worry.'

'Where's Loony?' said Snubby suddenly. 'He wants to say goodbye too. Where on earth is he? Loony, Loony, Loony!'

'He *doesn't* want to say goodbye,' said Miss Pepper firmly. 'I've shut him in my bedroom.'

The Lyntons got into the car. Snubby gave a yell and pointed up to Miss Pepper's bedroom window. Loony was there, his head squeezed through the half-open window,

203

trying his best to see what was happening. He gave a bark.

'He did want to say goodbye!' cried Snubby. 'Bark, Loony, bark!'

By a great effort Loony managed to push up the window a little way, and out came his shoulders and one paw.

'That dog will jump out next!' cried Mr Lynton and jammed down the accelerator. The car leapt forward and was off down the road. Mr Lynton had no desire to see Loony leap out of a high window!

Snubby tore upstairs and was just in time to stop Loony from flinging himself out of the window. 'That dog!' said Miss Pepper, as they all went back to the house. 'I can't imagine what the people at the inn will say about him. They said they didn't mind dogs – but they don't know Loony! Does he still go for brushes and mats?'

'Oh yes – and since he went to stay with your sister's dog, Loopy, last May, when we all went away with you after 'flu, he's taken to bringing down all the towels too,' said Diana. 'He caught that from Loopy.'

'Well, we'll simply *have* to stop him doing things like that at the inn,' said Miss Pepper, having a sudden vision of Loony piling all the visitors' towels out in the inn's garden, and then going back to fetch hair-brushes to put with them.

'I don't see how we *can* stop him,' said Roger. 'You simply can't reason with Loony. He just sits and grins at you with his tongue out, and thumps his tail on the floor. But you do love him, don't you, Miss Pepper?'

'I feel doubtful about that sometimes,' said Miss Pepper. 'Very doubtful. Now we'll all have to get very busy indeed, Roger and Diana, if we're going to be ready to go tomorrow. You'll have to help me pack.'

Loony came trotting down the stairs looking very pleased with himself. For once he had no brush or towel with him. Snubby followed.

'We're going for a walk,' he announced.

'Oh no you're not,' said Roger at once. 'Trust you to try and get out of fetching and carrying, Snubby – and lugging heavy cases about. You're jolly well going to stay here and help.'

'I'd much rather Snubby took Loony for a walk,' said Miss Pepper hastily, thinking it would be marvellous to get both boy and dog out of the way together. 'I'm sure Loony needs a walk.'

'Pah!' said Roger in disgust. 'Snubby always gets out of everything.'

'Go along, Snubby – but be back by teatime,' said Miss Pepper firmly, and Snubby went, followed by his faithful and adoring Loony, his long black ears flopping as he went – pad-pad-pad-pad.

The others spent a busy afternoon. Everything was packed. Diana neatly wrote a dozen labels, Roger tied rope round the trunk.

'I'll help you down the stairs with that,' said Miss Pepper. 'I've just got to find Diana's sandals to put into this last bag.'

Roger didn't want any help. He prided himself on his strength, and while Miss Pepper was hunting for the missing sandals, he dragged the trunk to the top of the stairs.

He set it flat and gave it a push. It cascaded down the stairs with a thunderous noise, arriving in the hall at top speed. Sardine the cat got the fright of her life as the trunk rumbled past where she sat on the stairs, waiting to pounce on someone coming down. She leapt in the air, and then tore like a streak of lightning into Diana's bedroom, as Miss Pepper was coming out in a hurry. Sardine shot between her ankles and landed on the bed, all her fur standing on end and her tail twice its usual size.

Miss Pepper rushed out on the landing. 'Oh, who's fallen downstairs! Are you hurt? Whatever's happened?'

The cook was standing in the hall, brought out of her kitchen by the noise. She looked in disgust at the trunk, which had slid along the polished floor to the front door.

'Starting to throw trunks at one another now, I suppose,' she said, and stalked back to her kitchen.

'What's the matter?' asked Roger, surprised. 'I just shot the trunk downstairs, that's all. Jolly good idea – no lifting or carrying. I thought it would save us trouble, Miss Pepper.'

Miss Pepper gave him such a glare that he disappeared into his room. Without a word she walked back to Diana's room, and picked up some socks.

'For two pins I'd leave them to themselves!' she thought, her heart still beating in fright. 'Really, if Roger starts doing things like this my life won't be worth living. Snubby's bad enough.'

Roger came humbly into the room. 'I'm sorry, Miss Pepper,' he said. 'I didn't know it would crash down like that. Let me take those cases. I can carry them down for you one by one. You have a rest now, do.'

'It's all right,' said Miss Pepper thinking that the three children had their nice ways after all. 'But I do wish you'd remember that you're in your teens, Roger, and be a bit more responsible.'

'You sound like my form-master,' said Roger gloomily. 'Don't preach, Miss Pepper. You're too nice to preach.'

Miss Pepper laughed and pretended to box Roger's ears. He ducked, grinning. He was very fond of her, as they all were, and hated it when she was vexed.

At last everything was finished. It was teatime and Snubby arrived back punctually with a tired Loony and an enormous appetite. He went straight into the kitchen to find the plump, good-natured cook.

'Cookie! Have you made any of your gingerbread for

me? Don't say you haven't! I've been thinking of it all the term.'

'Go on with you,' said the cook. She opened the larder door and took out a tin. She lifted the lid and showed Snubby a great flat slab of sticky-looking home-made gingerbread. He gave her a hug round her waist.

'You're my very best friend,' he said. 'You don't mind if we eat it all, do you? I mean – it's a real compliment, really, if we eat up every single crumb. Isn't it, Cookie dear?'

'Go on with you!' said the cook again. 'You'd talk the hind leg off a donkey, you would!'

'Why, is one of your legs coming loose?' inquired Snubby at once, and dodged out of the way as the cook took up a frying-pan and threatened him with it. Snubby's silly jokes usually went down very well with the good-tempered cook, and Mrs Lynton always said that they had more and better cakes when Snubby was with them than at any other time.

'It's a wonder I did any work at all this afternoon,' said the cook, taking the gingerbread carefully out of the tin. 'That cousin of yours threw trunks down the stairs, and my word, they made a noise. I nearly had a heart attack!'

'Oh I say – good old Roger!' said Snubby, breaking a bit off the end of the gingerbread. 'Strong man he's getting, isn't he? Wish I'd been there to see him throwing trunks all over the place.'

'Now take your fingers away from my gingerbread,' said the cook. 'And take that dog out of my kitchen. I never in my life knew any animal that could slink into the larder when the door's shut, like that dog of yours can. He's a living miracle!'

'He is. You're right,' said Snubby, wholeheartedly. 'I'm glad you appreciate him. Oh golly, here's Sardine. We'd better go.'

They left hurriedly. Sardine considered that the kitchen

belonged to her, and hissed and spat spitefully if Loony stayed too long!

Teatime passed very pleasantly, because there were hot scones and honey, and gingerbread and some coconut buns. After that they all tidied up their rooms and put away everything. Loony helped by gathering together all the loose mats and putting them in a pile on the landing for people to fall over.

'I really think it's about time for Loony to grow up a bit,' said Diana, picking herself up after stumbling over the mats in the darkness of the landing. 'He's nearly two years old, and reckoning that in human years, it means he's in his teens. He ought to be more responsible.'

Roger grinned at Miss Pepper nearby. 'Another preacher!' he said. 'Loony, do you hear what Di says?'

'What's the time?' said Miss Pepper, looking at her watch. 'It's gone eight. I think you'd all better go to bed now. We've got a long day before us tomorrow. I want a bit of peace and quiet, too, to write letters.'

'All right – we'll go.' said Diana. 'I always think it's thrilling, the night before we go away. Thinking about the sea and bathing and prawning, and walks . . .'

'Woof!' said Loony, at once. He always joined in the conversation when he heard that word.

'Clever dog!' said Diana. 'Come on – let's all go to bed.'

Chapter Three

Off to Rubadub-on-Sea

The next day was truly exciting. Usually the three children went off for their holidays by car, but they much preferred the train.

They found an empty carriage, and each bagged a corner. Loony shared everyone's corner in turn, breathing down their necks in excitement.

It was a long way to Woodlingham, where they had to change trains. The journey was a cross-country one, involving many long stops at various stations at which bits and pieces of the train were added or subtracted.

Snubby, of course, was intensely interested in these stops, and talked to every engine-driver, guard and porter that he could see.

'Do you know,' he announced once, as he returned from a chat to the driver, 'do you know that of all the fifteen carriages we started with, only two of the original ones are left now – ours and the next one? Such a lot have been shunted off. But some have been added, of course.'

'You make it sound like a maths problem,' said Diana. 'So long as they leave our carriage on the train that's all I care about.'

'Just like a girl,' said Roger scornfully. 'No interest in railways at all. I call it all very thrilling. We start with fifteen – we shunted off six at Limming and added five. We left another three at Berklemere, and got two more added on at Fingerpit. Now let me see . . .'

'This sounds like a riddle now,' said Miss Pepper sleepily. 'If we shunt off six and add two, and leave five somewhere, and forget to take on the rest, please tell me the name of the engine-driver!'

'Ha, ha, joke,' said Snubby politely. 'I say, isn't it time for lunch yet?'

They got to Woodlingham at last and woke up Miss Pepper, who had fallen sound asleep. 'It's a good thing we're *respon*sible people,' said Roger. '*Some*body's got to look out for the station we change at.'

'Don't be idiotic, Roger,' said Miss Pepper. 'I can't imagine how I could have gone to sleep in this rattling, rumbling old train.'

The train to take them to Rockypool came in at last. Snubby went to talk to the engine-driver, having found out that there was a ten-minute wait before it drew out of the station again.

He didn't notice that another engine came backing up to the end of the train. He didn't notice it being hooked on. He suddenly heard the whistle of the guard and the voices of the others calling him frantically.

'Snubby, quick, we're going. SNUBBY!'

Snubby leapt into the very last carriage, dragging poor Loony in by his collar. 'Gosh!' he said to a surprised old country-woman there. 'I nearly missed it! How was I to know the thing was going to go off the other way? Peculiar way trains behave here!'

'Ar,' said the old woman wisely.

'I mean – it came in with the engine at the front, just as usual – and it leaves the station with a perfectly fresh engine, at the *back*,' said Snubby, working himself up into a grievance because he felt so foolish. It's time somebody spoke about these things.'

'Ar,' said the old lady, nodding her head. Snubby looked at her. In his experience people who said nothing but 'Ar' made extremely good listeners. So he aired his views at great length and enjoyed himself thoroughly. He didn't even get out at the next station or the next, to find his way to the carriage where the others were. He was afraid they would tease him unmercifully about being so nearly left behind.

Two men got in at the third station. Snubby looked at them closely. They were naval men, he saw. Aha! Probably they belonged to the Secret Submarine Harbour. What a scoop for him if he could make friends with them and get news of the harbour to retell proudly to the others. The men opened newspapers and began to read.

'Excuse me, sir, but are we very far from Rockypool?' began Snubby. 'I've got to get out there.'

'You'll see the name of the station when we come to it,' said one of the men gruffly.

'I say, sir, I suppose you don't belong to the Secret Submarine place, do you?' Snubby tried again. 'I've always been interested in submarines. Used to sail them in my bath, and . . .'

'You probably do still, I imagine,' said the other man. 'Shut up!'

Snubby subsided, grieved. He examined the men carefully, pretending he was a detective. Both clean-shaven. One with a mole on his right cheek. One with crooked eyebrows. Actually he thought they looked nice men. It was a pity they wouldn't talk. He sat and stared at them thoughtfully.

'Anything wrong with my face?' inquired one man at last. 'What about looking out of the window for a change?'

Snubby scowled. He woke up Loony, who was sound asleep under the seat, bored with this long journey. He lugged him up on the seat and began to talk to him. He couldn't very well talk to the old woman, because she was now snoring in her corner, her mouth wide open.

'Shut up!' said one of the men again. 'What a babbler you are!'

The old woman woke up unexpectedly. She gave a little wheeze of laughter.

'That's right, he is,' she said. 'Babbles like a brook, he do. I couldn't get a word in till you come along, misters.'

Snubby glared at her indignantly. He got out at the next station with much dignity, and made his way to the compartment where Roger and Diana were hanging out of the window.

'Why didn't you come before?' demanded Roger. 'Was there somebody interesting in that carriage?'

'Rather!' said Snubby, climbing in. 'There were two men from the Secret Submarine place – and my word, the secrets they know!'

'As if they'd tell *you* any!' said Roger at once.

'All right. If you're feeling like that I won't tell you a word,' said Snubby exasperatingly. He sat down in the opposite corner. Roger stared at him. He couldn't believe that any one would tell Snubby anything interesting in the way of secrets – but on the other hand Snubby was so friendly that people *had* been known to relate most amazing bits of information to him.

'Go on – tell me what you heard,' said Roger. 'Who were the men? What were they like?'

'They wouldn't tell me their names.' said Snubby. 'So I didn't press them. But I can tell you exactly what they were like. You just never know when it'll pay you to be really observant.'

He described the men exactly, down to a mole, crooked eyebrows, two overlapping teeth, bitten nails on one man's hands, and misshapen little finger on the other man's.

'Jolly good,' said Roger, thinking for the hundredth time that his fat-headed little cousin could be quite sharp, for all his idiotic ways. 'You ought to go into the police force!'

Snubby was about to air his views on how lucky the

police force would be to get him, when the train slowed down at a station.

'Rockypool!' yelled a porter, and Miss Pepper stood up quickly.

'Ah – here we are. Roger, go and see if our trunks and cases are *still* in the luggage van. I can hardly believe we have the same luggage van as when we started, but still, you never know!'

Roger disappeared to find out. Snubby and Diana handed down the smaller cases and parcels, and they all got out of the carriage. Loony got his lead entangled round Snubby's legs as usual, and made him cross.

Roger came back. 'The luggage is all there,' he announced. 'Safe as can be. What about a taxi, Miss Pepper? Shall I go and see if there's one?'

'It's already ordered,' said Miss Pepper. 'I asked the innkeeper's wife at Rubadub to order one for us. It should be waiting.'

It was. As they walked to it Snubby nudged Roger and nodded his head towards two men walking nearby. Roger looked at them and immediately recognised a good many of the big and small characteristics that Snubby had recited to him. He stared at the men with interest. Like Snubby he thought it must be thrilling to work on anything secret.

Their taxi was waiting. The driver got down to help the porter in with their things. He strapped on the trunk, and put the cases in front.

'Is it far to Rubadub?' asked Snubby. The man shook his head.

'Matter of three miles,' he said. 'The railway don't go any farther than this.'

They all got into the old musty-smelling taxi. Snubby stuck his head out of the window to take a look round. The country they passed through was rather wild and desolate – heath and moorland with pools of water shining here and there.

They rumbled along. Snubby looked at Loony anxiously.

'I think he's going to be sick,' he said.

'Oh *no*!' said Miss Pepper, in despair.

'He'd better go in front with the driver,' said Snubby, and he knocked on the glass. 'Hey – stop a minute, will you? I'm coming in front with you.'

The taxi stopped. Snubby got out, carrying Loony, who looked very surprised. The two of them were soon in front with the driver, sitting on a pile of cases.

'Now I can see fine,' said Snubby to the driver, and grinned happily.

'Well I never!' said Diana, who heard this. 'I bet Loony wasn't feeling sick after all. It was just that Snubby wanted to sit in front and see everything.'

'Well, never mind,' said Miss Pepper, who was feeling tired, and not very anxious to cope with the inexhaustible and irrepressible Snubby. 'We'll soon be there.'

It didn't seem long before the taxi drove into a little town by the sea. It was set in a semi-circle of cliff, looking out to a small bay. There was a good promenade, a fine little pier, a stone jetty with boats and a sandy beach.

'It looks grand!' said Diana, pleased. 'And oh, look – is this lovely old place the inn?'

'Yes – this is the Three Men in a Tub Inn, in the old town of Rubadub!' said Miss Pepper. 'Out you get – we're here at last!'

Chapter Four

The Strange Old Inn

They all tumbled out of the taxi. The driver gave a shout to someone called by the extraordinary name of Dummy.

'Hey there, Dummy! Come and collect these things, will you? Your people have arrived.'

The children stood and looked at the Three Men in a Tub Inn. It had an old, old sign, but whether it was of three men in a tub, or of anything else it was quite impossible to tell, it was so dark and dingy.

The inn looked like something out of a story. 'If you told me we were back in the Middle Ages I'd believe you!' said Diana, staring up at the inn. 'I feel as if I've gone back hundreds of years when I look at this quaint old place!'

It was a rambling old inn, set back against the cliff, almost nestling into it. Its leaded, diamond-paned windows gleamed brightly. It had tall chimneys, and a roof so covered with grey-green lichen that the red tiles only showed through here and there.

The front door might have belonged to a castle! It was enormous, very stout and strong, and had a great knocker in the form of a sailing ship. Snubby, of course immediately wanted to go and bang on it, but before he could do so the old door creaked open and a face looked out with round eyes and a button of a mouth.

At first the children thought it was the face of a child, but when the whole person appeared they saw that it was a grown-up! A grown-up not as tall as Roger, the head rather big for the body, and the face an odd mixture of child and grown-up.

'Come on, Dummy. Stir yourself,' said the driver, undoing some of the cases. Dummy ran out clumsily. He wore the dress of a hall-porter or odd-man – thick, navy-blue trousers with a line down the side, a leather apron and waistcoat over a dark shirt. He grinned at the children, holding his face sideways as if half-shy.

He appeared to be enormously strong! He lifted the trunk with ease, jerked it on his shoulder, and went back into the inn with it.

'That's old Dummy,' explained the taxi-driver. 'He's a good chap, but never properly growed-up, I don't reckon. Strong as a horse, and gentle as a child – unless he gets into one of his rages, and then all I say is, I'd rather meet a lion than Dummy!'

'I liked him,' said Diana 'He had a nice sort of smile.'

'He gets on well with children,' said the taxi-driver. 'But when grown-ups go for him for being a bit slow, like, he mutters and mumbles and growls and scowls, and looks as if he'd like to throw them over the cliff. And see you don't ever laugh at old Dummy. Anyone who laughs at Dummy comes to a sticky end, so I've been told.'

Miss Pepper thought that the taxi-driver had talked quite enough. She saw Snubby drinking in every word, eager to ask about the people who 'had come to a sticky end.'

'I think that's all,' she said, taking out her purse. 'Thank you for meeting us.'

The driver touched his cap, and pocketed the fare and the generous tip that Miss Pepper had given him. Then he drove away.

Dummy appeared again to take the rest of the cases, and brought with him the innkeeper's wife. She was a large, plump woman with rather a gloomy face. She had so many chins that Snubby was quite lost in admiration. She did her hair high up on her head, and really looked rather majestic.

216

'Good afternoon,' she said, advancing on the little company. 'Your train must have been very punctual for once in a way. It's usually so late that I didn't expect you for another half-hour. Come this way. Your rooms are all ready.'

'Oh, thank you, Mrs er – Mrs . . .' said Miss Pepper, rather taken aback by the ponderous plumpness of the inkeeper's wife.

'My name is Glump,' said that lady. 'Mrs Glump.'

'What a wonderful name!' murmured Diana, as they all went into the big, dark hall, following Mrs Glump. 'And doesn't it suit her?'

'Yes – mixture of 'glum' and 'plump,' said Snubby with a giggle. 'I wonder if there are any little Glumps. Come on – up the stairs we go. My word, aren't they uneven and steep?'

'Mind the bends,' said Mrs Glump, in her stately voice. 'Oh my – what's that?'

It was only Loony, escaped from Snubby's hand, tearing up the stairs, pressing himself against her legs as he passed her at sixty miles an hour. He liked this place. He knew he would find plenty of strange, unusual smells here.

'I'm so sorry – did he scare you?' said Snubby in his politest voice. 'That was only my spaniel. He's excited because he's come to a new place. You don't mind dogs, do you? Miss Pepper said you took dogs.'

'I take *well-behaved* dogs,' said Mrs Glump, leading them down a twisting corridor, lined with stout old doors. 'I have a dog of my own, very well trained and most obedient.'

'What's his name?' asked Roger.

'We call him Mr Tubby, short for Three Men in a Tub,' said Mrs Glump. 'My husband's idea of a joke. It took me a very long time to see it. But now that he – the dog,

217

I mean – is old and fat, I must say that his name suits him very well.'

She went up a few more stairs and came to a small square landing, out of which opened four or five doors.'

'This is where I have put you,' she said, and opened one of the doors. 'This is the best of the rooms. Perhaps Miss Pepper would like it.'

'Oh, I *should*!' said Miss Pepper in delight. 'I once had it when I stayed here as a child. Oh, the view – it's exactly the same as it always was!'

She went to the leaded casement window and flung it wide open. The children crowded beside her.

The room looked out down a steep cliffside to the golden sands below. The sea was cornflower blue that August day, and the sound of the waves below came softly up to the window.

'Like someone sighing,' said Diana to herself. 'But I expect on a stormy day the noise of the waves would be terrific. Oh, I hope my room has the same view as this!'

It had. It was a much smaller room with a strange slanting ceiling. Big beams ran crookedly across the walls, which were whitewashed. There was almost the same view as from Miss Pepper's room, but a little farther west.

The boys pronounced their room to be 'smashingly super,' and called Diana to see it. It was a big room with a built-in oak cupboard, an old double bed that looked as if it had once been a four-poster but had had its four upright posts taken off, and a very uneven floor that would trip the boys up hundreds of times before their visit was over!

'This place has got a lovely old *feel*,' said Diana. 'Don't you think so, boys?'

'Rather,' said Roger. 'Like Hampton Court or the Tower or somewhere frightfully old. You can feel that things have happened here for years – the walls still remember them!'

'Funny. I feel like that too,' said Snubby, rather astonished. 'And I feel this has been a happy place, too – enormous meals and things.'

'You *would* think that,' said Diana. 'If the walls could talk to you, all you'd want them to tell you about would be the meals people had downstairs.'

'I wouldn't mind having a meal now,' said Snubby. 'Do we unpack? Where's Miss Pepper?'

Miss Pepper came in to see what the boys' room was like. She immediately shooed Loony off the big bed. 'Snubby, you heard what Mrs Glump said about well-behaved dogs, didn't you?' she said. 'For goodness' sake tell Loony he can't behave here as if he was at home. Mrs Glump would have plenty to say.'

'It's a marvellous name, Glump,' said Snubby. 'Sort of gloomy and gluggy and gurgley and . . .'

'Oh, don't be *silly*, Snubby,' said Miss Pepper. 'Hurry up and unpack and come down to tea. Mrs Glump said it would be ready when you are.'

'Well, I am now,' said Snubby at once.

'No, you're not. You've got to wash yourself and brush your hair – it's like a red-haired mop – and for goodness' sake brush your shorts too. You look as if you've been scrambling about under all the carriage seats on the train.'

'I shall go all gloomy and glumpish if you scold me as soon as we get here,' complained Snubby. 'I feel glumpish already.'

Diana gave a little squeal of laughter. 'Oh, Snubby – that's a lovely word. Much better than gloomy. Do you feel down in the glumps?'

'Not really,' grinned Snubby. 'Hey, Loony, get off that bed. Didn't you hear what pepper-pot said?'

'You'll get into trouble with Miss Pepper if you begin calling her that,' said Roger. 'She won't stand cheek from you. I say, it's a shame our room doesn't look out over the sea, isn't it?'

'Yes. But it's got quite an *interesting* view,' said Snubby, looking out of the small casement window. Chimneys and roofs and other people's windows.'

It was rather a peculiar view, really. Their part of the inn was higher than the other part, and they could see across uneven roofs and into attic windows here and there. They could see tall chimneys rising up too, one of them with wisps of smoke coming out.

'I wouldn't mind exploring this roof some time,' said Snubby, washing his face vigorously. 'I'm good at exploring roofs. You never know when that kind of thing comes in useful.'

'You're an awful fathead, Snubby,' said Roger. 'Look, that dog's on the bed again. I think really it would be best to drape it with an old rug or something. I don't see *how* we're to keep Loony off it. Come on, Loony – teatime.'

They called Diana and Miss Pepper, and went down the twisting, uneven stairs, moving rather cautiously because of the sharp bends in the stairway where one side of the stairs narrowed to an inch or two. Loony, of course missed his footing and fell headlong down, bouncing merrily from stair to stair.

'Can't you behave, Loony!' hissed Snubby. '*WHAT* will Mr Tubby think of you?'

Chapter Five

After Tea

They had tea in the dining-room of the inn. This was a large, rather dark room, with heavy oak beams across the ceilings and walls. It had a colossal fireplace, now filled with foxgloves, and an amazing number of doors, all polished oak.

Snubby saw that the tea was good and fell upon it ravenously. New brown bread and butter and home-made damson jam disappeared down his throat without stopping.

'You're a greedy pig, Snubby,' said Diana. 'You get worse instead of better. I say, isn't this a heavenly room? It's got stags' heads all round, and big glass cases of fish. And look at those funny old prints – and did you ever see such a selection of horse-brasses hanging down each side of the mantelpiece?'

'Horse-brasses?' said Snubby, pausing in his munching. 'I say – I collect those. I must have a look at them and see if there are any I haven't got.'

'Ass! You've got about nine, that's all, and there must be seventy or eighty there,' said Diana. 'Look at that old clock, too, Snubby. It's enormous.'

It was an old grandfather clock, the biggest the children had ever seen in their lives. It almost reached the ceiling, and its tick was so loud that it could be heard all over the room – TICK-TOCK, TICK-TOCK. When five o'clock came it burst into the loudest dong-dong-dongs that the children had ever heard, except from Big Ben. It was quite deafening.

'Miss Pepper, is everything just like it was when you

came here as a child?' asked Roger. 'Was that clock there then? Do you remember it?'

'Oh yes – and I remember someone hiding inside the big pendulum case at the bottom once, and frightening the life out of me by growling inside there like a dog,' said Miss Pepper rashly. Snubby had already pricked up his ears at this idea, of course.

'That's a smashing idea,' he said at once. 'I'll remember that.'

'No, don't,' said Miss Pepper, with a groan. 'Please, Snubby, behave yourself here. I'm almost sure I knew Mrs Glump as a child, and I don't want her to put you down as a lot of hooligans and think that I can't manage you all.'

'Gosh – did you really know Mrs Glump when she was a girl?' asked Snubby in wonder. 'Was she older than you?'

'About the same age,' said Miss Pepper. 'She was a funny shy little girl then. See – what was her name now – oh yes – Gloria.'

'Gloria Glump!' exclaimed Diana, in delight. 'It can't be true.'

'Sh!' said Miss Pepper, afraid that Mrs Glump might hear Diana. 'She wasn't Glump then. Her name was Gloria Tregonnan, as far as I remember. Her family have had this inn for hundreds of years, so it's said.'

Mrs Glump suddenly appeared at the door. 'Have you enough tea?' she inquired in her ponderous voice. 'Oh dear – why, there's hardly anything left. Er – shall I send in some more?'

'No, thank you,' said Miss Pepper, feeling suddenly certain that a good part of the tea had gone under the table to a ravenous Loony. That must have been why he had been so very quiet! She frowned at Snubby, who was just opening his mouth to protest that *he* could do with some more to eat. He shut it again.

'Now, while I unpack, you can go and explore the beach,' she said. 'And if it's wet, please tie your sandshoes round your neck. You hear me, Snubby?'

They rushed off. Miss Pepper poured herself out another cup of tea and drank it quietly. Mrs Glump reappeared.

'Handful, aren't they?' she said sympathetically. 'My, children aren't what they were in our day, are they? We had to be seen and not heard.'

'They're not bad children at all,' said Miss Pepper loyally. 'A bit high-spirited at times. Are you very full now, Mrs Glump – many visitors here?'

'Well, we're not over-full at the moment,' said Mrs Glump. 'There's a big new hotel built down in the town now, you know – near to the pier – and that's taken a lot of my custom away. We're old-fashioned here at Three Men in a Tub, and a bit out of the way.'

Miss Pepper looked at one or two tables with napkins folded by the plates, and dishes of fruit. 'You seem to have a few visitors besides ourselves,' she said.

'Oh yes – I've two or three of the pierrots staying here,' said Mrs Glump. 'There's a very good pierrot show on the pier every night, you know. They call themselves "The Rubadub Rollicks," whatever that may mean. "Come to the Rubadub Rollicks for a Rollicking Show," is on posters all over the place.'

'Oh, the children will like to go and see them,' said Miss Pepper. 'Is there a funny man?'

'Oh yes – very funny,' said Mrs Glump. 'They'll love him. He's staying here, as a matter of fact. And there's a conjurer too – strange thing to have in a pierrot show, but he goes down quite well, I believe. He's here too – and Miss Iris Nightingale, the singer from the show. That's not her real name, of course, she chose it because it's a good name for a singer.'

'You've got some quite interesting people,' said Miss Pepper, enjoying the chat. 'Anyone else?'

'Well, there's an old fellow called Professor James,' said Mrs Glump. 'I would like you to warn the children not to upset him, please, Miss Pepper. He doesn't like dogs, not even my well-trained Mr Tubby. He's rather deaf, and he's got a very hot temper.'

Miss Pepper made a mental note to warn all the children, especially Snubby, and to keep Loony strictly under control when Professor James was about.

'And there's Miss Twitt,' said Mrs Glump. 'That's the lot. She's all right, but she's what I call a *gusher*. Gushes over children and dogs and cats and the pretty butterflies and the darling birds, and all that. I wouldn't want the children to laugh at her.'

'Oh dear!' thought Miss Pepper. 'I hope they won't. I'll have to give them quite a talking to tonight.'

She told Mrs Glump how, long ago, she had known her as a shy little girl, and the innkeeper's wife nodded her head in pleasure. Well, well – to think she and Miss Pepper had known each other as girls!

'The inn is very little changed!' said Miss Pepper. 'I shall love being here again!'

She went up to unpack. She looked at the glorious view from the little window and sat down to enjoy it. It all looked so very peaceful and serene! What a lovely quiet part of the world this was!

Just as she got up again, a muffled explosion shook the inn. Miss Pepper sat down again suddenly, feeling scared. What in the world was that?

She went out on the landing, feeling alarmed. Dummy was there, carrying somebody's case. He grinned shyly at her.

'What was that awful noise?' asked Miss Pepper.

'Boom-boom-boom,' said Dummy, delighted. He put

down the case with a crash that made Miss Pepper jump. 'BOOM!' he said, and did it again.

'Don't' said Miss Pepper. 'I just wanted to know what made that loud noise.'

Dummy took Miss Pepper by the arm and led her to a little door. Behind it was a stairway. It led steeply upwards. He went up it and beckoned Miss Pepper. In surprise, she followed. The staircase led up to the roof, through a small trap-door which had a piece of glass set in it, like a small skylight.

'Boom-boom,' said Dummy softly, pulling Miss Pepper beside him, their heads sticking out of the skylight trap-door.

She was now so high that she was almost on a level with the top of the cliff behind the hotel, where it suddenly slanted downwards. There was a deep cleft in it at one place, and the skylight opening looked directly through the cleft to the sea on the other side of the cliff.

It was surprising to see right over the cliff to the sea away on the other side. Miss Pepper gazed curiously. She remembered that the Secret Submarine base was somewhere over there, closely guarded on all sides, land and sea. Experiments, top-secret experiments, went on there. Perhaps the muffled explosion she had heard came from one of these experiments.

'Booooom-ooom!' The far-away noise made her jump again. Before the noise came she had seen a little cloud of either smoke or spray rising from the sea on the other side of the cliff. The noise made her certain it was an explosion of some sort.

'Boom-boom,' said Dummy, who seemed quite unable to say anything else, pointing and grinning.

'Yes. Very interesting. Thank you, Dummy_____ M____ Pepper. Dummy gave her his engaging side____ and his bright blue eyes looked shyly at her.

him on the arm. What a peculiar little man he was – more like a gnome or brownie than a human being!

She made up her mind to tell the children what she had seen when they came home. They would be thrilled! She went to unpack once more, humming. The weeks seemed to stretch away before her, full of sunshine and walks and reading, and looking after three interesting madcaps of children.

They were having a lovely time by themselves. They had explored the sandy beach, which was studded with hundreds of pinkish shells. They had climbed a few rocks, and Snubby had slipped into a pool and sat down heavily. Now he dripped water wherever he went.

They went down the promenade, and came to the pier, where they examined all the notices.

' "Come to the Rubadub Rollicks for a Rollicking Show," ' said Roger, reading the biggest poster, "I say, we ought to go and see them. I love pierrots. Look, it says there's a conjurer too. Matthew Marvels. We'll have to go and see *him*!'

They examined the photographs of the twelve pierrots. The children thought they looked fine.

'So long as the girls don't *sing* too much,' said Snubby. 'An awful waste of time when you've got a conjurer and a funny man as well. I don't mind the dancing so much – but all that singing's boring.'

'Loony's gone on the pier,' said Roger suddenly. 'Loony, come back! Loony, Loony!'

Loony was halfway down the pier. He took absolutely no notice of the shouts. He had smelt an enticing fishy smell somewhere at the end of the pier and he was going to examine it if it was very last thing he did.

'We'll have to spend tuppence and fetch him,' said Snubby in disgust. 'Anyone got tuppence?'

'Yes. *You* have!' said Roger. 'You don't get tuppence

out of me that way. Spend your own pence on your own dog.'

So Snubby had to fork out tuppence and go and yank a disappointed Loony out of a pile of decaying fish at the very end of the pier.

'Can't you hear the seagulls yelling at you, idiot?' said Snubby severely. 'That's put there for them. What a dog you are! Can't even understand the rude names the gulls are calling you!'

Chapter Six

The Other Guests

They got back to the inn about seven o'clock. Miss Pepper had said they must be in by then because the inn served dinner, and everyone was expected to come in on time for that.

'You *are* nice and early,' she said, hearing them come up on the landing, and going to her door to greet them. 'Did you have a good look round?'

'Rather! It's a super place,' said Roger. 'Did you hear any bangs, Miss Pepper? We did, and a man told us they were from the Secret Submarine base. He says it's very hush-hush. I wish we could see over it.'

'People don't see over hush-hush places,' said Miss Pepper. 'You might know that. Look, as you're in so early, I'll show you something. Dummy showed it to *me*.'

She led the way to the door behind which was the little staircase. They all went up it wonderingly. Wherever did it lead to? Roger gave an exclamation when he reached the top and pushed up the trap-door to peer out.

'My word – we can see the Secret Base through that cleft in the cliff! How exciting!'

'Let me see!' said Snubby impatiently. 'Di, do pull ̇ ̣ ̣ ̣ down. He's pawing so hard at my shorts he'll make where ̣ ̣ ̣ ̣ ̣. Gosh, Roger – what a view! I say, is that 'Yes. I ̣ ̣ ̣ ̣ ̣ came from, Miss Pepper?'

must have bee ̣ ̣ ̣ ̣ smoke – or spray, I think it 'I shall sit up ̣ ̣ ̣ ̣ ̣ ne,' said Miss Pepper.

announced Snubby ̣ ̣ ̣ ̣ he third one,'

'No, you won't. You'll just come straight away down now,' said Miss Pepper.

They all climbed down the little wooden stairway and went out of the door at the bottom, on to the landing. A man was just coming up to it from the lower stairs. He was a tall, thin man, with a long, cadaverous face, and deep-set, rather staring eyes. He looked in surprise at the children coming down the little stairway.

They stared back at him. Diana didn't like his eyes. She thought they seemed to look right through her, and she shivered. Who was he?

'Good evening,' said Miss Pepper politely. She thought he must be one of the other guests.

'Good evening,' said the man shortly, opened the door and disappeared into his room. He shut the door with a soft click.

Miss Pepper thought over the guests that Mrs Glump had told her about, and came to the conclusion that the man could only be one of the pierrots who was staying there. Surely he wasn't the funny man, the comedian of the party? He didn't look as if he had ever laughed in his life. Then it must be Mr Matthew Marvels, the conjurer. Well, he certainly looked more like a conjurer than a comedian!

'That must be Mr Glooomp,' whispered Snubby with a giggle. 'Didn't he look the picture of gloom? Lost a shilling and found a farthing, I should think.'

'Hurry up and change into something clean.' said Miss Pepper. 'And do remember that you have dinner, not supper, and are supposed to look _kind_ of place? and tidy, and must put on _we fell in a rock-pool._'

'Oh dear,' gro___d Miss Pepper, 'Snubby bring Anyway, ___

me your shorts to dry when you've changed into clean, dry ones.'

When the gongs boomed out over the house, the three children were all ready. Loony was too. 'I've brushed him and washed the sand off him' said Snubby, proudly. 'He looks fine, doesn't he? I want him to make a very good impression on Mr Tubby Dog.'

They were the first down in the dining-room. A most appetising smell of tomato soup came from the kitchen. Snubby sniffed loudly, and then caught Miss Pepper's eye.

A very portly dog waddled into the dining-room. He was enormous – a bull-mastiff with a most gloomy and lugubrious face, wrinkles and folds of flesh hanging down his cheeks.

'This must be Mr Tubby,' said Snubby, eyeing the big dog with awe. 'I say – look at his wrinkles. Good evening, Mr Tubby, let me introduce you to Loony. Mr Tubby – Mr Loony.'

'Woof,' said Loony, scared but polite.

'Grrrrr,' said Mr Tubby, and lifted the skin from his top teeth in a horrifying manner. Loony backed hurriedly into a waiter who was bringing in the soup.

Mr Tubby walked to a rug by the fireplace and subsided there gradually, with a few rather human-sounding groans. He eyed everyone with a superior and contemptuous air, looking extremely miserable. Then he laid his great head on his paws and let out a sigh that blew along the floor like a draught.

...gazed at Mr Tubby in awe. What a dog! What decided to... a dog! Loony felt extremely small and by's feet.

The waiter laid half. He lay down heavily on Snub-one. They had just b...

...up in front of every-
...guests walked

into the room. Miss Pepper glanced at them, recognising them from Mrs Glump's description.

Mr Marvels the conjurer came first. He was the man they had met on the landing. Then came a man with a comical face, ears that stuck out and a broad smile. He winked across at the children, and joked with the waiter. He must be the funny man, decided Miss Pepper.

Then came a pretty girl of about twenty, who sat at the table with the conjurer and the funny man. She must be Iris Nightingale, the singer.

Finally came an old man with a beard, and a middle-aged lady fluttering with scarfs and bits of chiffon, and with a bow in her over-curled hair.

'Professor James – and Miss Twitt,' thought Miss Pepper, drinking her soup. The children stared round at all the newcomers.

'Now,' said the Professor, stopping just inside the room. 'Where's that dog? Nowhere near my table, I hope.'

Mr Tubby didn't even deign to raise his head. Professor James stared at him with dislike and Mr Tubby stared back sorrowfully and contemptuously.

'Ha! There you are!' said Professor James, advancing to his table. 'Well, keep on the rug. Waiter, what soup is it?'

'Tomato, sir,' said the waiter, a bright-eyed youth who had already exchanged a few winks with the irrepressible Snubby.

'What's that? Speak up, my man,' said the Professor. 'Everyone mumbles nowadays.'

'Tomato, sir,' said the waiter, a little more loudly.

'Bless the man – can't hear a word!' said the old fellow.

'He said "TOMATO," ' said Snubby helpfully at the top of his voice. Everyone jumped violently including the Professor.

'Who's shouting?' said the Professor angrily. 'Enough to deafen anyone!' He glared around at the children's table. Snubby got ready to confess at the top of his voice that it was he who had shouted, but Miss Pepper frowned so hard at him that he desisted.

'I should like some more tomato soup,' he said in his normal voice.

A little laugh came to their ears. It was from Miss Twitt, who was sitting at the next table. She leaned over to Miss Pepper, one or two necklaces and bracelets jingling merrily.

'Isn't he *sweet*? Trying to be so helpful! And how nice to see such a healthy appetite!'

Snubby looked so completely horrified at being called 'sweet' that Roger and Diana had to laugh.

'Such nice-looking children,' gushed Miss Twitt. 'Are you their mother?'

'No. I am merely in charge of them' said Miss Pepper, politely but coldly. Miss Twitt was the kind of person to avoid, she could see! She would rapidly drive the children to rudeness. 'My name is Pepper, Miss Pepper.'

'And mine is Twitt. Miss Twitt,' was the reply. 'We'll have to get together, Miss Pepper, when these rascals are safely in bed. I do *so* love children, don't you? *And* dogs, of course. Dear creatures!'

Loony decided to see who this gushing, talkative person was, and he appeared from below the table. This was the signal for a fresh outburst from Miss Twitt.

'Oh, the darling! Oh, I *do* love cockers! Come to me, my pet. I'll take you walky-walkies one day, shall I?'

Loony gave her one disgusted look and retired under the table. Mr Tubby gave what sounded remarkably like a snigger, got up very slowly, and lay down on his rug with his back to Miss Twitt.

'And what are the children's names?' went on Miss Twitt, who could apparently talk and swallow hot soup at one and the same time. 'What's the little girl's name?'

'I'm Diana. And I'm not a little girl,' said Diana. 'You sound as if you think I'm six!'

'I'm Roger,' said Roger gruffly.

'And I'm Snubby, Miss Twitter,' suddenly beamed Snubby. Diana gave a giggle.

'My name is Twitt, not Twitter,' said Miss Twitt. 'And how do you like Rubadub, children? Such a very quaint name, I always feel!'

'Yes, so *twee*, Miss Twitter,' began Snubby. 'Oh, what pretty dinky beads you wear, Miss Twitter.'

'Snubby,' said Miss Pepper, in such a fierce voice that he subsided at once. Miss Twitt looked at her in surprise.

'Get on with your meal, children, and don't let me hear another word,' said Miss Pepper, afraid of the effect Miss Twitt would have on them if they entered into any lengthy conversation.

Snubby was really scared when Miss Pepper's voice took on a certain tone. He began on a plate of cold chicken and ham and salad, unusually silent.

'Please, mayn't we talk now?' asked Diana after a while. 'If we just talk to one another, I mean?'

Miss Twitt was now having an animated conversation with the funny man, who played up to her valiantly. Miss Pepper judged it was safe to let the three children use their tongues.

'Very well. But I've warned you,' she said. 'Don't go into the lounge after supper, please. Leave it to the other guests.'

'Right. We'll all go for a walk then,' said Roger. '*I* don't want to go into the lounge.'

None of them did. Oh dear, thought Miss Pepper, this was going to be rather a *difficult* holiday!

Chapter Seven

Fine News

The three children and Loony set off once more for a quick walk. Miss Pepper had said it must only be a short one, as it was getting late. It was still light, of course – but as they turned down to the promenade they saw one of the buildings along it blazing with lights.

'It's a kind of fair,' said Roger. 'Let's go and have a squint at it.'

'Oooh – it's got those Dodgem Cars,' said Diana, thrilled. 'Do you remember, we once had rides in them when somebody took us to a Play Camp. You kept crashing into me, Roger.'

'Let's have a go now,' said Snubby at once. But no one had any money on them, so they could only stand and watch. It was a very small fair – it could really hardly even be called that. There were automatic machines standing round the wall, where you could lose any amount of pennies. There was a stall to buy ice-cream and candy-floss. There was a machine that played tunes if you put money into it – loud, blaring tunes that never seemed to stop!

'A juke-box,' said Snubby, airing his knowledge. He looked at the list of tunes on it. 'Oh look – it can play twenty different tunes. How super! I wish they had one of these at the inn.'

'Goodness – Professor James would have a blue fit!' said Diana.

'Yes – he'd go up in smoke at once,' agreed Roger. 'So would Mrs Glump, I should think. Pity we haven't any money tonight.'

'I don't believe Miss Pepper will let us come here much,' said Diana, looking at the people who were swarming in. 'They look a pretty rough lot, some of them.'

A good many sailors had come in, and were climbing into the Dodgem cars with yells and whistles. One of them lurched roughly against Diana.

Roger immediately took his sister out of the place. He had been taught always to look after her, and he suddenly thought that this place wasn't right for Diana to be in at night.

'Here – where are you going, Roger?' asked Snubby in surprise. 'We've only just come.'

'Well, we're going,' said Roger. 'Come on. Let's go and see if the pierrots have begun their show.'

They must have begun because a sound of very sweet singing came down the pier as the three children stood at the turnstiles. 'That's Iris Nightingale,' said Snubby. 'I bet it is. I thought she looked sweet.'

'Snubby's lost his heart to her!' said Diana. '*I* thought the Funny Man was the nicest of the three. I loved the way his ears stuck out – they were rather pointed too – like a brownie's!'

A sound of a banjo being played now came from the pier – jig-jig-jig-jiggy-jig-jig-jig! Snubby at once pretended he, too, had a banjo and began to play it earnestly, making a peculiar noise through his teeth as he did so.

'Oh stop it, Snubby,' said Roger. 'I suppose you think you're very funny.'

'Well, I do rather,' said Snubby, still going on with his banjo playing. 'Everyone roars when I play my banjo at school – a pretend one, of course. I can play the zither too – listen!'

He pretended to be holding a zither, and twanged the strings with much feeling, imitating the sound of a zither as he did so. He really did it very well.

A man strolling down the pier suddenly stopped and

listened. He was dressed in pierrot clothes and had obviously left the show for a breath of air. He watched Snubby with amusement.

'Hey there!' he called. 'Aren't you the kids at the inn? You're not bad at that fooling, youngster. Why don't you go in for our kids' competition each week – I bet you'd win it!'

Snubby stopped his imitation of a zither, and grinned at the man. 'I didn't recognise you in your pierrot get-up,' he said. 'You're the Funny Man, aren't you?'

The man suddenly waggled his big ears, which startled the children considerably. He also made a most peculiar face which Snubby immediately longed to copy.

'Yes, I'm the Funny Man,' he said. 'But it isn't always funny to be funny. I get bored, you know.'

He did a few ridiculous dancing steps on the pier, fell over his feet and sat down suddenly with a surprised grin. The children roared, and Loony nearly went mad trying to get off the lead and streak through the turnstiles.

'You know, we have fun in these kids' competitions,' he said, getting up in one quick movement. 'Anyone can go in for them. Five bob prize for the best girl, five bob for the best boy. You ought to come along and try. It doesn't matter what you do – dance, sing, conjure, play the fool. That young fellow there would win the prize for playing the fool in no time!'

He nodded at Snubby, who didn't quite know whether to take this as a compliment or not!

'Snubby's *always* playing the fool,' said Roger. 'It's the one thing he really works hard at. Isn't it, Snubby!'

Snubby gave Roger a punch. The man grinned and turned to go. The dance music had stopped and he was due back in his place. He threw his cigarette over the side of the pier.

'So long!' he said. 'See you in the morning at the dear

old inn and Ma Glump seeing that we all use our knives and forks properly, and don't speak with our mouths full.'

'Makes you feel quite in the glumps, doesn't it?' said Snubby, remembering the joke he had made before. The Funny Man laughed.

'You ought to come and be my partner,' he said. 'The Funny Man and the Scream of a Boy. So long!'

He went quickly up the pier. Snubby stared after him. He wasn't sure whether the man thought he, Snubby, really was funny or whether he was just making fun of him.

'Showing off!' said Roger to Snubby, in a tone of disgust. 'How you can show off like that I don't know, Snubby. Come on – it's getting late. Miss Pepper will be sending out a search party soon!'

They went back to the inn. Miss Pepper met them at the door. 'Roger! Diana! Who do you think has just telephoned?'

'Who?' asked everyone at once.

'Barney!' said Miss Pepper.

'BARNEY!' said all three children in delight. 'Is he anywhere near then?'

'Come in and I'll tell you what he said,' said Miss Pepper. She took them into the lounge which was now empty.

'I was sitting here,' she said, 'when Mrs Glump came and said there was a Mr Barnabas on the telephone for you – but would I like to go instead. I couldn't think who Mr Barnabas was at first!

'I went, and it was Barney, of course,' said Miss Pepper. 'He's been ill. He sounded very lonely indeed, and I think he was longing to get in touch with the only friends he's got – you three. He gave me a telephone number and said would you ring him when you came in. It's a call box and he's waiting there now.'

'Quick – we'll telephone this very minute,' said Diana.

'What's the number? Dear old Barney! I'd so love to see him again!'

Miss Pepper gave them the number and they rushed off the the hotel telephone. Barney! How lovely! If only he was somewhere near and could come to Rubadub!

Barney was their circus-boy friend. They had met him by accident, with Miranda, his clever little monkey – and had been firm friends ever since. He was all alone in the world, and kept himself by taking jobs in circuses and fairs. Now he had been ill – he was lonely. The three children longed to ask him all his news.

Roger and the others crowded into the little telephone box. Roger rang the number. Barney's voice answered at once. 'Hallo! Is that you, Roger?'

'Hallo, Barney! Where are you? I hear you've been ill. Are you all right again? How's Miranda?'

'She's fine,' said Barney. 'I got a chill or something – sleeping under a hedge in the rain. I had to lie up in a barn for a week or two – and Miranda looked after me!'

'Good old Miranda!' said Roger, having a mental vision of the little monkey sponging Barney's face, and bringing him cups of water to drink! 'Where are you, Barney? How did you know we were here?'

'I telephoned your home,' said Barney. 'Your cook told me. Listen – I can get a lift almost to your place tomorrow. Just a stroke of luck. I've been a bit lonely lately – that chill, I suppose.'

It was so unlike Barney to admit that he felt lonely that Roger knew at once he must be feeling very miserable. He remembered how he had felt when he had the 'flu in the spring – and he had been surrounded by people eager to help and comfort him. Barney had had nobody but Miranda!

'You come down here,' urged Roger at once. 'Come and stay at our inn. Oh, wait though – I'm sure Mrs Glump wouldn't have Miranda. Blow!'

'I can't possibly come and stay where you are,' said Barney at once. 'For one thing, I've no money and for another, they wouldn't have me there. But I can find some kind of a job, I'm sure, and I can always sleep on the beach in this fine weather. I'd like that.'

'All right. Anyway – *COME*,' said Roger. 'We'll be on the look-out for you. Oh, Barney, how super to have you here! Give our love to darling Miranda! Loony will be thrilled to see her.'

'I'll come,' said Barney. 'Goodbye, Roger.' There was a click in Roger's ear as the telephone receiver was put down at Barney's end. Roger put his down too. The others immediately plied him with questions.

Roger squeezed out of the box with the other two pressing on him, so eager to hear what he had to say that they couldn't wait to get out of the box properly.

They all went into the lounge, where Miss Pepper was waiting for them. Roger told them word for word what Barney had said.

'So he'll be here in Rubadub tomorrow,' he said exultantly. 'Good old Barney! It will be grand to see him again, and Miranda too.'

'Smashing,' said Snubby, who was very fond of the sturdy, self-reliant Barney, and his amusing mischievous little monkey.

'Now go to bed, please,' said Miss Pepper, who was longing to go herself. 'And please *do* be down in time for breakfast!'

Chapter Eight

Dear Old Barney

The children slept so soundly that they didn't even hear the loud breakfast gong. Miss Pepper came bustling into their rooms just after it went, only half-dressed, with her dressing-gown still on!

'Wake up, do!' she said. 'I've overslept as well. Dear me, we shall make a very bad impression on Mrs Glump if we are so late the first morning. Can you be very quick?'

'No,' said Snubby sleepily, and turned over.

'Barney may be here at any time,' said Miss Pepper artfully.

Snubby shot out of bed at once. 'I'd forgotten old Barney,' he said. Miss Pepper left the boys dressing quickly, made sure that Diana was also getting up, and went to finish her own dressing. They were so late that only Miss Twitt was in the lounge!

She greeted them beamingly. 'You poor things! Did you oversleep? The dear children must have been so tired – and the dear dog too!'

The dear dog was not in the least tired. He trotted up to Miss Twitt, removed her napkin from her knee and made off with it. It was a silly trick he had picked up, most annoying to everyone. Miss Twitt gave a little squeal.

'Oh, naughty, naughty! Bring it back then.'

'LOONY!' roared Snubby, in his most stentorian voice. 'BRING IT HERE!'

Miss Twitt almost fell out of her chair at this roar, and the noise brought the contemptuous-looking Mr Tubby to the door. He gazed in inquiringly, looking more miserable than ever, with his baggy wrinkles falling over his doggy face. Loony backed away from him and dropped the napkin. Mr Tubby sniffed at it, picked it up and took it to his rug. He lay down heavily on it, creaking and groaning.

'There, Loony! He'll take *you* next and drop you on his rug and lie down on you,' threatened Snubby, hoping that he wouldn't have to go and rescue Miss Twitt's napkin from the formidable Mr Tubby.

'Dear Mr Tubby,' gushed Miss Twitt. 'Isn't he a *remarkable* dog? I do love dogs, don't you, Miss Pepper? I love cats, too, the dear dainty things!'

'You'd like our cat Sardine then, Miss Twitter,' began Snubby. 'She likes to trip people on the stairs in a very dainty way. Oh, and Miss Twitter, you'd love a monkey that belongs to a friend of ours.'

'Yes, dear, I'm sure I should,' said Miss Twitt. 'But my name is Twitt, not Twitter.'

'I just *can't* remember,' said Snubby, deliberately not looking towards Miss Pepper, who was wearing a fierce and warning frown. 'It reminds me of a song I know – twit-twit-twitter little bird – something like that anyway. I do so *love* birds, don't you, Miss Twitter. I think they're sweet.'

'Snubby, will you go and get me a handkerchief, please,' said Miss Pepper desperately. How could she stop this awful chatter of Snubby's? It was sending Diana into helpless giggles, and Roger was grinning from ear to ear. Even Miss Pepper, angry as she was, couldn't help thinking that Miss Twitt deserved to have fun poked at her – how very, very silly she was! Twittering away like that.

Snubby gave a surprised glance at Miss Pepper. ''Tisn't often you forget *your* handkerchief,' he remarked. He caught her eye and decided to say no more. He went meekly off and returned with a handkerchief. Miss Twitt beamed and looked as if she was about to make a remark about helpful little boys. Miss Pepper charged in desperately before she could say a word.

'I wonder when Barney will arrive, Roger. Did he say any time? We must look out for him.'

This was such an interesting theme of conversation that all three immediately forgot about Miss Twitt, and she soon left her table and went out of the room with a swish of skirts, a rattle of bracelets and a sudden waft of rather strong perfume.

'Pooh!' said Snubby. 'What's that awful smell?'

Miss Pepper took the opportunity of explaining very clearly and concisely to Snubby exactly what she thought of discourtesy and impoliteness, and threatened such dreadful things that Snubby sank back in his chair, amazed.

'I say!' he said feebly. 'I'm sorry. She kind of sets me off, you know, with her twittering. She's too good to be true. Miss Pepper, you don't really mean to say you'd make me go without cake for a whole week, and only let me have one helping of anything? You couldn't be so cruel.'

'I could and I shall,' said Miss Pepper severely. 'I will not have rudeness even if you mean it to be funny rudeness. Now, finish up that toast and marmalade for goodness' sake. I don't want to sit here till dinner-time.'

They all bathed that morning. The water was warm, and although there was little wind, there were very satisfactory waves some way out to dive through.

'I like to cut through a wave just as it's breaking,' said Diana. 'It spills its green colour all over me. I say – it's going to be super here, isn't it?'

They kept a look-out for Barney and Miranda, but they didn't appear that morning. They all went on the beach in the afternoon to read and laze. The sun shone down on them and they began to turn a lobster red. They were all in swimsuits and Miss Pepper thought they would feel very uncomfortable if they got much more burnt!

'Loony wishes he could take off his coat and wear a swim suit too,' said Diana, patting the panting dog. 'Hasn't he got a long tongue when he hangs it out? Do you want an ice cream, Loony?'

'Woof,' said Loony at once, scrambling up. 'Ice cream' was one of the words he understood very well! But as everyone was too lazy to go and buy any, Loony lay down again mournfully. Fancy raising his hopes for nothing! He began to pant heavily once more, making Diana feel hotter than ever.

One by one they fell asleep in the sand. Diana lay on her back, her sun-hat fitted over her face. Roger lay on his side, curled up comfortably. Snubby lay on his tummy, and his back got redder and redder. Miss Pepper slept in a dignified manner in a deck chair, with a sunshade over her head.

Somebody came scampering over the sands. Somebody leapt right in the middle of Snubby's back and jumped up and down there, chattering. Loony gave an enormous bark and planted his front paws on Snubby's back too.

Miss Pepper woke up with a jump. Snubby woke too and yelled angrily. 'Get off, idiot! Who's that banging my back? Get off, I tell you, it's sore!'

He rolled over and somebody suddenly cuddled into his neck, making a little chattering noise of welcome.

'MIRANDA!' yelled Snubby. 'Oh, Miranda, it's you! Hey, look, Miranda's here. Where's Barney?'

The whole group then became extremely wide awake and lively. Loony went mad, of course, and raced round and round them, kicking up sand as he went. Miranda leapt from one to another, chattering and hugging and snuggling.

Snubby stood up and looked along the promenade. He

saw a figure he recognised at once. 'Barney! Barney, here we are! Come on, Barney!'

By this time every one on the beach was aware that a boy with a monkey had arrived, and was being loudly welcomed by his friends! Barney jumped down from the promenade and made his way over the sand, grinning. Diana flew to meet him.

'Barney! You've come! Oh, Barney, you've gone thin!'

Barney sat down with his friends, his face beaming. His strange, wide-set eyes were as brilliantly blue as ever and his corn-coloured hair was the same thick mop. His wide mouth smiled happily as he looked from one to another of his friends.

'It's grand to see you,' he said. 'It seems ages since May when we were at Ring O'Bells together. And now we're at Rubadub-on-Sea! You're looking fine, all of you.'

'You've been ill, poor Barney,' said Diana. 'You look thin and you're not as brown as usual.'

'Oh, I'm better now,' said Barney. 'Miranda looked after me, as I told you. I got a chill, I think – sleeping in the rain. I lay in a barn and coughed for days. The farmer let me be there, and Miranda fetched and carried for me! She went to the farmhouse each day and brought back the bread and stuff the farmer gave her. You should have seen her carrying mugs of milk too – never spilt a drop, did you, Miranda?'

Diana's eyes suddenly filled with tears. She could see Barney lying alone and ill with only a little monkey to see to him. How *awful* to be as alone as that – no mother, no father, no friends to rally round! Dear little Miranda – how worried and puzzled she must have been!

'You must have been awfully lonely,' said Snubby who, because he had no parents, understood a little more than the others what it meant to be on his own – though Snubby had plenty of kind relations!

'Yes. I'm not usually lonely,' said Barney. 'I wished my

mother wasn't dead. And I wished I could find my father. Just imagine having a father alive somewhere, and you don't know who he is or where he is! He doesn't know anything about me, I know – but all the same we belong, don't we?'

Miss Pepper was listening. She knew all about Barney's history, of course – how his mother, a circus-girl had married an actor, and had run away from him after three months to go back to the life she loved, in the circus. Barney had been born six months later, but she hadn't bothered to let his father know, afraid that he might want to have Barney for himself.

So Barney had grown up thinking that his father was dead – and it was only when his mother was ill that she had told him her secret – how she had run away from his father, and had never even told him about his son! But no doubt his father was alive, and Barney must look for him, she had said.

And Barney *had* looked for him, but had never found him. What was he like? Was he still an actor? He had acted in Shakespeare's plays, that was all Barney knew. If only he could find the one person who really belonged to him!

'We'll find your father for you,' said Diana, unable to bear the loneliness in Barney's voice. 'We will, we will! *SOMEHOW* there must be a way, Barney!'

Chapter Nine

Lazy Afternoon

Barney felt better at once when he had told his troubles and fears and longings to his three friends. He had brooded over them after his illness and hadn't been able to get them out of his mind.

'But now you've told us all about everything, and we'll all do our best to get things right for you, you'll feel different, won't you?' said Diana anxiously. She could never bear people to be miserable.

'I feel different already,'said Barney, half ashamed of telling his troubles. 'I shall feel a mutt tonight when I think of all I've told you.'

'Well, what's the good of having friends if you don't share your troubles?' said Roger sensibly. 'It simply means you trust us.'

'Yes. It means that all right,' said Barney. 'But *you* don't share your troubles with me – you never seem to have any. Perhaps people don't when they've got families to belong to.'

'Oh yes they do,' said Snubby feelingly. 'You wait till you get into trouble with Uncle Richard like I do – and get one of his whackings. That's trouble all right. Unfortunately I can't ask anyone to share it.'

'Don't forget that friends share their good things as well as their troubles,' said Miss Pepper. 'Seeing we're all friends together, what about sharing our tea, and a few ice-creams?'

'Golly – is it teatime already?' said Snubby, sitting up hurriedly. 'Fancy – I was so pleased at seeing old Barney, I actually forgot all about tea!'

'What a wonderful compliment to Barney,' said Diana, stroking Miranda, who was surely the happiest little monkey in the world at that moment. 'I shouldn't think anything or anybody made you forget about a meal before.'

Barney laughed. This was the sort of silly family talk he loved and never had unless he was with his three friends. All that answering back and idiotic jokes and teasing – it was lovely to him, though Miss Pepper, of course, often got tired of it.

The children had brought tea down to the beach. Mrs Glump had graciously said that she would have it packed up for them, and had supplied a quite enormous number of sandwiches, buns, slices of fruit cake and some home-made shortbread biscuits that really melted in their mouths.

'This is some tea!' said Snubby, with much appreci-ation. 'I wouldn't have thought Mrs Glump would have given us such a spread. But she's not as glumpish as she looks.'

'She probably hoped that by giving you far too much to eat at teatime, you would eat less at dinner,' remarked Miss Pepper, with amusement.

'What a hope!' said Snubby. 'It doesn't make the slight-est difference as far as I am concerned. You know I always feel frightfully sorry for you grown-ups, Miss Pepper. It must be awful never to have a really good tuck-in because you feel it might be rude or greedy.'

'You'll hate being grown-up, won't you, Snubby?' said Diana. 'No big meals. No half-dozen ice-creams one after the other. No munching of chocolate bars half the day. No . . .'

'Don't,' said Snubby in alarm. 'Come on, Barney, have another sandwich.'

But Barney's appetite was not what it once had been. Miss Pepper thought he must indeed have been very ill.

247

She wondered what he was going to do now. She wished she could have him at the inn and feed him and look after him a bit. But that was impossible. Nobody there would think of having Miranda, for one thing, and Barney would certainly not be parted from her.

Also, he was rather down-at-heel and untidy. He had does his best to look clean and neat for his friends, but he had had no money for some time, and it was impossible even to buy new sandshoes. So he wore none, and his feet were brown and bare. His shirt was torn and had no buttons, and his grey flannel trousers were patched about the knees and frayed at the ends.

But what a fine boy he was – good-looking, trustworthy, intelligent and straightforward. A boy any father could be proud of. Miss Pepper looked at Barney and sighed. She felt sure that Barney would never find his father, but she hadn't the heart to say so.

'Barney, I *wish* you could come and stay at the inn with us,' said Diana.

'I couldn't,' said Barney. You know that. Anyway, I've got myself a job.'

They all stared at him in admiration. A job already! How *did* he do it!

'What job?' asked Roger.

'Well, there's a kind of small fair in the town,' began Barney. 'With Dodgems cars and things.'

'Oh yes! We went there last night!' cried Diana. 'Have you got a job there, Barney?'

'Yes. I'm good at machinery, you know,' said Barney. 'I'm in charge of the cars – got to keep the machinery oiled and all the cars in running order and so on. It's an easy job for me. I like fairs, too – it's my life and always has been, going about with fairs and circuses!'

'Well, you'll be able to be with us quite a lot, won't you?' said Snubby eagerly. 'This fair isn't open till after tea.'

'Yes, I guess I can be with you quite a bit,' said Barney, pleased. 'I won't come to the inn, though. They'd look down their noses at me – I don't look very ship-shape at the moment. But when I've got a bit of money I'll soon spruce myself up.'

All the three wanted immediately to offer Barney every penny they had, either as a gift or as a loan – but they said nothing. Barney was surprisingly proud. It made him feel ashamed and embarrassed if they offered too much.

However, Miss Pepper had an offer to make and she made it briskly.

'There's one thing you can certainly do, Barney. Borrow a swimsuit from Roger – and while you're bathing I can sew buttons on your shirt and mend the frayed ends of your trousers. They look quite clean, so I shan't need to wash them.'

'Well – thanks,' said Barney, flushing. 'I'm not too good at doing things like that.'

Roger rushed off and fetched a swim suit from the inn. Barney went behind a rock and came out again almost immediately in Roger's bathing trunks. He handed his shirt and trousers shyly to Miss Pepper.

'Thanks a lot,' he said. 'You're really kind. Gosh, it's wonderful to be back with you all again. Loony too – mad old Loony!'

Loony's cup of joy was full and running over now that he had Barney and Miranda as well as everyone else. He raced round the beach at top speed, barked as he passed the others, dodged round Miranda, barked in her ear, and then went off again at sixty miles an hour.

'Express train act,' said Snubby. 'He'll probably be tired out in a minute and come and flop down beside Miranda – and she'll play a few of her tricks on him.'

It happened exactly as Snubby had said. Loony, quite exhausted, and panting like a train going uphill, flung himself down on the sand by the others. Miranda leapt on to his back and pulled up his big, floppy ears. Up he got and tried to shake her off, but she hung on, chattering excitedly.

Loony tore off with her, hoping to jerk her off, much to the amusement of everyone else on the beach. But Miranda stuck on, enjoying her ride immensely, bumping up and down on Loony's back as if he were a little black racehorse!

He suddenly remembered how to get rid of the annoying little monkey! He rolled over on his back and Miranda promptly sprang off, afraid of being rolled on. She scampered back to Barney and leapt into his arms before Loony could catch her.

A man came slowly up to them – a tall, thin man whom the children recognised at once. It was the conjurer belonging to the pierrot show. He had watched Miranda and Barney and an idea had suddenly struck him. He saw that Barney was dressed poorly and guessed that he had to work for his living.

'You boy,' he said, when he came up, pointing to Barney.

'Do you want a job? I'm a magician – a conjurer with the pierrot show on the pier. If you like to come there with your monkey as my assistant, I'll give you good wages. What about it, son?'

'Sorry, sir. But I've just got a job,' said Barney. 'Down with the Dodgem cars. But if it doesn't turn out well, I'll come and tell you. I've got to stay there a week though.'

The conjurer nodded and walked away. Barney turned to the others. 'Did you see his eyes?' he said. 'I bet he's a strange fellow. I guess I wouldn't like to work with those piercing eyes on me! They'd send shivers down my spine. He's the kind of fellow who can see out of the back of his head!'

'All the same, I think it's marvellous to be offered a job just like that!' said Snubby enviously. 'I bet nobody would ever offer *me* a job out of the air. I bet it would take me months to find one.'

It was a lovely lazy afternoon. Miss Pepper went for a walk about six o'clock and left the little company alone. They told Barney all about the guests at the hotel, especially Miss Twitter. They told him about the funny little hall-porter, Dummy. Barney looked up at once.

'Dummy? What's he like? Tell me.'

They described him. 'Little – with a big head and round blue eyes – a button of a mouth – and frightfully strong,' said Roger. 'He's not properly grown-up, I think – sort of half-child, half-adult. I like him. The taxi-driver told us he got into awful rages at times. Why – have you ever met him?'

'Well, it *must* be the Dummy I once knew,' said Barney. 'He was in a circus with me some years ago. He was always very fond of my mother, who was kind to him. I left the circus and never knew what became of him. Dear old Dummy! I liked him – he was really just a kind-hearted child – but he certainly could get into savage tempers. He was dangerous then, with his extraordinary strength. I've seen him pick up a man and throw him into the air!'

'Goodness!' said Roger, startled at this new light on Dummy. 'Well, you'll have to go and see if it's the Dummy you know. We'll tell him about you.'

Miss Pepper came back and called them. 'Dinner time,' she said. It was the one call that always made them hurry! 'Good-bye, Barney, see you tomorrow!' Snubby yelled. 'Look after yourself!'

Chapter Ten

A Word With Dummy

Miss Pepper wouldn't let the children go down to the little fair after dinner. 'No,' she said. 'It will be Barney's first night. He ought to have nothing to attend to but his job.'

'We shan't disturb him!' said Snubby indignantly. But Roger saw Miss Pepper's point. It wouldn't be fair on Barney when he was busy learning a new job to have three friends, to say nothing of Loony, trying to get his attention, or embarrassing him by watching him at work.

They decided to go and find Dummy and see if he knew Barney. Mrs Glump was surprised when they asked if they might talk to Dummy.

'We think we've met a friend of his,' explained Roger. 'We just want to talk to him and find out.'

'But you won't get anything out of poor old Dummy,' said Mrs Glump. 'He hardly ever says a word. He can imitate noises. Boom-boom – bang-bang – ch-ch-ch, like a train – mew-mew like a cat. But he doesn't talk.'

'Could we see him, all the same, though?' asked Roger.

'He'll be out in the back-yard,' said Mrs Glump, not very graciously. They went to the back of the dark hall, pushed open a baize-covered door, and went into a great kitchen. A door led out from there into the back-yard. It was a horrid little place, full of piled-up rubbish of all kinds, empty bottles, crates, boxes, old decaying vegetables, and a large tabby cat.

The cat immediately vaulted up to a high wall when Loony appeared. Loony, of course, felt sure he could jump the wall and began to fling himself at it madly.

Dummy was there, sweeping up the rubbish when Loony rushed into the yard, Dummy turned round and saw the children, and his face became just like an amiable child's.

'Woof-woof' he said, pointing to Loony.

'Hallo, Dummy,' said Snubby. 'We want to ask you something.'

Dummy's face clouded over. He obviously didn't like being asked questions. They confused his mind. He didn't mind being told to do things – be he couldn't bear to be asked anything. That meant he had to think of an answer.

'It's all right, Dummy,' said Diana, noticing his frown. 'We just want to tell you something. We met a friend of ours today who thinks he once knew you. A boy called Barney.'

Dummy thought hard and then shook his head. The children were disappointed.

'It can't have been the Dummy that Barney knew,' said Roger. 'And yet – Barney said he was exactly like our description of *this* Dummy!'

Diana suddenly had an idea. She turned back to Dummy, who was regarding the three children anxiously.

'Dummy,' said Diana, 'Barney had a monkey – a dear little monkey called Miranda. Do you remember *her*?'

A brilliant smile transformed Dummy's anxious face. He threw down his broom and clasped his arms together, rocking them as if he were holding some small creature.

'Monkey!' he said at last. And then with a great effort he brought out the word 'Barney.' He nodded his head up and down violently, swept with sudden memories. 'Barney, Barney, Barney,' he said. He pulled at Diana's arm. He pointed round and about as if asking where Barney was.

'He's got a job down at the little fair – where the Dodgem cars are, you know,' said Diana.

'Is good, good, good,' said Dummy in a transport of

delight. Then he caught sight of Mrs Glump at one of the windows and snatched up his broom again. He began to sweep wildly, sending the rubbish here, there and everywhere.

'Come on – we'd better go. We've excited him so much that he won't be able to sweep anything up properly if we don't go away,' said Roger. 'I wonder what time he goes off duty. I bet he'll go straight down to the fair to find Barney.'

'I do like Dummy,' said Diana. 'I'm sure he'd be able to talk all right if people were kind to him.'

'I'm going to be very nice to him to make up for all the people who probably haven't,' announced Snubby, rather fiercely. 'I like him too. He reminds me a bit of Loony – sort of faithful and loyal and all that.'

'He's not a *bit* like Loony,' said Diana. 'Loony's crazy! Look at him now, still thinking he can jump over that wall. Loony, come here. That cat is laughing at you.'

They disappeared through the kitchen door, and came out in the hall. It was dark there. They debated what to do.

'Let's see if there's anyone in the lounge,' said Snubby. 'If it's empty we might go in and play cards. But if Miss Twitter's there I shall run for miles!'

Miss Twitter wasn't there. But Professor James was. Fortunately, however, he was fast asleep in the big arm-chair. 'We could bring our cards here and just play a *quiet* game for half an hour,' said Diana. 'He's asleep – and besides he's deaf. He probably won't hear a single sound.'

Roger fetched the cards. They sat down round a little table to play, and Roger dealt out the cards. He glanced round at the old Professor to see if he was soundly asleep. If he still was, they could talk in normal voices.

They played two games and then gathered up the cards, wondering if there was time for more. Snubby remembered the little stairway up to the roof, where a view could be got of the sea on the other side of the cliff.

'I wish we could get out of that skylight, walk across the roof to the cliff, and then sit down in that cleft to see the Secret Submarine Base,' he said. 'We might spot something quite interesting.'

'We shouldn't,' said Roger. 'It's too far away. It's a funny little staircase, isn't it? I wonder what it was first used for – I mean – it doesn't seem to serve any useful purpose.'

'There used to be smugglers here in the old days,' said Snubby. 'Miss Pepper told me. I wouldn't be surprised if that old staircase up to that roof had some use then – you know – signalling that a smuggling ship had come in.'

'Or it might have been used by wreckers,' said Diana. 'The men who used to send ships on to rocks by wrong signals, so that they could make money out of the wreck.'

'Horrible creatures!' said Snubby. 'I can't understand people like that.'

'You might have done it yourself if you'd lived in those days,' said Diana.

'I would not,' said Snubby, raising his voice. 'How can you say such a thing?'

Roger was listening idly, flipping the cards in his hands. He happened to glance into a mirror opposite him, which clearly reflected the old Professor, who was in a chair a little way behind him.

Had he got his eyes open? It looked exactly as if he had! It looked as if he were wide awake – and yet he hadn't said a word to stop them playing or talking! Roger turned quickly – but no, the old man's eyes were fast shut.

Roger was puzzled. Had he been mistaken? It really had looked as if the reflection showed the old man with his eyes open – why should he pretend to be asleep?

The other two were still arguing. Snubby was angry – how could Diana think he would ever be a wrecker?

'Don't shout,' said Diana. 'You'll waken the old man.'

'I don't care,' said Snubby rudely. 'I just wish Loony would jump on him and give him a fright. It's awful for a dog to have to lie as still as a mouse under a table!'

Roger looked into the mirror again. There – he was *sure* the old man had his eyes open again! He was looking at Roger's back, listening to what was being said about him.

Roger turned round quickly – but again the old man's eyes were closed there too. He was puzzled. Why was he pretending to be asleep? Just to listen while they went on talking? But then, he was deaf, wasn't he? What was the point then?

Roger gave it up. If an old gentleman liked to pretend he was deaf and asleep, and listen like a sneak to what others were saying, then he could get on with it.

He suddenly determined to find out for certain if the old man was deaf – and asleep. He leaned across the table, and winked at the others. They knew something was up, and looked at him expectantly.

'Listen,' said Roger in a sinister sort of voice. 'There's no one about except that old fellow there, who is deaf and fast asleep. We can have a few words about What We Know.'

'Aha, yes,' said Snubby, wondering what was up but quite prepared to fall in with any silly game of Roger's. 'About the Man Who Whispers, you mean. And the one with the False Passport.'

'That's it,' hissed Roger. 'Once we find out their Password, we can get going. We must look out for a man in disguise.'

'Yes. But you can tell him by one of his little fingers – it's crooked,' said Snubby, remembering one of the naval men he had seen on the train and putting him into his silly story.

Diana stared open-mouthed at the two boys. What in the world was all this? Had they gone mad?

Roger looked hurriedly into the mirror. The old man's eyes were wide open. He was certainly listening now. Well, much good it would do him! If he began believing all they said it would give him a lot to think about!

A voice came in at the door, making them all jump violently. It was Miss Pepper.

'Haven't you gone upstairs *yet*! Oh dear – is that the Professor there? I didn't see him at first or I wouldn't have spoken so loudly.

'It's all right,' said Roger, getting up. 'He's fast asleep!'

Chapter Eleven

More About Barney

Next day was rather exciting. For one thing, Barney had discovered that Dummy *was* the old friend he had once known. He was very pleased about it.

They all met down on the beach in the morning. Miranda was excited and talkative. She began to dig herself a little hole to sit in, imitating the children. Loony watched her, his tongue hanging out. Miranda suddenly reached up a quick paw and pulled it hard. Loony yelped.

'Well, keep your tongue in then, Loony,' said Snubby. 'It's just an invitation to Miranda if you stand over her, hanging it out half-way down your chest. You're a very silly dog to let a monkey get the better of you.'

Loony wandered away, offended. Barney began to tell them about Dummy. 'I was just finishing my work at the fair last night,' he said, 'when my boss said "Chap to see you, Barney." And in walked old Dummy!'

'Was he pleased to see you?' asked Diana.

'Pleased! I should think so. He took both my hands in his and worked them up and down as if they were a pump handle!' said Barney. 'Then Miranda spotted him and she knew him at once. Miranda never forgets anyone, you know. She took a flying leap on to his shoulder, and he cradled her in his arms just like he did when she was a tiny little thing. He crooned to her like he always used to. I nearly howled!'

'Did he talk to you at all?' asked Roger. 'He doesn't seem able to talk very much.'

'Well, he's not British, to begin with,' said Barney, 'and he never was much good at picking up our language.

258

But he can talk when he wants to, if he's happy and people are friendly. He couldn't say a word to me at first but he said plenty later on, when he came back to my lodgings with me.'

'What did you talk about?' asked Diana curiously. 'Your old friends?'

'Yes. And my mother,' said Barney. He paused. 'Dummy didn't know she had died. He cried when I told him, because he was very fond of her. She was so kind to him. But he said I'd grown quite unlike her.'

'How?' asked Roger.

'Well – she was dark and I'm fair. She had brown eyes and I've got blue. She was little and I'm tall. I am sorry I wasn't like her.'

'You must be like your father then,' said Diana, looking at Barney's strange blue eyes. 'That will make it easier when we try to find him. We'll look for someone just like you!'

'I wish I *could* find him,' said Barney. 'A father's no end of a help when you're growing up. Of course – I might not like him. He might not like me either. He might even be ashamed of me.'

'Why did your mother run away from him?' asked Diana. 'Was he unkind to her?'

'I don't know. I guess she couldn't live in a house after she'd lived in a caravan all her life,' said Barney. 'I guess she hankered after the life she knew. But I wish she'd sent word to my father when I was born. It's awful to think he doesn't know about me. He might not believe my story, if ever I do find him.'

'What's your surname, Barney?' asked Roger, suddenly realising that they didn't know.

'Lorimer,' said Barney. 'My full name is Barnabas Hugo Lorimer – what a mouthful! But Lorimer isn't my father's name – it's my mother's. She used her own name again when she ran away, and I never even knew it wasn't my rightful surname till just before she died. She didn't tell me my real name – I don't think she thought to tell me, and I never thought of asking her, because I somehow thought Lorimer was her married name, you see. I never realised it would be important.'

'What about your birth certificate?' asked Diana, remembering hers. 'That would have everything on it, wouldn't it?'

'What's a birth certificate?' asked Barney, looking startled. 'I never heard of one before. Anyway, I haven't got one, whatever it is.'

There was a silence. The three children were all thinking the same thing. How hopeless to try and find a man when you didn't know in the least what he was like, or how old he was, or even what his name was! Why, he might be staying in the same town and none of them would know!

Roger made up his mind to ask Miss Pepper's help. She would know how to set about things. Anyway, they did know that Barney's father acted – or used to act, in Shakespeare's plays. That was something.

Loony appeared, carrying some article in his mouth. 'Now what's he got?' said Snubby. 'Loony, if you bring that dead crab again I'll make you eat it. It was a bad enough crab yesterday and today it'll be worse.'

It wasn't a crab. It was a man's hair-brush! Snubby took it out of Loony's mouth and glared at him. 'Bad dog! Didn't I tell you when you come to stay at an inn or hotel you don't pinch people's brushes? You're not at home. Whose brush is this, I'd like to know!'

'Woof,' said Loony, pleased with himself.

'Do you mean to say you've been all the way back to the inn, popped upstairs, found an open door and grabbed a brush?' said Snubby. 'You must be mad!'

'He's just showing off,' said Diana. 'He's trying to show Miranda something she can't do.'

'Don't say that!' said Barney quickly. 'You know how she imitates every one. I don't want *her* arriving with brushes. I should get into awful trouble.'

'So will Loony,' said Snubby severely. He smacked the surprised spaniel on his nose with the brush. 'Why have you always had this passion for brushes? You are *not* to take brushes, towels *or* mats away, Loony!'

Loony backed hurriedly away from another smack and sat down on Miranda. He got up again just as hurriedly, feeling sharp teeth in his tail. He yelped and leaped on to Snubby.

'Don't play musical chairs with me and Miranda,' said Snubby, pushing him off. 'I'm still cross with you.' He examined the brush. It had the initials M. M. on it in silver.

'Matthew Marvel,' said Diana tracing them with her finger. 'He's the conjurer. His bedroom is on the same landing as ours. Loony must have found his door a bit ajar, pushed it, and gone in. I believe he thinks that all the rooms there are his to wander round. I found him in there yesterday.'

'Well, I'll return it to dear Matthew some time today,' said Snubby. 'I don't feel I can go back this very minute. Let's bathe!'

So they bathed. Miranda wouldn't go into the water, but danced up and down at the edge of the waves, holding up her little red skirt, much to the amusement of all the children nearby. Loony leapt into the water boldly, trying to keep up with Snubby. Barney swam the best. He was already feeling much better, partly because he was happy again. He thought warmly of his three friends – no, four, counting Loony. Whatever happened, he would never, never lose them.

'Can you come out with us this afternoon, Barney?' asked Roger, as they lay drying in the sun after their bathe.

'Oh yes. I'm not on duty till half-past five,' said Barney. 'What are you doing?'

'We haven't thought,' said Snubby. 'I'd like to take a boat out, I think.'

'Yes. Good idea,' said Roger. 'I say – let's row out to Rubadub Whirlpool – I'd love to see that.'

'What's that?' asked Barney, interested.

They all told him at once. 'It's not very far out – it's towards the cliff that separates our little bay from the Submarine Bay,' said Snubby, when Barney had disentangled all the descriptions of the whirlpool.

'Right. We'll get a boat and go there this afternoon,' said Barney. 'I'd like to see that. I've never seen a proper whirlpool before.'

It was lunch time, so they parted and Roger and the others hurried back to the inn – not because they were late, of course, but because they were overcome with hunger! They ran upstairs to wash and tidy themselves.

'I'd better return Mr Marvel's brush,' said Snubby. 'I hope he's not in. If he isn't I could steal into his room and put it back. Then I shouldn't have to explain Loony's idiotic behaviour!'

Snubby knocked quietly. He listened. There was no sound from inside at all. He turned the handle of the door quietly and slid in without a sound, the brush in his hand.

He stopped suddenly. Mr Marvel was there after all. He sat at a table strewn with cards on which were many numbers of all kinds. He was studying them, and the writing rapidly. Snubby didn't quite know what to do. He gave a polite little cough.

Mr Marvel leapt to his feet immediately and turned a furious face on Snubby, covering up the cards with his hand. 'What is it, what do you want, how dare you sneak in like this?' he demanded in a harsh voice. Then he realised that it was only Snubby, and forced a smile on his long, lean face.

'You silly boy – you startled me! I was just working out one of my conjuring tricks – lost in thought – deep in meditation – and you gave me such a start. What is it you want?'

'I'm sorry to say, sir, that my dog took your brush out of your room some time this morning,' said Snubby, still feeling a little scared of the furious face he had just seen. 'I've brought it back.'

'Oh, thanks,' said the conjurer, and took it. He put it down and pulled Snubby to him. 'Why don't you wash your ears, boy?' he said.

'I do,' said Snubby indignantly.

'Well, well – you've got potatoes growing behind each one,' said the conjurer, and removed two small potatoes from behind Snubby's ears. Snubby stared, open-mouthed.

'And why keep watches in your mouth?' said Mr Marvel, with a little laugh. 'Anyone can see them and take them – like this!' And he inserted finger and thumb into Snubby's mouth and brought out two small watches.

'I say – look, I say,' began Snubby, amazed.

'And whatever is that bulging out your shorts' pockets?' asked the conjurer. Snubby looked down, astonished. His pockets were bulging out untidily! He put in his hands and pulled out two carrots from one and an apple from the other. He held them, staring in amazement.

'Food for a little donkey,' said Mr Marvel, and laughed softly. 'You do like carrots, don't you? Have them with your dinner!'

Chapter Twelve

Rubadub Whirlpool

The others had gone down to lunch. They couldn't wait for Snubby. Nor could Loony, who was also feeling decidedly ravenous. Miss Pepper looked coldly at Snubby.

'You've been a long time,' she said. 'What happened to you?'

'Oh, nothing much,' said Snubby airily. 'Mr Marvel found some potatoes in my ears, and two watches in my mouth and some fruit and vegetables in my pockets, that's all!'

'Do you mean he did some magic tricks on you?' asked Diana. 'You lucky thing! But I don't believe he took any watches out of your mouth.'

'Well, I *wondered* what that ticking noise was that I heard this morning,' said Roger. 'Gosh, Snubby, you might have let *me* take them out of your mouth.'

'He was pretty furious when he suddenly turned round and saw me standing there,' said Snubby. 'He shot out of his chair, and covered up some cards with his hand as if I'd come to sneak in on his magic. He said I'd disturbed him working out a magic trick. I can't make out if I like him or not.'

Mr Marvel came into the room at that moment, and Miss Pepper signed to Snubby to change the subject. The Funny Man also came in, with Iris Nightingale in a very pretty blue and white frock and that took Snubby's eye at once. He grinned at her and she smiled back.

'She's *aw*fully nice!' he said. 'I had a word with her this morning. She says we really must go to the show and she'll sing me my favourite songs.'

'Well, I only hope she knows "Ride a Cock-horse to Banbury Cross" and "Where did you come from, Baby dear?" ' said Roger solemnly and rather loudly.

'Shut up. She'll hear,' said Snubby fiercely. 'You want a bang on the head, Roger.'

'Snubby, behave yourself,' said Miss Pepper, much to his indignation. He sat back, sulking, scowling at Miss Pepper. A bird flew in at the open window and fluttered round the room and then flew out. Snubby saw a way of annoying Miss Pepper, and paying her out for insulting him in public.

'Oh, did you see that dear little dicky-bird?' he said, turning round to Miss Twitt with a sweet smile. 'I'm sure it twittered. I do so *love* birds, don't you, Miss Twitter.'

For once in a way Miss Twitt looked at him coldly. 'It's funny your little boy has such a bad memory for names, isn't it, Miss Pepper?' she said. 'But there – not all of us can have brains, can we?'

'One in the eye for you, Snubby,' said Roger in a low voice. The Funny Man had heard all this and he gave a guffaw which exasperated Snubby. At all costs he must change the subject. 'Miss Pepper, we're going to get a boat and row to Rubadub Whirlpool this afternoon,' he said loudly.

'Then you must go with a boatman,' said Miss Pepper at once. The three children stared in dismay.

'Oh *why*?' asked Roger. 'You *know* we can manage a boat by ourselves perfectly well.'

'I don't know anything of the sort,' said Miss Pepper. 'And anyway you are *not* visiting whirlpools by yourselves.'

'Quite right,' said an unexpected voice. 'A most dangerous place. Far better for children to keep away from it!'

It was Mr Marvel speaking. Professor James put his hand behind his ear and spoke loudly.

'What's that? What's that you're talking about?'

'RUBADUB WHIRLPOOL!' shouted Snubby, and made everyone jump.

'Ah, very dangerous place,' agreed the Professor. 'Shouldn't let them go, Mam.'

'Nor should I,' said Miss Twitt, shuddering. 'Whirlpools suck people down, don't they – and boats too. Down, down, down – it's terrible to think of.'

'But, Miss Pepper – there are big advertisements all over the place saying it's just an afternoon trip in a boat,' protested Snubby angrily. 'We won't go alone if you don't want us to – but do be a sport and let us go with a boatman.'

'Try Binns,' put in the Funny Man. 'He's the man I use. First-class fellow in a whirlpool. Always rows the boat the other way round in a pool so that you can keep quite still and watch it sucking things down. Binns for Brains, I say.'

Nobody knew quite how to take this, but Miss Pepper came to the correct conclusion that he was merely being funny. She looked hesitantly at the beseeching children.

'All right – I'll take you down to the jetty and see you safely into a boat myself with a boatman. In fact, I might even come myself.'

'Good,' said Roger. 'That's settled then. We all go. Barney and Miranda are coming too.'

'They set off after lunch and met Barney and Miranda. The Funny Man stopped Miss Pepper as they went out.

'Why don't you bring the kids to our show tonight?' he said. 'We've got our weekly competition on for children, and one of these might win a prize. Snubby's bright enough anyway! Tell him to bring his banjo and zither. He'll bring the house down with them!'

He walked on. Miss Pepper was surprised. 'But you haven't *got* a banjo or a zither, have you, Snubby?' she asked. 'What does he mean?'

'Oh, he's just being an ass,' said Snubby. 'Do let's go

tonight, though, Miss Pepper. I'd like to go and see the conjurer anyway.'

'And he *does* want to hear Iris Nightingale sing to him,' put in Roger, and fled away at top speed as Snubby turned on him.

Miss Pepper found a boatman at the jetty who looked sensible, and strong enough to deal with whirlpools if necessary. She asked him if he could take them.

'Oh, yes, Mam, that's right I can,' he said cheerily. 'And don't you be afraid of being sucked under, Mam – I can always pull you out again. I got a fine boathook, see?'

This didn't sound too good, but Miss Pepper felt that she couldn't possibly draw back now. So in they all got. Barney and Miranda had joined them by this time, so there was a real boatload.

'Do you mind the dog and the monkey?' said Miss Pepper.

'Not a bit. Only wish I'd brought my parrot. Be a bit of company for her, like,' said the boatman with a huge guffaw of laughter. 'Here you, lad – take an oar, will you?'

Barney rowed as well as the boatman. They shot out over the little bay and veered to the left.

'The whirlpool is round behind that clump of high rocks there,' said the boatman at last. 'We go between two sets of dark, high rocks, and then the way opens out – and there we are, on the whirlpool, if I don't stop rowing!'

Loony was a bit of a nuisance. He kept racing from one end of the boat to the other, looking forward at the bows, and backward at the stern. Miranda sat on Barney's shoulder, enjoying the rhythmic to and fro movement as he rowed.

They rounded the clump of high rocks. As they came round them the children saw that there was a narrow, very crooked channel winding between them, down the very middle. It was as if the rocks had been cleft in half, letting the sea run right in.

The high rocks cut off the rays of the sun now and again, as the boat made its way carefully through the winding channel. After a little while the children heard a noise – a boiling, rushing, hissing noise that sounded excited and angry.

'Rubadub Whirlpool,' said the boatman. 'We goes careful here!'

And carefully they went, feeling a sudden pull on the boat as if the distant pool was putting out suckers to drag them to it!

They rounded a bend slowly – and the boatman slewed the boat quickly round to a ledge where a post stood. In a trice he had thrown a rope over it. The boat was held fast.

The whirlpool was not far from them. The channel had suddenly widened right out into a big rounded pool. It seemed alive and angry. It boiled and bubbled and threw up spray, it swelled up, and then, with a horrible sucking sound, it drained down low. Then up it boiled and bubbled again.

'That's one of the finest whirlpools I ever did see,' said the boatman. 'And I've seen a-many in my time. Anyone want to get out and walk along the ledge to see the pool properly? I'll show you the rock that gives the name of Rubadub – it's like a scrubbing board.'

They all got out eagerly, even Miss Pepper, who was really fascinated by the restless, tortured waters of the strange whirlpool. They climbed up on to the ledge where the mooring-post was, and followed the boatman along another ledge that ran at the side of the high, enclosing rocks.

This ledge led them to a small platform of rock immediately over the pool. From there they had a truly wonderful sight of the boiling, sucking waters. The boatman took a piece of wood up and threw it down into the pool. The waters swelled up, bubbling, and then were sucked under again. When they swelled once more, the piece of wood was nowhere to be seen.

'Sucked down,' explained the boatman. 'It'll never be seen again. You be careful you don't slip any of you'

Miss Pepper began to wish they were safely back in the boat, but the old man hadn't finished with them yet.

'Now you watch,' he said. 'Next time the pool swells up and then goes right down again, look across there to the rocky side opposite. You'll see Rubadub Rock.'

They watched the waters swell and subside – down, down, down – exposing the rock on the other side. And sure enough, it was straight and oblong in shape – and ribbed just like a scrubbing board!

'Old Neptune's scrubbing board,' said the boatman. 'I guess he used to send the mermaids here to scrub out his best clothes – rubadub-dub!'

'They'd be sucked down!' said Diana with a shudder.

'Oh, they'd like that. That'd be a game to them,' said the boatman enjoying himself. 'Do you know what folks say, Missy? They say that in the time of the smugglers and the wreckers, this was a mighty fine place to throw your enemies!'

'Don't!' said Diana. 'I shall dream about it tonight! Is there anything else to see?'

'Oh yes – the Blow-Hole!' said the boatman. 'I'll show you the Blow-Hole. Follow me – I'll show you something mighty odd.'

Chapter Thirteen

The Blow-Hole

He took them to the back of the little platform, and walked on another ledge alongside the high rocks. He came to some natural steps in the rocks and climbed up them to the very top of the outcrop of rocks.

It was windy up there. The breeze whipped Diana's hair across her face, and made Miss Pepper clutch at her scarf.

From this rocky height they could see over the Submarine Bay. 'You know what goes on there, I don't doubt,' said the boatman. 'Secret Submarine work. No one's allowed there, not even us fishermen, though as a boy I knew every corner.'

A stone enclosure guarded the whole of the bay. No ships could get in or out without the secret openings being unlocked. Men kept guard in little stone shelters along the top. There was a flash from one of them.

'See that?' said the boatman. 'That's one of the guards turning his glasses on us. But he knows we can't get farther than this. If you go over the top of these rocks, any nearer the boy, you'll be blown up. They're mined.'

'This all seems extremely dangerous,' said Miss Pepper.

'Bless you, Mam, you couldn't get near the mined bit!' said the boatman reassuringly. 'There's hundreds of yards of barbed wire.'

'What about the blow-hole?' asked Roger.

'Ah yes. Now – you look over there, see?' said the boatman, and he pointed towards the land, out of which ran the crop of enormous rocks they were standing on.

Suddenly they saw a great spout of water gushing up with a roar. It fell back immediately.

'What was it?' asked Diana, startled.

'I told you. A blow-hole,' said the boatman. 'Haven't you ever seen one before? There's a-plenty round our coasts, some big, some little. There's a long passage through the rocks from the whirlpool to the blow-hole – and when it's high tide – as it is now – the whirlpool waters get sucked down, and some of them are forced by the tide and the suction through the passage and out of the blow-hole. Watch – there'll be another spout in a minute.'

There was. Snubby felt very thrilled. 'Why is it only at high tide it comes?' he said. 'Why doesn't it come always? Gosh – there goes another! It's like a whale spouting!'

'At low tide the level of the water sinks below the passage,' said the boatman. 'So no water gets along it. But when high tide swells up the waters again – whooooosh – they force themselves through the tunnel and out of the blow-hole!'

'Where's the entrance to the passage?' asked Roger. 'I suppose it's not visible at high tide?'

'No. Not at all,' said the boatman. 'But I can show you just about where it is. There's an extraordinary old tale about it.'

'What?' asked Snubby at once. He never could resist extraordinary old tales.

'Well, it's said that some smugglers once wanted to get rid of one of their enemies so that his body would never be found again,' said the boatman. 'And they carried him here at dead of night. They threw him into the whirlpool and fled away, back into the bay over there, where the submarines are now.'

He paused, and Snubby urged him on. 'Go on – what else?'

'Well, the fellow they threw in was a strong man, a

giant of a chap. He wasn't going to be sucked down without a struggle. So, before the waters could suck him right down, he flung himself to the edge of the pool and got a grip on a rocky ledge. But he couldn't haul himself up.'

'Did he escape all right?' asked Diana. 'Do say he did!'

'The tide went down, and the fellow had to change his grip to lower and lower ledges,' said the boatman solemnly. 'He couldn't seem to drag himself out, you see. The tide went down and down, and the waters of the whirlpool sank lower and lower. And then the man found himself standing on a ledge at the entrance to what looked like a dark little tunnel in the rocks. I guess it must have been moonlit that night!'

'It was the entrance of the passage that goes to the blow-hole!' said Roger.

'You're right. It was. And up that passage crawled the man right till he came to the blow-hole itself! He scrambled out, made his way back to land – and my word, didn't his enemies stare when they saw him walking down the street. They ran for their lives!'

'I bet they did,' said Snubby, enjoying the tale. 'Serve them right, the beasts. I hope they all got caught.'

'I never heard tell,' said the boatman. 'There she blows!'

And once again they turned to see the blow-hole send out its sudden high gush of water. 'That'll die gradually down as the tide falls,' said the boatman. 'Well, now, we'll go back. I'm not allowed to take you any farther, and even if I wanted to, there's too many mines about for my liking!'

They watched the blow-hole once more and then went back to where they had left the boat. The whirlpool was still performing its endless rhythm, and was boiling away merrily, making a strange, gurgling, groaning, rushing sound.

'Definitely glumpish,' said Snubby. 'Look at Loony – he's as quiet as a mouse. He's scared, aren't you, Loony-dog?'

Certainly Loony wasn't at all drawn to the whirlpool. He strained away from it as far as ever he could, held tightly on the lead by Snubby.

Miranda was curled up inside Barney's shirt, fast asleep. She didn't even wake when they reached the boat.

'You didn't show us where the entrance hole was,' Snubby reminded the boatman.

'No. Nor I didn't,' said the man. 'Well, while I untie the boat you slip along and look down into the pool. When the water gets sucked down, watch out for a rock with a great knob-like piece on it. The entrance is below that.'

Snubby and Roger and Barney went to look. They spotted the knobby rock at once, but could not see any sign of the entrance, of course, because the tide was still very high.

'A jolly interesting afternoon,' said Roger. 'Kind of trip I like. Something to write about when my form-master gives us his usual essay at beginning of term – "Describe an interesting day in your summer holiday." I can let myself go about this. I'll put in the tale about the Fellow Who Came Back too. Horrible business it must have been, crawling through that tunnel in the dark – never knowing when the tide might turn and send a long arm of water after you.'

'All this has made me hungry,' said Snubby. 'Anyone got any chocolate?'

Nobody had, so Snubby had to endure his hunger till they reached land. Miss Pepper paid the boatman and they went to have tea at a tea-shop Snubby had spotted that morning.

'It said "Lobster Teas," ' he explained. 'It's just about

273

what I feel like. Why don't we ever have lobster teas at home?'

'Simply because it's easy to catch lobsters by the sea and it isn't inland, idiot,' said Roger. 'And let me warn you that if you eat more than one lobster you'll probably dream you're being sucked down in that whirlpool tonight.'

'It'll be worth it,' said Snubby, and was most bitterly disappointed when Miss Pepper refused to let him have more than half a lobster. Miranda liked lobster too. She daintily ate the little bits that Barney held out to her!

They all went for a good walk after tea. They examined the programme for that night's pierrot show as they passed the pier.

'Looks jolly good,' said Snubby. ' "Fred the Funny Man Keeps You Laughing. Matthew Marvel Mystifies you with Magic. Iris Nightingale sings like her name. Judy Jordan and John Jordan in their Wonderful Dancing Act. Bertram Deep the Baritone, and other talented Players. Philip Drew at the Piano. GREAT WEEKLY CHILDREN'S COMPETITION TONIGHT. LET US RECOGNISE YOUR TALENTED CHILDREN EARLY. Two prizes of five shillings." '

The others read the notice with Snubby. It certainly sounded a good show. They all felt just in the mood for it.

'Super!' said Snubby, rubbing his hands together. 'I could do with five shillings. Can't think where my pocket money disappears to.'

'Well, I could tell you,' began Roger, but Snubby didn't want to hear. 'Barney,' he said, 'if you went on the platform with Miranda, you'd bring the house down.'

'I'll be at work, you know that,' said Barney.

'Yes, I know. Well, I suppose I'll have to uphold the honour of the family,' said Snubby, and began to pretend to play his 'banjo' again, making a horrible metallic, buzzing noise between his teeth. 'Zizz-ziz-ziz-ziz-ZIZZ, zizz-ziz-ziz-ziz-ZIZZ!'

'*Not* here, please, Snubby,' said Miss Pepper. 'Is that how you intend to uphold the honour of the family? I shan't know where to look if *you* go up to perform!'

'I prefer your zither,' said Diana.

'Or what about my mouth organ?' said Snubby, and pretended to take a mouth organ from his pocket. He wiped it and put it to his mouth. Terrific noise ensued, extremely like a mouth organ. Anyone would really have thought that Snubby was playing one!

'That's *enough*, Snubby,' said Miss Pepper, as a little crowd of interested children gathered.

'You know – I could really make a jolly good living at this kind of thing, if I stood at a good corner,' said Snubby. 'I could put a hat down. I bet it would soon be full of pennies!'

'You're too full of yourself!' said Diana. 'Come on – chase Loony and forget all the marvellous things you think you can do – but can't!'

Chapter Fourteen

At the Pierrot Show

'I say!' said Snubby, at dinner time that night, calling across to Iris Nightingale, 'I say – we're coming to your show tonight. We'll clap like anything.'

'Good,' said Iris, smiling at him. She really was very pretty. 'We'll put on our very best show for you.'

'And be careful to wash your neck, young man, in case I find more potatoes growing there,' said Mr Marvel.

Snubby scowled as everyone laughed. He determined not to give the conjurer one single clap that evening. Mean fellow – talking about unwashed necks in public!

'I'm coming, too, tonight,' put in Miss Twitt. 'It's the children's competition, isn't it? I do so love seeing the little dears march up on the platform to give their funny little recitations and songs. The pets!'

Snubby's heart sank. He didn't at all like the idea of having Miss Twitt watch his performance. She would be so silly about it afterwards, he was sure.

Miss Twitt turned towards his table and spoke to Miss Pepper with her usual beaming smile. 'And are any of your dear children going to perform?' she gushed. 'The little girl, now – I'm *sure* she can dance beautifully.'

If there was one thing Diana hated it was being called 'a little girl.' She glanced despairingly at Miss Pepper.

'Do you mean Diana?' said Miss Pepper. 'I wonder why you call her a *little* girl, Miss Twitt? She is almost as tall as you are, and very grown-up indeed!'

Diana could have hugged Miss Pepper! She looked at her gratefully. Why didn't all grown-ups know that boys and girls hated to be referred to as 'little'?

'Why don't *you* go up and sing on the platform, Miss Twitt?' asked Snubby, innocently. 'I'm sure you could twitter like a blackbird.'

The Funny Man gave a guffaw and turned it into a coughing fit. Miss Pepper looked fiercely at Snubby, but Miss Twitt actually took it as a compliment.

'Well, I *did* sing beautifully as a child,' she said coyly. 'Fancy you guessing that! He's quite a cute little boy, isn't he?' she said, turning to Miss Pepper.

'You'll have to take Iris's place when she has a night off,' said the Funny Man. 'You would give everyone a surprise.'

'Oh dear no, I couldn't sing like dear Iris,' said Miss Twitt, fluttering nervously. 'Ah, here comes the pudding – pineapple and ice-cream – how very nice!'

Miss Twitt was usually only silent when she was attacking her food, and the same thing applied to Snubby. Miss Pepper heaved a sigh of relief when she saw the young waiter put a really enormous helping of pineapple and ice cream in front of Snubby. How did Snubby always get such big helpings? Miss Pepper supposed that, as usual, he made himself well known to the staff, and as so often happened, made himself a firm favourite.

The show began at eight. The Conjurer, the Funny Man, and Iris had coffee quickly and then went to get ready.

'We'll have our coffee in the lounge together, shall we?' said Miss Twitt to Miss Pepper. But Miss Pepper had had quite enough of Miss Twitt.

'I'm not having coffee tonight, thank you,' she said. 'I'll go and sit outside in the evening sun with the children.'

She found them wanting to start off for the show at once. 'We do want good seats,' said Snubby. 'I can't see how a conjurer does his tricks unless I'm right at the front. Miss Pepper, let's go now. Have we got any chocolates to eat?'

'No, we haven't,' said Miss Pepper. 'There's no need to suck sweets or chocolates at the show – especially after such a good meal.'

'Oh well, never mind. I think I've got a piece of chewing-gum,' said Snubby, searching his pockets.

'Then please give it to me,' said Miss Pepper. 'If there's one thing I hate more than another it's to see people's mouth moving up and down, chewing gum – looking exactly like a lot of cows chewing the cud!'

'Gosh! Now I know why cows do that,' said Snubby. 'It's just as good as chewing-gum to them. I never thought cows could be so sensible. Anyway, Miss Pepper, you don't look at me while I'm chewing.'

'Shut up, Snubby,' said Roger. 'You go on and on and on like a babbling brook. Let somebody else get a word in. And keep an eye on Loony. He's disappeared into the inn. He'll be bringing out something he shouldn't, I bet!'

Loony appeared, eagerly wagging his stump of a tail. He was dragging a small mat. He laid it down at Snubby's feet.

'Look at that!' said Snubby in disgust. 'He's started his idiotic tricks all over again. Take it back, crazy dog!'

Loony tore off, but without the mat. 'Now he's gone to get another!' said Diana. 'Miss Pepper, can't we start now?'

'Yes,' said Miss Pepper, getting up from the seat. 'We'll leave Snubby to cope with the mats.'

Snubby snatched up the mat and tore indoors. He collided with the Professor and Miss Twitt inside the hall.

'Oh – sorry,' said Snubby. 'Frightfully sorry. I didn't see you. Are you going to the show? See you there, then!'

'What that boy wants is a good caning,' said the Professor, annoyed. 'Always rushing about at top speed, shouting at the top of his voice – no manners at all!'

'Ah, yes – but children *will* be children,' said Miss Twitt. 'Dear little things. I do so love them, don't you?'

'No, I don't,' said the Professor. 'I should like to drown them all.'

And having made this remark loudly and with much feeling, he said no more, but walked slowly off with Miss Twitt, who jingled and jangled as she went, and left behind her a very strong scent of Sweet Pea perfume.

Snubby soon caught up the others, with Loony tearing at his heels, his ears flapping wildly. He slowed down, panting. They came to the pier turnstiles and paid to go in. Then they made their way to the concert room, which was about halfway down the pier. There was a very good platform, and, in the open air, rows and rows of seats. The roof had been drawn back as it was so warm. In wet or cold weather it could be drawn right across, so that the concert room became an enclosed hall.

'This is fine,' said Roger. 'Are we going in the very front seats?'

They were all taken, however, so the children had to be content with middle seats in the second row. They sat down expectantly. Miss Pepper bought two programmes between the four of them. They studied them in silence.

Professor James and Miss Twitt joined the audience, but they sat halfway down the hall, as by that time all the front seats were taken. Evidently the Rubadub Rollicks were popular! Miss Twitt waved her programme to the children, and they waved back politely.

At exactly eight o'clock there was the sound of merry music from a piano on the curtained stage. Then the curtains swung back with a flourish, to reveal the twelve Rollicks on the stage, all looking very jolly and bright, except for the conjurer, who looked his usual gloomy self. He did, however, manage a smile as they all rose to their feet for the opening song.

The pianist was excellent, a bright young fellow who immediately singled out Snubby, and gave him a broad wink which made Snubby feel very proud.

The programme followed a very usual course – songs, dancing, patter, a little sketch or two, much silly talk from the Funny Man, and, of course, the conjuring.

Iris proved to have a very sweet voice. Snubby clapped her so hard that his hands felt quite sore. He went on clapping long after everyone else had stopped. Roger poked him hard with his elbow.

'Shut up! Everyone's looking at you!'

'Encore!' shouted Snubby, undeterred. 'Encore!' He was delighted when, at a word from the Funny Man, Iris got up to sing again. She gave him an amused smile.

The ordinary dancing was quite good, and the tap-dancing excellent. Snubby began to strum on his imaginary banjo when Judy Jordan began a tricky little tap-dance with clicking toes and heels. Miss Pepper stopped him at once, hearing the familiar 'Zizz-ziz-ziz' beginning.

But the best part of the whole show was the conjurer. He was quite brilliant. He didn't smile once as he went through his ritual, dressed for the act as an old-time Enchanter, with pointed hat and flowing cloak. He made Diana shudder, as with gloomy face and deep, gloomy voice he performed his act.

'He's really excellent,' Miss Pepper whispered to Diana. 'Absolutely in character with his magic! You could imagine him conjuring up genies and spirits and hob-nobbing with witches and goblins. He's really weird!'

The audience watched him in silence. He did unusual tricks. He picked most extraordinary things out of the air – a rose-spray – a pack of loose cards – quite a large book – a bonnet, which he presented to Iris with a deep bow!

He took up his wand and announced that he was about to conjure up fire. He muttered a string of peculiar words that sent shivers down Snubby's spine – and then, hey presto! flames sprang up above his head, burning brilliantly. He really did the most extraordinary things!

'And now,' he said, putting down his wand, 'now I

propose to show you my wonderful mind-reading act. Magic, my friends, pure magic!'

Chapter Fifteen

Mr Marvel – and Snubby

'You watch this,' whispered somebody in the seats behind the three children. 'It's marvellous!'

Iris stepped forward and bowed. Apparently she was to be Mr Marvel's assistant. 'Blindfold me,' commanded the conjurer. Iris took a very large black scarf and blindfolded Mr Marvel well and truly. Even Snubby was absolutely sure that nobody could see a thing under that scarf. It made the conjurer look very sinister indeed!

The mind-reading act followed the usual ritual. Iris collected articles from the audience, walking down the rows of chairs, smiling, putting her fingers to her lips.

'Mustn't give anything away!' she whispered. 'No hints, nothing that might help Mr Marvel. This is a true and honest test of his powers!'

She went back to the stage. Mr Marvel, still blindfolded, was twisted round by Iris so that he stood with his back to the audience. She stepped to the front and held out a little gold brooch, given to her by a young girl.

'What do I hold in my hand, Mr Marvel?' she cried. 'Tell me! Let your mind read what I hold!'

Mr Marvel began to swing his great cloak so that it flowed round him like black waves. He began to mutter in a deep, growly voice that made Loony, who was fast asleep under Snubby's chair, wake up at once.

'I see – what do I see – mirrity-marrity-mingle-o – I see, ah yes, I see – something small – something round – something that shines like gold – abblety-gabblety-mingle-o – it IS gold!'

'Ah, but what is it?' cried Iris, still holding up the little brooch. There wasn't a sound in the concert hall, as Mr Marvel began to mutter again. He suddenly swung right round, his cloak flying out round him.

'A brooch. A little brooch.'

There was a loud storm of clapping. Snubby forgot that he didn't mean to clap, and clapped hard; Roger and Diana clapped even harder than Snubby. Then Iris swung Mr Marvel round with his back to the audience again, and this time she held up two things for them to see. One was a silver ring with a yellow stone in it and one was a watch.

'What do I hold now, Mr Marvel?' cried Iris. 'Two things I hold for your mind to read. Tell me what they are!'

There was muttering and mumbling again, and the cloak swung this way and that. To the three children it all seemed very weird and magical indeed. Mr Marvel brought the house down by guessing both articles quite correctly. He waited till the applause had died down and then said:

'Wait – I see something else. The watch, I see the watch – on the back it has the letters A. G. S. Yes, I see A. G. S.'

'You're quite right,' said Iris in an astonished voice, looking at the back of the watch. Everyone clapped again. A few more articles were held up and correctly described, and then came the last part of the magician's act.

'And now,' said Mr Marvel solemnly, his long thin face looking even longer beneath his pointed hat, 'now we come to Numerology. My excellent assistant, Miss Iris, has a pack of cards with her. Each card bears a high number. She will shuffle the cards and pick one at random, showing it to you in silence. I will see it in my mind's eye within thirty seconds or less, and tell you the number she holds in her hand.'

Iris took up a pack of cards. They all had plain-coloured

backs of yellow. Snubby sat up suddenly. Why, these were the cards that he had seen in the conjurer's room when he had taken back his hair-brush. He must have been studying them then. But what good would any study do if he didn't know which one Iris was going to pick out.

Iris picked out a card and held it up silently. The number on it was printed in black ink, in large figures across the card. Everyone could see perfectly. The number was 673589255.

The usual muttering noise came from Mr Marvel. Then he groaned. 'It is difficult. Where's my wand?'

Iris gave it to him. He made various passes with it in the air. 'Come, genie of the numbers, come to my aid!' he cried, in such an anguished voice that the audience felt scared.

'Ah! AH! Now I see the number! Wait, wait – it comes! The number if 673589255!'

Iris was still holding up the number. Mr Marvel had guessed it correctly. There was a shout of applause, and clapping and stamping of feet. Wonderful!

'Let's have another number!' shouted a voice.

'Only one more,' said Iris. 'This is a great strain on Mr Marvel.'

It certainly seemed to be by his writhings and mutterings and passes in the air with his wand. But he at last guessed the number correctly again.

'It is – it is – 864592643!'

'Gosh – he scares me,' said Snubby to Miss Pepper. 'I'm going to be jolly polite to him in future. He's a wonder.'

There was a merry song and dance next, to remove the tense atmosphere that Mr Marvel had so cleverly created. Then Iris stepped forward again.

'Now comes the end of our programme and perhaps the best part,' she said with her engaging smile. 'The Children's Competition. As usual we have two prizes of five shillings, one for the cleverest boy, and one for the cleverest girl.'

A jingling noise from the Funny Man proclaimed that the money was ready and waiting. 'Can I go in for it, please, Miss?' said the Funny Man pathetically. 'I can sing "Three Blind Mice" well, I can, really.'

Iris went on with her little speech. 'We don't mind what you do – sing, dance, recite, play our piano, tell us a funny story – or even do a bit of conjuring that will put Mr Marvel into the shade. Now come along – who will be first?'

Two small girls and a boy pushed their way eagerly to the stage. Another girl followed, and two more boys. Roger gave Snubby a nudge. 'Go on! Do your stuff too, Snubby.'

But Snubby was unaccountably overcome with nerves, and he glowered at Roger. 'I'm not going to make a fool of myself, so shut up.'

The children proved very ordinary indeed. Two of the girls played the piano, thumping hard and strong. One boy sang a comic song, of which nobody could hear a single word.

Another small girl did a competent little step dance, but was obviously so conceited that nobody clapped very much except her fond and admiring Mamma.

Then a boy about Snubby's age gave a recitation at top speed so that nobody could follow it at all. He then retired from the platform, also at top speed quite overcome by his effort.

The third boy refused to perform at all. He stood up on the platform the picture of misery.

'I've forgotten me words,' he kept saying. 'I've forgot me words. Mum, what's me words?'

Mum had apparently forgotten them, too, so the small boy left the platform in tears.

'Now now, children!' said Iris reprovingly. 'I'm *sure*

285

there's somebody else who can try for the five shillings. We do badly want another boy.'

'Let *me* try, Miss, do let *me* try,' urged the Funny Man, putting on a little-boy voice. 'I'm top of my form, I am, for singing and whistling.' He pursed up his mouth to whistle, but hard as he blew, no sound came. So he produced a big whistle from his pocket and blew, making Iris jump violently. Everyone laughed, he was so idiotic.

'One more boy!' urged Iris. 'Just one. Then we shall have had three girls performing and three boys.'

The Funny Man came to stand beside Iris. He looked straight at Snubby. Then he pointed at him. 'Look, Iris,' he said, 'there's the World's Wonder down there. See him? Chap with red hair, turned-up nose and freckles! Finest banjo player the world has ever seen. Pays a hundred pounds for each of his banjos. Whew!'

Everyone craned their necks to look at Snubby. He went scarlet to the roots of his hair. 'Come on, son!' cried the Funny Man. 'Come on up and play your banjo. Tell us your tune and the pianist will accompany you.'

'Go on, Snubby,' said Roger. 'You've got to, now. Those other boys were frightful.'

Snubby went up to the platform, half annoyed, half pleased at the Funny Man's patter. He stood facing the audience. The Funny Man solemnly placed a chair beside him. 'To put your leg up on,' he informed him. 'That's a heavy banjo you have there. Rest it on your leg, mate. Now – what's your tune?'

Snubby suddenly entered into the fun of it. He laughed. 'I'll play you "What's the time when it's twelve o'clock," ' he announced, and put his leg on the chair. The song was very popular just then, a silly jigging tune, admirable for the banjo. The pianist nodded. He knew the tune well.

'I must tune up,' said Snubby, and he solemnly tuned up the string of his imaginary banjo, making twanging noises as if he really were screwing the wires to their correct pitch. People began to laugh.

'Right. Ready?' said Snubby to the pianist. 'Not too loud, please. Tune all through, the chorus twice.'

He brought his hand down on imaginary strings and made a startling twanging noise. Then off he went, twanging away with his right hand, and with his mouth making a most remarkable banjo-like noise he followed the tune absolutely correctly. Snubby could make his noises very loudly, and the pianist did not drown him at all, but followed him perfectly,. They made an excellent pair.

'Twang-a-twang-twang-twang, twang-a-twang-twang,' went Snubby, and ended off with what sounded like a marvellous chord. He put down his leg and bowed solemnly.

He got more applause than any other member of the show had been given, even more than Mr Marvel! Everyone yelled for more.

'One more – can you manage it?' asked the Funny Man, delighted. 'Any other instrument?'

'I've happened to bring my zither,' said Snubby solemnly, and put down his imaginary banjo and took up his imaginary zither. 'I'll have to sit down for this, please.'

He sat down, and once more he and the pianist gave an extraordinary performance together. Snubby reproduced the harp-like sounds of a zither perfectly, and instead of a jiggy song, he chose a romantic tune, 'If I could only give you the moon.' He didn't sing it, of course, but made the sound of a zither playing the tune. It was most remarkable. Everyone listened intently.

Fancy *Snubby*, the crazy idiotic *Snubby* holding a big audience like this with just a little make-believe! Roger and Diana felt swollen up with pride in their cousin!

The tune ended. The Funny Man bowed to Snubby. 'Quite a maestro!' he said, and Snubby wondered whether he was being rude or complimentary. He had never heard the word before. But the Funny Man was delighted with him. He turned to the audience. 'And now to give out the prizes,' he said. 'We award the girl's prize to little Lorna Jones for her step dancing.'

There was very slight applause. Certainly little Lorna had been good, but nobody had liked the little show-off.

'The boy's prize goes – of course – to our young friend here, for . . .'

But the rest of his words were drowned in claps and stamps and cheers. Snubby, redder than ever, bowed, and took the five shillings. What an evening! Whoever would have thought that his crazy habit of strumming imaginary musical instruments would have brought Snubby such applause?

Chapter Sixteen

What Happened in the Night

Snubby walked home in a whirl of excitement. 'Now don't let all this go to your head,' said Roger, afraid that Snubby might become quite unbearable. 'After all, you can't *really* play the banjo or the zither – and you can only pick out 'chop-sticks' on the piano. You're no musician, really.'

'And for goodness' sake don't play banjos and things all over the hotel,' begged Diana. 'They won't like it a bit if you do.'

Snubby took not the slightest notice. 'I've been wondering if I could do an organ,' he said. 'Or a drum.'

'*No*, Snubby,' said Miss Pepper firmly. 'Oh dear, here comes Miss Twitt. Hurry!'

But Miss Twitt was determined to pile praises on Snubby. 'The little wonder!' she said, as she hurried up to them. 'What a little marvel! The clever little boy. He's a born player, isn't he, Miss Pepper?'

'Well – I wouldn't say *that*,' said Miss Pepper. 'He can't play a note actually.'

'Fancy that! It just shows how wonderful he is to make people think he *can* play!' prattled Miss Twitt. 'I *quite* thought it was a real banjo, you know. He really *ought* to join the pierrots, oughtn't he? Everyone would come to hear him!'

Miss Pepper glanced at Snubby and was horrified to see a pleased and fatuous smile on his face. He was drinking it all in!

'Snubby's little tricks are quite all right to amuse his

289

friends at school,' she said firmly. 'But that's really all they are. It's silly to think them anything else, Miss Twitt.'

Fortunately they had now reached the inn. 'I want a drink,' announced Snubby. 'All that twang-a-twang has made me thirsty. Can I have a lemonade, Miss Pepper – two if you like. Oh, I say – wait a bit, though – I'd forgotten my five shillings. Drinks all round, please. What'll you have, Miss Pepper? Miss Twitt? Orangeade? Lemonade? Or go a splash and have a ginger beer?'

Diana began to giggle. Snubby really could be very funny. Miss Pepper ordered the drinks and then sent all three children, and a very sleepy Loony, up to bed.

'It's late,' she said. 'Very late. Take your orangeade with you. No, Snubby, I don't care if you have five shillings or ten shillings, you can't have more than one orangeade. No, Loony can't have one either. Water is good enough for him.'

Snubby went off sorrowfully. He had hoped to stay downstairs until Iris, Mr Marvel and the Funny Man came back, and also Professor James who had still not returned. Praise from them would be worth a hundred times more than fulsome words from Miss Twitt.

Snubby was too excited to go to sleep that night. Roger snored gently and peacefully while Snubby tossed and turned, his mind full of wonderful plans. He would practise more and more imaginary instruments to play. He would broadcast – perhaps he wouldn't though, because people might think he was *really* playing a banjo or zither or guitar – they wouldn't be able to *see* that he hadn't really got one.

Well, what about television then? That would be the thing. And what about a drum? He was sure he could make that big BOOM-BOOM noise. He began to practise it very softly. Then he couldn't resist doing a very loud BOOM!

And then a most frightening thing happened. As soon

as Snubby had delivered his BOOM, another BOOM came – a terrific one, muffled and very frightening. The inn shook. Snubby sat up in bed, scared.

'Bombs!' he thought. 'No – can't be. Of course – it's an explosion in the Submarine Bay. Some experiment like the one we heard the other day.'

He thought for a moment. 'But wait a minute – this is the middle of the night – about half-past two, I should think. They wouldn't experiment then, and wake everyone up.'

The noise hadn't however, awakened Roger, who was in his deepest sleep. It hadn't awakened Diana either. Miss Pepper had heard it, and had sat up, listening. But as there was no more sound she had lain down again.

Snubby felt restless. He couldn't possibly lie down and go to sleep tonight. A thought flashed into his head. He would go up that little stairway that led to the skylight, open it, and peer out. He *might* be able to see something through that cleft in the cliff – something down in the Submarine Bay!

He slipped out of bed and went to the door. He opened it and went out to the dark landing. Nobody seemed to be stirring. Perhaps they hadn't heard the noise then.

Snubby stole to the little door that shut off the steep staircase. He opened it quietly. 'Yes – there was the staircase – he could feel it with his foot though he couldn't see it. He went up cautiously. It was a clear night and Snubby could see stars shining through the little square of glass set in the middle of the trap-door that opened on to the roof.

He opened it, pushing it back carefully, so as not to make a sound. He looked out.

Gosh! Something *had* happened down in the Submarine Bay. Snubby could see quite clearly through the cleft in the cliff. Far away, on the other side of it, was the bay, and something was burning there, on the water. Searchlights were playing here and there. Snubby held his breath. Something had happened. Some awful accident, perhaps. He wished he could see more.

'Perhaps if I climb right out of the trap-door I can find a higher place to see from,' he thought. 'It would be easy.'

He climbed to the topmost stair and found it simple to get out on the roof, which, just there, was flat. Snubby looked round. There was a rise in the roof just to the right of him, where a set of chimneys rose up together. He could sit on the little rise, beside a chimney.

He made his way cautiously across the rise in the roof, and crawled up it on hands and knees. Now he was by a chimney. But the wind swept him that side, so he crawled round in between two chimneys where he was well protected. One chimney was warm – good!

But to his disappointment he couldn't see much more of the bay than he had seen before, although he was now a little higher. Searchlights were still criss-crossing, and the flames of whatever was burning were still as high. Perhaps a submarine had exploded and was on fire.

Snubby cuddled up to the warm chimney, feeling daring to be out on the roof in the middle of the night. He suddenly sniffed the air.

He could smell something. What was it? Cigarette smoke! Couldn't be! No one else was up on the roof in the middle of the night – smoking a cigarette too!

He craned his neck round the chimney, and saw, in the distance, a tiny glow, the red, burning end of somebody's cigarette. Somebody else had heard the explosion then and had come to see what could be seen.

He soon saw that the glowing end was just where the trap-door opened on to the roof. Somebody must be standing on the stairs there, looking out and smoking. Snubby was just about to give a low call to tell them that he, too, was there, and had heard everything, when he stopped himself.

No. He'd get into a frightful row for being out on the roof at night. If Miss Pepper heard of it she would be furious. There wouldn't be any second helpings for the rest of the holidays! Silence was best. But *who* was it there? Snubby screwed up his eyes, but he could only make out a blob of a head with the glowing end of the cigarette in front.

After a while the smoker finished his cigarette and threw it down the roof. Snubby heard the soft creak of the stairs. Somebody was going down them – but that somebody had shut down the trap-door first! Snubby's heart missed a beat or two. He could imagine himself sitting out on the roof all night – falling asleep – rolling down the roof – oh, how simply horrible!

He crept across to the trap-door. As he got there, a light sprang in the window of a room some distance away. Snubby stopped. Who was in there? Probably, whoever it was, was the smoker of a few minutes before – he must have returned to his room and switched on his light. Snubby decided to see who it was.

He crawled to another position, and found that he could look right across the roof into the lighted room. The curtains were drawn across, but there was a space about a foot left in the middle.

'Gosh! It's Professor James!' said Snubby. 'What a good thing I didn't let him know I was up here. He'd have told Mrs Glump and Miss Pepper and got me into an awful row!'

He tried the trap-door with a trembling hand. Had the Professor slipped the catch into place, so that it could not be opened?

With an enormous sigh of relief Snubby found that he *could* open it. Thank goodness! He swung it back, and then clambered on to the narrow wooden stairway. He closed the trap-door quietly and then climbed down the stairs. He opened the door at the bottom, went on to the landing and back to his room. Roger was still fast asleep.

Just as he was about to shut his door he saw a line of light under a door nearby. It was Mr Marvel's door. So he had heard the explosion too. Snubby debated whether to go in and have a chat about it – surely Mr Marvel would welcome him now that he had given such a fine performance in the show!

He decided against it, however. Mr Marvel wasn't quite the person to enjoy a midnight chat. He might start to do a bit more unpleasant magic on Snubby.

Chapter Seventeen

The Next Day

In the morning the whole inn was agog with the news of the explosion in the night. So were the papers.

'GREAT EXPLOSION IN HUSH-HUSH BAY,' said the headlines. 'WAS IT SABOTAGE? ARE OUR SECRETS SAFE? INHABITANTS OF SURROUNDING TOWNS ALMOST HURLED FROM THEIR BEDS.'

'What a lie!' said Snubby. 'The bed just shook, that's all. And you didn't even wake, Roger. I did.'

'Did you?' said Roger. 'Was it really a big explosion?'

'Terrific,' said Snubby. 'Tremendous. Louder than thunder. I got out of bed and went up that stairway to look out of the trap-door – and I saw something burning like anything. And searchlights going like mad over the bay.'

'Sh! Miss Pepper will hear you,' said Diana. 'She'd be furious if she thought you went wandering about at night – especially up to the roof.'

'She didn't hear,' said Snubby. He glanced round. Old Professor James was nearby reading a newspaper. He was deaf so he wouldn't have heard either. Mr Marvel and the Funny Man were also near – they would have heard, but probably they didn't know about the staircase anyway.

'I did something else too,' said Snubby, lowering his voice. 'I got out on the roof and sat beside a jolly warm chimney. Somebody else came up the staircase and looked out too. The old Professor, I think. Fancy him hearing the explosion and not you, Roger!'

'I expect the vibration woke him, not the noise,' said

Diana. 'I say – it's pretty serious, isn't it? One of our newest submarines blown up to the surface – and then burnt to nothing! I do wish you'd woken me up, Snubby!'

'You'd have hated seeing it,' said Snubby. 'Is it sabotage, do you think? I mean – would it be possible for anyone to get into the bay and do a thing like that to damage us? I should have thought things were much too strict and closely guarded.

'It was probably an accident,' said Roger. 'You can't have successful experiments without accidents. Look at the things that happen in the lab at school!'

'Oh well – we *plan* some of those,' said Snubby. 'A bit of well-planned trickery! All the same – I'd like to know if it *was* an accident. I don't want to think of people somewhere around planning to blow up more submarines – especially while we're staying here.'

'Why? Are you afraid of being mixed up in another mystery?' asked Roger with a grin.

'*Afraid!*' said Snubby with scorn. 'I *like* mysteries. I dote on them. But this isn't a mystery, it seems to me. I bet it's an accident.

Whether it was or not they didn't learn from any of the papers that morning or evening. The Press seemed to shut down on the incident, which annoyed the children very much.

That afternoon was wet. The rain poured down and the children looked gloomy.

'It's a glumpish afternoon,' said Snubby. 'What shall we do? Shall I practice my banjo?'

'Not unless you go up on the roof or somewhere far away,' said Roger. Snubby had produced his imaginary banjo, zither, guitar and harp at different times that day, and Roger and Diana were getting a little tired of the remarkable twanging, zizzing, buzzing sounds produced by Snubby.

'Let's go up that little stairway and see if the poor old

submarine is still burning,' said Snubby. 'I promise I won't take any musical instruments with me!'

They ran upstairs to their landing and went to the little door that enclosed the staircase. Snubby turned the handle. But the door wouldn't open!

'What's the matter with it? Is it stuck?' he said, and pulled violently. All that happened was that the handle came completely off in his hand and he sat down heavily on a startled Loony.

'Ass! You *would* do that!' said Roger.

'Things always come off in my hand,' complained Snubby. 'Now what shall we do?'

'You'll have to go and own up to Mrs Glump,' said Diana. 'Go on, Snubby. If you were brave enough to get out and sit on the roof last night, surely you're brave enough to confess to Mrs Glump.'

So Snubby had to go and find Mrs Glump. She was in a peculiar little den, adding up rows and rows of figures, and didn't look at all pleased to see Snubby. He explained what had happened.

'But why did you pull at the handle so violently?' asked Mrs Glump, resting her face on her four or five chins, and looking most majestic. Snubby wished he had a few chins he could look majestic with too. He felt very small beside Mrs Glump, and she made him feel like a naughty little boy.

'Well, I pulled hard because the door stuck,' said Snubby. 'It's locked, I think.'

'Locked! But the key would be in the lock anyway,' said Mrs Glump.

'There wasn't a key. I looked,' said Snubby. 'I'm sure it's locked, Mrs Glump. I thought *you* must have locked it. I'm sorry about the handle. I've still got one and sixpence left out of the five shillings I won at the pierrot show yesterday. Would one and six pay for a new handle?'

'I expect so,' said Mrs Glump. 'But I'm sure Dummy

has an old one he could fix on quickly. Go and ask him. And I hear I must congratulate you on winning the prize yesterday. Let me see – you played the banjo, didn't you?'

'Not a real one. My imaginary one. Paid a hundred pounds for it!' said Snubby with a grin, and immediately began to play a jigging, strident tune, twang-twanging in a most lifelike manner.

Mrs Glump began to laugh. She had a very curious laugh. It seemed to begin somewhere deep down and then rumbled all the way past her magnificent chins, and came out as a very hearty affair indeed.

Snubby stopped, bowed and grinned. 'You're a caution,' said Mrs Glump. 'Get on with you! Go and find Dummy about the handle. And don't shut my door too violently in case the whole door comes off in your hand.'

Snubby went out, pleasantly surprised. She wasn't really glumpish at all! He made his way to the kitchen to find Dummy. He was polishing some horse-brasses one by one and making a very good job of them.

'Hello, Dummy. Can I help you? I collect horse-brasses too,' said the cheerful Snubby. 'I say, did you hear about me winning the five bob at the show last night?'

Dummy listened and nodded. 'You,' he said. 'You win. Good boy.'

'My word, you *are* a chatterbox today,' said Snubby, rubbing vigorously at a brass.

'What you do?' asked Dummy earnestly.

'This,' said Snubby, and played his imaginary banjo again. To his enormous surprise, Dummy also picked up an imaginary banjo and began to twang it, making a most peculiar noise as he did so, almost as good as Snubby's!

'Here – what's all this?' said a voice, and the face of the young waiter poked round the door. 'Some band performing here?'

Dummy fled at once, out into the back yard. He sat

down, blinking his eyes, confused. Years and years ago he had had a real banjo and he could play it. But when he had fallen from the rope, during a wire-walking act, he had hurt his head – and after that Dummy was different. Poor Dummy!

He sat till his mind cleared a little. He began to smile. Yes – he remembered his old banjo – and the tunes he played. He twanged imaginary strings again.

Snubby came into the yard to find him. 'Oh, there you are, Dummy. I say, I forgot to tell you what I wanted you for. Have you got a spare door-handle? I've somehow pulled off the handle of the door that shuts in that little stairway leading to the roof.'

'Roof,' said Dummy. He stared at Snubby and then suddenly leaned forward. He whispered loudly in his ear. 'Mind bad men up there! Bad men!'

Snubby drew back, startled. Dummy smiled and nodded at him. Then his face grew solemn again. 'Bad, bad, bad,' he whispered again. 'Dummy see. Dummy watch. Dummy follow. Bad!'

Snubby looked at Dummy doubtfully. Poor old fellow – what peculiar imaginings had he got now? He couldn't imagine Dummy watching people and stalking them! Snubby decided to humour him.

'Snubby see. Snubby watch. Snubby follow,' he said, equally solemnly. 'Gosh, we sound like Red Indians or something. Dummy, where's an old door-handle? Let's find one and go in. I'm not too keen on sitting out here in the rain – twang-a-twang-twang-twang, zizz-a-zizz-ziz-ziz. Ker-plonk! There – I knew a string would bust if I played out in the rain. See that?'

He held out his imaginary banjo, and Dummy laughed delightedly. It was the first time Snubby had heard him laugh. It was a ripple, just like a very young child's. Snubby patted Dummy on the back.

'That's right. Laugh your troubles away! Have you got a door-handle, for the third time of asking?'

Dummy had. He produced one from a shed and went upstairs. He was clever with his fingers and had soon fixed it on the door. He gave it a pull.

'Locked,' said Snubby. 'And the key's gone. Who did that? And why? I tell you, Dummy, there were mysterious goings on up here last night!'

'Indeed? And what were they?' said a voice.

Snubby jumped and turned round. Mr Marvel the conjurer was standing outside his door. Snubby thought furiously. No – he wasn't going to give anything away and get himself into trouble.

'Oh, nothing,' he said airily. 'I was just putting the wind up old Dummy. I say, sir – that was a wizard act you put on last night. How did you guess those articles – and the initials on the back of the watch? Beats me!'

'That's *my* secret,' said Mr Marvel. 'Did you hear the explosion last night?'

'Yes, I jolly well did,' said Snubby. 'Did you?'

'No, I didn't,' said Mr Marvel, which surprised Snubby very much. Hadn't he seen a line of light under Mr Marvel's door when he, Snubby, had come down from the roof to go to bed again?

'I saw a light under your door though,' blurted out Snubby, and could have kicked himself.

'Indeed? And what were *you* doing out on the landing at that time of night?' said Mr Marvel at once.

'Just peeped out to see if any one was awake after the explosion, said Snubby. 'I say, sir – how *did* you guess those numbers last night?'

But Mr Marvel was gone. Snubby was left staring at a closing door. He made a face at it. All right – *be* snooty, Mr Marvel! You *were* awake last night! Snubby shook a furious fist, marched into his own room, and slammed the door.

Chapter Eighteen

The Time Goes By

After the first few days the holiday began to slip away fast, as holidays always do.

A week had gone by before any of the children realised it. It had been a good week – bathing, boating, paddling, walking – messing about with Barney and Miranda. Loony had enjoyed himself too.

He dug violently every morning, covering everyone with sand. He then ran into the sea and got thoroughly wet. Then he came back and shook himself really vigorously, showering everyone with drops of sea water.

He had also developed a new and most irritating habit. Having been smacked hard for attempting to bring brushes, towels and mats on to the beach, he cast about for something that nobody could possibly object to.

He brought along a strange dog each day to play with him. The first time he brought a peculiar-looking mongrel with very short legs and a large head.

'Look at that,' said Snubby. 'Poor creature. If its legs were much shorter they wouldn't touch the ground!'

'Ha ha – very old joke,' said Diana. 'All the same, it *is* a peculiar dog.'

'It's a bit of a smelly dog,' said Roger, as the dog sat down heavily on his legs. 'Get off, Smelly! Go away!'

But Smelly had no intention of leaving his good friend Loony. They went crazy together and nearly drove Miss Pepper mad as they tore round and round her deck-chair. They had to put up with Smelly all day, and were amazed to see Loony sharing all his tit-bits with him.

The next day Loony trotted off the beach and returned

with a second friend – a bulldog with a face a bit like Mr Tubby's. He wasn't as bad as Smelly, and he liked to sit as near every one as possible.

'I wish you wouldn't *dribble* all over me,' Snubby said to the bulldog. 'You want a bib or something. Miss Pepper, do bulldogs always dribble or is this one just doing it on purpose?'

'He's dribbled over me too,' said Diana. 'I remember a teacher at school who had a bulldog and he dribbled as well. Loony, next time you bring a friend, bring one who doesn't smell *or* dribble!'

The bulldog was very sweet-tempered until he took a fancy to a bone that Loony was gnawing. Then he gave out such blood-curdling growls that even Snubby drew back. Miranda was with them at the time and she leapt on the top of Barney's head in fright.

'Go away,' said Miss Pepper firmly to the bulldog. 'That's Loony's bone. Go away!'

The bulldog calmly picked up the bone and waddled off. Snubby gave Loony a poke with his foot.

'Coward dog! Couldn't keep his own bone! Cowardy custard!'

Loony hung his head. He crept off the beach when no one was looking. He returned looking quite a different dog, bright and cheerful, accompanied by three small dogs of the terrier type, all very alert and inquisitive.

'Oh, stop it, Loony! Have you gone potty?' said Snubby, surveying the four dogs in disgust. 'What do you want to go and pick up half the town for? Shoo! Scat! Clear off, all of you. No, not you, Loony. You're going to be tied up to Miss Pepper's deck-chair for the rest of the day.'

'Oh no, he's not,' said Miss Pepper at once. 'You did that two days ago and he made my chair collapse. Tie him to your foot!'

Barney was rather quiet after three or four days. He

didn't encourage the others to go to the fair. 'It's a rough place,' he said. 'Don't come. I don't like the men who run it either. They're cheats. They're in some racket or other, too, but I don't know what it is.'

'Why don't you leave them, Barney?' said Diana anxiously. 'I *knew* you weren't pleased with the job. Don't stay with dishonest men.'

'Oh, I'm used to that type,' said Barney. 'You can't knock about as I do without coming up against them all the time. Anyway – where would I get another job?'

'Don't you remember – the conjurer belonging to the pierrot show said he'd take you as an assistant,' said Diana, remembering.

'But he's got Iris,' said Snubby. 'I don't know why he said he wanted another assistant!'

'No. Perhaps he doesn't,' said Diana. 'When's your week up, Barney? Tomorrow, isn't it?'

'Yes. I get paid then,' said Barney. 'Two whole pounds! I can buy some new sandshoes and a shirt.'

'Well, *do* leave then,' said Diana. 'I don't like that place either. I'm *sure* you could get a job somewhere else!'

But Barney wouldn't say he would leave. It wouldn't be easy to get another job in Rubadub, and he did so want to be near his friends.

That night Iris didn't go to the show. It was her night off. She sat in the lounge and played cards with the children, looking almost as young as Diana. Snubby sat next to her, wishing he could deal her the best cards in the pack. Loony sat on her feet. He agreed with his master that Iris was a very nice girl indeed.

'What will Mr Marvel do without you tonight?' asked Diana, watching Roger deal the cards. 'Does he do his mind-reading act when you're not there to help?'

'I don't know,' said Iris. 'I don't care either! Surly fellow. I don't like him.'

'Why?' asked Snubby.

But Iris wouldn't tell why. 'He used to have a helper,' she said. 'A youngish fellow. Then he suddenly went, I never knew why, and Mr Marvel asked me to take over till he got someone else. I said I'd try for two weeks. But I don't like it and I'm not doing it any more. The two weeks are up now.'

Diana now knew why Mr Marvel had asked Barney to be his helper. He had been afraid that Iris wouldn't go on with him after two weeks.

'Has he got anyone instead of you, do you know?' she asked suddenly.

'Someone came to see him today. I expect he was after the job,' said Iris. 'He'll probably get it, too, because Mr Marvel must have someone. He can't do that mind-reading act without an assistant.'

'Why not?' asked Snubby. 'Anyone from the audience could be called up – or one of the other pierrots.'

'No. He wants a proper assistant of his own,' said Iris. 'Look, are we playing a game of cards or is this just a chatter party? I've got such a wonderful hand that I'm longing to play it!'

Diana didn't play very well that night. She was thinking hard. Suppose they went to Mr Marvel and begged him to take Barney instead of the other applicant? If they could tell Barney they had the job for him, surely he would give notice at the little fair tomorrow, and join the pierrots? He would make a wonderful assistant!

She could hardly wait to tell the others when they went to bed that night. They listened in silence.

'Yes,' said Roger. 'I think we ought to tell Mr Marvel that Barney doesn't like his job, and will he take him instead of the other fellow, whoever he is. But *you'd* better ask him, Di. You're better at that kind of thing. You catch him all alone tomorrow morning and put your case!'

So, the next morning, when breakfast was over, Diana went to look for Mr Marvel. He was sitting in a garden shelter, reading the paper. He looked up as she came shyly in.

'Please can I speak to you, Mr Marvel?' she said. 'It's about that friend of ours, Barney. He doesn't like his job. I'm sure he'd come as your assistant if you still want one. Please have him instead of anyone else. He's a very hard worker and very clever. He'd do *anything* you want him to, anything.'

Mr Marvel put down his paper and looked at the earnest Diana. 'I'm looking for a *servant*, really,' he said. 'Someone who will do errands for me, see after my clothes, take messages, as well as help in my act.'

'He could do all that,' said Diana eagerly. 'Do try him, Mr Marvel.'

'What's his full name?' asked the conjurer, taking out a fountain pen and notebook.

'Barnabas Hugo Lorimer,' said Diana. 'Actually that's his mother's name. He doesn't know his father's.'

'How strange,' said Mr Marvel.

Diana plunged into Barney's story, and Mr Marvel listened with interest. 'So you see,' finished Diana, 'Barney is all alone in the world, he can go where he likes and take what job he likes – but oh, I *do* wish he could find his father!'

'I've no doubt I could do that for him!' said Mr Marvel, putting away his fountain pen. Diana gasped and stared.

'What do you mean? How could you? How would you set about it? Surely you couldn't, if even Barney doesn't know anything about his father – not even his name!'

'My dear young lady, I have been in the theatrical world for more years than I like to remember,' said Mr Marvel. 'I have only to ask a few of my friends if they knew of a Shakespearian actor some fifteen or so years ago, who is probably very like Barney in feature – he has

305

a most remarkable face, that boy. I'm quite certain I shall have news within a very short time!'

'Oh, Mr Marvel!' cried Diana, her eyes shining. 'Oh, it would be wonderful! Will you really do that?'

'If Barney comes to me, does what he is told and proves himself useful and trustworthy, then I shall certainly do my best,' said Mr Marvel. 'It rests with the boy himself. I'm not likely to take any trouble though, unless he does well with me.'

'Oh, Barney will do well, I know he will!' cried Diana joyfully. 'Let me go and fetch him, Mr Marvel. Then he can give in his notice today, and come to you tomorrow. Oh, thank you, thank you.'

She flew off, her heart singing. Oh, Barney, Barney, suppose your father is found quite soon! Oh, wonderful Mr Marvel, kind Mr Marvel – why had she ever thought she disliked him?

She found Barney down on the beach, waiting for her and the others. She flopped down beside him and told him her news. 'Please go to the inn now, this very minute, Barney!' she begged. 'He's there, waiting for you. Barney, just suppose he really *can* find your father for you! He seemed quite certain he would!'

'You're a good friend, Diana,' said Barney, his eyes shining. 'Come on, Miranda – we'll go and try our luck!'

Chapter Nineteen

Barney Gets the Job

Barney got the job. Mr Marvel appeared to think he could try, at any rate. It seemed a wonderful job to Barney.

'I shall get you new clothes instead of those rags,' said Mr Marvel. 'I will pay your lodgings for you. You will have three pounds a week – to start with. A good assistant is worth more than that to me, if he does what he is told!'

'Yes, sir,' said Barney, hardly believing his ears. He'd be rich! He could save a bit of money! Miranda should have a new skirt!

'But you understand, of course, Barnabas, that I am a magician, a conjurer, don't you?' said Mr Marvel. 'You understand that my secrets are *my* secrets, and if I have to let you into any of them, you must never say a word to anyone about them. Not even to those three friends of yours.'

'I wouldn't dream of it,' Barney assured him.

'And about your father,' went on the conjurer. 'I think I can find him for you. In fact, I am certain I can. I shall cause inquiries to be made immediately and let you know where he is. He may no longer be an actor, of course.'

'Yes, sir. I know that,' said Barney. 'Oh, sir – I'd do anything in the world for you if only you'd find out about my father – and make him believe I'm his son.'

'I think I can do that all right,' said Mr Marvel. 'I know many strings I can pull. Now, be a good boy to me in every way – and probably by the end of the season you won't want a job any more – because your father will want you instead!'

Barney walked unsteadily to the beach. He could hardly

believe his good luck. What a job! And what a reward! He sat down and told everyone about the interview.

'Well, I must say that Mr Marvel is going to do a lot for you,' said Miss Pepper. 'He must be a kindly fellow, although he looks so solemn and mournful. Well, it's time you had a bit of luck, Barney!'

That was a very happy morning. The sun shone, the water was calm and warm, and everyone was in high spirits. Loony disappeared, as usual, and all the children wondered what friend he would produce this time.

To their enormous surprise he brought back Mr Tubby – the gloomy, lugubrious Mr Tubby. How he had managed to persuade him to join the family circle nobody could think.

Mr Tubby, however, drew the line at monkeys. Children he would put up with, and a courteous, polite dog like Loony, who deferred to him in every way – but not monkeys. Certainly not monkeys. He stared mournfully at Miranda, who stared back, surprised at such a big dog. She suddenly dipped her hand into a bag of peanuts Barney had bought for her, and threw a pawful at the surprised and annoyed Mr Tubby.

He gave a deep, enormous 'WOOOOF' that startled everyone for some distance around. He cast a look of scorn at Loony, turned his back on them all, and lumbered back to the inn.

'There! Now he knows what awful friends you've got, he'll never speak to you again, Loony,' said Diana with a squeal of laughter. 'Oh dear – how marvellous of Miranda to throw those peanuts straight into his miserable face!'

Barney gave in his notice, and got his week's money. He didn't buy himself clothes as he had planned. If Mr Marvel was going to buy those, he'd buy something else. So he bought a fine handkerchief trimmed with cobwebby lace for Miss Pepper, a book for Diana, a propelling pencil for each of the boys and a ball for Loony. That was so like Barney!

He went to his new job with delight. It would be easy after the one he had just had, which was a dirty one, as well as hard and heavy. And there would be the thrill of seeing how Mr Marvel set about finding his father!

Mr Marvel bought Barney some excellent clothes, and Barney appeared at the inn looking very well dressed for the first time in his life. He grinned shyly.

'Do I look odd? I feel odd! Look at my tie. First time I've ever had one!'

He was full of Mr Marvel. 'He's a funny chap – his bark's worse than his bite. But my word, he's generous! He's already written to somebody who might know my father.'

Everyone's opinion of the conjurer had gone up skyhigh. The children told Miss Twitt and the Professor all about how Barney had got his new job. Miss Twitt prattled away, as pleased as they were. But the Professor merely grunted.

'Well, if anyone wants to work with a conjurer I suppose he can! Dangerous job. Mark my words, young man, it's a *dangerous* job!'

He glanced sharply at Barney as he spoke. Barney smiled politely. 'Oh, there's nothing out of the way about conjurers, sir. I've been at circuses with sword-swallowers, fire-eaters and the like – they are all quite nice fellows, really.'

The Professor gave one of his best snorts. He leaned back in his chair and shut his eyes. The chat was at an end!

Barney began work with the conjurer. He found it quite pleasant. He had to brush and sponge Mr Marvel's very considerable wardrobe, and to do that, he had to go to his room in the inn. He had to do his shopping for him, and clean all his many pairs of shoes. Mr Marvel was always complaining that Dummy didn't do them properly.

The conjurer frightened poor Dummy by shouting at him and calling him names that Dummy didn't understand. 'Dunderhead! Nitwit! Fumblehands!' No wonder Dummy wouldn't clean his shoes properly for him!

Mr Marvel initiated Barney into the mystery of his art. He told him what he wanted done on the platform, what cues Barney had to follow and so on. Barney was quick in the uptake and understood everything very easily. He was deft with his hands too, and soon felt that he could do some of the tricks himself that Mr Marvel did.

'He's a better-class conjurer than you usually find in little shows like ours,' he said to the children. 'He could get a job in London easily. But he prefers the seaside in summer.'

'Has he heard anything about your father yet?' Diana asked eagerly.

'There hasn't been time,' said Barney. 'But he wrote two more letters yesterday to old friends of his. It would be much easier if I knew my father's name, of course!'

A few days went by, happy and peaceful – and then a rumour flew through the little seaside town. 'The police are here! Scotland Yard, they say. It's about a submarine that blew up. It *is* sabotage – someone got to know too much, passed it on – and the result was the blowing up of the submarine!'

The three policemen, all in plain, sober clothes, actually stayed at the inn! This was a terrific excitement. Everyone knew they were the police, of course, and Snubby spent ages staring at them. Had they found out anything? Did they suspect anyone in Rubadub? It was said they had visited the little fair. Had any of the men there something to do with the sabotage?

'Barney always said they were dishonest men,' said Roger. 'It might be one of them that the police are after.'

Mrs Glump placed a special room at the disposal of the solemn detectives. As Snubby passed the door once, he saw the Professor coming out. He didn't see Snubby, and went slowly up the stairs with bent head. Snubby watched him.

'I bet they've been questioning him! I bet they suspect him! And I bet they're right too! Wasn't he up on the roof that night, watching the blaze? Ought I to tell them?'

On second thoughts he decided not to. After all, he hadn't actually *seen* the Professor – he had only seen the glow of a cigarette, and noticed the Professor's light switched on in his room later on. Regretfully Snubby decided he had better not barge in. But he would keep his eyes open!

Dummy vanished completely when the police arrived. He was absolutely frightened out of his wits. As soon as he knew the three men were detectives he went to earth like a rabbit.

Nobody could find him. Mrs Glump was cross and worried. 'He did that before when a policeman in uniform arrived one day to ask about a lost dog,' she said. 'Why he's so scared of them I don't know. Oh dear – just when we've got three extra guests in the house too.'

Barney offered to help, if Mr Marvel would let him. Mr Marvel agreed at once, and went to the police to offer Barney's services if they wanted a good honest lad to clean their shoes and do any other jobs for them. Mrs Glump, too, was only too glad to accept the offer.

'Thank you,' said one of the detectives. 'Right. If you can spare him we can make good use of him. We hear he was down at the fair. We'd like to ask him a few questions about the men who employed him.'

But except that he knew they were dishonest, Barney could give the police very little information about the men.

'What about the men who go there?' asked one man.

'Did you see any of them getting in touch with your employers?'

'Yes, sir. But I never heard what was said,' said Barney. He gave quite a good description of one or two sailors who had visited the place two or three times and spoken to his employers.

'You're employed by a Mr Marvel now, I believe,' said the man. 'Getting on all right with him?'

'Yes, sir. He's very good to me,' said Barney. 'It's a nice job.'

'Right. You can go,' said the man, and Barney went. He had a room high up in the attics now – he was actually living in the inn with the children, though he had his meals with the staff, of course. It all seemed very wonderful to Barney. Things were going well. And soon Mr Marvel might hear news of his father. That would be the best thing of all!

Chapter Twenty

Next Morning

'Miss Twitt's all of a twitter this morning,' announced Snubby, the next day. 'The police have interviewed her. She's terribly excited about it. She says they asked her all kinds of questions.'

'I bet they didn't get anything sensible out of her, then,' said Roger. 'I wish they'd interview *us*. Not that we've much to tell them. They've talked to Barney. I don't see why *we* should be left out.'

'It was only because Barney worked down at the fair,' said Snubby. 'He thinks the police imagine he might have overheard some strange talk. I say – I do wonder where old Dummy's gone. I miss him.'

'I expect he's streaked off at top speed, and is at the other end of the country by now!' said Roger. 'Barney says most circus folk try to keep clear of the police. For all we know, Dummy may have thought they were after him for something.'

'He's left all his things behind, the waiter told me,' said Snubby. 'Poor old Dummy. I did like him.'

Miss Twitt sailed up, jingling as usual. A tremendous perfume of Gardenia came with her. She was, as Snubby had so aptly said, 'all of a twitter!'

'Pooh!' said Snubby, under his breath, as he got the Gardenia full strength. He removed himself from the room at once, with Loony gasping at his heels. Snubby held his breath till he got outside the door, and then blew out vigorously. Miss Pepper, who was coming in, looked at him in amazement.

'What's the matter, Snubby? Don't you feel well?'

313

'A bit knocked out, that's all,' said Snubby, leaning against the wall, fanning himself with his hands. 'Miss Twitt's in there – with a new smell!'

'Oh, don't be so idiotic, Snubby,' said Miss Pepper. 'I do wish she wouldn't use so many perfumes, I must say – but there's no need to make such a song and dance about it!'

'Good idea!' said Snubby, and produced his imaginary banjo. He began to strum, making his twanging noise, and did a ridiculous step dance in time all round the hall. Miss Pepper began to laugh.

'You're a born comic,' she said. 'Oh dear, I don't feel as if I want to hear about Miss Twitt's interview with the police all over again. I've had a few words with them myself.'

'Gosh! Have you really?' said Snubby, forgetting his banjo. 'I say – why are they interviewing everyone here? Do they think anyone has got anything to do with the sabotage?'

'I don't really know,' said Miss Pepper. 'They've apparently got *some* clue they're working on. I think they're trying to find out how information and orders are passed out and into the Submarine Base. It's practically sealed off from the outside world, you know. Everyone is searched and checked before he goes out. But it can't be anyone *here* – nobody here has anything to do with the Submarine Base.'

'I bet I know who it is,' said Snubby mysteriously, his mind flashing back to the night of the explosion. 'I bet I do!'

'No, you don't, Snubby,' said Miss Pepper. 'You're just being silly. Oh – good morning, Mr Marvel. Have you been interviewed too? Snubby here thinks he knows more than the police!'

'And what do you know, young man?' asked Mr

Marvel, with his peculiar smile, that never reached his eyes. 'Which of us is the saboteur?'

'What's *that*?' asked Snubby. 'Oh – the fellow who did the damage? Aha! That's *my* secret!'

He sauntered off, strumming his banjo again. He wasn't going to tell either Miss Pepper or Mr Marvel his suspicions of Professor James. They'd only laugh at him. But wasn't the Professor just the person to be mixed up in Big Secrets? He must know an awful lot about scientific things – and any information passed out he would understand – and he could learn it by heart, probably, and then tear up the message.

But how could any message get to him? Well, that was up to the police to find out. Or perhaps he, Snubby, could do a little snooping and find out something.

'I could creep over the roof and peep in at his window, to see if he's doing anything suspicious,' thought Snubby, and a swirl of excitement came over him. 'I *say* – that would be a smashing thing to do! I'll tell Roger. He could come with me.'

Roger was rather doubtful. He agreed that the Professor was the most suspicious person in the inn. He had already told Snubby how he had seen him in the mirror a night or two ago, wide awake, listening to their conversation, although he was pretending to be asleep.

But all the same, creeping over the roof at night to snoop through his window didn't seem too good. 'A bit sneakish,' said Roger.

'Rot,' said Snubby. 'If he's a traitor of some sort he deserves to be spied on. If you're not game to do it, I'll do it with Barney. He sleeps up in the attics, and he could easily snoop about at night.'

'You and Barney aren't going to have all the excitement,' said Roger jealously. 'I'm jolly well joining in.'

They spoke to Barney about it. He agreed that it would

315

be exciting to do some snooping round on their own. He thought the old Professor was up to something too.

'He's not such an old crock as he makes himself out to be,' said Barney. 'And he's not as deaf as everyone imagines either!'

'We know *that*,' said Roger. 'Right – we'll keep an eye on him – several eyes, in fact. When shall we do our bit of roof-crawling?'

'Wait till the bobbies are gone,' said Barney. 'I've no doubt they're doing a bit of snooping round too. I saw one of them coming out of the Professor's room yesterday – I bet he'd been doing a rummage round.'

'All right. We'll wait a day or two,' said Snubby. 'They won't be here very long. I say, how does Miranda put up with staying in your room by herself?'

'She's as good as gold,' said Barney. 'She knows I'm on a job, and she just tucks herself up on a cushion by the window and waits till I'm free to go to her.'

'We can always have her when you're busy, you know,' said Roger. 'Shall we have her now? We're going down to the beach.'

'Right. You take her,' said Barney gratefully. 'I've got a lot to do. Dummy may have been a bit strange in the head, but he certainly managed to get through a lot of work! I must hurry or I shall never get done in time!'

Miranda was perfectly happy to go with Roger and the others. She knew Barney was busy and couldn't rush round with her on his shoulder all the time. So she played happily on the beach. Diana bought her a tiny spade, and Miranda dug with it valiantly, scattering sand all over Loony as soon as he came near.

Loony was still bringing new friends. He brought a tiny Pekinese that day, with a funny little snub nose.

'Isn't that Peke like Snubby?' said Diana. 'Miss Pepper, do look at him – he's got *such* a look of Snubby, same untidy mane, same turned-up nose, same . . .'

Snubby threw a bucket of water over her in rage and she screamed. 'Don't, you beast! I've got hot in the sun and that water felt icy-cold!'

'Serves you right,' said Snubby, pushing away the snub-nosed Peke. 'Keep off. You're not my little brother, even though you think you are, after Di's silly remarks!'

Loony dug up a bone he had buried the day before, and proceeded to lie down and gnaw it. The Peke immediately ran up. Loony growled.

'You be careful, Peke,' said Roger. 'The only time when Loony feels brave is when he's got a bone to protect!'

The Peke suddenly grabbed the bone from beneath Loony's nose and ran off with it. Loony barked in rage and ran after him. The Peke turned, dropped the bone, and faced Loony, yapping fiercely.

'Look at that!' said Diana admiringly. 'What a tiny thing to be so lion-hearted!'

Loony ran at the Peke. But the little dog stood his ground and yapped and snapped. He suddenly ran at Loony, snapping his teeth and snarling.

And Loony put his tail between his legs and fled! The Peke picked up his bone and waddled off with it in triumph. He didn't appear again.

'*Well!* Loony ought to be ashamed of himself!' said Roger, disgusted.

'Oh, many a bigger dog than Loony has been put to flight by a Peke,' said Miss Pepper amused. 'They aren't afraid of anyone or anything. Poor Loony!'

Loony arrived back after about twenty minutes, looking very much ashamed of himself. He sat down by Snubby and looked at him mournfully. Snubby put his arm round him.

'It's all right, Loony. I still love you though you really are a fathead.' said Snubby, pulling Loony's long ears gently. 'But don't bring any more strangers here – one dog's quite enough!'

Barney passed them, on his way to do some errands for Mr Marvel. He had to go to the dressing-room at the concert hall on the pier to arrange Mr Marvel's stage properties for the next show. He whistled merrily.

Miranda shot up the beach and was on his shoulder in a trice. 'I'm going on the pier,' shouted Barney. 'I'll have a few minutes with you when I come back.'

'We'll come with you,' called Roger.

'No, don't, I can get on without paying now, but you can't,' shouted back Barney. 'It'd be a waste of money! See you later.'

Barney sounded busy and happy. He had been a success with Mr Marvel at the show. He had been provided with a small silken cloak with stars and moons on it and a round silken cap, rather like the pierrots wore, but with a brilliant star in front of it. He looked extremely handsome in cloak and cap, a simple black tunic and long hose!

'He's a better assistant than I was,' Iris told the three children. 'He gets on with Mr Marvel better too. And I must say that Mr Marvel is very good to him – much nicer to him than he ever was to me. Maybe Barney is cleverer at helping him with his tricks than I was. He's got some new ones since I helped him.'

Barney felt that he had decidedly gone up in the world! A job at the inn near his friends – a job on the stage in fine clothes – other new clothes too – and a very fine wage! Barney was very pleased indeed with life.

Chapter Twenty-One

A Trick – and a Plan

Two or three days went by, days of brilliant August weather when the sea and sky were both deep blue and only a few cotton-wool clouds strayed overhead like lost sheep.

The children were burnt a deep red-brown, and even Miss Pepper began to turn colour too. They all had enormous appetites, and Mrs Glump began seriously to wonder if she was making any money out of their stay at all! Snubby's appetite seemed quite insatiable.

'You're eating all day long,' said Diana. 'Honestly, I don't believe you ever stop. And when you can't find anything to bite and swallow, you take that horrible bit of chewing-gum and work on that!'

'Well, it's a comfort,' said Snubby, chewing hard. 'Though it hasn't any taste left now, unfortunately.'

'You're disgusting,' said Diana. She really did think Snubby was dreadful with his chewing-gum. She spoke to Roger about it. 'Can't we get it out of his pockets and throw it away?' she asked him. 'Couldn't you wait till Snubby's gone down to bathe and then take it?'

'No. He takes it with him in his mouth!' said Roger. 'But Diana! I'll tell you what we'll do! Listen!'

He whispered to her. She chuckled. 'Oh *yes* – that'll cure him! Go and buy some now.'

So Roger sped off the beach while Snubby was bathing, and bought a little packet of plasticine. He opened it and took out a small stick. He broke off a bit and began to mould it and squeeze it to get is soft. When he squeezed it flat it really looked remarkably like Snubby's chewed bit of gum!

He and Diana waited their chance. Then Roger substituted the new bit of plasticene for the old bit of chewing-gum, wrapping it up carefully in the bit of paper Snubby kept for his gum.

'Now we'll see what happens,' he said to the delighted Diana.

But unfortunately Snubby did himself so well at meals that day, helped out by an ice-cream or two and some sweets, that he didn't remember his precious bit of chewing-gum. So the bit of plasticene stayed in his pocket, waiting.

After tea that day Barney came to them, his face shining with delight.

'Listen!' he said. 'Mr Marvel's had a letter back from one of his friends. He says he thinks he knows my father.'

'*Barney!* Not really!'

'Oh, Barney – how wonderful!'

'Gosh – good old Marvel!'

Miss Pepper smiled at the excited boy. 'How does the man who wrote to Mr Marvel know that it's your father?' she asked.

'Well,' said Barney, 'he said that for one thing this man he thinks is my father used to be an actor and was very fond of Shakespeare's plays – and for another thing his Christian name is Hugo! And that's my second name, you know. My mother must have given me that name after my father!'

'That's very likely,' said Miss Pepper. 'What did he say your father's surname was?'

'He said it's Johnson, but he doesn't know if that's the name he chose for acting, or whether it's his real name,' said Barney. 'Isn't it grand, Miss Pepper!'

'Is he like you to look at?' asked Roger.

'He didn't say,' said Barney. 'He's trying to find out a bit more. He thinks my father was called up in the last war, so he's asking actor friends of his, who were also called up, if they heard of him anywhere.'

'It's jolly exciting, all this,' said Snubby. 'I do wonder what your father's like. He might not be an actor at all now. He might have stayed in the Army – or gone into the Navy or Air Force. He might be an admiral or a general or anything!'

'He might equally well have fallen on hard times and be playing a barrel-organ in the street,' said Barney. 'I wouldn't mind – so long as he was my father! To find someone who really belongs to me would be wonderful. I never even had an aunt or uncle on my mother's side, I never even remember a granny. You just can't imagine what it would be like to me to find people who were my own.'

Barney thought the world of Mr Marvel. To think he was taking all that trouble! He would be grateful to the conjurer as long as he lived. Barney shone all his shoes till they reflected everything around. He brushed all the conjurer's clothes till they hadn't a speck on them. He cleaned all his stage properties meticulously and never forgot a thing, Mr Marvel had never in his life had such a willing and trustworthy assistant!

The police went at last. All three detectives slipped out one morning and were not seen again. They were there at breakfast, and then appeared no more. Mrs Glump heaved a sigh of relief.

'There's nothing for them to snoop about here,' she confided to Miss Pepper. 'Down in the town, perhaps, yes – particularly at that Fair. Such a rough lot do go there – especially sailors. That's where any mischief is planned, I don't doubt.'

Roger, Snubby, Diana and Barney met on the promenade that morning to discuss the departure of the detectives. They thought they might begin their snooping now.

Snubby had dreamt about roof-crawling till he could hardly stop thinking about it.

'Let's have an ice-cream while we're waiting,' he said. But no ice-cream man came in sight.

'Oh well – I'll have a spot of chewing-gum,' said Snubby and put his hand into his pocket. Roger looked at Diana and winked. This was the first time Snubby had done any chewing since they had changed over the gum for plasticene! It had exasperated them considerably that Snubby should have shown no interest in his chewing-gum for the last day or two. Still, they could wait!

He took out the piece of paper and unwrapped it. He slipped the grey bit of plasticene into his mouth without even looking at it. He began to chew.

Diana felt she must begin to talk or she would dissolve into some of her helpless giggles. 'Isn't the sea grand today,' she began. 'And look at the little frilly white waves at the edge – just like lace. And . . .'

Snubby looked at her in surprise. 'What a lot of babble,' he said. 'You sound like Miss Twitt. She babbles like that!'

He was chewing hard. Then a peculiar expression came over his face. He chewed more slowly. Diana felt an enormous giggle forming in her middle. Roger began to talk fast now, much to Barney's astonishment.

'We'll have to make some plans. We might be able to do something tonight. I thought the Professor looked rather down in the mouth today. Maybe the police . . .'

Snubby wasn't listening. He wore a look of great disgust. His mouth fell half open, and he looked desperate.

'Ugh!' he said, and suddenly spat the plasticene right out of his mouth and on to the beach below.

'Snubby!' said Barney, amazed. 'You nearly hit that woman on the beach. Whatever are you thinking of?'

'I'll have to get a drink of water,' said Snubby, looking very green. 'I'll be back.'

Diana's giggle burst out of her and she sank back, holding herself tightly. Roger roared loudly. Barney, who hadn't been told the joke, stared in surprise.

Neither Diana nor Roger could explain what the matter was. 'Snubby's face!' gasped Diana. 'Oh dear!'

'Come on – tell me the joke,' said Barney, beginning to laugh himself at the sight of Diana and Roger. At last they were able to tell him. 'But don't say a word, will you, Barney?' begged Diana. 'If it cures him of chewing-gum it would be too marvellous for words. *Don't* tell him.'

Snubby came back, looking better. He sat down on the seat again. 'What was the matter?' asked Barney, trying to keep a straight face.

'It was my chewing-gum,' explained poor Snubby, tickling Miranda under the chin. 'I think I must have suddenly turned against it, it was *horrible*. I just *had* to spit it out, I couldn't help it. I'm never going to chew gum again, never. Gosh, it made me feel as sick as a wet hen!'

Diana wanted to giggle again. But it would never do to give the game away after Snubby had made such a wonderful resolution. He was never going to chew gum again! It was too good to be true.

'I got a drink of water,' said Snubby. 'In fact, I drank the whole jugful that was on our table. I couldn't seem to get the taste out of my mouth. Who would have thought I'd turn against chewing-gum like that? Well, I felt so sick at even the *thought* of chewing-gum that I made up my mind I'd go up to my room, get the rest of the packet, and throw it away. So up I went.'

'Good for you,' said Roger, approving heartily.

'And listen to this,' said Snubby, dropping his voice suddenly, and looking round furtively as if he thought the promenade might be full of listeners, 'Just listen to this. When I got up to my room, there was old Professor James on our landing! He must have been in somebody's room!

He doesn't sleep on that landing. He's no business to be there.'

The other three were extremely interested. Another black mark against the Professor! 'Did he say anything?' asked Roger.

'I said to him, "Hallo, Professor, lost your way?" ' said Snubby. 'He just scowled at me and didn't answer. He went downstairs then.'

'He might have been trying to get up those stairs,' said Roger.

'He couldn't. The door's locked and the key is lost – or stolen,' said Snubby. 'It all looked jolly suspicious, anyway. What about doing our snooping tonight? We might see something interesting if we crawled over the roof and peered into his window – always supposing he hasn't drawn the curtains right across.'

'Yes, we will,' said Roger. 'Not Di, though, I'm not going to have her rolling off the roof!'

'I don't particularly want to come!' said Diana. 'I'll keep a look-out for you, if you like. But how are you going to get on the roof if you can't get up that little stairway that leads there?'

'Easy,' said Roger. 'Our window gives on to part of the roof. We can easily get out there and crawl over to where we can peep into the Professor's window.'

They all felt very excited. Snubby gave the surprised Loony a loving thump. 'Roof-crawling, Loony!' he said. 'But not for you, old chap! It's a shame – but I just feel you'll have to be left out of our trip tonight!'

Chapter Twenty-Two

Along Comes An Adventure

Miss Pepper couldn't think why the children seemed so mysterious that night. They gave each other winks and meaningful looks, and Snubby kept talking about cats on roofs.

'Why do cats like roofs, Miss Pepper?' he said. 'Do they go and warm themselves by the chimneys?'

'Why should they?' said Miss Pepper. 'Very few chimneys are warm – only those that have a big fire down below. Don't be silly, Snubby.'

Roger gave Snubby a kick to warn him to stop. But he went on. 'I once knew a nice warm chimney,' he said. 'It was a lovely place to sit.'

'That'll do, Snubby,' said Miss Pepper. 'If you've got one of your silly fits on, leave the table.'

'But I haven't had any pudding,' said Snubby. 'All right, I'll stop twittering.'

Miss Pepper made an exasperated click. But Miss Twitt was engrossed in cold meat and salad and didn't hear Snubby's silly remark.

Barney had a disappointment for them that evening. He met them after their dinner. 'I've got to go to the show now,' he said, 'but I just came to tell you I won't be able to join you tonight. I've got to take a bag with something urgent in it over to the next town after the show.'

'Well, you'll be back before midnight I should hope!' said Roger, surprised.

'No, I shan't,' said Barney. 'I've got to stay the night at Pearley, at the place I take the bag to. It's some clothes

Mr Marvel wants altering in a hurry – some of his stage clothes. He says the old woman I give the bag to will alter them that same night and give them to me to bring back tomorrow morning. Apparently she is always willing to do that for him. So I shan't be able to join you, unfortunately. I'm catching the last train to Pearley. I'm taking Miranda, though.'

'What a nuisance!' said Roger. 'Well, we'll roof-crawl without you. You can join us another time. I just don't feel we can put it off after getting so worked up about it.'

'Of course not,' said Barney. 'I must fly. So long!'

The grandfather clock in the dining-room chimed a quarter to eight. 'What shall we do this evening?' said Diana. 'It's fine. Shall we go for a walk?'

'No. I'm tired,' said Snubby. 'All that swimming we did, I suppose. And I don't want to make myself any tireder because of tonight, I want to be jolly wide awake!'

'Well, let's read then,' said Diana. 'I've got a good circus story I want to finish. It's got a monkey in it, like Miranda.'

It was decided that Diana need not keep awake or do any looking-out for the two boys. There wouldn't be much chance, they thought, of anyone knowing they had crawled out of their bedroom window or of anyone trying to stop them.

'Di, get Miss Pepper's alarm clock for us out of her room,' said Roger. 'We plan to roof-crawl after midnight, and we're sure to fall asleep before then. We'll have to have an alarm to wake us up.'

'Well, set it and put the clock under your pillow then, or it will wake up everyone on our landing!' said Diana. 'I expect Miss Pepper will go to bed just after we do – she's such an early bird – and when I know she's asleep I'll creep in and borrow her clock.'

Everything went as planned. They went up to bed at a

quarter to nine, and Miss Pepper yawned and said she really thought she would come too. Diana winked at Roger. Good!

She slipped into their room with the alarm clock at just after half-past nine. 'Will you believe it, Miss Pepper's asleep already,' she whispered. 'Here you are. I half wish I was coming now.'

'Well, you aren't!' said Roger. 'We'll tell you all about it in the morning, if we discover anything interesting.'

Roger put the clock under his pillow. The alarm would go off and waken him but nobody else. It awakened him all right, and he sat up in bed, startled. Of course – it was only the alarm going off! He scrabbled under his pillow and switched it off. Then he woke the snoring Snubby.

It was difficult to wake Snubby, so Roger got Loony to do it instead. Loony leapt on to him and licked his face lavishly. Snubby sat up and pushed him off.

'What on earth . . .' he began, and then remembered. He scrambled out of bed.

'Don't make a row now, Snubby,' warned Roger. 'And tie Loony to the bed or he'll try to jump out of the window after us. He won't howl, will he?'

'Not if I tell him not to,' said Snubby, and tied Loony up firmly. Loony whined a little, but then lay down patiently.

The two boys climbed out of their window. There was a moon, but the sky was very cloudy, so the light was fitful. They sat on the roof outside their window and looked round.

Not far off was the Professor's window. It had a light shining in it, but tonight the curtains were drawn more closely together and only a small crack showed.

'Still – it's enough to peep through,' whispered Roger. 'Come on. Keep to the flat parts, or you'll roll away. It's easy going here.'

They crawled slowly, dragging themselves along cautiously in a sitting position. There was no danger where they were, but still it all *felt* very dangerous and exciting. Snubby's heart began to beat quickly.

Just as they came really near to the Professor's lighted window, his light went out! The room was in darkness. How maddening!

'What shall we do?' whispered Roger. 'Wait a few minutes, do you think?'

'Yes. Let's get by that tall chimney there. We'll be out of sight if he comes to the window,' whispered back Snubby. So they crawled silently to the big chimney. Unfortunately it was not a warm one. Still the night was not cold, so it didn't matter!

They stood by the chimney, hoping against hope that the light would be switched on again. And then Snubby suddenly clutched Roger so violently that he made him jump almost out of his skin.

'Roger! Look! What's that!'

Roger looked in the direction that Snubby was facing. He stiffened in surprise. Some distance to the right, and higher up than they were, a light was flashing. Flash, flash, flash. Flash, flash.

'Signalling,' whispered Snubby. 'What window is it that the signals are coming from? I say, Roger – this is extraordinary!'

'Let's get nearer that window,' whispered Roger. 'This is very important, Snubby. For goodness' sake don't make any noise. Let me go first.'

Keeping in the shadow of chimneys when they could, they made their way very cautiously indeed towards the window from which the signals came. It certainly seemed very high up. What window could it be? It must be the highest one in the inn!

Roger clutched Snubby by the arm and put his mouth excitedly to his ear. 'Snubby! That's not a window! That's the skylight trap-door opening off that little staircase! Why didn't we think of it before?'

So it was. The boys could now clearly see the trap-door thrown back, as the moon sailed out from behind a cloud.

'Who is it signalling?' said Snubby. 'We *must* find out, Roger. Gosh, the police were right. There *is* someone here who's acting jolly suspiciously. Is it Professor James? It's funny his light went out just before we saw the signals. I suppose they *are* signals?'

'Of course,' said Roger, watching for the next series of flashes. 'Those flashes can be seen quite clearly by any watcher in the Submarine Bay if he is in exactly the right place to receive them. That cleft in the cliff might be *made* for signals to and fro! Maybe that is why it *was* made originally – for smugglers or wreckers to signal news or warnings. Whoever is out in a boat on the very spot that can be seen from that high trap-door window is no doubt receiving important messages!'

'It *must* be the Professor,' said Snubby. 'How can we find out for certain, Roger? We simply must!'

'Well, we daren't go any nearer than this,' said Roger. 'We don't want to be seen. It's important that the man shouldn't know we've been watching him. I know – you slip back into our room and hide somewhere on the landing. Then you'll see the man come down and spot who he is!'

'Jolly good!' said Snubby. 'I'll do that. You stay here and watch.'

He crawled away from Roger very carefully and quietly. He was strung up and excited. Why, this was another adventure! All of a sudden, in the very middle of the night, there was a smashing adventure! You just never knew when adventures might come along.

He came to the window and climbed in. He made his way to the door, fell over Loony, who was very pleased

329

to see him again, and made much more noise than he meant to.

'Shut up, Loony!' he whispered, trying to push the excited dog away. 'That's my face you're pawing. Be quiet. SHUSH!'

At last Loony quieted down. Snubby opened his door and looked out. The landing was in complete darkness. Not a sound was to be heard. Snubby debated where to hide. He wasn't afraid of being seen, the landing was so dark – but if the man had a torch, he might pick out Snubby in its light if he didn't hide himself well.

He shut his door softly. He tiptoed across the landing to a window hung with long curtains. He crept behind them and drew them carefully round him. He stood and waited, his heart working like a piston.

He waited there for a few minutes, his ears strained for any sound. Nothing happened. No noise came, not even the creak of a bit of furniture in the night.

Then Snubby thought he heard a sound. What was it? It was rather like somebody very cautiously clearing his throat. Surely that fellow hadn't come down the stairs so quietly that Snubby hadn't seen or heard him! He listened again.

There! The tiny noise came again – it was a little sniff this time. Snubby stiffened with fright. Good gracious! There was something on the landing. He was certain of it. Where? Who could it be?

And then the door enclosing the little staircase opened slowly. A little moonlight came through the skylight at the top of the stairway, enough to show Snubby that someone was creeping out of the door. Then it shut just as softly. Who was it? Snubby hadn't been able to make out – but he was absolutely certain it was old Professor James!

Chapter Twenty-Three

Snubby is Not Lion-Hearted

Snubby, hidden behind the long curtains, heard the little creak-creak of the boards under the landing mats, as somebody went cautiously by. He longed to make absolutely certain that it was the Professor.

He would follow him and see if he went down to his bedroom on the next landing. So he slid out between the curtains and took a step or two towards the head of the stairs. He had completely forgotten there might be somebody else hidden on the landing!

He heard the creak of a stair some way down. He came to the head of the stairs and began to go down very cautiously himself.

But one of the stairs creaked so loudly that the man he was following heard it. He was now on the landing below. He took fright.

He ran down the remaining stairs at top speed and landed down in the hall. Snubby ran after him.

And somebody ran after Snubby! That somebody who had been hiding on the top landing, as well as Snubby, was coming down the stairs, close on his heels!

Snubby felt a hand clutch at him. He was suddenly terrified. He tore into the big dining-room, which was dimly lighted now and again by the moon. He must hide!

He heard a noise coming from the hall. Somebody was struggling there – struggling with somebody else, panting, trying to keep as silent as possible.

Snubby heard a gasp as one of the two fighters struck a blow. Then came a groan. He gazed desperately round the big dining-room. Where, oh where could he hide?

Whatever was going on was something desperate, and he didn't want to be mixed up in it. Who was the Professor fighting?

He was standing by the grandfather clock. It suddenly made the loud whirring noise that meant it was going to strike.

Snubby almost jumped out of his skin. His hair stood on end – and then, with a wave of relief he realised that it was only the old clock. The old clock – why – the old clock would hide him!

Snubby felt for the clasp that fastened the door of the clock over the great pendulum inside. He opened it and got inside, almost falling in, he was so anxious to hide. The fighters were now in the dining-room, swaying this way and that, and they crashed against a table. Snubby pulled the clock door shut and stood trembling inside. The pendulum tried its hardest to swing to and fro with Snubby pressing against it, but it couldn't. It gave up, and the clock suddenly stopped its loud ticking.

But nobody noticed that, certainly not poor Snubby. He could only hear his heart beating, far more loudly than any grandfather clock!

There was a crash as a chair went over. Both the fighters fell on the floor, judging by the thudding and wriggling that went on. Snubby longed to peep out and see who the two were, but he didn't dare to push the clock door open even a crack. It was not Snubby's night for being lion-hearted!

A dog began to bark. It wasn't Loony. He was too far away to hear any noise. It was Mr Tubby, shut up in Mrs Glump's little den, with his enormous basket.

The fighters stopped for a moment. Then there was the sound of scampering feet, a click – and silence. One of the fighters had evidently gone. Which one?

Snubby listened with both his ears. The one who was

left tiptoed to the hall. Snubby then heard him going up the stairs – creak; creak-creak.

He was gone. Snubby wondered whether it was all right for him to go and find Roger. He was simply longing for Roger! Snubby was always very brave in the daytime, but at night things were somehow different.

He pushed open the door of the clock. He climbed out. At once the pendulum began to swing again and the clock ticked once more. Tick-tock, tick-tock, slowly and deliberately.

Snubby tiptoed to the door in his turn. He didn't like it a bit. He wished he was safely back in the clock. He stopped, thinking he heard a sound. He had! Oh goodness gracious, who was that now? How many more people were there prowling about tonight?

It was somebody in the hall. The moon shone out at that moment and Snubby shrank back into a deep shadow, waiting there, shivering. If anyone was in the hall he could jolly well show himself first!

A pair of curtains draped over a big hall window suddenly moved. Snubby nearly screamed. He stood there in his corner, hardly daring to breathe. Who was coming out of the curtains?

But nobody came out. Instead, something was poked through and a brilliant light suddenly shone on poor Snubby, making him gasp. He was caught in the beam of a powerful torch!

It was too much! He tore up the stairs two at a time, gasping and panting, fearing that the one behind the curtain would chase him. But nobody came after him. When he got safely to his room he sank down beside Loony, trembling and terrified. What an awful night! However many suspicious people were there creeping about the inn? It seemed suddenly to have become a perfect hot-bed of extraordinary happenings!

Loony licked him and licked him, whining because he

didn't understand why Snubby was so scared. Snubby remembered Roger. He would still be out on the roof, wondering why in the world Snubby was such a long time. Snubby, feeling much better now, decided to go and get Roger and tell him of the astounding happenings down in the inn.

He climbed out of the window. The moon suddenly swept out again and he saw Roger standing by a chimney. Was he still watching for the flashing signals? Or was he looking into the Professor's window? He would be back in his room by now, no doubt.

He crawled to Roger. 'What an age you've been!' said Roger crossly. 'The flashes have stopped long ago and there's been no light in the Professor's room, so there has been absolutely nothing to see. What have you been doing? Did you see who came down the stairs?'

'There's too much to tell you out here,' whispered back Snubby. 'Come back to our room. But, I say – let's peep into the Professor's room first. I've got a reason.'

'Got a torch?' asked Roger, Yes, Snubby had. They could shine it quickly into the room.

'But suppose he's there?' said Roger. 'He'll be angry.'

'He won't do anything,' said Snubby. 'He'll be too scared! Come on – it's important.'

They crawled to the Professor's room, and switched on the torch through the crack in the curtain. The light fell on the bed. No one was sleeping there. Snubby swept the light of his torch swiftly over the little room. It was quite empty, but the door was shut.

'Whew! He's not back yet! Where did he go to then?' wondered Snubby. 'I certainly heard him creaking up the stairs after the fight.'

'What fight?' asked Roger, astonished.

'Let's get back to our room and I'll tell you all about it,' said Snubby. 'Come on.'

They were soon in their room, and once again Loony gave them an enormous, over-generous welcome.

'Before I tell you everything I must just see if the door of the staircase leading to the roof is still open,' whispered Snubby.

He and Roger crept out to see. They shone their torch on to the door. It was shut. It was also locked. And the key was gone!

'The one who has the key is the man we want to look for!' said Snubby. 'He's the light-flasher – must be – because he's the only one with the key. And the lock must be well oiled too, because I never even heard him turn the key in the lock.'

They went back to their room – but on the way Snubby paused. 'What's that?' he whispered. They both listened. Roger gave a chuckle.

'Only the conjurer having a nice little snore!' he said. 'I often hear him at night – don't you?'

'Little does he know all that took place here tonight,' said Snubby. 'I wish old Barney was here.'

Once more they went back into their room and once more Loony flung himself on them rapturously. He simply couldn't understand what game the two boys were playing, but so long as they kept coming back to him he didn't mind a bit!

They sat on the bed, Loony between them. Snubby began to tell his story – how he had hidden on the landing – and had heard someone sniff, and had known there was someone else hiding there; how he had seen the staircase door open, but hadn't been able to see who came out; how he had tracked the fellow down the stairs, only to find somebody trailing him behind.

'And when a hand clutched me I got the wind up,' said Snubby. 'I flew into the dark dining-room and got inside the grandfather clock.'

'*What!*' said Roger, hardly able to believe this extraordinary tale. 'You got into the clock? You didn't, Snubby!'

'I did. And the pendulum stopped and the clock didn't tick,' said Snubby. 'And then the two fellows, whoever they were, began to fight. They rolled round the dining-room, they knocked over tables and chairs, they crashed into the clock, they . . .'

Snubby's imagination was beginning to run away with him. He went on, embroidering his tale as he talked. 'They were getting quite desperate, and groaning and grunting, when Mr Tubby barked. He simply barked the place down. I wonder you didn't hear him.'

'Don't be silly. You know I was up on the roof. Go on,' said Roger. 'I can hardly believe all this. To think I was out of all the excitement! Weren't you scared, Snubby?'

'Pooh, *scared*! What do you take me for?' said Snubby grandly. 'It takes a lot more than that to scare *me*. But that isn't all, Roger. When Tubby barked, one of the fellows shot away somewhere – towards the kitchen, I think, because I heard a door click. The other went upstairs. I heard him go. I'm sure it was Professor James, though where he is now beats me. Gone to do a spot more flashing perhaps!'

'Is that the whole story?' asked Roger.

'Not quite. When I got out into the hall, meaning to follow the Professor up the stairs, I heard a sound,' said Snubby, thoroughly enjoying himself. 'And gosh, there was a *third* person hiding! He suddenly pointed a torch at me from behind those big hall curtains, and got me full in its beam. I just turned and hared up the stairs at top speed. I'd had just about enough.'

'I should think so,' said Roger. 'How very extraordinary! What *can* be going on? We'll have to do something about this, Snubby. My word, *what* goings-on!'

Chapter Twenty-Four

A Great Deal of News

The two boys were so very tired after their late night that they both overslept considerably. Miss Pepper came to wake them just as the breakfast gong went.

'Well, really!' she said. 'You'll have to go to bed much earlier if you oversleep like this. That's the breakfast gong, listen!'

They didn't remember the events of the night before as they stared sleepily at Miss Pepper. It wasn't until she had gone out of the room that Snubby sat up and suddenly remembered everything.

'Gosh! Do you remember last night? What are we going to do about it?'

'We'll tell Barney first, when he comes back from Pearley,' said Roger. But they didn't see him until almost lunch time. They debated whether to go to the police or not, as the morning went by and there was still no sign of Barney and Miranda.

Then at last they saw him. He was hurrying along the promenade, Miranda on his shoulder. He waved eagerly to them and then jumped down to the beach. Miss Pepper had gone for a walk, so the four children were alone.

'I say,' said Barney, his eyes bright. 'I've great news!'

'What?' asked all three.

'My father's been found!' said Barney. 'Already! Isn't it marvellous. Look!'

He showed them a letter. Attached to it was a typewritten document, looking very official. Barney pointed to it. 'Read it,' he said.

' "Hugo Paul Johnson," ' read out Roger. ' "Aged 40.

337

Born in Westminster, London. Married Teresa Lorimer. Worked as producer and actor, mainly Shakespearian plays. Called up to the Navy for World War. Remained in the Navy on Secret Service. Present whereabouts secret."

The typewritten document was signed by someone in the Services. The three children read it again and again. Well, how wonderful! Barney's father was found at last. Except, of course, that his whereabouts were secret.

'Oh, Barney – I'm *glad* for you!' said Diana, and gave him a sudden hug.

Roger and Snubby were very much moved too. They shook hands solemnly with Barney, feeling that the occasion called for some ceremony to mark it.

'What does the letter say?' asked Diana, 'the one this document is pinned to?'

'Nothing much. It's just from one of Mr Marvel's friends to say he's managed to get the information he asked for, and sends it herewith,' said Barney.

'If only we knew where your father *was*!' said Diana. 'That's the only thing missing now. Can Mr Marvel find that out too?'

'He *has* found it out!' said Barney proudly. 'And all because of something very extraordinary too – he doesn't mind my telling *you* this, but you must absolutely swear you won't tell any one else.'

'We swear,' said all three breathlessly.

'Well,' said Barney, dropping his voice. 'Mr Marvel is more than he seems. *He's* in the Secret Service too.'

There was a dead silence as they all took this in. Barney laughed at their astonished faces.

'I thought that would amaze you,' he said. 'He is a jolly good conjurer, and uses his gift for that as a cover for his Secret Service work. There's been spying and sabotage going on down here – and he was sent to see if he could trace anything. Extraordinary, isn't it?'

'Gosh, yes!' said everyone.

338

'*And*,' said Barney, his face glowing even more, '*and* one of the men he's in constant touch with happens to be this very Hugo Paul Johnson – my father! Though he didn't know it! He says he's never seen him, only been in touch with him – and where do you think my father is now?'

'Where?' they all said, hardly able to take all this amazing news in.

'In the Submarine Bay!' said Barney. 'Isn't that incredible! To think he's so near and I never knew it!'

'It sounds exactly like a story,' said Diana. 'Oh, I feel as if I want to hear it all again!'

She did hear it again. Barney repeated it from beginning to end – he couldn't talk about it enough. He was so happy about it, so glad that his father was alive and near him!

'Are you going to see him?' asked Diana.

'Yes,' said Barney. 'But I don't know how or when yet. Apparently there are some very hush-hush enquiries going on at the moment about this blowing up of the submarine. There are traitors among the men over there, and yet they have been checked and double-checked. My father is helping to track them down, and he hands the information on to Mr Marvel, who sends it to the proper quarters.'

'It's too exciting for words!' said Snubby. 'I do hope you'll soon see your father. I bet he's exactly like you! You'll recognise him at once!'

'I hope so,' said Barney. 'I shan't know for a day or two how it can be arranged for me to meet my father – all the men in the bay are under close supervision since the explosion, and no one is allowed to leave the base on any consideration whatsoever. But Mr Marvel says that if it's possible he'll arrange a secret meeting *somehow* – he'll wangle it if he can. And he will too. He's a marvel, that man – and that's not a joke, it's the truth!'

'Barney, we've got some news too – and I bet it would interest Mr Marvel,' said Roger, remembering the night before and what happened. He began to tell him everything, helped and hindered by Snubby, who kept interrupting and adding various bits.

Barney listened in amazement. Diana had already heard it all, of course. 'My word!' said Barney. 'That really *is* news! What a pity I was away. I could have joined in it all! I had to take those clothes to the old dame who altered them. I didn't get back till after breakfast and then I had lots of jobs to do. My word – what a tale you have to tell!'

'We thought we ought to go to the police,' said Roger. 'What do *you* think, Barney?'

'I'll tell you what *I* think,' said Barney. 'Let me tell it all to Mr Marvel and see what he suggests. Then, if he thinks you should go to the police, he could go with you. They'd be sure to believe every word you say if Mr Marvel is with you!'

'Oh yes – that's a bright idea!' said Roger pleased. 'Will you tell him, then? Don't forget *anything*, will you? Even the smallest detail might be important. It's a pity he slept through all the excitement – we heard him snoring away in his room when at last we went back to bed.'

'Do you know it's a quarter past one?' said Diana suddenly. 'No wonder the beach is so deserted. Oh dear – Mrs Glump won't be at all pleased with us – late for breakfast and now late for lunch!'

'She'll give us her most glumpish look,' said Snubby. 'Come on, Loony – eats, boy, eats! Dinner, bone, biscuit!'

'Woof!' said Loony happily, and they ran back to the inn at top speed.

'Barney, come and tell us what Mr Marvel advises as soon as you know,' said Diana, as they parted. 'We won't say a word to anyone till you've told Mr Marvel.'

Miss Pepper was thrilled to hear about Barney's father.

She spoke to Mr Marvel about it. The children hadn't told her anything except that Mr Marvel had traced Barney's father and hoped to arrange a meeting. They hadn't, of course, said anything about Mr Marvel's secret work.

'What wonderful news for Barney, Mr Marvel,' said Miss Pepper to him after lunch. 'It's so good of you to take such an interest in him.'

'He's worth it,' said Mr Marvel. 'A good, trustworthy boy. There are difficulties in the way of arranging a meeting, but it can be done – it can be done! I shall do my best for Barney, you may be sure!'

Barney himself appeared at that moment, eager to talk to Mr Marvel and tell him what the children had related to him.

'Can I have a word with you, please, sir?' he asked. 'It's rather important.'

Mr Marvel got up at once. 'Excuse me,' he said politely to Miss Pepper, and disappeared into the inn garden with Barney. They were there a very long time. Miss Pepper couldn't understand why the three children hung about so, instead of going down to the beach. At last she got cross and chivvied them all out.

'You won't even have time for a bathe before tea if you hang about much longer!' she scolded. 'Whatever is the matter with you all? You *are* a lot of dawdlers!'

Barney joined them in an hour, looking really excited. 'Sorry I couldn't come before,' he said. He glanced at Miss Pepper, half asleep in her chair. 'What about a walk? I could do with one!'

'Yes, do go,' said Miss Pepper. 'I'm getting tired of Loony digging holes all round me. Stay out to tea if you want to. I haven't brought it with me this afternoon as Mrs Glump didn't seem very pleased about you all being so late for meals today.'

'We'll have some tea somewhere at a shop,' said

Snubby. 'A lobster tea! And I shall have a *whole* lobster,' he added as soon as Miss Pepper was out of hearing.

They went beyond the pier and found a very deserted spot. 'Now,' said Roger, sitting down comfortably, 'what did Mr Marvel say? Tell us every word!'

'Well, first of all, I must warn you that I can't tell you *everything* Mr Marvel has planned, or is planning,' said Barney. 'It's so very secret. But I'll tell you everything I'm allowed to – and you must absolutely swear and promise not to say a word to anyone till Mr Marvel says you may.'

'We absolutely promise,' they all said together. They sounded so solemn that Loony added a grave deep WOOF too.

'Well,' began Barney, 'he was *most* interested, of course, in the story, you told me of last night. He could kick himself for being asleep! He was horrified when he heard about the signal flashes! He says something or other must be being planned again – another explosion, or a theft of valuable plans, or something.'

'Did you tell him we suspected Professor James?' asked Diana.

'Yes. And he says we're right to. The detectives who came down suspected him too, but they can't prove anything against him. They told Mr Marvel that. They know him well, of course. Mr Marvel can't quite understand about the fighting. He says one must have been the Professor, of course. He doesn't know who the third person is, but he thinks it may be someone in the pay of the Professor. But do you know who he *does* suspect? You'll never, never guess! Have a try.'

Chapter Twenty-Five

More Exciting Still!

'Does he suspect Mrs Glump?' asked Diana after a pause.

'No. Try again. It's someone we know quite well.'

'The Funny Man?'

'Oh, no! Try again. And don't suggest Miss Twitt because it isn't her either!'

'Give it up,' said Roger. 'You tell us.'

'*Dummy!*' said Barney. 'He says Dummy isn't half as stupid as he seems to be. He's a very, very useful go-between, Mr Marvel says. He's hand in glove with the Professor.'

'I don't believe it,' said Snubby, shocked to the bottom of his heart. 'I liked Dummy.'

'Well, do you remember how he disappeared immediately the police came? That was a guilty conscience, Mr Marvel says,' said Barney. 'He was afraid of being caught.'

'I just don't believe it,' said Snubby. 'I never, never shall believe it. Dummy wasn't like that.'

'It shows how much cleverer he was than we thought him to be,' said Roger, amazed. 'Yes – I believe it. I always thought it was funny that he ran away as soon as the police came.'

'Well, I *don't* believe it!' said Snubby, getting into quite a rage about it.

'Don't work yourself up, Snubby,' said Barney. 'You don't know how dishonest and deceitful people can be, even when they seem quite the opposite. You haven't knocked about the world as I have.'

'That isn't the point,' said Snubby in one of his obstinate moods. 'The point is not that I don't recognise *bad* people when I see them – I grant you I may quite well be taken in by them – the point is that I know a *good* person when I see one. And I know Dummy was good, even though he was strange in the head.'

'Well, have it your own way,' said Barney. 'As he's gone, there's not much point in arguing about him. It's quite certain we'll never see him again! He's probably a hundred miles away by now. I liked him too – but there you are! I was wrong.'

'Are we to go to the police?' asked Diana.

'Not yet. Not till Mr Marvel has collected one last bit of evidence he needs,' said Barney. 'I have a feeling it's the names of the men who are traitors and saboteurs that he's waiting for now. He says he hopes to get this last piece of evidence soon. Perhaps tomorrow. And *I'm* to be in on that! I can't tell you how or why – that's really a terrific secret. I shall be able to tell you all about it afterwards. It's all tied up with how I'm to meet my father for the first time.'

Barney was quite breathless after his long speech. Roger and Diana were too thrilled for words. Snubby still looked sulky. He simply couldn't believe that Dummy was bad.

'Let's go and have tea,' said Diana, and Snubby at once looked more cheerful. Barney gave him a smack on the back. 'Sorry about Dummy,' he said. 'But these things happen, you know.'

Snubby didn't answer, but gave an awkward grin. After that he was more himself again, and he kept his word and ate a whole lobster for his tea.

'How you can do a thing like that I *don't* know,' said Diana. 'You'll dream tonight all right. We'll hear you yelling and calling for help! And it'll only be the lobster paying you out for your greediness.'

They were all restless and excited for the rest of that

day. Miss Pepper stood it until after dinner and then announced that they had better go to the pierrot show again. 'I really must get rid of you,' she said. 'You're so fidgety and restless. Go along with you – I'm sure Barney will like you to see him helping Mr Marvel, now that he's got used to it.'

So off they went to the pierrots. The Professor was there again, too, but not Miss Twitt. They all looked with great scorn at the Professor. Ho! He didn't know that they knew all about his horrible doings! However, he took no notice of them at all, but merely slumped down in his chair, only waking up a bit when Mr Marvel came on to do his conjuring, with a very handsome, finely-dressed Barney as assistant.

Barney certainly was excellent, deft, good at any patter necessary, and first class in the mind-reading. Once more the conjurer identified articles taken from the audience, and once more he guessed the long numbers correctly. There were more numbers tonight – six, instead of three. The audience clapped and clapped again, but Mr Marvel would guess no more than six.'

'It is tiring,' he said apologetically to the delighted audience. 'Mind-reading and number-guessing are the most difficult things to do!'

That night the boys quite meant to sit up and wait for anything else that might happen. But unfortunately they were so tired with the night before that they didn't wake, even when Loony had a bad dream and began barking in his sleep. 'Yip-yip-yip!'

Snubby had terrible dreams. He was set upon by men behind curtains, he was involved in a terrific explosion, people sat hard on his tummy, somebody chased him up thousands of steep steps up which his legs could hardly crawl. Oh dear – that lobster tea!

Nobody heard anything during the night at all, not even Barney, who said he was so excited that he hadn't been able to sleep. Mr Marvel had had another long talk with him, and had promised that when the morning letters came he might be able to tell him if and when he could arrange with him to meet his father.

Barney saw Mr Marvel after breakfast. His eyes asked an eager question. Had the letter come? Mr Marvel nodded. 'See me at eleven o'clock, when you can get ten minutes off,' said Mr Marvel. Barney went off whistling, Miranda on his shoulder. Not even a scolding by Mrs Glump for taking things out of the larder made him down in the dumps.

'I took nothing,' he said. 'I never do. I'm not that sort. Sorry, Mrs Glump, but if you think I'd take pie and cakes, when you give me them for nothing, don't keep me! I'll go!'

But Mrs Glump didn't want to lose such a good worker. She still had no news of Dummy and felt sure he would never come back. So she said no more to the indignant Barney and began to wonder if the bright-eyed young waiter was quite as honest as he seemed.

Barney went off to meet Mr Marvel at eleven o'clock, when he had a break of ten or fifteen minutes. The conjurer was impatiently waiting for him. He took the boy by the arm and walked with him to a deserted part of the promenade. They sat down in a shelter.

'I've arranged everything, Barney,' said Mr Marvel. 'It's all planned out well. By this morning's post I had the letter from one of my men telling me that the names of the saboteurs, the men who blew up the submarine, have all been ascertained. But they're dead secret, of course.'

'Yes, sir,' said Barney.

'They are being sent from the Submarine Bay to me,' said Mr Marvel. 'Tonight. They will be delivered by hand. But not here, of course, with so many people like Professor James about. Too dangerous! I am to meet the man who brings the names, away out at sea.'

'I see, sir,' said Barney, excited.

'I can't row,' said Mr Marvel. 'So I want you to row me out, Barney, and row me back. Can you do that?'

'Easily, sir,' said Barney.

'And, as your reward, Barney, I will tell you this,' said Mr Marvel. 'The man who brings the secret document is – your father!'

Barney couldn't say a word. He could only gaze excitedly at the conjurer. So Mr Marvel had done what he promised! Arranged everything so that he, Barney, could meet his father face to face! His heart swelled with gratitude.

'Now, not a single word of this to anyone, my boy,' said Mr Marvel. 'You understand that it has been difficult for me to arrange for it to be your father who brings the list – I have done it because of you. So on no account must you say a word, not even to your three friends, as I told you before – because I myself would get into serious trouble if my plans leaked out.'

'You can trust me, sir,' said Barney, looking straight at Mr Marvel with his brilliant blue eyes, more brilliant than ever now, with excitement and happiness.

'Yes, I think I can,' said Mr Marvel. 'Barney, be down on the beach at midnight. It will be moonlight then. I will tell you where to row. I shall be there with a boat which I will go and arrange for now. Goodbye, my boy – and remember – not a word to anyone!'

'Sir – before you go – just one more thing,' said Barney. 'Will my father know me? Does he know he'll meet me tonight?'

'As soon as he has given you the package safely, you can ask him,' said Mr Marvel. 'I think you will find that he knows you, Barney! If he doesn't, then come back to me, and I will put things right. He may have found it all very difficult to believe. After all – he didn't even know that he *had* a son!'

347

He left Barney and went to speak to a boatman about a boat. Barney sped back to the hotel, afraid that he had taken too long for his break. The children were down on the beach. Nobody was about. Barney began to sing at the top of his voice as he polished up some silver.

Mrs Glump suddenly appeared, looking extremely 'glumpish' as Snubby would say, 'Barney! What in the world are you thinking of, making a noise like that!'

Barney couldn't tell her what he was thinking, though he was bursting to tell somebody. He was thinking of that evening – the mysterious trip in the boat – the meeting – the man who was his father. What would they both say? Would his father be pleased with him?

Barney looked at himself in the kitchen mirror. Would his father have his bright blue eyes and corn-coloured hair? He did hope there would be some likeness between them.

The day dragged along for Barney. It went quickly enough for the others. They bathed and swam as usual. They took a boat round the pier and back. They prawned after tea and caught a magnificent collection of enormous prawns which Snubby said he would ask Mrs Glump to cook for them.

They didn't see Barney till just before dinner. He grinned happily at them.

'Any news?' asked Roger.

'Yes, plenty. Good news too,' said Barney. 'But I can't tell you any more. You understand why, I know. Things are going to happen tonight! I'll tell you all about it tomorrow!'

Chapter Twenty-Six

The Meeting on the Rocks

Barney went to bed at half-past ten that night. At least, he went up to his room – but he didn't even lie down or try to get a little sleep, because he was so excited. This was to be such an important night. He was helping someone in the Secret Service – he was also finding his own father!

Barney walked restlessly up and down the little attic room. Miranda was puzzled. What was the matter with him? She sat on his shoulder while he walked, occasionally nibbling his ear gently, just to let him know she was there.

'What shall I call him?' wondered Barney. 'Dad? Father? Pa? And I wonder what he's like. Will he want me to go and live with him? Shall I find I've got aunts and uncles – and perhaps cousins. No – I mustn't hope too much. So long as I just find my father that's enough for me!'

Eleven o'clock. Half-past eleven. Twenty to twelve. Time to go!

The boy crept downstairs cautiously, Miranda still on his shoulder. He couldn't leave her behind, she would hate him going off at night without her.

He made his way quietly down the back stairs and into the kitchen. He undid a little garden door and slipped out like a shadow.

Soon he was down on the little private beach belonging to the hotel. He knew the boat would be pulled up there somewhere, waiting. In the house the big grandfather clock chimed the quarter to twelve. Barney was early.

He waited on the beach. The moon came out from behind a cloud and flooded him with silvery light. It was a beautiful night. The tide was rapidly going down. It would be easy to row out to sea.

Then he heard a slight noise behind him. It was Mr Marvel. 'You're there – good boy,' said the conjurer's deep voice. 'Let's go.'

The boat was a roomy one. Mr Marvel sat on one seat, and Barney sat on another, with an oar in each hand. A heap of tarpaulins lay in the stern of the boat, and coils of rope in the bow.

They were soon on the little waves that swelled up near the shore. Barney rowed strongly out to sea. This was one of the greatest nights of his life, he thought. What a piece of luck that he had met Mr Marvel!

The moonlight dripped from the oars with the sea-water, as Barney rowed. 'Over towards that great ridge of rocks,' ordered Mr Marvel. 'Look – that ridge stretching out form the land.'

'Why, that's where we rowed out to the other day,' said Barney. 'We went to see Rubadub Whirlpool. It was a fine sight.'

'Ah, good,' said Mr Marvel. 'It's just near the whirlpool where I am meeting this man – your father!'

'Oh, well – that's easy then. I know the way perfectly,' said Barney, and rowed vigorously. Farther and farther out they went, until they came to the end of the great ridge of high rocks. Now Barney knew he must find the entrance to the channel that led to the pool. He pulled over to the rocks and looked for the narrow, rocky entrance.

'There it is!' said Mr Marvel. 'Swing round a bit more, Barney. That's it. Now we're heading straight for the channel.'

Soon they were right in the winding little waterway. It looked quite different now, from when Barney had last seen it, on a brilliant sunny day. It looked bigger, darker, more mysterious. The level of the water much lower too, because it was now just about low tide. It would soon be on the turn.

Barney pulled right up the channel till he heard the sucking, gurgling sound of the strange whirlpool. Then he looked for the mooring post he knew was there.

'Ah – there it is,' he said. 'Ill just fling the rope over that post, sir, then we shan't get pulled along to the whirlpool. Once down there we'd never be seen again!'

The boat came to a standstill, held by its rope. Barney jumped out. 'What do I do now, sir?' he asked. 'How does my father get here – by boat down the channel too?'

'No. He swims here,' said Mr Marvel.

Barney was amazed. 'Swims! But how can he? And why? The bay is completely built round by a stone enclosure, surely? And there are great gates built under water to prevent anything from coming in!'

'You father is a remarkable man,' said Mr Marvel. 'He will swim right under the gates and then strike out for these rocks. He has done it before now. It is the only way that he can bring secret information to us. He is a very brave man.'

'But why must he do it all so secretly?' asked Barney. 'He might be seen and shot by one of our guards on the stone enclosure.'

'Quite!' said Mr Marvel. 'I can hear someone coming. Now, you know what to do! Meet the man, say the password – "Moonlight Night" – and then take the parcel he gives you. It will be wrapped in waterproof cloth. Give it to me and then go back to talk to your father. I don't want to be present because it will no doubt be a thrilling meeting for you both.'

Barney nodded. He was feeling tense and excited. He, too, could hear someone coming – climbing over the rocks, panting and exhausted after a long and tiring swim. He waited, his heart thumping painfully.

A man came over the top of the ridge of rocks. Except for bathing trunks, his body was bare and dripping with sea water. It glistened like silver in the moonlight. Barney gazed at him.

He was a big fellow with great square shoulders, and a head of dark, curling hair which was drying already.

'Password,' he said sharply, when he saw Barney.

'Moonlight Night,' stammered Barney. He couldn't see the man's face because the moon chose to go behind a big cloud at that moment.

The man took a package from the back of his bathing trunks. It was wrapped in waterproof cloth as Mr Marvel had said. He threw it to Barney.

'Catch,' he said. Barney caught it, and then hurried to give it to Mr Marvel. The conjurer caught it deftly.

'Good boy. Now go and talk to your father!' he said. Barney turned, almost trembling with excitement. But the messenger was already climbing back over the rocks again! Barney called to him.

'Wait! Wait! Don't you know who I am?'

The man turned. 'Why should I?' he asked.

'I'm your son,' cried Barney. 'Didn't Mr Marvel tell you! He said you were my father!'

The man threw back his head and laughed. It was a harsh, mocking laugh. 'What's he been stuffing you with?' he said. 'You don't want to believe a word he says. I'm not even married.'

The moon sailed out for a second and Barney caught a sudden glimpse of the man's face. He recoiled in horror. It was a mean, traitorous face – no, no, surely not his father! Barney stared in horror and dismay. The man laughed again, a contemptuous, amused laugh, and then turned to go.

'Just one of his jokes, I reckon!' he called as he went.

He disappeared over the top of the rocky cliff, still laughing.

Barney felt suddenly sick. He sat down on a rock. He had left Miranda in the boat – but she suddenly came scampering up to him, chattering in her odd monkey way. She leapt into his arms, and snuggled to him.

'Oh, Miranda,' said Barney. 'It wasn't him. I can't make it out, I'm all muddled. I don't understand anything at all. Oh, Miranda!'

Then a sudden flame of anger shot him to his feet. Why had Mr Marvel deceived him like that? What was the point of it? He would demand an explanation – and if Mr Marvel couldn't give it, Barney would give away his secrets!

He went back to the mooring post, a furious rage making him tremble. But there was no boat there!

'Where's the boat? Miranda, what's happened? Where's the boat?' cried Barney, feeling as if he were in a nightmare.

He ran along the ledge that led to the exit of the channel between the rocks. If he could catch Mr Marvel he would fight him, strike him till he cried for mercy, throw him out of the boat if he couldn't explain properly what all this meant!

The boat was rounding the end of the rocks as Barney got there. Barney leapt straight into the water, Miranda still with him, and began to swim towards the boat. He shouted.

'Mr Marvel! Wait! I've something to ask you. WAIT, I SAY!'

Mr Marvel went on rowing. Barney was a very strong swimmer, and so full of rage that he swam twice as fast as usual! He reached the boat, and tried to hang on to the edge.

Mr Marvel hit out at him with an oar, and Barney got a crack on the head. 'Keep off!' he shouted. 'I've no more use for you, don't you understand that? You were a fool to believe all my pretty tales! You deserve all you got!'

'Mr Marvel! Wait! I don't understand!' shouted poor Barney, still bewildered.

And then, quite suddenly, he *did* understand. He saw it all! Mr Marvel had used him for his own purposes. He wasn't in the Secret Service. He was a spy, a traitor, in league with other traitors in the Submarine Bay. He had been afraid when he had found out that Barney and the others knew so much – so he had stuffed up the boy with the silly tale of his father. He had got the secret packet he wanted, and now he was off by himself with it, and would escape easily, because Barney would be left marooned on the Whirlpool Rocks.

'Traitor!' yelled Barney, beside himself with rage 'Spy! Wait till I get you!'

'You can't,' called back Mr Marvel mockingly, rowing away. 'I've got what I want, thanks to your kind help – and now I'm off to give it to my headquarters – but *not* the names of those who blew up the submarine! Oh no! I've got the plans of the next secret submarine, not a list of names I already know! And long before anyone sees you on these rocks and rescues you, I shall be hundreds of miles away. You were a very stupid boy, Barney. Oh, VERY stupid!'

Barney could have cried with rage. He saw that he could not catch up the boat now. There was nothing for it but to swim back to the rocky reef with Miranda, and hope and pray that someone would rescue him in a day or two.

But wait – what was happening in the boat? There was a yell from Mr Marvel, and the boat rocked violently. Whatever could be happening?

Chapter Twenty-Seven

Marooned Beside the Whirlpool

Barney clambered on to some rocks and stood up to see what was going on in the boat. The moon now shone as clear as day, and Barney could see everything.

There were *two* men in the boat, not one! Who was the other? Whoever it was, he had attacked Mr Marvel and was struggling desperately with him. The two men rocked to and fro in the boat and the boat rocked too, almost overturning. Barney was amazed.

Where had the second man come from? Had he crept into the boat out of the sea? Barney held his breath as the two men struggled together. He could hear their panting clearly. Miranda, wet through, crept inside his dripping shirt, frightened.

There was a sudden splash. One of the men had fallen into the water. Was it Mr Marvel? Oh, let it be Mr Marvel; Barney strained his eyes to see.

But alas, Mr Marvel was sitting down, rowing away for dear life. The man in the water was struggling and yelling for help.

'He can't swim!' Barney said suddenly, full of horror. In a trice the boy dived into the water again and was swimming strongly to the struggling man.

He slid his arm under the man's back, and began to lifesave him, pulling him towards the rocks. Fortunately the man was now so exhausted that he didn't struggle with Barney or drag him under. The boy took him to a rocky ledge, climbed up and dragged the other man up too.

He looked down at him as he lay there, his eyes shut,

his chest heaving up and down as he tried to get his breath. Barney saw who he was.

'Dummy! *DUMMY!* Why, it's you. Well, I'm blessed. This beats me. *DUMMY!* Where did you come from? Good gracious, is this all a mad dream?'

Dummy opened his eyes and saw Barney. He managed a very weak smile. Then he sat up suddenly and looked out over the moonlit sea. Away in the distance was the little black speck that showed where Mr Marvel and his boat were, on their way to land.

Dummy sent out a string of foreign words after the conjurer, and shook his fist violently. Then he turned and patted Barney's knee.

'You save Dummy,' he said. 'Good boy, Barney, he save Dummy.'

'Dummy – for goodness' sake tell me where you came from so suddenly,' said Barney. 'I can't understand a thing!'

'Dummy in boat all the time,' said Dummy. 'Dummy know that man is bad, bad, bad, Dummy know he spy. He flash lights, and then – boom-boom-boom. He makes bad things come, that man.'

'Go on,' said Barney. 'Why didn't you tell anyone?'

'Dummy silly, Dummy not brave,' said the little fellow. 'But Dummy watch and watch. And one day that man see Dummy watching, and he say, "Ah – I get police. They take you away, Dummy." '

'And then one day the police did come and you thought they had come for you and you hid away. Poor Dummy!' said Barney, suddenly seeing light. 'Where did you hide?'

'Down in cellars,' whispered Dummy, as if he thought somebody might be eavesdropping on the rocks. 'And at night Dummy come up – eats pies and cakes in larder. Bad Dummy! And Dummy watch all the time at night. Dummy fight with that man too one night!'

'Gosh! So it was you who followed Mr Marvel and

356

Snubby the other night – and fought the conjurer!' said Barney. 'But who was the third fellow? Goodness, this is a peculiar business – everyone watching everyone else! But I still don't know how you got here like this tonight, Dummy.'

'Dummy see that man with boat,' said the shivering little fellow. 'Dummy hear him tell you things and Dummy afraid for you. So . . .'

'So you slipped under the tarpaulins and waited to see what was going to happen!' said Barney. 'You must have given Mr Marvel a horrible shock when you pounced on him. It's a pity he didn't fall into the sea, and not you. As it is, he's won his little game nicely – got rid of me and all I know – made me a fool – and now he's off with those secret papers, and will escape to do a whole lot more damage. He's too clever, that chap!'

Dummy put his hand into his shirt and drew out something with a sly look. 'Papers,' he said proudly. 'Dummy have them!'

Barney gave a yell. 'Dummy! That's the packet the other fellow gave me! How did you get it away from Marvel?'

'He put in bag, and then put bag near Dummy,' said Dummy. 'So Dummy open the bag and take package.'

'Oh, Dummy – you're a wonder!' said Barney. 'He hasn't got his secret papers after all! And unless he looks in his bag for them he won't even know they're not there! Dummy, I could hug you.'

Miranda poked her head out of Barney's wet shirt and chattered a little. Dummy stroked her soft little head. 'We stay here long, long time?' he asked Barney.

'Till someone picks us up,' said Barney, gloomily. 'Gosh, isn't it cold out here in the wind, for all it's a summer night! Let's get down into that sheltered channel. There's a little cave-like place near the whirlpool we could shelter in. I wish we had a boat! Then we could row to land, and catch that hateful fellow!'

They made their way down to the channel. It was certainly more sheltered there. They walked along the moonlit rocks almost to the whirlpool. 'Come and have a look at it in the moonlight,' said Barney. 'I suppose it will be pretty low now it's low tide.'

They went to the whirlpool. Certainly it was very low down in its ring of rocks now, and looked quite different from what it had looked the other afternoon. It sucked and gurgled away a good way below them, lighted brightly by the moonlight.

'Hole down there,' said Dummy, pointing. 'Big, big hole!'

Barney looked. 'Yes – that's the entrance to the tunnel that runs all the way to that blow-hole, Dummy.'

But Dummy had no idea what a blow-hole was. He shook his head. Barney looked below the rock that had a great knob sticking out of it, watching the dark place that must be the entrance to the blow-hole tunnel. He suddenly remembered the old tale that the boatman had related to them.

He stood and stared intently at the hole. The whirlpool's waters were about six inches below the bottom of it. Was that old tale true? Was it really possible to squeeze through the blow-hole tunnel at low tide?

'Dummy, I'm going down to that hole. It leads into a rocky tunnel,' said Barney suddenly. 'The tunnel leads to land – we might be able to escape that way.'

'No,' said Dummy, shrinking back. 'No.'

'Well, listen – there's just a chance I could get back before Mr Marvel escapes,' said Barney. 'He might think there's no hurry for him to escape immediately, as I'm marooned here. Dummy, I must take that chance. But you can stay here and I'll try to send out a boat for you tomorrow – if I get through safely.'

'Dummy go too,' said Dummy. 'Barney brave. Dummy poor silly man, but Dummy go with Barney.'

'Right,' said Barney, only too glad to think he would have company in his dangerous struggle through the rocky tunnel. 'We must go now if we're going. The tide is creeping in! Once it gets much above the level of that hole, the water will be pushed and sucked along it to the blow-hole – and that wouldn't be at all pleasant for us!'

Barney leapt down like a cat, and Dummy watched him stand in the entrance of the dark little tunnel. Then he bent his head and disappeared inside.

Dummy then dropped down, lightly but clumsily, almost missing his footing. He shuddered as he just prevented himself from dropping into the angry pool a few inches below. Dummy thought it looked alive and ready to clutch at him.

He went into the tunnel. 'Barney!' he called, suddenly overcome with fright. 'Barney!'

'Here!' cried Barney. 'Just in front of you. Follow me. Miranda has hopped down and she's leading the way, bless her! Her monkey eyes can see better than mine in the dark. Feel your way, Dummy – there are all sorts of unexpected knobs and ledges waiting to jab you or trip you up.'

Barney sounded more cheerful than he felt. It was a horrid little tunnel, and he had to walk bent almost double. It was wet too, and smelt strongly of something sour and bad. Pooh!

Miranda kept running ahead, then coming back and touching Barney's knee to make sure he was following. She didn't seem a bit scared.

It was difficult to work, going along the narrow, low-roofed tunnel. In one place it was so narrow that both Barney and Dummy had to go sideways to get through. Once or twice Barney became panic-stricken. Suppose they got held up somewhere? There wouldn't be time to get back before the tide came in – and they would meet the first big surge of water driven up the tunnel to the blow-hole! That would be horrible – they would surely drown! Or worse still, they might be dragged down by the water that ran back to the whirlpool, and end by being sucked into the pool itself!

Barney shivered with cold and fear as he made his way up the tunnel as fast as he could. It was pitch dark, of course, and he had to feel his way at every step. Miranda, however, had no difficulty at all. She went ahead and then came back, then went ahead again time after time.

'Wait, Dummy!' called Barney suddenly. 'The roof's gone down low here. I can't even squeeze under it bent double. We'll have to crawl through it. I hope to goodness it doesn't go for far like this, I shall feel smothered to death!'

The roof went down to within two feet of the floor of the tunnel at this point. Barney wriggled painfully along on his tummy, hoping against hope that the tunnel would get no smaller. Why had he believed that tale of the boatman's? It was only a tale probably. He began to doubt if he and Miranda and Dummy would ever get out of the dark, damp tunnel.

At last he was through the narrow bit. The roof rose up again. Thank goodness! Barney stood up once more and knocked his head against the roof. Then Dummy gave a shout. 'There's water behind me, Barney! It's coming, it's coming!'

Chapter Twenty-Eight

A Night of Surprises

Water! That meant that the tide was coming in rapidly then. Water was being sent up the tunnel already! There was no return that way. They could only push on as quickly as possible, hoping that no great surge would race up the tunnel and overwhelm them.

Barney went on grimly, bruising himself badly as he struggled on as quickly as he could. Then he, too, gave a cry.

'The water again! That's the second time! It reached *my* feet then. Keep close to me, Dummy. We may have to help one another.'

The water retreated again. The tide was not yet high enough or strong enough to send a wave all the way along the tunnel to spurt out of the blow-hole. But at any moment a bigger wave than usual might come, and they would be swept off their feet, smothered with the surging water.

'It's wider here.' gasped Barney. 'We can go more quickly. I'm getting so tired, my legs will hardly move along. Are you there, Dummy?'

'Yes, Dummy here!' came Dummy's scared voice. 'Dummy hear water, Barney, water!'

The water ran beyond them that time and then retreated again. Barney stumbled on – and then, oh joy! What was that shining ahead of him? A moonlight opening! The blow-hole itself surely!

Dummy gave a shout of warning. 'Big one coming. Barney!' Sure enough it certainly *was* a big wave that time. It almost felled them to the ground, and Dummy bumped right into Barney. Miranda leapt into Barney's arms in fright just in time to escape the swirl of water.

'Up to our knees that time,' said Barney grimly. 'Come on – just a minute more of this and we're out!' He struggled to the moonlit opening. It was quite round, and so big that he could easily get out. He climbed out thankfully, and pulled himself to a rock above the hole. He must have a rest for a moment, it was no good, he simply must!

There was a loud yell from the cave, and a roar of water. Dummy was caught! This was the first wave powerful enough to rush all the way down the tunnel to the blow-hole itself. It had terrific force.

In terror Barney waited. The water burst out of the blow-hole like a spout from a whale. With it came poor Dummy, yelling in fright. He was thrown up in the air like a ball, and then landed with a thud beside Barney, who was covered in spray.

'Oh, Dummy killed, Dummy drowned!' wept Dummy 'Oh save poor Dummy.'

'You're all right,' said Barney. 'We're both all right. Just did it nicely. Well, Dummy, I should think you are the first man ever to be thrown out of a blow-hole!'

Dummy went all to pieces. He wept and blubbered and sobbed like a child of three. Barney had to put his arm round him and comfort him. 'It's all right now, I tell you. We're going to the inn now. We'll get something to eat and drink, and we'll feel fine!'

'Kind Barney,' said poor Dummy, and nestled up to him like a child. Barney gave a weak grin. What a night! After all his great hopes, all he had was poor little Dummy sobbing on his shoulder!

He got up at last. His legs felt wobbly after his long struggle in the tunnel. 'Come on, Dummy. Back we go. I'll look after you while you're with me.'

Dummy followed him like a dog. Barney knew roughly

where he was – at the beginning of the great ridge of rocks, where it jutted out from the land. He had only to make his way a little inland, and he would strike a path that led back to the inn.

The blow-hole was very active now. Giant spouts of water came up continually with a tremendous noise. Barney watched one or two. How weird it was – and how horrible it would have been to be caught in the middle of that tunnel when the blow-hole was in action!

He and Dummy and Miranda made their way landwards. It was not very far. There was a little path made by people who sometimes came to watch the blow-hole, and Barney followed it thankfully.

They came at last to the inn. 'Let's go in the side gate,' whispered Barney. 'Do you know if any door is open, Dummy? Which one did you come from tonight?'

Dummy knew an old forgotten entrance, a low wooden garden door that led into a tiny passage. He opened the door and the two went silently in, with Miranda inside Barney's shirt, trying to sleep after her adventure in the tunnel.

'I wonder what's the best thing to do now,' wondered Barney. 'Telephone the police, I should think. Oh goodness, what's that!'

They had now made their way to the kitchen, meaning first of all to get themselves something to eat and drink. The moonlight shone in at the window – but standing by the larder was a stout, formidable figure, half in moonlight, half in shadow. There was a click – and the room was flooded with electric light.

'And what's the meaning of this?' said the furious voice of Mrs Glump. 'Raiding my larder again, I suppose? You too, Dummy! Where have you been all this time? I've a good mind to telephone the police! I was watching for my larder thief tonight – I knew I'd get him sooner or later. For shame, Barney! What will your friends say?'

Barney interrupted desperately. 'We have got to tele-phone the police ourselves!' he said. 'We want them to arrest Mr Marvel. He's a spy, a traitor! Mrs Glump, let me fetch Miss Pepper – she'll tell you I'm not likely to tell you fairy tales!'

'I'd rather fetch someone else,' said Mrs Glump aston-ished. 'If there's anything in what you say, I'll certainly fetch him – or better still, we'll go to him! But mind – if you're lying to me, you'll have the police on your track immediately. Such goings on in my inn! I never did hear the likes!'

'Who is it you want to go to?' asked Barney, puzzled.

'Professor James,' said Mrs Glump, which astonished Barney considerably. Professor James! Why, they had suspected him too! He was probably hand-in-glove with Mr Marvel, so what was the use of getting *him*?'

But Mrs Glump was not to be argued with. She hustled them both in front of her and pushed them up the stairs, dripping wet as they were. She knocked at Professor James's door.

'Come in,' said a low voice, and a light was switched on immediately. To Barney's amazement the Professor was sitting in a chair, fully dressed, in the darkness. What-ever for?

'These two have turned up dripping wet with some tale about Mr Marvel, sir,' said Mrs Glump. 'They wanted to telephone the police. So I thought the best thing to do was to bring them to you, sir – knowing what you've warned me to do.'

'But what's the use of telling *him* anything.' said Barney. 'He might be hand-in-glove with Mr Marvel for all we know! We've spotted him doing some very funny things anyway. I don't want to tell him what's happened tonight. It's absolutely urgent to find out if Mr Marvel has come back and to arrest him before he gets a chance to escape.'

'What do you know about him?' rapped out the Professor, in such a sharp, imperious voice that Barney got a shock. He looked at him sulkily.

The Professor spoke again, more gently.

'Listen, boy. You can trust me. I'm working for the police. Mrs Glump can tell you that. I'm here investigating some very queer things, and some very queer people. It's your duty to tell me what you know.'

Barney was bewildered. 'Mr Marvel said *he* was on Secret Service work, working with the police too, sir.' he blurted out. 'He said *you* were one of the people they were watching. But oh, sir – this is very urgent. We've got secret papers here, sir. I don't quite know what they are – plans, I think. They ought to be taken care of quickly.'

'Where are they?' demanded the Professor, who suddenly seemed years and years younger, eyes, voice and everything! Barney was astounded at the sudden change in him.

'Here,' said Barney and put them on the table beside the Professor. He pounced on them, ripped open the waterproof case and pulled out a folded document. He opened it hurriedly and pored over it. He let out an enormous sigh of relief and leaned back in his chair.

'Thank God!' he said, and it sounded as if he meant it from the bottom of his heart. 'Our newest and finest plans! Blue-prints worth a fortune to an enemy. We know they had been copied – and that the fellow was only waiting to pass them out of the Base. Boy, you don't know what it means to have this document in my possession! But this is all very extraordinary! How on earth did you get hold of them?'

'Sir – it's rather a long story,' said Barney. 'Couldn't you arrest Mr Marvel first and get him safely under lock and key?'

'You needn't worry. He was seen when he came in late

tonight.' said the Professor. 'There is a man outside his window, on the roof – and one on the landing outside his door. He's safe enough. We were closing in on him, anyhow. But this is just what we wanted to bring matters to a head. Now – what about your story? Would you like to tell it here, to me – or shall I get the police in just to satisfy you that I'm to be trusted?'

'It's all right, sir. I believe you.' said Barney. 'But I've been so taken in by Mr Marvel that – well – I began to feel I couldn't believe anybody! I say sir – was it you who shone that torch on Snubby the other night after he had come out of the grandfather clock?'

'It was,' said the Professor. 'I, like Snubby and Roger – and Dummy here – have been doing my little bit of snooping too. So *that's* where Snubby was – in the clock! Bless us all, what a boy! It beat me to think where he had gone to!'

Mrs Glump noticed that Barney and Dummy had begun to shiver. 'Sir,' she said, 'what about going down to the kitchen and letting me poke up the fire for these two? They're shivering. We can lock the doors on ourselves. These two ought to get dry clothes and something hot inside them.'

'Down to the kitchen then,' said the Professor obligingly. 'I could do with something hot myself, Mrs Glump. All this prowling about at night is cold work.'

They all went down to the kitchen, and Mrs Glump locked the doors. She gave Dummy and Barney dry blankets to wrap themselves in, while she dried their other clothes beside the fire. She set some milk on the stove to heat, and got some meat-pie from the larder.

'Not so bad, Mrs Glump,' said the Professor eyeing the pies. 'Now – what about a heart-to-heart talk while we put away these? You begin, Barney!'.

Chapter Twenty-Nine

In The Morning

It was a strange hour the four of them spent, down in the warm kitchen. Barney told his whole tale, and Dummy occasionally added a few words. He was scared of the Professor.

'It seems to me that you children have been doing quite a bit of investigating yourselves,' said Professor James. 'All that roof-crawling! Extremely dangerous, I should think. And trying to peer into my window! Well, well – you fancied yourselves as a lot of detectives, I suppose?'

'Not really,' said Barney. 'I'm sorry we suspected you, sir – but what with one thing and another – you know, not finding you in your room that night – and feeling sure you weren't as deaf as you pretended to be – well, we were right on the wrong track, of course, I see that now! I say, sir – who locked that staircase door and took the key?'

'Marvel, of course,' said the Professor. 'He used that skylight at the top to signal messages to his friends in the harbour, and when he knew you children were messing about up there, he locked the staircase door! He is a bold and wily fellow, is our Mr Marvel. His real name by the way, is Paulus, and he really *is* a conjurer – a very good one too.'

'Yes, but, sir – he doesn't *really* guess those articles I held up,' said Barney. 'He taught me various ways of putting the question to him. "What have I here?" meant something in the jewellery line, for instance, and "What do I hold in my hand?" meant a watch – and so on. And sometimes, sir, he used to have a pal in the audience who

367

lent something – usually with initials on, so that it seemed marvellous when he guessed them.'

'I know all that,' said the Professor. 'In fact, much of his work in that guessing was only a cover for the giving out of code messages. For instance – those long numbers! They were merely a message in code to a sailor in the audience, who would pass on the code messages to higher quarters on his ship – a traitor there, you see!'

'Yes, sir. I see,' said Barney. 'But he didn't *guess* those numbers, sir. He told me which cards to hold up each night – they were marked in some way so that I knew – and he knew them too, of course. I thought it was a mean trick to play – but there, he was a conjurer, and tricks are their trade!'

'He worked the message into the number code first,' said the Professor. 'It took up a lot of his time! May I have another pie, Mrs Glump? Thank you. Most delicious. Well, my boy, your tale is very interesting, and you must be very tired after your struggle through that blow-hole. You're a brave lad, very brave. I'm sorry about that father business – that false letter describing your father – the false meeting – most disappointing for you. You'll have to try again somehow, won't you?'

'No, sir,' said Barney. 'I'm not trying any more. One disappointment's enough. I don't want to talk about it, please, sir. Anyway – I'm glad that fellow I saw *wasn't* my father!'

'You can't give me any really good description of him, can you?' said the Professor.

'Not really,' said Barney. 'Just a big strong-looking fellow with a mean face, and I think his hair was curly – oh, and he had a crooked little finger, I noticed. Not that that's much use!'

'It may be, it may be,' said the Professor, jotting down a few notes.

'Sir – what will Mr Marvel do when he opens his bag

and finds he's not got the secret package, after all?' asked Barney.

'I've no idea. Go off his head, I should think,' said the Professor. 'However – he's safe enough now, even if he takes it into his head to creep down to hunt in the boat for his lost package! But I've no doubt he's fast asleep, thinking he has everything safe – and that you are well and truly marooned on the cliffs. Nice fellow, Mr Marvel!'

'Can I tell Diana, Roger and Snubby about all this?' asked Barney.

'Not till tomorrow,' said the Professor. 'Then we shall have everything nicely finished up, I hope. Go to bed now, boy – what's your name – Barney. You've done well. Pity your father doesn't know it all – he'd have been proud of you.'

Barney said good night to the Professor, Mrs Glump and to Dummy, who was sitting blissfully half asleep in front of the fire. Mrs Glump had told him she would be very glad to have him back in his old job, and that not another word would be said about hiding away in the cellars – or taking food from the larder at night!

Barney was soon in his attic, fast asleep, tired out with excitement and with struggling through the rocky tunnel. He would dream about that many times in his life!

Next morning Snubby and Roger were awakened by a great commotion outside on the landing. There were shouts and yells, and the noise of a struggle. Then it sounded as if two or three people had rolled down the stairs together.

The two boys leapt out of bed, and, followed by a barking Loony, they ran out on to the landing. They saw a peculiar sight. Mr Marvel was struggling half-way down the stairs with two burly policemen! One had spent the night in a convenient cupboard, the other had come to relieve him – and had arrived at the very moment that Mr Marvel, shocked to discover the precious package was not in his bag, was about to hurry downstairs to examine last night's boat.

He was in a great hurry – but the policemen were not. They stopped him and suggested he should go back to his room and rest a little longer. Mr Marvel had no intention of doing this, of course, and a very interesting struggle had developed on the landing, resulting in all three falling headlong down the stairs together.

Barney, attracted by the noise, came running up the stairs to see what was happening. He had been helping Dummy with the before-breakfast jobs. Mr Marvel suddenly caught sight of him.

It gave him a dreadful shock. What! *Barney* here, large as life, when he ought to be shivering out on the rocks waiting until the next boat trip came to visit the famous whirlpool? He simply couldn't believe his eyes. He sat on the stairs and gaped at Barney.

'Where did you come from?' he said weakly.

'From the kitchen,' said Barney promptly. 'Lost something, sir?'

Those words, of course, told Mr Marvel that he had not only lost something but that Barney had got it. He gave up at once and went quietly with the two angry policemen, wearing a most bewildered look.

'What's it all about, Barney?' said Snubby, in open-mouthed amazement. 'Why have they taken Mr Marvel? Have they got the Professor as well? Did you row out to the rocks? What about your father?'

'I can't answer all those questions at once,' said Barney. 'But I've got a whole lot to tell you. See you after breakfast!'

Nobody saw Mr Marvel again. That plausible, wily, traitorous rogue was dealt with in a way that made it quite impossible for him ever to do any damage to anything or anyone again. Everyone in the hotel was horrified when they knew that the conjurer was a traitor and a spy.

370

Iris Nightingale wept and shivered. 'I never liked him. He was deceitful and cruel.'

The Funny Man stopped being funny for a whole day, and didn't smile once. He was truly shocked.

Miss Twitt sank back into a chair and said she knew she was going to faint. She had felt in her bones that that man wasn't what he seemed. But as nobody paid the slightest attention to what she felt in her bones, she soon stopped thinking she was going to faint and listened with open mouth to all the news going round.

The three children could hardly believe their ears when Barney told them of his night's adventure. 'Crawling through that blow-hole! Ugh, how simply terrifying!' said Diana.

'Smashing! I wish I'd been with you,' said Snubby.

'Fibber!' said Diana. 'You'd have hated every minute.'

'I'm sorry about your father,' said Roger. 'That was a hateful trick to play on you. Don't give up hope, though, Barney. We'll still go on looking.'

'I'm not going to bother any more,' said Barney, his face clouding over. 'After all that looking forward to seeing him – and to meeting him for the first time – and then for it to be nothing but a trick! No – I've finished with looking for my father. If he wants me, he can look for *me!*'

'But he doesn't know about you!' said Diana.

'Then we'll never know one another,' said Barney, and he looked very obstinate. 'And listen, you three – I don't want you to mention my father to me any more! Do you promise?'

'No,' said Diana. 'Don't be silly, Barney. Oh, Barney, don't look like that.'

'Well, I mean it,' said Barney. 'I tell you, I've realised it's just a stupid dream of mine. I've done without a father all these years, and now I've made up my mind I don't want one. I don't want any of you to mention him again. See?'

'All right,' said the three reluctantly, seeing that Barney was really serious. What a pity! But after all, it must have been a terrible shock to have that awful, heartless trick played on him by Mr Marvel.

'What was the fellow like, who gave you the package?' asked Roger.

'I couldn't see very well,' said Barney. 'I wish I'd noticed more about him – but the moon went behind a cloud just then. I know the Professor thinks I've fallen down a bit there – if I could have described the man properly, he'd have been able to put his finger on one of the main traitors in the camp. All I saw was that he was a biggish man, with possibly curly hair – and a crooked little finger.'

Snubby suddenly gave a yell. 'A crooked little finger! *I* can give a full description of him then – listen!'

He shut his eyes, visualising the two naval men he had seen in the train coming to Rockypool, where they changed for Rubadub.

'Yes – here he is – a clean-shaven fellow – with a big mole on his right cheek – two teeth overlapping each other in front – hairs growing out of his ears – and a misshapen little finger! There – if the police can find that man in the Submarine Service, he's the traitor who gave you the secret papers last night, Barney!'

Chapter Thirty

What More Could Anyone Want?

An astonished voice spoke behind them. 'And how do you know all that, young man?'

They all turned. It was the Professor's voice – but could this be the Professor! This spruce, upright, keen-eyed fellow with brown hair instead of grey and no beard?

He laughed at their astonished faces. 'I can be myself now,' he said. 'Good disguise, wasn't it? I was always afraid that Snubby, in one of his wilder moments, might pull off my beard or wig – but mercifully he didn't! Well, Snubby, what about it? Is that true what you were saying just now – or a little invention on your part? Actually, there *is* a man of that description, but we'd no actual proof of his being mixed up with this business.'

'He was in naval uniform when I saw him, sir, and I noticed everything about him, just as I said,' said Snubby. 'You find him and pin him down – and tell him Barney saw him last night – you'll have got him all right!'

'I rather think you've hit on the right man,' said the Professor. 'Excuse me – I'm going to telephone and use your bit of information immediately – mole on right cheek – overlapping teeth . . .'

Out he went, quite a different man from the old Professor they had known so well. What a very extraordinary thing! Why, Miss Twitt might turn out to be a policewoman or something! Surely nobody could *really* be quite as silly as Miss Twitt always seemed!

'I'm going to see Dummy,' said Snubby, getting up. 'I was the only one of us who didn't believe it when Mr

Marvel said Dummy was bad. I'm going to shake hands with Dummy and tell him he's a fine fellow.'

And off went Snubby to find Dummy. He was out in the shed in the back-yard, peeling potatoes, and looking very happy indeed.

'Shake, Dummy,' said Snubby, holding out his hand solemnly. 'Shake! You're a fine fellow! Loony, put up your paw and salute Dummy! That's right. Now, three barks for Dummy – yap-yap-yap, WOOF!'

Loony obliged at once. Dummy was really very touched. He patted Snubby on the arm.

'You good boy,' he said. 'Funny boy. Good friend to Barney.'

'It's a pity about his father, isn't it?' said Snubby. 'He says he's given up all idea of trying to find him now. You know he really thought he was going to meet him last night, Dummy, don't you?'

'Meet father?' said Dummy, looking bewildered. 'Barney have mother, not father.'

'Oh, I forgot. You knew Barney's mother, didn't you?' said Snubby. 'What was she like? I say – did she ever tell you anything about Barney's father?'

Dummy frowned, trying to think back so many years. 'Dummy think,' he said slowly. 'Snubby – you play your banjo again, and make me think.'

Snubby guessed what Dummy meant. He had known Barney's mother in the years when he, Dummy, had played the banjo. The twang-a-twang-twang noise and the sight of Snubby strumming away would bring back memories of those years.

'Twang-a-twang-twang-twang, twang-a-twang-twang-twang!' went Snubby softly, and Dummy sat, lost in thought.

'She so kind to Dummy,' said the little fellow. 'She tell Dummy her troubles and she make Dummy tell his. She tell Dummy about Barney's father – just a little bit.'

'Did she tell you his name?' asked Snubby quickly, resuming his twang-twang noise at once.

'Oh, his name was Barnabas too,' said Dummy, his eyes lighting as he remembered. 'Barnabas Frederick Martin – so many times she said it.'

'What was he like?' asked Snubby, breathlessly. 'Have you ever seen him? Twang-a-twang-tang-twang!'

Dummy shook his head. Snubby strummed on violently. 'Did you ever hear where he lived? Where his home was? Twang-twang-a-twang-twang, zizz-zizz-zizz!'

'He had home, yes – nice home, she said. In Cherrydale,' remembered Dummy. 'His mother cross because he married circus girl. Unkind to poor Tessie. Made her run far away.'

'Now we're getting somewhere!' thought Snubby, exultant. 'Who would have thought old Dummy could say so much. I'll know how to make him talk another time – twang-twang-a-twang!'

'Dummy!' called a voice, and Dummy jumped. He was brought back to the present so violently that he looked quite ill for a moment. It was the bright young waiter. 'Hi, Dummy – where have you put the dusters? Eaten them or something?'

There was nothing more to be got out of Dummy after that. He put on the worried look that meant he wouldn't be able to answer a single question. But Snubby had found out enough. His first thought was to rush to find Barney and tell him the news.

But no, on second thoughts, he wouldn't. Barney might be still obstinate. He might refuse to listen. Of course, Dummy's story *might* have nothing in it. Perhaps, on the whole, he had better tell Miss Pepper. Grown-ups came in jolly useful at times. They always seemed to know what to do in matters of this kind.

So Snubby was soon pouring it all out to an interested

and surprised Miss Pepper. She sat and thought for a minute.

'Cherrydale,' she said. 'I have a friend living near there. I could telephone her and see if there ever was – or still is – a family of the name of Martin, with a son called Barnabas Frederick. I'll go and do it now. Oh, Snubby, it would be too wonderful if it were true!'

It took half an hour to get through to her friend and find that yes, there *was* a family called Martin living at Cherrydale – an old lady and gentleman, and a son called Barnabas, and an unmarried sister of his called Katherine. There was also a married brother with four children.

'Miss Pepper! Barney's not only got a father then. He's got a grandmother and grandfather, aunts and an uncle, and cousins!' said Snubby. '*Miss Pepper!* This is smashing! What do we do next?'

'Leave it to me,' said Miss Pepper firmly. 'And don't say a single word to Barney about it, for goodness' sake. He couldn't bear a second disappointment.'

So Snubby left it to Miss Pepper, and quietly and efficiently she went about the very delicate business of contacting Barney's relations. Four days later she called Diana, Roger and Snubby to her room. She shut the door.

'I've news for you,' she said. 'Barney's father is coming down here today. He's longing to see Barney and to know if he really is his son that he never even heard about. Oh, children – I've seen a photograph of the father – and he does look so like Barney!'

'Good old Barney,' said Diana, with sudden tears in her eyes. 'When's the father coming?'

'This afternoon,' said Miss Pepper. 'I've arranged for Barney to be on the beach with you. I shall send his father there when he arrives – and you three will simply disappear when you see him – and Loony too, of course. You understand?'

'Of *course*,' they all said fervently. Dear Barney. It *must* be his father, it *must!*

All four were on the beach that afternoon. Miranda was playing with her little spade. Loony was waiting for her to put it down so that he could run off with it.

Diana was keeping a watch on the promenade. She suddenly gave Roger a nudge. He looked up.

A man was standing up there, tall and well-built. He had thick, corn-coloured hair, brushed back. His eyes were very wide set, and brilliantly blue. His mouth was wide, and his face was brown. He was a grown-up Barney! He stood there, looking rather nervous. The three children rose up silently behind Barney and went to the promenade. Loony followed, astonished at the sudden move. Barney looked round, also astonished.

The man jumped down to the promenade, and walked down the beach. Barney stood up and faced him, wondering what he wanted. Then he stared incredulously. Why – this man was so like him! Who was he? What did he want!

'Your name is Barnabas, isn't it?' said the man.

'Yes,' said Barney.

'So is mine,' said the man. 'I'm looking for a son I've lost for fifteen years – and I hear you've been looking for me.'

'Yes,' said Barney again, almost in a whisper. 'Are you – are you really my father?'

'Just as much your father as you are my son,' said the man, deeply moved as he looked at this fine-looking boy with the brilliant blue eyes so like his own. 'And you've got a monkey, I see. How strange!'

'Why strange?' said Barney, fondling Miranda, who had leapt up to his shoulder.

'Because your grandmother has a monkey too!' said his father. 'How pleased she will be to have a new grandson,

Barney. And your aunts and uncles to have a new nephew. And your cousins to have my boy for a cousin!'

Miranda suddenly leapt on to the man's shoulder with a little chattering cry. She began to nibble his ear.

'Let's go for a walk and talk,' said Barney's father, and he took the boy's arm. 'You've much to tell me. We've got fifteen years to catch up on! It's a long time!'

They walked off together, Miranda still on the man's shoulder. The other three watched them go from a distance. Diana swallowed hard.

'It's come all right,' she said. 'Barney's got what he wanted. He won't need us any more.'

'He will,' said Snubby. 'Barney's our friend for ever. Isn't he, Loony?'

'Woof!' said Loony solemnly, gazing after the two walking alone on the sands.

'A holiday – a mystery – an adventure – and a happy ending for dear old Barney!' said Roger. 'What more could anyone want?'

'An ice cream,' said Snubby promptly. 'Who's coming to buy one?'